These are the stories I've been waiting for. The characters in THREE ALARM FIRE wreck you, tug at you, slide into your heart and take up arms. Reading Juan Carlos Reyes' work feels like shining sunlight onto complex human emotions, as if the soul could be gently removed from the body, examined, polished, and put back a little better than before. I adore this. —A. Rafael Johnson, author of *Absinthe Party at the Fly Honey Warehouse* and *The Through*

Juan Carlos Reyes writes with wit and precision and an off-kilter brazenness that is refreshingly original and disturbing in a good way. He gets inside the psyche of his characters and they get under your skin. It's fun and harrowing stuff. —Mark Haskell Smith, author of *Elephant Crunch*

THREE ALARM FIRE is a daring book, alive with myriad voices. Family dramas and inner city conflicts unspool like detective stories, academics exchange metaphysical theories about language, characters get swallowed by our broken online discourse, and literary hoaxes contaminate our reality with their fictions. This is a collection of alternate histories and alternate perspectives. The stories spread across the page like brilliant fire. —John Englehardt, author of *Bloomland*

In his debut story collection, Juan Carlos Reyes builds worlds upon the page that extend beyond the page. These are stories cast in streetlight and starlight, stories whose characters don't reflect life but embody it fully. The pages tremble with aliveness. And every story roars. —B.J. Hollars, author of *Year of Plenty: A Family's Season of Grief*

Haunted by violence yet reaching for connection, these stories reveal characters in states of longing and wonder. With THREE ALARM FIRE, Juan Carlos Reyes proves that he is unafraid to inhabit the minds of those fumbling towards belief in their own humanity. As readers, we are compelled to think through their choices—and with them, our own. There can be no greater gift from literature. —Kristen Millares Young, author of *Subduction*

Three Alarm Fire is a heartrending and urgent collection. Youth, neighborhoods, relationships, and literary culture itself are found in disarray. National tragedies exist both at the periphery of the lives found in these spellbinding stories and in their front yards, streets, basements, and screens. Juan Carlos Reyes' prose is tender, deeply understanding, and captivating. While reading, I found myself imagining what stories might emerge if Don DeLillo and Clarice Lispector spent an afternoon together in a small café talking about dying empires and the types of love that still bind us. These are those stories, and so much more. —Michael Zapata, author of *The Lost Book of Adana Moreau*

Reyes delivers the existential battle between function versus imagination with striking elegance and skill. —Rigoberto Gonzalez, author of *The Book of Ruin*

How to do justice in a few words to the beauty and elegance and strangeness and sadness at play. Jeffrey Eugenides meets Dumitru Tsepeneag meets Magdalena Tully (channeling Italo Calvino). —Laird Hunt, author of *Zorrie*

Reyes's voice is supremely confident, and his alternative universes recall the harrowing landscapes of Coetzee and the playfulness of Borges. —C. P. Heiser

In the bold, experimental stories of Juan Carlos Reyes's Three Alarm Fire, reading is a riddle that results in salvation.

Shifting in register from abject horror to cool irony and featuring slippery, compelling details, this is a book filled with sudden, slicing truths that takes challenging the act of reading itself as its raison d'être. Emotions roar out of its pages, pure, raw, and bristling. Long, meandering sentences are placed at the fore, with the prose doubling back on itself, bounding forward again, and experimenting with language and meaning. Conversations run without punctuation marks or tags; different consciousnesses bleed together.

Surreal and unsettling, Three Alarm Fire is an intrepid hybrid collection that highlights how people and relationships are riddles. —Elaine Chiew, *Foreword Reviews*

Thank you, Lise!

THREE ALARM FIRE

THREE AL
ARM FIR
E THREE AL
A R M F I R E

stories by Juan Carlos Reyes

Hinton

Three Alarm Fire: stories
© 2024 Juan Carlos Reyes

Cover illustration & design: Vladimir Verano
Book design: Vladimir Verano

print: 978-1-60944-156-2

ebook: 978-1-60944-157-9

Published in the United States by
HINTON PUBLISHING
SEATTLE, WA

marcus@hintonpublishing.com
hintonpublishing.com

Hinton is an imprint of Vertvolta Press
vertvoltapress.com

Please contact the publisher for Library of Congress Catalog Data

C O N T E N T S

Contents

ELEMENTSOFABYSTANDER

Elements of a Bystander

ELEMENTS OF THE NIGHT

He asked me until I gave in. Until I told him about the things he'd thought he'd heard. He was precocious enough to imagine stories in the sounds and hanging wires beneath the moon and ledge. His windowpane was old enough to jitter with passing traffic. The fire escape clung, and barely, to bricks stacked so long ago that every element of the night, compared to their birth, made for a different world. The neighbor's potted plants on the fire escape rattled as if begging for attention. I can only imagine now the things my son must have felt and thought he couldn't see, so he imagined hearing them as he waited for me to come home, curled over his knees on the windowsill. The curtains draping over his shoulders. The passing headlights lighting his cheeks one birthmark at a time.

As soon as I closed the front door, I turned around and saw him standing in the kitchen light. I thought maybe he'd wet his pants, because even though he hadn't in years, he stood stiffly and avoided my eyes. As soon as I hung my purse on the coat rack, I said that if he wanted I could turn on the bathroom light. He shook his head. I said that if he wanted I could make him a sandwich. He didn't reply, and so I said, I'm hungry so let me know and I'll make one for you and for me both. He nodded.

His bony elbows hung to his sides like they belonged to a different boy. His arms maybe hoping to belong to a different eight-year-old face that seemed suddenly so much older that night than it had the night before. He crossed his arms and pursed his lips and he adjusted his feet so his toes hugged the floor, Where were you, he said, I'm right here baby, Why are you so late, I'm home now baby.

I went to hold him, but he stepped back. My hands stuck by his shoulders, and closely, so he could feel his own skin and its distance from mine. It didn't matter that I didn't know what he was feeling. My hands didn't leave his side, even if all they ever did was wait until he fell into my arms angry or crying or confused after old age had come and gone to take his bones, Ma I was waiting for you by the window, he said, I know but why were you doing that, I said, Ma you're late, The street can get dark and lonely baby and you shouldn't just be staring at it, I didn't know where you were, You know I always come home, But I heard sounds ma and the things I heard were real clear, Well I'm right here now baby, But it's late, But I'm home, But with the sounds I heard I didn't know if you were coming back.

I had to pause to let his eyes sink even further into the space between us, The world is always making sounds honey and I always come back home.

I never expected a boy to feel so much. His father never had. But his father hadn't the chance to feel much before he passed on. He just felt enough, I guess, for me and for us. And I miss him. Without him to let me in on secrets I couldn't read and the hall of ghosts I suspect but can't see in my son, I hadn't the slightest clue what to expect of boys. Least of all mine. My boy who I've always tried so hard to look into. But there he stood, in the kitchen light, still and feeling things that I had no idea about. I knelt at his feet. I picked up his chin. My full pocket poked my thigh. I didn't work too hard to adjust my leg because the pinching didn't matter so much as the things he was feeling that I didn't know.

I hadn't seen his eyes since I walked into the apartment. He'd kept them from me. His small frame stood poised in the light, stern, near enraged but not there yet because I'm sure he didn't know exactly what it was he was feeling. His cheeks in the shadow of a bowed face that seemed to temper the tremor of his voice. Imperatives and questions that he maybe wanted to believe were a kind of interrogation even though he probably knew his body couldn't handle the tension. Especially not the recoil of statements bigger than him, I couldn't go to sleep, he said, Did grandma try putting you to bed, I said, Yeah but I heard things through the window ma and they weren't coming from her, But did you wake her up and tell her you could hear things so she could help you with them, No, And why not, Cuz I just wanted to tell you, Well we all make sounds honey, So tell me what the sounds were, I don't know the sounds you're talking about baby.

He nodded, Can you see'em ma the sounds, I don't know honey, They sounded so real like you could touch'em, They probably really were as real as they get baby, I heard'em, Were they like footsteps, I think so.

I turned his chin to the light. I nudged his face up so I could see his eyes. I've always wondered how much his words were just a mirror to the tones I use and the turns I take to be his mother. I leaned my face into the light so he could see the wrinkles by my eyes. He's traced them since he was a baby, like he was counting the doubts I've amounted to, Ma I think I heard what scared sounds like, he said.

I wished just then that he'd never learned how to stay up, how to defy the power of the night, I said, So tell me what you think scared sounds like, Like the sound was meant for me, he said, And what's that like for you, Like my hair could run away, Sometimes we fight for our bodies to be ours baby, Why does scared do that, Do what baby, Make you disappear, It only makes you think that baby, I didn't think you'd be coming home tonight.

I grabbed his hand.

I tucked him in. I slid next to him and settled on one of his extra pillows. I laid on my side and I watched him bunch the sheets, So what do you want to know, Does scared look like anything I know, It sometimes looks like you wouldn't expect, Can it see, Only if you can see *it*.

I had a story in mind to tell him. Of a woman who runs away from scared at night. He glanced over at his curtains without so much as blinking. I can usually read a room, but this boy, my boy, can scramble the composition of a place with just a look into its corners. His eyes, when they seem to expect something, can water a space so his imagination blooms.

He looked from his feet to my face like he wasn't buying my discretion, Where does scared come from ma, That's a tricky question baby.

I told him that sometimes scared is so easy to see that no one believes it's there. That nobody ever believes scared can be so naked. So honest about what it wants.

His right hand trembled and I reached for it. I pressed it between both of mine, and I soothed his fingernails, a caress my mother showed me into my teens whenever I couldn't manage the things I wanted to tell people and so couldn't say a word. I stiffened a lot as a kid. In front of so many people that all that tension felt like a confrontation. With everybody. In place of things I had to say, I had stories about things that didn't happen but could have. Things that should have happened if for no other reason than that things had to be said. Like about those places we see and go to or don't and shouldn't.

He looked at his extremities again. He played with the arches of his feet, with the wiggle of his toes, Can we make it out of something if scared comes running, he said, Usually and it helps if people who can help us actually do just that sometimes they get scared too, I said, How come, How come what baby, How it's so hard to do something when people see scared, I don't know, Is scared very different every time it comes, It's not always so different, Is it hard because people don't know what to do, That's just it baby people kind of always know what they should do when they see scared but don't always do it.

There was a woman, I told him, that one time, when she saw what scared really looked like, it was still early enough to do something about it. But that it was almost not early enough. And that's the thing about moments we find ourselves scared honey, I said.

Sometimes we find ourselves close to touching it and we might not always see it in time before it touches *us*, I said.

I let his hand go and grabbed the other, gently. I traced his fingers to feel again what expectant trembled like. The woman, I told him, stiffened up when she saw scared coming for her. She'd been walking on the street. Coming home from work. She was tired. But happy. Satisfied. She'd worked hard. And as she was walking, past the playground, past the gas station, past an apartment building, past a basketball park, she started feeling like she wasn't alone on the street anymore. Like it wasn't just cars on the street anymore. She turned around, and even though there were a lot of cars crowded and parked on the curb, pressed right against each other's bumpers, she saw something crossing the street. And when it came out from behind another car, there it was. Scared. Right there with two feet and two hands. A face, too, but a face like a shadow when it swallows another shadow.

Scared had crossed the street, and it started following her. So she turned back around. Looked straight forward again, the way she had been doing. At first she walked like she'd been walking already. Normal. Steady. But scared had been making up some ground, and that means that scared was starting to turn the space between them into the space behind them, I didn't know anybody could do that, he said, Sometimes the world surprises us baby and sometimes a breath can become a memory when everybody starts moving too fast.

So she started walking faster because she realized what was happening. That scared had come after her. There's never anyone to see what's happening at night, and the woman yelled when scared got really close. Like four cars away and then just over three cars away. But there was nobody outside. It was just night, and the front doors were locked, and the front stoops were empty, and a lot of the windows were closed, so what's a woman to do in a story like this except shout. To make sure anybody that could hear her, anybody at all, actually could hear what it sounded like to be scared. And to give them a chance to face scared in the face with her. Just like she was doing.

The woman screamed so loud that she looked crazy to anybody looking. So crazy, maybe, that scared probably thought twice about getting any closer than he already had. She screamed like she was talking to herself. She had these big expressions, so if scared could see her face, he'd be impressed by the corner of her lips. By the bigness of her nostrils. She made her eyes big, too, so if scared could see them, he'd be confused. She screamed like she was having a conversation, the rudest conversation, with herself. She interrupted herself. She scolded herself. She asked herself some questions, Like what questions ma, he said, Like *Did you remember to leave dinner out for the kids, you wild lady? and I bet you don't remember what time you got married, you crazy girl.*

It was like she was laughing at herself, chuckling real loud about the weather, about groceries, about the flickers of light in the windows, about the breeze coming and going. She shouted about the friends she had made and the people she loved and the places they shared. All. To. Her. Self. And I reminded my boy that sometimes screaming is something people can do when scared shows up, when they want scared to go away, Just saying something can make scared look a little smaller and make it sound like something we can all meet with our heads up and our eyes open, I said.

A truck rumbled past us outside the building. From three stories up, I could feel the brakes steam like they wanted to fog the window. The axles ground like they wanted to bore holes in the brick. The bedroom pane shivered. The fire escape shook. The potted plants rattled like they wanted to be tipped to the sidewalk. Anything, perhaps, to get rid of the exhaustion that kept them awake at all hours of the night.

My son grabbed my fingers. He started poking at the callouses. It's funny to see sameness happen. I've always poked at the callous on my own palms since I could remember anything about remembering. It was like an exercise in concentration. I could only imagine how his imitation games cut the distance between us or how he thought they made for understanding us better or how he could use them to make his own self, So she made it home right ma, I'm getting there baby.

I pulled his collar up. With the imperfect window frame and the cracks that let the air in, I wanted to make sure he didn't get cold, What happens if you touch scared or if scared touches you, he said, Holding onto something usually helps, I said, Like to throw it you mean, Maybe or just to hold something in your hands to help you feel safe, Do you mean that you're ready to hit scared with it, Sometimes but mostly to feel like you're back in your body and like you're holding onto something to bring you back home, Like what ma, Like a memory or like hope.

Like the woman in the story who had had her house keys, I told him. She reached for them in her purse and she shook them. High up in the air. Jingling them like a present. Like she was ringing to get the moon's attention. And then just as fast she pressed the keys hard into her hand to feel the pain of being awake. Alert. The faster she walked, the harder she squeezed. And after all that, after the shouting and the crazy and the keys, scared slowed down a little, but only slow enough to keep pace. Like scared didn't want any more attention on him, but like he also thought he could go back to going unnoticed. Like he could go back to being hidden by the night to keep doing what he'd wanted to do. And so the woman kept walking. Fast. Alone. And that's the thing about the night. It's always moving fast when we find ourselves all alone.

In the lull of the story, he tugged my hands. He pressed them between his own like he was trying to clean them, but stories have a funny way of sticking to you, And scared never got closer right ma, I'm getting there, Cuz she was loud and she could see where she needed to go and she could touch the keys in her hand that made her feel safe right ma, Scared got so close that she could smell him baby, What'd he smell like, Like a lot of scared things do, Like what, Like an addiction or like an oily road, I don't understand, When you know what you're doing isn't right and you do it anyway.

The smell of scared cooked like fuel. The woman's feet started rushing, even more than they already were, the end just in sight and like a tempo that knows how its ending will echo. The smell compelling the replay of everything she'd ever done, every choice she'd ever made, like a movie trying to convince you that you could still trust its stories. And that you could trust your own opinions of them, Could I have done something if I was there, he said, We can always do something baby if we're there when scared comes around, So what can I do if I see it too, You can yell, What do I yell ma, You can yell anything you want to baby so just as long as it's big.

In the end, things got real wild for the woman. She'd been walking so fast that she could almost smell home. As if the odors of the night could blend with the scents of her lit kitchen and she could taste the tears of her kid and the corrections of her mother, Cuz mas are always teaching you and mas are always making you better right ma, he said, They're always trying baby.

The woman could almost touch how close she was to the linens and the towels and the cabinets that mattered, and she could probably fly there, too, if she could just put her mind to it, but because it was too late, and she was too tired, she could only manifest the energy to keep her eyes scanning the earth and her legs climbing over the bad news she didn't want know about.

And so, at last, and like an impulse that falls out of the sky, she crossed the street. She hadn't thought about it before she did it. She just shook her keys again and shouted, loudly, for a friend who wasn't there, and she gripped her purse tight so it wouldn't fall as she ran across the street yelling at nobody, at nothing but wind, that it was so great to see them and could anybody believe the coincidence of finding each other there in the dead of night at that hour and at that place with everything else that had gone on in the world, what with all the bad news of things and the good news of things and the news of things that seemed to spread like fire when we weren't careful about what we said and how we said it.

There was nobody across the street, but still scared slowed down. He slowed down real hard until he stopped altogether. Just at the sight of it all, And then what happened ma, The woman ran across the street and then started walking the opposite direction, But wasn't that the opposite direction of home, It was but she decided to take the long way, And so did she run home, The woman turned around two blocks later and saw scared standing right there in the same place where he'd stopped, So scared didn't come after her, Scared just got stiff like he didn't know what to do, So like getting away from scared means you gotta do something opposite, Something like that baby, But what would have happened if scared had come after her, I don't know but she would have done something new all over again, What do you mean, Like maybe if she'd seen him closer she'd have reached for something else to make her safe and yell at something else so people could know what scared sounded like and if he got close again then she'd smell him for inspiration to get a taste of home and trust what she was doing was all right.

My son nodded, a little knowingly, I hoped, a little absently, I'm sure. Like processing stories taller than him was the formative process that turns ruminating boys into mature ones. Boys with more deeply set eyes and who wanted to find themselves a little bit less uneasy about the night.

After he fell asleep, after waiting for the dark to settle his breathing, I didn't shut the door behind me. Not completely. Even if he was only asleep, I wanted him to hear whatever soft racket I'd be making in the kitchen. He's always been keen to sounds. Some of them, after all, can comfort and keep us dreaming.

On the kitchen table, I laid out the bread and cheese and turkey. I filled a glass of water. I sat down, and right away my lap burned. My skin pinched with a poke, and so I reached into my pocket and took out the keys. I settled them on the table. My palms were still red. The lines on them hurting. I wasn't sure anymore how hard I'd squeezed, but for certain hard enough for the keys to leave an impression on my lifeline.

I got up for an ice cube and took it to the window to stand in front of the fan. It felt good. Outside, there was no traffic shaking. All three traffic lights on the intersection shivered in the breeze but so unevenly. The yellow always came and went like it rushed to let everything through. The green was short like it didn't know how to give you room to run. The red so long like it dared you to test its patience. Dared you to challenge the night.

I sat down again at the table. I rested my hands on the wood, palms up, again, icing them now with two cubes and an easier heart rate. The clock over the microwave ticked seconds away, and the microwave, unplugged, seemed to enjoy having its eyes closed. Like it could only find rest in the absence of touch and motion. Not only because the world had fallen asleep but also because the night, in its earnestness, could only really be shut out when you put it to rest in a corner. When you found a home for it where nothing, and no one, could shake its heart and dangle it over a hot stove.

ELEMENTS OF THE PASSIVE VOICE

Should have asked dad a long time ago to throw out the clock. It ticked loud and I was up and it was midnight.

That scream, man. All drunk. At this time of night, a scream like that don't just tell you that night was never asleep like you were. It screams it at you.

Probably happened that I left the window open because the pillow was cool. My tongue, too. My tooth, too, and it hurt. And a breeze on my fingers when I scrunched the pillow. I don't know what has to happen, what has to go wrong, for somebody to be able to hear the sound a pillow makes when it's so still.

The pillowcase had a tear. Or maybe just bad stitching coming apart. Like me. Like I was just waiting there rubbing loose threads between fingers because what else was I supposed to do. I wasn't going back to sleep. My mouth hanging open saying nothing. Like just waiting for another scream.

People say it all the time. You hear a scream, a real scream, then something happened and that something's going to turn into more screams. Especially if you don't do nothing. But what was I going to do. People never tell you what to do.

And I don't doubt there's a pattern to this stuff. Rhythm. I hear it all the time that things happen all over the world. People scream. And enough people say it, too, that it must be true. But I don't always leave the window open so I don't know.

I wanted to go back to sleep, but all of it was just loud. The clock and pillow and socks at the edge of the bed that maybe slipped off while I was sleeping. Sleep that whoever was screaming didn't want me to have.

And then another scream. And damn if I didn't sit up and straight.

I pointed my chin straight, too. With a scream like that, you go straight all the way everywhere. That's when I opened my eyes. I was scared that whoever it was that was screaming would see me right then but whatever. It's harder to be scared with your eyes open. And who cares if whoever was screaming saw the color in my eyes, the shape, my eyebrows even.

And besides I didn't have a choice. I couldn't just hear something twice and go back to sleep. I was stuck, though. I didn't have a plan. No one ever tells you what to do when your eyes open. People just tell you to pay attention, to listen. They never tell you what to do.

But I guess the least I could do was get up. Or maybe just, like, leave my eyes open. Like that was good enough, and I guess for a minute I wished it was. But the longer I sat there thinking about everything, the clearer the scream was that I remembered. The clearer it got just playing in my head in all that quiet and getting worse every time.

I turned my body to the window. All tight like that. My whole body at once. And it just got tighter when I stopped moving. My lips and fingers. I didn't want to be committed, man, but like at that moment, I realized I think I was. That whoever was screaming outside probably saw that my hips got locked. My elbows stiff. My teeth tight and grinding. That whoever was screaming could see me through the walls and all the way up here in the highest apartment on the block.

People never tell you what to do when you think something's going on. When you hear screaming. Like if I got up to look what was up, what was I going to do. And what would have happened if I did nothing. If I just kept looking and that's it. What if I'd frozen seeing what was happening. Would have been like I was participating, man, and I'm not like that. That's not me.

But my breathing got heavy like I was finally paying attention and that's more like me. To realize that. Like whoever was screaming was realizing, too, and hearing my breathing. At that point, I guess, what couldn't she hear. Whoever was screaming probably heard the bed squirming and me squirming on top of it. The sheets buzzing, too. All hot and all.

And then a thud on the outside wall. Like a pound because it came from all the way down on the sidewalk beneath us. Maybe dad had heard it, too. But I didn't hear nothing in his room. And then a screaming like another thud, and damn if people never tell you what to do in these situations. When you hear somebody screaming. Especially like that. People just think maybe other people should know what to do. But who really ever knows what to do anymore.

Rooftops way outside the window and the antennae and the tar sheets. The fire escapes. It was all there. Whoever was screaming probably thought she could make it to the top of those buildings with that scream. Or bring the rooftops down to her. Even dig up the pavement like it was nothing.

And then another scream. The biggest one yet. Octaves higher, man, and to my window, to my room, like the scream knew it had to be frantic. Not just like it was frantic but also like it knew it had to be even more frantic than it was. Like it wanted to be a kite and catch a wind or something and just get out of there. Far away from there, from here, and who knows where this all was by now. Like we'd been picked up and moved to space while I was sleeping. Somewhere people don't sleep. Somewhere these things happen all the time and people just scream. Somewhere I just wasn't ready for. Like I wasn't old enough for that kind of war.

And if that scream had seen me, it would have pointed, accusing me for not being ready. It would have said, Why ain't you screaming too. And what was I going to say. That I didn't know what to do. I don't think that that screaming wanted to hear the truth. That I wasn't nobody.

Windows high across the street were lit like a fake orange. I couldn't see nothing beneath the seventh floor of that building. Not from where I was on the bed. And I counted from the top to make sure. One and two and three windows from the top. Highest buildings on this street all the same yesterday and today.

And then all of a sudden, footsteps, like whoever was screaming was running, too. At least, trying to run. And footsteps like it, like *he* was running, too. And I thought the whole thing was a bad idea. Because whoever was screaming should have stayed in the light where people could have seen her, especially the people who knew what to do when these things happened.

And then nothing for a little bit and then all of a sudden another scream. A bad one, man. So bad.

I don't think even my knees could have moved after that, not even to run from somebody running after me. Not left or right or wherever. But I had to try, I guess. I had to try to just get up. Just getting up was something I could do. Maybe something I had to do. But damn if all this breathing wasn't so hard because nobody ever tells you what to do when these things happen. They just say, You got to do something.

My elbows shook for like a second, but I finally threw the sheets off when whoever was screaming screamed again. A scream like the worst of them, man. It cried like *Help me* and hard. Like the first screams were just practice for that one. Like it was begging. Like it was small and sorry for being small. Like it wasn't nothing compared to the moon, and I know what that's like. Like you want to do something but what you going to do. Everything's hard, and there's nothing you can do. Ever. Like you're smaller than everything and your hands don't mean nothing and your arms don't mean shit. Like your words don't mean nothing.

Putting my feet down was something I could do, I guess. But my whole body got cold fast on the floor, too. Like the building stretched until the window was far away. So far, like, whoever was screaming would have had to have screamed louder to just get me to make it there. Not even to get me to fly to hold her because that just wasn't me. I ain't ever jumped for nobody. There ain't no ledge that could have caught us anyway.

And I stopped not too close to the window. Like two feet, but not three because I wasn't all coward. I was closer, but it was important I wasn't too close. I would have been toast, like chalky, burnt-bread toast, if whoever wasn't screaming had seen me. If anybody had seen me, really, but especially him. People always say that whenever whoever was screaming was a she, whoever it was who wasn't screaming was always a he.

I had a hard breath at the window, and a breath had to count for something. I could count as low as the second floor windows across the street and that had to count for something.

And then came like an angry groan, man, and it just came and left and then came again, and my body shook all funny like it wanted to get hard. And all over, too, from chest to toes, and I didn't know what was happening, but I was getting hard but not hard all the way. They were some wretched notes, too, and then another scream that croaked like *Help me*. Like it came after a bad slap.

I backed from the window and my heels backed into the desk chair. I was halfway into the room when I realized I was halfway into the room. Further from the window than the pillow. Right next to the phone. And I thought maybe it was something I could do, pick it up. *Pick up the phone*. But then who was I. I wasn't nobody to make that call. I had no information. What was I going to say. It didn't make no sense to just say, Not sure for sure what's going on but something's on. That was stupid because I didn't know nothing. I couldn't have just said, Hey operator it's some strange shit going on outside my window on the street on the sidewalk on the concrete but I can't describe nothing because I don't know nothing and I ain't nobody. Whoever the police was that answered crazy calls at midnight from strangers about stuff going on would have been like, Who's this. They would have been like, Why ain't you got more to say. I knew a lot of things for my age, but not nothing like this.

This kind of thing was too important to get wrong. And what if I'd gotten it wrong.

For example, I should have been counting the screams. I was stupid for not counting. That would have been responsible, but damn if I wasn't terrible. I tried to remember, too, like it could have been five, ten. Fifteen, maybe. My eyes were wide open and I should have known. I should have paid attention. And that just proves I ain't nobody, man. Nobody good.

Besides, somebody had to have gotten it right. Like somebody should have heard the screaming, too. Somebody better than me. Somebody better that would have known to have started counting when it all started. Stood to reason, too, because nobody's ever alone. People are always saying that ain't nobody ever alone in how they feel, what they feel, in life, in all that stuff. If I heard something, then somebody else had heard that something, too, and that meant somebody out there was calling the police and it wasn't just on me. It was good to think about it like that. And who knows maybe a whole lot of people were calling the police. Better people than me. Good people who knew the right things I couldn't know. Even though for my age, I knew a lot of things already. But, me, I didn't know nothing like that.

And then whoever it was that was screaming started crying. Clear as day, too. And whoever had called the police had probably started calling back. Details mattered. Crying in all that groaning. Groaning that came and puffed and puffed again and then left and came back. Ain't nothing right about any of that. So whoever had called the police had to have called back to give all those details.

And my body just stopped what it was doing. No tingling, nothing. No hardness, no close to hardness, just sadness. And tiredness. And I hoped whoever it was that was calling the police knew that. About my body just feeling like that. And I hoped they'd said that the woman crying had gotten to crying soft. And that the crying had traveled high and that it came interrupted like whoever was crying was stopping every second to swallow or breathe or because of something in her mouth. Like maybe the words were getting too tired to go anywhere. Like all that begging was just getting tired of getting nowhere.

And damn if I wasn't tired of not seeing. Of getting a full picture of everything going on. So I shifted one foot and the other and ran. I stormed that window, man. I straightened my body. My arms got limber. And I looked everywhere good. Left and right and down to the corners. All the sidewalk I could see. Short and tall buildings, windows with shades and without shades. But I had to get on my toes to see to the concrete right-right below, and there was a lot of shadows but nothing moved. So I got up on tips real high. And then a scream like a-that-was-it-and-dead kind of scream. The worst of them. The worst of whatever eight, ten, twenty, however many there were.

I hit the floor fast, too. I hoped somebody was calling the police again because that scream jumped to the window like it wanted to break the glass. I hoped whoever was calling knew to say that, too. Details mattered. And I hoped they'd figure to say what was happening to their body like what was happening to mine. Arms like soft and an ankle that didn't quit. Wasn't easy at all backing against the radiator. My heart was loud, and then something like a bad whip, like *fwap* from way down below, and not like any *fwap* that had come before. And I just knew, man. I just knew whoever it was that wasn't screaming, that that guy must have seen me and just gotten mad and just had had it. Like I just made it worse.

And, man, I hoped whoever it was that was calling the police didn't tell nobody it was my fault. Because details mattered but not like that. Or I don't know. Maybe it was important to say it was me. Or maybe it was and maybe it wasn't. Maybe whoever it was that was calling the police should have told them it was me that needed to go, that needed arresting because I didn't even call in the first place. And that I'd made it worse and needed confessing. But damn if it shouldn't have been me to make that call. This was my fault and so I had to call. And I tried, too, man. I really tried. I tried for the phone but damn if it didn't happen. Nothing happened. My feet just got heavy. Like after all that had happened only so much was clear. That my place was right there on the floor.

ELEMENTS OF A BLOCK PARTY

I rushed downtown. That's what I was told. Rush downtown. Dad didn't even have to explain his afterward sigh. Of course, I said, and then I hung up.

I fumbled my keys in the kitchen on the way out. I almost lost my wallet down the stairs. At the turnstile, I forgot to slip my card, and so my hips felt the jab. On the platform, I stared into the void between beams waiting for the train. Waiting was the hard part. *Rush downtown*. The wait between trains, however short, was awful. Finally inside a car, though, wasn't any better. I sat across from a line of men staring into their hands. The women beside me stared into the window. The streaking glare, the grinding, labored to every stop. I found them all numbing, blinding.

Two years ago, my sister spent a night on a park bench. She told us she waited. She never confirmed for what. Through evening and moon, she sat in one place. She watched the center fountain empty out, first of water and then of musicians. She sat watching dog walkers, obsessive and distracted, And other types too all types, she said. She watched the homeless settle into their benches, fashioning their own designs for sleep. Maybe for dreams of hoping they had something to dream about. She admitted that on a few occasions she had to watch certain men creep onto the bench next to her, wait there, for something or just her. Sometimes they slid their hands across the seat. They always stopped, either their reaching fingers or eyes, when she turned to watch them. I can imagine her look. A stern, fixed look that held nothing, wanted nothing, was nothing.

When I stepped above ground again, I fought to find a place on the sidewalk. The playground just outside the station reveled in the sun. Waiting on the corner for the green light to turn, the flood of people fending each other off hadn't even the decency to look up. No one had to push, but too many people did. An older man was almost nudged into a bus. Near death made us, made me, more conscious of my feet. My bouncing heels. My toes. My impatient knees.

Waiting, I heard the children behind me scamper and bounce. They tossed sand. They climbed. They shook their butts off swings. Too jittery for a permanent seat at their age and that was okay. At my twenty-five, though, that much motion was not okay. It was unstable. Unbecoming. It would have made me childish.

One year ago, my sister rode a subway train from end to end. Three complete round trips. She never got up once. She didn't once change seats. I asked her later if maybe she'd been reasoning to get off at the right stop as the right stop came and went and she just got caught up in the logic of it all. The mind wanders far off track precisely because it's grinding too hard to stay on the tracks. Perhaps there had been a rhythm to the screeching wheels and the brakes and the opening and closing doors, and it all felt like a lost day. But she said, I was fine. And then she said, I don't know though. I said that perhaps she subconsciously thought Coney Island had been too muggy to get out and walk. Or maybe Jamaica Boulevard had been simmering. No, she said, I rode the train I did and I missed my stop and that was that. But the stop you wanted was in Manhattan. I know, she said. And you never got off the train did you. I know, she said.

I left the crowd behind me. I crossed the street and then straddled the curb on the next block. Rushing means you have no steady bearing on what is and what is not adjacent to the space you need. At that pace, in that ocean of people, I would have collided and sunk. So I stayed on the curb, and it ran alongside everyone, only very lonely. No one else was challenging the pavement, the traffic, like I was. In that solitude, listening to yourself rush also means you can listen to the hesitation no one sees but you. You can hear the reluctance in your shoes. You can feel your hands cautioning you. What's the hurry, you say to yourself. *Rush downtown.* But consciousness of all that speed makes you aware of the words the sky can snicker when it hangs there tickled at your hurry. It can make you aware that the windows whirring by you have nowhere to be but there looking at you.

Just yesterday, my sister didn't leave work. She stayed on after her shift and just sat at an outdoor table with the same cup of coffee until it grew cold.

Until her boss sat next to her and encouraged her to leave because they were closing. Because he had to go home and he was done worrying about what was wrong with her.

She didn't get up. She only gave him my number and so he called me. He said that, at first, when she used to do that, he found it amusing. Sweet, even. Like she was thinking or processing something really important, and even though he wasn't sure what it was, he was pretty sure it mattered. But now, he told me, after three weeks of the same shit, she's been doing this too long, And I'm tired of it, he said, And she needs to leave and I don't want her back, he said.

I told him she's been doing that since she came back from Virginia. Maybe trying to keep her job, I told him that the stillness was part of her therapy. He pried, though. He wanted to know what had happened. He said he had a right to it. I didn't tell him that she'd been pimped. Against herself. That after she'd moved in with a boyfriend, he'd forced her into positions so cruel, she still can't illustrate all of them. She still can't remember the names. I told her boss I'd be there to pick her up. He asked me how long it had been since she'd been back from Virginia. He said he had a right to know that, too. I told him it had been almost two months. He said he thought I was lying. I told him I'd be there to pick her up. It wasn't his right to know it had been almost two years.

I knocked, but she didn't open the door. So I did. I tried to swing it lightly, but the hinges, even after so much greasing, dared you to tear them off. I had asked dad for my own set of keys almost four months ago. After she checked out of the hospital. He was too busy to check on her every day and the doctor specifically mentioned that after she transferred to independence, the doctor's own terms, we had to check on her every day. Maybe move in for a while. I'm sure that no one but me held his breath on that one. My parents weren't nearby and they had obligations. I had responsibilities, too, but, well, I was nearby. I wanted to tell the doctor, Now that's some kind of proposal. But I kept my mouth shut because the ink on that contract would fall to me if I spoke up. Which doesn't mean I didn't want to help. It just means I didn't know how. I was younger than she was and I didn't have the tools to deal with it and, after all, who does.

It did eventually fall on me, though. At least, the evening watch. And the night watch. And sometimes the morning watch. She needed checking on.

Every day. Even without emergencies. Especially when she wasn't picking up her phone.

I checked for her in the kitchen. The wall phone lay neatly wrapped in its cord. Like a mouse entrapped. A pest that had suffered its last squeal. A flame flickered on the window sill. The summer breeze was just enough to rumba without the candle going faint.

The television went on in the living room. I could barely hear sitcom audience laughter, but I stayed in the kitchen. She always welcomed me more easily when I didn't rush to her side or impose any questions. And it was also important she didn't think I'd rushed to get there. So I stood by the window a moment and then I turned on the fan to cool off. A minute later, I soaked a sponge and shifted plates around the sink. I grabbed a rag from the refrigerator handle. I rolled up my sleeves.

Later, when I poked into the living room, she turned to me, and I asked her, You got space there. I do, she said.

She pulled her blanket close, tucked it under her feet, left a patch on the couch I fell into, almost completely. The couch was so worn, I'd begun to think it once belonged to a Depression-era family. Only history, in the face of all that age, can feign to still be so soft.

She smiled. Her smile carried a certain smell of choice. The smile itself a reminder that she could have chosen to sneer or laugh or simply start crying. She didn't always smile that way. After so much time, though, she was probably still relearning how the gesture worked, and she said, I called him again today. Of course you did, I said.

The sitcom she'd been watching had taken some kind of turn. I'd barely been paying attention, but that essential turn made the audience especially quiet, What do you think about that, What do you mean what do I think about that, Well you didn't say anything when I said that, What am I supposed to say, I just want to know what you think, The same thing I thought the last time, So say it again, The guy abused you and left you homeless, I understand that but I also once knew a different kind of guy, Then get to know another different kind of guy, What I'm saying is that he used to be a different guy and I want to know what happened.

A stamping on the ceiling distracted me and it made her flinch. It sounded like heels or a broom. Maybe a belt or a dropped phone or a fall. I didn't have much to say about her phone calls anymore. Telling me like she wanted a reaction from me, however, bothered me. But we're still in that gray where reason's on hiatus. That's what the doctor said. When she pulled me aside, the doctor also said that it's sometimes hard to demonstrate to someone that recovery is in their hands when so much of their trauma never was. The process can be disillusioning, the doctor said, because the process is so, so long.

On the end table, a glass of water was sweating and so I picked it up for a sip, sip, How are you doing, she said, I'm good, I said, How's your girl, She's fine, How's work, It's good. Revealing no more than you have to was pretty much genetic for us. Her living room was quiet but never an uneasy silence. Even now she knew how to let comfort speak for itself, imposing only when she felt her neck anchored by obligation. The feeling that she was someone else's obligation.

During commercials, she muted the television. Rushing carries a tone especially distinct from a stillness that doesn't anticipate or wait for what it doesn't know. I could hear us repeating the same exchange again, I want to stop calling him you know. I nodded, It's okay, But what if it's not okay, The doctor's a pretty bright doc and she said it'll be okay, But what if next year I still don't know how to be alone, Then you don't have to be alone, But what if I don't know how not to be, Don't put it past yourself to learn.

A pigeon cooed on the ledge. It turned and stared at us, past us, How did the kitchen look, she said, It was tidy, I said, Why are you always so much older than me, I'm not, That's not what I'm saying, I guess being four years younger than you means I have your hindsight to appreciate without having to bear through mine.

She turned the volume back on, Did you see the flyers in the hall, You mean the neighbor's, There's something out in the courtyard tonight, This afternoon, Yeah that's what I meant, I've never met the neighbors, They seem okay enough, Okay enough isn't always good enough, I get that but it'll be okay, How can you say that, Cuz you'll be with me, What is that supposed to mean, Nothing that's consequential I'm only saying that I'll be there too.

She muted the television. Like she was waiting for me to press her. But I knew better. The doctor once told us to enjoy her silences. The doctor also said to expect nothing from them. Even replies.

The barbeque wasn't much. A dozen or so neighbors. A grill. Puppies. Swaying lanterns.

She introduced herself to a few people outright. And then she introduced me. She only recognized a handful of neighbors, and they all seemed fine enough. Even Virginia couldn't take that away. Her ability to meet a greeting straight on. She was never good at pretending to be coy, and we both hated people who pretended to be coy or wanted more than they deserved from hellos. She's always been good, too, at slipping away from extended hellos, anticipating conversations that want to pry, that offer nothing or at least nothing of consequence. She's always keen at finding those nooks, a corner or stairwell or bench, where no one bothers to go.

A guy about her age, scruffy top, glasses, grilled burgers on the center patch of cobblestones. An older woman approached him every so often, smiled, pecked, walked away. An older man lingered everywhere his dog led. A woman, her hands a collage of paints, made rounds to greet everyone, even us for a moment. But rounds never take long, so she disappeared when she had to.

I never intended to leave my sister alone. But after filling a plate of chips, I followed the modest steel art that trailed the courtyard edges. After the fourth or fifth sculpture, I realized I'd been alone and then looked around for her. I found her where she'd been, across the perimeter, clutching herself, a light sweater draped across her knees. Sipping tea.

The sixth sculpture was an old wood-burning furnace, cut down its center and pried open, the semblance of a steel heart fixture inside it. Its color, the color everywhere, was simply its rust. Even in its unity, it was disconnected from the steel figures sculpted elsewhere, all of them in stiff motion, a still-life human figure running or walking or dashing or flying, all of them captured for all time in a frenzy that decorated the place in a yearning to be somewhere else.

The woman making her rounds was making her rounds again. A dress to her calves, she glanced around lightly, airily, like she had no control of her smile, like it beamed against choice and will and threatened to carry her and whoever enjoyed it into a sunset without a phone to call home. She offered me a beer. She whispered to me about the grill, about the center table, about the ketchup, about the pita and the dip, *A cozy quaint celebration needs all* these things, What are we celebrating, Spring and the new season maybe, Merry Spring then, Merry Spring honey.

We clinked bottles. She bumped into me and said, Is that yours, and I said, Excuse me, Are you with her. She pointed across the courtyard, That's my sister, She's getting there isn't she, Excuse me, She's finding a way back to us isn't she.

My sister had unrolled her sleeves. She pulled her top buttons shut. She sipped her tea, rising fumes hazing her eyes. She gazed into the row of potted plants across from her as one of the dogs sniffed between petals, and meanwhile the woman making her rounds didn't leave me as quickly as she had the first time, I can tell she isn't sick, How can you tell that, Because I can tell these things honey.

I feigned wanting more chips, but she seemed to know the ploy and only roped me back in, People always need to see that kind of thing, What do you mean exactly, It's selfish I know but someone else's grievances put a boundary on the extent of ours.

I was already facing perpendicular. I'm pretty sure she got the point I didn't want to talk, but she seemed intent on refusing to acknowledge the point. After she paused for a sip, she waved to someone across the way and then made a point to speak to me while speaking to no one in particular, Without wounded children how can the rest of us know we've grown up. She smiled at me before she excused herself and twirled off. She had no reins on her smile. The smile that seemed to control her.

The dog sniffed around my sister's feet and moved on. When it returned for another smell, she stumbled out of her daze. She nuzzled the dog with her bare foot. It leaned her way but went back to sniffing a crack in the cobblestone. When she nuzzled it a second time, it settled by her chair, and she leaned over to whisper to it, cradling its ears, meeting their noses like she wanted to pamper it unabashedly. I made to leave to her. To sit by her again. But then she took a deep breath and sat up straight and stared firmly ahead of her. I kept my distance, carefully measuring the distance if she needed me. She still wasn't looking anywhere, but as now more people were making their rounds, her eyes were at least wide open.

Of Hearts & Minds

WARRIOR, NEW JERSEY

Oh you're from Jersey.

Dude says it like he's reciting a rehearsed exhaustion, like he invented an insult that can't even insult. He has to clear his voice, too, after he says it. Sometimes people like talking bigger than they are, like they can throw on a costume whenever they think they're undersized.

I want to say *Oh and you're a piece of work*, but then I'd be citing my own opera, a call and response too much like a song in a tenor two octaves too high for me. And I'd be affirming whatever it is he thinks he is. Silence is no kind of response, but at least silence can agree to agree to nothing.

I'd only just sat to eat. I'd only just settled my backpack between my feet under the table. I hadn't even been able to fold my slice of pizza. I barely got to look at it to catch the extra cheese before it slipped, and here was this kid getting all "ugh-heh-you're-from-Jersey-ugh" like he was saying something new.

He and I had only seen each other once before, in our afternoon social psychology course so overcrowded that kids have taken to sitting on the floor against the wall with their textbooks turned to the most random pages about family dynamics and abandonment theories. Even on the second day of class, some guy in the desk ahead of me had his book turned to the section on collective impulse to fascism inside the socio-psycho unrest chapter. Maybe he was trying to impress himself. Maybe he thought being a student meant putting on a studenty costume. Whatever the case, it was only the first week, and people were acting like they could breeze through a semester with just a page count.

But back to the "ugh-heh-Jersey-ugh" kid. We sat by each other on the first day of class, and he'd looked over my writing hand to catch something I'd noted in my notebook about in-group and out-group distinctions. This professor didn't play around. Day 1: syllabus and heavy shit. Day 2: clarity to our questions about the syllabus and then more heavy shit.

Meanwhile, this "ugh-heh-Jersey-ugh" kid—and it's important we establish the *ugh-ness* going on here before we proceed—when I caught him peeking at my notes, he smiled and nodded like we've been friends since middle school. Like I was supposed to be familiar with his mushroom breath from years of putting up with that almost comically scarce upper lip mustache.

He introduced himself and asked formally if he could crib my notes because he'd missed the last thing the professor had said. He complimented my handwriting, but I couldn't even remember his name. I'm sure he could have spoken one long sentence with just his name in it and I'd have still forgotten it.

Anyway, on only the first day of class, after a curt silence, he gets all, I'm from Queens. He even got all specific about his neighborhood. I didn't laugh even though I wanted to. The neighborhood he grew up in is barely in Queens. This kid was trying hard to qualify for a city kid, but my mother's worked for the same construction company in Flushing since I was a kid, and she's probably drafted the designs for half the buildings there. So I know Queens, and this kid is practically from Long Island.

That's the thing about kids from Queens. They carry a chip on their shoulder like they don't count until they've demanded to be counted, like they have to remind you where you're from before you can remind them that there isn't anyone keeping count. Which is different from Bronx kids who pronounce *the Bronx* with a nod as if preparing themselves for you to challenge that they're telling the truth, which you're not going to, if for no other reason than what's the point of challenging anyone about where they tell you they're from if they're not trying to lie to you. And Brooklyn kids say *Brooklyn* like they were born mumbling the word while latching onto their mothers, in a kind of *I don't need to know you* kind of singsong that's really just a mask that reckons they want to forget who you are before you have a chance to forget who they are. And Manhattan kids look down on just about everybody, because in their eyes if you're from Queens you might as well be from Connecticut, and if you're from the Bronx you might as well be from Buffalo, but like the hard core part of Buffalo, and if you're from Brooklyn you shouldn't remind people so much you're from Brooklyn, and if you're from Staten Island you might as well be from Delaware. Which brings me to Staten Island kids, who make absolutely sure to remind you that you aren't from New York before anyone reminds them that they aren't either, not really, and they always fumble through some haughty laughter like they're not somebody's insecure little cousin trying to jockey for position in mixed company every time somebody talks about their childhood.

Anyway, here we are at the dining hall table, and I can't even get to my second bite of pizza before mr.-lower-case-m "ugh-heh-Jersey-ugh" introduces me to some new kid who joins the table, and not only does this "ugh-heh-Jersey-ugh" kid over-pronounce my name, he gets my name wrong, which I find almost impossible because it's almost as easy as John. And then this "ugh-heh-Jersey-ugh" kid says, He's from Jersey, to the other kid that just joined our table, and the kid that's just joined our table looks at the other kid quite a lot confused, and then he asks, Did you say Hershey, I said Jersey, Cuz it sounded like you said Hershey like P-A Hershey, No I said Jersey.

The kid that just joined our table shrugs and says, Okay, like somebody had just told him about quantum mechanics when the only prompt for it was *hello*.

And then, finally, our important newcomer joins our table. Freshmen year, if anything, is one newcomer to the table after the next. Anyway, she joins us. She smiles and sits down and tells us her name. She's wavy-haired, a little frizzy-haired but nothing sloppy, with sunken eyes and bony hands. The "ugh-heh-Jersey-ugh" kid does the same thing to me except with this girl, and I swear it does actually sound like he's saying *Hershey*, but no matter because when this girl hears that I'm from Jersey, she gets all, Oh yeah me too where from. I tell her Jersey City, and she says she's from Warrior, New Jersey, and I say, Wait where, and my eyes must have bulged because she adds, Yeah it's the real name of a real place. She laughs at herself when the fork accidentally slips out of her hand and claps onto her tray.

Her whole demeanor unsettles the pattern that the "ugh-heh-Jersey-ugh" kid had been on, at least enough that he doesn't bother repeating it for the next person that joins us at the table. In fact, I don't hear from the "ugh-heh-Jersey-ugh" kid again for the rest of dinner.

In any case, I get into a conversation with Warrior, New Jersey, and I ask her what it's like, and she says it's just like any other suburb but also not much like a suburb at all because it's more like a town with just one Main Street, Of course a Main Street, she says, and only a few ATMs, a couple way-too-white sushi places, and a Dairy Queen, Of course a Dairy Queen, she says, right in the center of town.

Later when we ride the elevator back to our rooms, she notices the button I push and tells me we're just a few floors apart, and then she asks me to press her button. I don't think much of it other than that we'll probably be riding the elevator together often. A few days later, I hear a pebble ricochet off my open window, loudly and somehow without cracking the glass. We had run into each other in the elevator that afternoon, and I had said something like I needed to go grocery shopping because I'd been eating too many ramen noodles. When I poke my head outside the open window, I look to catch a flock of birds leaping off the building ledge and a second pebble just misses my forehead by maybe inches, millimeters even, and Warrior, New Jersey cackles so hard, she has to cup her mouth to keep from echoing down Manhattan. She shouts at me from her higher window, shouts that I should join her for some grocery shopping. I tell her she'll have to wait a few minutes so I can check with my mom to make sure I have cash in my checking account. I repeat what I'd just said but this time in my head, and I do a piss poor job of backtracking with the "Actually what I'd meant to say was..." routine, but she hadn't even been fazed the first time, Don't worry about it, she says, I can manage my own money I promise, I say, I don't care, So what now, Can you meet me in the lobby in ten.

I nod.

The next few weeks follow me in the same kind of way, a routine of pebbles on glass or straight shouting down the alley until one of us remembers we're modern people and start using the phone, You ready, No, What are you doing, Nothing really I guess, Meet you in the lobby in ten.

We take turns pushing the shopping cart. She never trusts me to grab the produce because she jokes that she doesn't know where I'd put my hands that day. I never trust her to pick out the right salsas because she doesn't know anything about salsas. She says I have no idea what a ripe avocado feels like. She can't believe how many bananas I eat. We usually go to three places for the best deals, and we only start using coupons when they start appearing in the campus newspaper, but we never clip them. Instead we just tear them in odd angles right there at the register.

We have a grocery store run after midterms, and I remember it well because I don't talk much. I nod when she recommends the pre-seasoned canned beans, and I don't argue with her when she says I should probably start making my own grilled cheese sandwiches with tomatoes in them because I'm running out of campus dollars and the pans in my cupboard are collecting dust.

She's polite about the whole thing. She doesn't ask about my mood when we're in the toiletries or frozen food aisle. Outside the store, right before we reach the curb, though, she says she wants to take a minute on the fire hydrant against the storefront window, and she puts her bags down against the side of the building and I set mine right beside hers. On instinct I pull out a pack and light up a cigarette and lean against the glass. She leans, too, and we face the street traffic like the stereotype of a City College moment.

Two no-longer-underage-kids trying hard to figure out how to be of age and meaningfully alive.

I don't know what to say. At this point in my life, I'm not yet comfortable telling anybody what I'd always thought were the most uncomfortable things about me, namely that my head spins from time to time, that too many interactions in a single day confuse me, that I don't know how to be alone, that too often throughout a day I go through mental replays about all the things I should have done and the words I should have said and the ways I should have moved just to have hidden the ways I didn't think I knew what I was doing.

But maybe, maybe, she knew a little bit about that. Or maybe she knew enough to know that I wasn't going to share much yet. In any case, she starts talking, sharing about her day, about the two exams from the day before, about the essay she has to submit the next day, and she talks and talks into what amounts to my absence. There's nothing better to call it. A silence can be like an emptiness that feels like an awakening when you only know how to be alone in the company of someone really close.

I look over at her and she glances at me without smiling. Maybe she's worried. Maybe she's trying to hide that she's worried. It's not easy to carry the burden of killing somebody else's time for them. But she does smile, and as a bus rolls by, she crosses her arms and contemplates whatever's going on across the street. She seems comfortable enough to enjoy the silence with me, and it's then, I think, that I learn about how a buddy becomes a friend, and then she interrupts me staring at her, which I don't know I'm doing until she tells me I'm doing it. She interrupts me contemplating the way she tucks her hair behind her ear like a firefighter kicking aside dry brush, and then she suddenly just gives a loud hoot. Like a military hoot. Like a barbarian kind of *hoo-hah*. And then just a silence again. She raises her eyes expecting me to be shocked, but maybe it's a weak smile I give back, because she goes, Oh, and then I go, Oh what, and then she says, I guess you really were listening to me, What else did you think I was doing, Maybe tuning me out because I tend to think too much out loud, I guess it was comforting to listen to you, Please tell me to shut up if you ever need me to shut up, I've never wanted you to shut up,

But you'd tell me right, I'm not sure I would, But you'd want to, Why would I want to.

As late October rolls around, the costume schtick sort of sneaks up on me. I don't know what to dress up in so I find a werewolf mask on a weekend trip back home, and on campus the Friday before Halloween, Warrior, New Jersey interrogates me about the simplicity of it all, What is that mask supposed to be of, A werewolf, That doesn't look like a werewolf, What does it look like then, It looks like a sick dog, I guess maybe it's a sick dog then.

I turn the mask around and take a good look at it. I bring it nose-to-nose with me, and then she says, We're not hoping to win any costume contests I hope. I tell her to shut up. I remind her that she said I should tell her if ever I needed her to shut up. She rolls her eyes.

The elevator stops on my floor and she reminds me to meet her in the lobby at seven o'clock the next day, Are we not doing the pebbles into the window thing anymore, Yes, Yes what, We're adults now and we shouldn't be throwing rocks into each other's glass anymore.

On Halloween night, we climb the scaffold of a building under renovation downtown to watch the Charade Parade, and our favorite costumes are the tandem sets like an oven mitt and apple pie, Martha and George Washington, and a condom and lube tube. We hold onto each other as we sit perched on a scaffold rail, even as the throngs on the sidewalk swell and the structure begins to shake. The whole thing seems to settle the more that people climb onto it, though it certainly doesn't alleviate my fear of heights to watch so many feet dangling over so many edges.

November gets colder, and the walk back to the dorms every day feels longer. We don't meet anymore at the florist before walking back to our rooms, not because she isn't interested in the daisies anymore, in the lilacs the florist lines up in benches by the front door, but because the shop is open air through Thanksgiving, and she can never just criticize the position of all the displays. She has to roll up her sleeves when she tells me where everything should go.

Her grandmother is a florist, and so Warrior, New Jersey sneers every time we walk past the shop because if there's anyone who knows her flowers in a flower shop it's the granddaughter of a florist. I'm sure Warrior, New Jersey could write a job performance review for the guy who runs the place and get him fired from his own shop. On the off chance that we do stop inside one afternoon, she points to all the daisy arrangements and rose bunches. She judges the combinations that biologically don't make any sense because they cause each other to rot sooner than they otherwise should. Some combinations cause each other's petals to darken and shrivel earlier than they otherwise should. Some combinations cause each other's stems to simply shed when they shouldn't. And then there's the fact that certain numbers don't go together, Do you mean like four lilacs and a dozen lavender stems because like really who does that, says Warrior, New Jersey. One time we stroll through the shop with our headphones on and the same Jill Scott album playing off our phones. I quietly switch over to Common when Warrior, New Jersey gets to talking about the decorative cactus plants on the windowsill. It's not like I don't want to listen. It's just that she's timing her own heavy beats and sighs to Jill's own, and I want to see what it feels like to listen to Warrior, New Jersey drive on about asynchronous blooming with her pauses on the offbeat.

It's weird the way it happens sometimes. How a friend becomes a woman.

One late afternoon in November, we spot each other on the corner outside the library. I think it's the third Thursday in November. Neither of us had actually been in the library. I was leaving the pizzeria across the street and about to turn the corner to the dorms, and she had just left the student center. I guess right that she had been aiming to go back to her room. I spot her first and wait hoping she smiles after she sees me. She does. But before we get to actually meeting up, before I get to the curb on her side of the street, mr.-lower-case-m "ugh-heh-Jersey-ugh" kid appears out of nowhere—thin air, I tell you—as if materializing from another dimension where it makes sense to be an exhausting prick. He brushes past me, long-stepping and bobbing his shoulder like he thinks he's about to mack some game, and instead of some smooth vibrato, he shouts too loud, Hey Jersey. His voice cracks, which is maybe why he goes, Hey Jersey, again, the second time with a kind of aggressive boredom to his voice that hopes somebody somewhere will agree the façade of passé feels cool. Warrior, New Jersey nods at him. She walks past him and right at me. And this "ugh-heh-Jersey-ugh" dude pivots like he's on ice. He eyes Warrior, New Jersey up and down as she walks away from him. His head bobs like he's bowing to a ghost of himself and so obviously that his face might as well have dislodged from his neck, and he follows it all up by saying, Hey Jersey, for a third damn time, this time with an inflection to "Hey" like he's a turkey trying to assure his flock there ain't no rain coming, like he's trying to tell us all something about tomorrow.

But Warrior, New Jersey—she nods without looking. She takes all of it in like she's heard people trying to shout obligations at her before, like she's seen too many kinds of things before, and like it's no more significant than a pigeon landing on her walking path that she knows that *it* knows is too small to posture, too small, at least without a flock to boost its ego. And she smirks at me. The kind of smirk that recognizes that we both recognize the same thing. The kind of smirk that seems to assure everybody around us that attention is capital, and when you give it away, you don't have anything left to barter with, and you have no more secrets to keep.

Warrior, New Jersey slows down as she gets close. I notice she looks tired. Like the thought of the rest of the week is heavy. Like the French-English dictionary in her backpack is as big as her backpack. Like the folder that organizes her course handouts is heavier even than the French-English dictionary. Like the ringed notebook day planner has so many checklists a whole calendar month will never be enough to complete every last bullet point.

She sighs heavy on me. She warns me that she won't be able to join me at dinner that night. That if it weren't cold as ice she'd start unloading on that very street corner and take a nap by the gutter. That if I don't agree to walk back to the dorm hall with her, she doesn't think she'd make it back without crashing into a tree or wall with the crossed eyes she gets from too much reading, And I've read so much today, she says, I've read like I'm running out of time, she says.

She's wearing a grey skirt, tall black and beat-up boots, and a thick beige jacket with its elbows and shoulders padded. Like if a runway show suddenly dropped a gauntlet on its models, she'd be ready. She's pretty. She's always been pretty. But sometimes a friend becomes a woman when you don't know how one thing multiplies into the next. When maybe you don't even know how the next million or hundred quintillion or googol factors into the equation. Maybe I've steeped too long in linear algebra, but sometimes the feeling blooms like dust and earth kicked up after a bomb. I'm not ashamed of the feeling. I'm just surprised I feel so unprepared for it.

Into the holidays and after we come back for finals, our time together gets unexpectedly softer. And undoubtedly quieter. Initially, I blame it on term papers, on exams. We study more. We read more. There's not a lot you can say when there's nothing more to say than *Why is this topic so hard?* or *Is this making any sense to you?* and *I'm so tired I can't even see straight anymore.*

We hadn't really studied together before. We'd always written our essays and finished homework on our own, but not because these obligations had been off-limits by decree or consent. It's just that we simply always studied and did our own work alone. Up until finals, we'd each just gone to our own rooms when thinking took precedence over jokes or banter or boredom. We never really talked about it. There just always seemed to come a time when it made sense to do our separate things. But when finals week came, our independent solitude suddenly became a shared experience, and the time wasn't just about swapping polite smiles and glances with the volume on mute. No. We were now confronting the spaces between the things we said and the seconds between the things that moved around us with a kind of consent that only the intense pressure of keeping good grades to keep our full scholarships could agree to. We needed to get things done. And maybe we needed the company of a familiar boat to help us navigate the choppy water. It was a kind of secondary silence, and it wasn't uncomfortable, either.

In the library, a shared table can feel like an ocean. In a study hall, brushing each other's shoes by chance warranted a kind of hesitation that obliged you to have to work that much harder to write your term papers and study for your finals without being distracted by the way your skin felt when denim touched corduroy. When your spirit touched somebody else's.

And then it happened. I don't think we put ourselves into a position that welcomed the percussion of bare faces and the melody of a quick kiss. She just leaned into my chest after her end-of-semester advising appointment like she had after her previous appointment and like she almost had after the appointment before that. This time, though, she'd been too exhausted to measure the separation between us, and the kiss, the world, just happened.

I didn't expect to put my arms around her when she leaned into me. And I don't think she met me in the stairwell thinking *Well, his lips are as good as any*. We were just too tired to not do something else, I guess. Her body's proximity to mine woke me up enough to meet her widened eyes and the smile that I think she'd kept herself from cracking open. And after the kiss, she leaned into me again and put her arms around me and said nothing. The saying nothing part felt just as good.

But let me rewind.

I'd been waiting for her on the couches outside the college advising center. I'd gotten exhausted with the book I had to read for my ancient civilizations course, mostly because it'd be years before antiquity would matter to me, but also because the book had been assigned by the professor who wrote the book, and who does that. I got tired of reading, so I packed my bag and hers, too, the one she left with me before she left for the appointment. Figured I had time for a walk up and down the stairs. I needed to feel my skin and blood again. But let me explain. I used to do this kind of thing a lot. Climb up and down stairs to release some of that nervous energy.

And so I went up a couple floors up, and then I descended a few floors, and when I got back to the advising center story, I leaned back against the stairwell landing wall and slipped on my headphones. My forehead rustled in the wool cap and so I scratched my itching hairline. The central heating unit on the fire escape platform between buildings shot on, and the pigeons that had sat on it for as long as I'd been in the stairwell jumped double-flips. I thought I'd be on the landing alone for a while, when suddenly Warrior, New Jersey opened the door from the main hall saying, I figured I'd find you in here. She looked disappointed about something, and when I asked her about it, she just said, I'm tired of talking, and I said, You and me both, and she said, I wish people weren't always demanding things of us, and then I said, You and me both.

I recognized the glaze that overcomes her eyes when the patience to listen runs its course. She walked softly right into me. She buried her forehead into my sweater. She looked up. She brushed the hair out of her eyes, and then she kissed my chin. And then she kissed my lips. After she kissed my chin, I might have leaned into her lips, but life is sometimes just one boring confession after the next, and that might have been mine. She exhaled after the kiss and then half-smiled after licking her lips, and then she said she had to wait for her adviser to meet with somebody else before she could go back in there. My appointment ran way over, she said. Let's go back to the couches outside the advising center, she said. Have you ever confused your legs for your brain, she said, As if every running thought were a marathon that didn't need to be run, she said.

I didn't know what she meant, so I didn't say anything. Silence is no kind of response, but at least silence knows when it has to agree.

When we sit again, she rests her hand on my hand. I stop myself from looking at my watch. I don't want to measure the minutes that have passed since the stairwell kiss because I'm afraid they haven't been minutes at all, just eternity turning the memories preceding an explosion into a reel of still portraits that all happen again and at once. I might put up a good face, but I don't ever know what comes next. The suddenness of how a woman becomes a partner is just another one of those nexts. How you come to terms with what a partner can even mean, for tomorrow and the day after—how you come to terms with the handbook you hadn't even realized you'd been writing, one that compiles definitions and revises the days gone by into a story that stretches those evenings out—nothing but a bunch more nexts that I can't see right now.

Warrior, New Jersey crosses her arms over her open coat. She laughs and says that if she knew she'd be changing her major, she'd have chosen her first set of courses with a different lens in mind. I nod and tell her that at least she has a lens she knows she wants to see through. She turns her head so her eyes land on my hair. She smiles. She reminds me I haven't combed my hair in a few days. I ask her how she can even be sure what day it is. She smirks and looks ahead. Our reflections in the advising center's glass wall stare at us. Transparency, it seems, knows how to contain us. It doesn't run away from holding onto us.

TO ADDRESS THE MATTER AT HAND

It would be an injustice to go on like this, with no mention of Paul Jean-Paul and his refusal to leave the library with no fewer than four books in his hands and one book under his arm and two others yet still in his bag. And you're probably asking, quite logically, as to why he hasn't already placed every book in his bag, particularly the ones in his hands, which he holds while crossing the street, which he presses to his chest as he rushes past traffic. But the question is more trouble than it's worth, seeing as you've probably already come up with an appropriate response, though I hope not to unfairly be expecting more than you'd like to contribute, because perhaps you have no answer for why young college men would read this much, to this grave extent, to this burdening madness of weight, crossing busy city streets at the risk of dropping one or even two books, and potentially losing life itself upon stooping to pick them up, why else would a young man read to this level of consumption and severity if it weren't for the mere supplication of a girl.

And don't argue with me, which I'm sure you are preparing to do, because you think, or because you might perhaps immediately propose, that this student is simply a good student, a socially delayed but academically refined one, you would probably suggest he is one of the good students, one of the proud ones, to which I must silence you, immediately, by saying simply, No, this here young man, Paul Jean-Paul, is most certainly not that kind of student. I know with absolute certainty he hasn't so much as cared, damn near hasn't even dared, to read for much of his nineteen years, at least not as much as he has read over the past few months, passing up, for most of his life, the drama comedy hubris and human meekness in literature for the arrogance of what youths call a full-court pick-up basketball game, or even for that immodest and thieving moment in which one girl or another or more than one suggest in no uncertain terms, Do you want to hang out in my living room, for which, in the past, Paul Jean-Paul has not only put aside books but also chores and homework and eating. And yet here we find Paul Jean-Paul reading, or at least hurrying to read, rushing across the street, walking briskly into a city park, plopping himself and his things and his coffee down, onto a bench, and then opening the top book of his pile, exhausted. He exhales. He wipes his brow. Clouds have come and gone over the city since the morning. Remnants of white remain amid the light blue, but the drizzle is gone, that light incessant rain that arrives and departs every day like scheduled flights over the ocean and back, across the Atlantic and back again like hungry cows over the same grazing plains. And so now, Paul Jean-Paul, after exhaling again and glancing across the park once, then twice, seeing nothing of interest but the same park fountain and the busy jungle gym and swings, opens the front cover of a book, something about the existential sea and its arrival at midnight or some other baffling metaphor of that inclination. Books are often like this, incorporating metaphors that either cloak or confuse things, though books are mostly clear about love, misspelling the word on its pages and always including some scrambled version of it in its letters. Coming back to Paul Jean-Paul, his finger trembles as he turns to the first page, though do not interpret this as some imperceptible weakness in his hands. It was simply the light spring winds. They can do that, make your hands move while simultaneously encouraging you as a whole and welcoming you into the given air you breathe. Paul Jean-Paul's focus, however, is not with the seasonal winds. It's with this new book and its title page, and then its opening page, and then for what, why is he reading this, his second book now in three days, what is all this for if not for the mere supplication of a girl.

And you're probably considering this girl, this young woman, her identity and looks and height, among other facets that come to mind when one thinks of a girl, not excepting her hair, whether it curls or waves or simply falls straight, and you're probably thinking, Oh how I've read this before, Oh how this consideration of a girl and her appearance is nothing new, to which I must say history is a repetitive mess, drowned in its failures and repetitions, a failure to contrive an alternate history and, in its detriment, repeating its every shortcoming. Considering this, you aren't alone, because Paul Jean-Paul is thinking it, too, seeing as he's had more than his share of repetitions and more than his share of swirling thoughts and failures and more than his indecent shared company of single young women, nothing outrageous, nothing insignificant, experiences from which he cannot assert to have succeeded at or learned anything from but from which he can certainly say, For better or for worse it was I who did this, all these experiences that have made him the young man he's become, the young man attending this university. And what a great place it is, with its flags and its science buildings and its hanging paintings, and Paul Jean-Paul has occasionally thought during his time there, For better or worse this place is going to make me, and though it's true, Paul Jean-Paul, it's not entirely true, but then again, no one is ever completely right. You can be certain, though, that Paul Jean-Paul is changing, having already changed into this young man here, the young man on the park bench, with his coffee beside him and his bag on the ground, the grass and tree behind him rustling in the city's afternoon breeze, a wind that very imperceptibly tussles Paul Jean-Paul's hair, and yet he adjusts his hair as if it had swung entirely out of place. Universities will do that. They'll re-make you all over though nothing was ever really maladjusted or misaligned or terribly incorrect. And universities will do this because boys at nineteen will have the tendency to do it to themselves anyway, create and recreate themselves, Wow what a girl she looks great she's eating vegetables she must like vegetables, and so what do these ythese young men do but start eating carrots from that very same eatery or celery from that very same diner, presenting a smirk or a smile as they pass by her, but then the girl unfortunately pays no attention because she's carrying two books in her hands that she must return to the library. I don't intend to describe this as exactly what happened with Paul Jean-Paul. His situation will become clear in time. I include this only to suggest that, at nineteen, young men embrace awful tendencies to create and recreate their jeans and collars and hair, which Paul Jean-Paul re-adjusts twice, all while settling into his book, by now on page seven. He exhales, as if hurrying through the words in a race, but what's the rush, and he takes a second deep breath and turns the page, but why the rush, Paul Jean-Paul, with a forced patience that does more to communicate Paul Jean-Paul's breezing wish to read through another book completely than to endeavor too long into the reading process. And if this moment is any testament, it's all too possible to never finish a book, because there isn't always enough time to appreciate a book's literary crumbs, and this is sadly the case because we often waste time, thinking while reading or mounting external considerations onto the characters in books that already carry so many considerations and worries, and *How unfair!* these characters must feel, having already been pushed around and told what to do by some writer, a novel's characters must also compete with the petty concerns of a reader, like laundry and groceries and clipping nails. But there are no superfluous concerns with Paul Jean-Paul, not with how fast he's reading, as there's no reality but this reality, and he can manage all other realities later, especially when the most pressing consideration here is not only the book on his lap but also the mere supplication of a girl.

And why this girl if she didn't request anything, and yet most young men insist the question was there, the supplication was present, Between the words, they say, In the silence, they say. I like her, thinks Paul Jean-Paul, but he didn't think it to mean what you think it meant. It was simply textual evidence he read, words on the page in the book he's reading that he quickly related to himself and then unintentionally doubled over in his own thoughts, as if its gesture were the very thing his eyes needed to embrace the view. He exhales. He stops reading. He picks his head up and looks around. A couple plays with their baby on the grass. A young woman rides her bike down the path. Half a dozen students idle at the base of a bronze bust, a monument to a person of relative acclaim, but it doesn't matter to these idling students. They care only about drawing a mustache in red ink marker beneath the bronze alloy nose and above the lips. And no one sees them. Well, to be honest, everyone sees them, but no one seems to care. And so Paul Jean-Paul veers back into his book, and that it's the seventeenth book he's read in five months is no laughing matter, and that he's read novels with such titles as *A Tale of Raven Lake* and *The Journey of Seven Squires Over the Atacama* and *Prosperity in El Paso* and even *The Geneva Conception* are all reasons to take this matter seriously, to offer Paul Jean-Paul the praise due him for reading with the hunger he does, for trying as hard as he does to relate to this girl who's already read these books, to some girl he believes has begged him to read these books, to his girl who isn't quite his girl at all yet, though I correct even my own insinuation here. No one person quite belonging to anyone else, unless of course one refers to a librarian or a security systems salesman, the former belonging to everybody and the latter belonging to thieves. And you're probably asking yourselves, how did this begin, why did it unfold this way, and so I'll explain to you. More precisely, I'll paraphrase. It was all because a young woman once invited Paul Jean-Paul into her dorm room, like friends, like all friends, And here's the book I was telling you about, she says, and he asks, Do you mean this one here, Yes and you can borrow that or take any other you'd like, and Paul Jean-Paul looked at all the books on the young woman's bookshelf, and then he scratched his brow. He scratched his head, a gesture he hoped the girl hadn't seen, and when he glanced at her, he noticed she'd been looking at the books, and so Paul Jean-Paul felt relieved. No one saw his masked troubled mind, least of all her, and, boy, was it troubled. There were all kinds of tumbling thoughts in his head, things like *Boy she sure likes to read* and *She's pretty and nice but she's not going to like me cuz I don't read* and then finally *Damn she looks good in those jeans.* And when something accustomed to running in no purposeful direction suddenly brakes at a fork in the road, with looming purpose in either direction but no signs explaining which goes where and why, that sudden braking doesn't happen without violent consequence to the foot on the accelerator, which sharpens into focus only after restrained frigid blood turns the skin blue and one is suddenly left colder and more alone. Have you read this one here, she asks, No I haven't, he says, How about this one, and the questions kept coming, politely and with friendly affection but too unyieldingly uncomfortable for Paul Jean-Paul's tastes, and every question was either

about whether he had read this book or this author or that poem and that poet, and after a minute or two, he just stopped saying No or shaking his head. It was simply rude to go on like that, technically disagreeing, and then he asked which her favorite book was, and that's when she reached for a book on the bottom shelf. She arose and handed it to him, and then she smiled, You can read it if you want. Paul Jean-Paul took the book, and I have no doubt this scene is familiar to you. After all, familiarity is an echo of something you've heard before, perhaps even read before, a resonance that imposes or a reverberation that kindles. But I'll stop there because repetitions can also be numbing. And so I'll just say this, the book this young woman gave Paul Jean-Paul was the first in the series of books he would read over the course of five months, and reading this particular book consumed all of eight days. After all, Paul Jean-Paul was a laboring reader, careful with his words, trying at every line to read even the space between letters, but then things changed and after reading several books he simply wanted to read more and dozens more and just finish them already. However, at first, he only knew he wanted to read this book, the book she had given him, at least to start his reading venture with it, because Paul Jean-Paul thought he had heard on that very first day in the girl's room, or at least thought he'd discerned in all the young woman's questions, especially in the tumbling thoughts that had muted his tongue, something akin to an appeal in her breath or something like a provocation or at least a consideration that sounded like the mere supplication of a girl.

And so this was how it started, this nonsense of book after book, the first he borrowed from her and the second he purchased and the third a library loan, which he returned promptly in exchange for three others that, by title alone, spoke to him in ways things often speak to us when they carry intention, because intention commands, and intentions have instruction and they force you to listen, even if said intentions have only been inferred. And then one day, Paul Jean-Paul's brother, a young man who was also Paul Jean-Paul's friend and roommate, asked how things had been, through which question the implication was simple, that is, How have things been going with that girl you like but that keeps treating you like a friend and do you think she likes you, Things are fine, You've been reading a lot, I know, Why have you been reading so much, I'm enjoying it, You've never enjoyed it before, I'm enjoying it now, Doesn't it seem strange to you, What does, That you didn't like to read all that much and now suddenly you do, You're getting annoying, And you're getting mad, I'm not getting mad, It's about that girl isn't it, I'm not getting mad, It is about that girl and she's making you read, She isn't making me do anything, So then why are you reading so much, Because I want to, Well I think it's because you want her to like you, Don't you have somewhere to go, I am like the voice inside your head after all okay, Listen I'm done I'm leaving, Are you thinking that she'll like you and then hug you and then suggest some coffee or dessert together and then say I love all that you're reading and I'd love to spend more time together, I'm not listening to this I'm leaving, I'm telling you the truth man and you better listen because she's not going to just take off her clothes and show you the matter at hand no sir you're wasting your time, and there was only so much Paul Jean-Paul could stand of his brother's words before Paul Jean-Paul picked up a five-pound barbell and tossed it in his brother's general direction, and because his brother jumped and slid out of the way, the barbell crashed into the wall and cracked open a hole.

And then Paul Jean-Paul slammed the door behind him and left the dorm room. He walked briskly to the elevator, his rushing steps seemingly tearing the carpet as he burned for the elevator doors, fuming, his cheeks turning red, and when he arrived to the elevator, he pressed the button to go down. He waited. The dormitory corridor was long. Papers and flyers were taped to the wall. They were scattered along it like confetti behind a parade. Paul Jean-Paul adjusted the bag on his shoulder. He gripped both straps firmly. He pressed his thumbs into the cotton vinyl. Someone suddenly opened her door and peered down the hall and, seeing only Paul Jean-Paul by the elevator, she hazily nodded and then went back into her room and closed the door. That was not Paul Jean-Paul's young woman. That most certainly was not Paul Jean-Paul's girl because Paul Jean-Paul's girl would have made some indication of a smile before she left back into her room and closed the door. She would have at least given some indication of a supplication, at least something Paul Jean-Paul could assume was such, but then again, just about everything the young woman said Paul Jean-Paul had construed as a supplication, and seeing as young men are no oracles, they are not only prone at mistaking a message, they are infamous for inferring one out of none. But you already know this. This is nothing new. Standing by the

elevator, Paul Jean-Paul felt a solitary pain in his hands, one which the young woman's supplications had never explicitly mentioned would be there. The supplication he had heard in the questions she asked him, in her voice and in everything she did carried no indication that all his reading would relegate him isolated from even here, the very place where he stood, and I won't bother you with more metaphor or contemplation because, having read at least this far, you know exactly what I mean.

Paul Jean-Paul waited for the elevator. He adjusted the bag on his shoulder, he gripped the book in his hand, and he half-stared at the sealed doors. And then he heard the familiar bell that accounts for an approaching elevator, and then at last the bell rang on his floor. The doors opened. He stepped into the elevator. He turned around, exhaled into the empty car, and watched the doors start closing. And then someone reached inside and kept the doors from closing completely. She pushed the doors open and then she slowly stepped inside. It was a young woman, it was *the* young woman, Paul Jean-Paul's young woman, the very one whose supplication has exhausted this story and the very one who will end it. The young woman stepped into the elevator and smiled, but then her lips gave way to tired eyes, a warm weariness Paul Jean-Paul had become all too familiar with and enjoyed. He smiled, only so much as to invite an eased silence, just enough to motivate himself, more than was needed to encourage time, to claim it and use it and elongate its space. They stood by each other. The elevator started down. Her brown hair hung like a river over her shoulders and cheeks. A depth beneath her eyes lent her olive face a shine that contrasted the shadows, I haven't seen you in days, she said, I've been reading, Nothing terrible I hope, You'd approve I think, You should tell me about it one day, I will.

IN DEFENSE OF UNNAMEABLE THINGS

I sat at my colleague's breakfast table recently, not exactly an amorous morning, awakening as we usually did on a Saturday to her snoring and my agitated semi-slumbering feet. We do this sometimes, fall asleep to wine and stumbled, heavy love making, and then we wake up the following day, hating we did either so late into the night, but at least thankful my eyelids could help me surface words.

Breakfast comprised partially buttered toast and hurriedly mixed coffee. I tried making some hash, and though some of the shredded potato burned, I salvaged enough to blend with applesauce and get our eating going, the habit itself, particularly on a Saturday, feeling more like a touch-and-go tasting and less like a devouring.

Me and my incomplete morning thoughts had been stumbling into each other quite a bit since I served coffee, as I'd started on some topics of literature and the classics, the various continents and their offerings, the various myths and their generous affairs among the gods, their fitting pains among the mortals. I'm sure it was Sidney Wang's most recent translation of Ae-cha Kwong's *The Heights and Havocs of Women* that got Olivia and I going about the wonders and tragedies of long sentences in literature, into which we proceeded with Lionel Ferreira's novel *El Mandado Colombiano*, having read both for a faculty book club we organized that semester, a rather niche book club, if I might say, but one particularly important to us as we usually have to suffer, amongst colleagues and students alike, the traps and travesties of a so-called canon, a limited kind of North American-ness that prefers its own reflections, a certain but thorough lamentation about how even intellectuals want to be practical with their so-called identities.

The conversation, especially after Olivia's half-argument that reframed Ferreira's terse expressions amidst comma-ridden pages as a kind of experience for the reader that supplanted the experience of the character, the narrator's *joie de vivre* being its own reason for the book to be at all, a persuasive approach in which she cited various lines across the novel's whole second act, took a ripe turn for us, especially as Olivia swirled her orange juice like she would have a glass of grenache. And I picked up from there, citing my own lines from Wang's translation, a brilliant adaptation of the original Korean particularly because it turned Kwong's em dashes into American English-language commas that set appositives, in sequence, like a snake molting across a desert strip, leaving dried curls of its skin across the sand behind it, separated by brush and stones and sticks.

We never actually disagreed with each other, but it did feel at times like a breathless "I can do you one better" approach between mouthfuls of ham and eggs, our conversation, at times, like its own poor impression of those long sentences we suddenly couldn't get enough of, though she didn't always have the same patience with my trains of thought as I'd had listening to her thoughtful pacing, interrupting me, as she often liked to do, to ask me if what I'd really meant to say was X and me having to interject to remind her that she'd interrupted me before I was able to arrive to X, So what you want to say is that the breathless overwhelming declaratives succeed in spite of themselves in Ferreira's work but succeed more intentionally in Wang's translation, she said, Olivia if you could just bear with me, I said, I would hope that someone who started us on this trajectory could keep up with the woman who could run laps around him on any track, I guess in the end I really should start at the beginning that I've loved these long sentences since I was a child, I can appreciate your appeal to compassion here, I'm also going for intellect so thank you for the cheeky sarcasm, But I can also see that you appear to want me to take it easy on you by replacing the man in front of me with the impression of boy in my mind, You crack me up, I am only stating the obvious, Fine then tell me what you really want to say, What I need you to start doing Bolívar is to cite your sources and stop pressing the point by appealing for sympathy.

I smiled. I was certainly an easy target at times, Would you like me to use the French press for the next pot of coffee, What I would love my love is for you to cite your sources.

She smiled, sipping just enough of the last drip of coffee in her mug to wet her lips and softly swallow. Fine then, I said, and I grabbed a notebook from the dining table, where she kept many half-used notebooks and their corresponding pens. She was both beautiful and mind-boggling in these smallest of ways. She loved leaving thoughts scattered in all these half-full pages in half-full notebooks across her house, and she also assigned a pen to each notebook, and even though I never saw a fast and hard rule, a specific pen applied to a specific notebook, in practice, that's exactly what it looked like. She almost always intuitively reached for the assigned pen or pencil every time she picked up one of her various notebooks in whatever room we found ourselves to be in. And, so, when I picked up the notebook and then pen that I did, I very much glanced over at her for approval, turning into a boy seeking permission in that moment, and she did not negate my decision. Instead, she offered a certain grin that, I admit, I had to keep myself from grinning in response to.

In the end, one never loses the need for approval no matter how old you get, least of all after you've shared the entirety of your body with someone.

I pulled the notebook open to an empty page, and I started to write, or at least tried to start writing, from memory, a sentence or two from Uriah Tomer's *Crimes of a Thousand Cuts*, the first of his novels that featured the wayward detective Amit Adah, and in which Tomer was known to let his narrator unpack traumatic childhood experiences that had led to the character's insomnia, hermeticism, and cocaine habit, What are you doing, she said, I'm forming a thought my love, I said, Decent enough choice Bolívar, I remember how much you love that book after all.

And she did. We had previously considered Tomer's long sentences for how well they unpacked everything and nothing at all, as if they existed as simply for the experience of reading as for the complicated nature through which they revealed hard truths about parenting, early sexual encounters, and loneliness, and she said, But be careful however not to compare apples with oranges darling, Olivia honey what else am I supposed to do.

She smiled, of course, as if contemplating the minor differences between obstruction and flirtation, Fine then go on, she said, Thank you, I said, But I must say that Tomer's prose feels like its own environment challenging the expectations of the narrator, Exactly and I particularly enjoy the way his sentences hold tensions articulating every feeling at once as if no one feeling could exist without another. She nodded, despite how much she disliked the notion of juxtaposition, particularly the popular belief that language and feelings in opposition hold the most weight.

I never did quite finish writing the sentence I was trying to remember, but I did note the jitter in my body, the good kind of jitter, that feeling in which your body remembers the first reading of something, the joy that memory sparks and in which your body feels again those old feelings of loving a book, especially those feelings of a book's binding and its ability to hold, forever, the allusions of all the language within it, and she said, So now that we've covered that source what next Boli, and I said, How about Marcelo Ricotta's *Hornet's Bulb*, I don't remember that one, We read it together not long ago, I remember everything when it hasn't been that long ago, Then perhaps it was long ago enough.

She laughed, and said, Well I was hoping to engage in the kind of comparisons that carry a kind of physical strain in their words, Like the strain of remembering, I said, I guess, she said.

The emotional maneuvers of a long sentence, like an extended moment across a kitchen island, as you and your other avert your eyes from the clock, captures something of a feeling, and whether or not you call it unnameable, you can't always call it explicit, Language is body as much as head Boli, she said, You don't have to speak to *me* in riddles my love, I said, I would say we are both riddles worth uncovering wouldn't you say.

I tipped my mug into hers, a passive toast to bridge an active compliment.

She stared at me from across the table, eyes half closed, tilting her mug sideways as if to demonstrate what was and was no longer filling its well. When she bit into her toast, her eyes remained on me, fixed, as well as on words in both long gone and looming books within and beyond her walls. The kitchen window hung open, and even at eight forty-five in the morning, the beach just beyond the hedges lingered in a perpetual sunrise, a forever kind of looming day relative to the geography we enjoyed, always cloudy with a soft chance of light, You're missing the game aren't you Boli.

I paused, I certainly am but talking literature is its own kind of game too.

I got up to run another liter of boiling water, and I left my phone behind, refusing to check for the score, the game by then likely well past ten minutes, I know you want to Boli, We don't keep score Olivia, You know that's not what I mean you fool.

I laughed. We both did. In the company of a humor that intrigues you, there are no differences between obstruction and flirtation, Would you humor me for a while, I said, What else have we been doing Boli, she said.

I offered that eternal hand gesture, the circling flip of a left hand, and *only* the left hand, because the right, as a symbol of conduct and order, holds no capacity for relieving tension or learning from a shared presence or saying *touché* without the tongue, Let's presume a game of sorts, I said, What kind of game, she said, A game that supposes fútbol were a long sentence sample, Explain, By which I mean a phenomenon so regionally specific as to suggest various *soccers* might exist in a single match and various forms of tension in the compounded meaning of one long sentence after the next physically represented by the continuous action before a pause before someone—likely a sweeper or defender—stalls the action by letting the goalie handle the ball and then lob to center field to get the action going again, In English please Boli, Let's imagine every long sentence were a soccer game worth reveling in and worth revealing.

The water boiled quickly, and Olivia, having filled the French press independently with enough scoops to double the strength of the last pot of coffee, returned to her stool at the counter, You don't have to explain the game to me Boli, Imagine this a thrilling long-awaited goal after near endless repetition of pass-dribble-pass, So what you're saying is that the long-winded sentence can establish expectations through a series of observations and passing perspectives one to the next or at least through some manner of free association or figurative repetition.

I raised my eyes to suggest we move forward with brewing the second pot of coffee.

Olivia leaned back in her chair and sighed, Can you please continue with your citations Boli, They're coming my love, After your claims I suppose, Indeed, and so I continued, Long-form sentences elongate and explore moments in ways that other briefer forms of prose are incapable of, You can't just choose to confine the long sentence's advantage to merely an attribute that a tiny poem could equally do, Hold on my love because a poem simply cannot achieve the lengthy continuity necessary to affect a reader like a long-awaited soccer match goal or a multitudes-containing sentence, Brevity is not dead Boli, Exhilarating long-awaited scores are nothing without the extensive void before them.

Olivia left the point unanswered as she poured herself another cup, a slow pour, without a splash, in that elegant way women of a certain slim height, particularly with one marriage behind them, can achieve with a glide from moment to moment separated by only the commas of their ruffled sleeves.

Her kitchen, the same as other rooms in the house, was a consummation of wall-mounted shelves, and she reached for a book over the buffet table, grabbing a copy of Édison Hidalgo's second edition of *La Historia de los Partidos*, an Uruguayan volume I hadn't yet read through or even browsed, though Lord knows I've wanted to, as I have so many other books in her ownership, mingling emotions with language in the company of her rooms, minutes across her shelves, generously and plentifully, able to change the way you breathe and touch and smell and taste.

I didn't ask, of course, where she got the book. Most of her books had once been her ex-husband's reading tendencies which, in time, become a wife's and then divorcée's leisure habits after a full split, especially when that full split emerges so suddenly, provoked, as bad splits are wont to do, with a younger pregnant infidelity, the man so foolish in his decision-making that Olivia refused him entry outright to retrieve his books after the final court documents were signed and delivered. Reading habits, too, can help someone come to terms with the spirit of differences that imploded a marriage, the habits and tastes that could maybe explain why those differences led to unnecessary rifts that led to stubborn silences and the kinds of choices you don't take back.

She flipped through bulks of pages at a time as I frothed the creamer for our coffee, and then she stopped at page six hundred eighty-four, and then again six hundred eighty-six, and then she handed me the tome and said, Start at the third full paragraph and continue to the next page and disregard the depth chart that divides the paragraphs, I think I love you, I said, and then she said, Just *read* you fool, and as the steamer whirred, I dipped my nose into the binding, Read and observe the language that so easily transitions into and retains its own defining context, she said, and I did, reading through sentences steadily increasing in shape and size.

If there were a book that could prove all our points at once, this would be it, Why do we even bother talking after this, Sports writing can be an achievement all its own when it reads just like the game feels like it's played, she said, and then I said, The effects in these sentences feel like they expand time, Which begs the point Boli that perhaps we should limit our discourse to whether or not the long-form sentence can embody a soccer match, I love your mind my love, Get over yourself Boli, she said, and so I said, Well then please propose a claim, That long form prose embodies the game better than other textual forms, With Hidalgo's text here as exhibit number one, Yes, And the implication is that there's always something exhilarating to be communicated through a match, That's one interpretation, And that even a draw can offer its own experience of accomplishment, Let's just say that the text must carry a stretch of perspective and not just spurts of it.

Pouring coffee can feel like a religious experience, one not unlike a priest meandering the aisles with incense and shuffling feet, airy and with a rhythm both monotonous and expectant, as if waiting, like the process of a long sentence, was in itself, regardless of outcome, its own kind of divine intervention, And I quote here my love *By the 1983 European Cup's end, not even the West German faithful lust for home believing their team's extra time one-nil victory was anything but an unearned mistake, the kind of unremarkable victory one couldn't even attribute to chance, because even chance comes with a burden of fairness, and the West German team's complete demise into poor ball control, clinically tasteless passing, and not a single shot on goal left everyone just scratching their heads at their only goal, caused by the ball lost in the scrum by the English goal, batted between toes and heels, the kind of goal that left everyone just plain confused, because how does one even celebrate that kind of mess, a thought certainly not lost on the West German forwards who wandered around the goal posts looking around, at the referees and at each other, unable to celebrate their sudden advantage and perhaps prepared to receive red cards, the full lot of them, for playing generally uninspired, awful football.*

Hearing that, I had to recall in that moment the Moroccan Elaid Mansouri's *The Anxieties and Corporeal Emotions of the Worldly Footballer*, for his ability to communicate an understanding of the pitch, especially to those who've never been on one, as it pertains to something he calls 'field mentality,' those of the footballer and of the audience, that is, the series of instincts and of actions-reactions, or a spectator's call-and-response relationship with the footballer, that accumulate to weave the events of a full game into one bound thread, though, in his extensive elaborations, Mansouri interrogates words like *thrilling* and *exhilarating* and *mesmerizing*, all of which, he argues, *are an ear-sore when you a hear a commentator utter it, and you want to twitch at the mention of such a slur or at least shirk at the thought of it, because 'thrilling,' in the end, is merely the description for a completed thought, a goal, the kind of punctuation that makes the series of misfires and ugly fouls and even uglier tackles worth it all, but what reader in any right mind would call a period or a question mark 'thrilling' merely because it ended a sentence, merely because it put meaning to the life of every word that came before it.*

When she leaned back in her chair, Olivia reclined as if on a mound of leaves, which is only to say that the backrest, as old as the chair was, since before she married, seemed to give completely into her arching back, about as far as she was willing to bend, I propose a trip to the archives Boli, Do you mean right now, Why not, Well firstly because neither one of us is dressed to so much as even take a walk to your mailbox, Well we don't need to wear much to hole ourselves up in a library, Perhaps, And perhaps we could scour the shelves like guerrillas mounting sporadic assaults on ideas and their labor, What do you intend for us to find, Poems my love, I should have guessed as much myself, The kind of poems that can impose the power of perspective without all that complicated haze of a personality that often becomes too much to bear in prose, So you want to disprove the premise we're on, I only want a comparable set of texts against which to test our ideas, So then I imagine that the central question becomes can a poem capture the heart of this most beautiful game better than long form prose, Correct my love.

Later that day, early afternoon, we visited the library. We started in the lobby, this tall atrium that cuts vertically up the building culminating in a stained-glass dome, a collage of triangles and trapezoids and hexagons and all of them impossible to cut symmetrically. I'd glance up occasionally as we compiled a surprising list of poets and their odes (and one elegy) at the Information Desk counter, standing there, I'm sure of it, to avoid sitting down any more than we already had that day. It was revealing, I think, to see just how spiteful Luxembourgians have been of their national team, predicting its demise almost monthly in their newspapers, particularly in *Le Weekend Suisse*, where one amateur writer praised the team's ambitions during its most recent, disastrous European friendly, the poet embarking into a kind of alternate reality, detailing in narrative poetry the hypothetical situation of a terrorist railway bomb murdering the whole team of young promising midfielders, of which the sole survivor would be goalkeeper Lorenz Tredent because he hadn't let up a goal the defense hadn't provoked by fouling in the box and producing a penalty kick for the other side. The satirist Jules Chevalier has stated of populist poetry (in last summer's edition of *New York Poetry League*) that it is *the first resort of a kind of unnameable feeling for people, the first thing people reach for when there's a private or public loss, which in the case of football, for which passions not only inspire love and anger but also resentment and residual physical frustration, can be felt throughout a family or community, and the fact that fans are increasingly likely to funnel their emotions into opinion pieces or editorials to their local paper in the form of a poem must certainly explain a kind of progress for literacy.*

We also found the example, one we were *also* not looking for, of a Singaporean magazine sponsored by a consortium of night markets, featuring their vendors and product manufacturers and which included profiles of clothing designers, taste makers, and chefs, a magazine aimed at tourists and available for free around the city-state. The Singaporean national soccer team had, as of this writing, not fronted a competitive team at the regional stage, much less the global one, and so locals, as you might imagine, lost their minds when two years ago, their national team was able to claim, as its singular success this decade, a nil-nil draw against Japan. Though the game was only a friendly, tons and tons of poems, by email and post-mail, flooded the central publishing office of the *Night Market Bazaar*, praising the team and elaborating on particularly notable moments of the match, which, from the Singaporean side, largely meant that a defender was not carded for an aggressive slide tackle or that a striker was able to recover their dribble after temporarily getting it batted away or that a sweeper was able to catch up with a Japanese counter-attack, of which there were many—so many—and rip the ball into the stands. The magazine published a host of these over the next two issues, the monthly unable to feature the excitement too prominently beyond that, tasteless as it would have been to keep voicing those everyday poets long after their relatively bland excitement had died out and, also, because less than two months later, Singapore lost a foul-heavy friendly to New Zealand.

Of the poems we needed books for, we charged ourselves with finding examples before we arrived to the library, to likewise determine what was available in the stacks and what wasn't, as something wholly original emerges reading the works in print, whether or not in their original collections. Our university library's translated works collections was limited, as one could expect from a U.S. institution of higher learning, so we settled for what we could find, though what we found felt like a breadth of personhood and niche interests—Samuel Poacher's "Raining Horns," Ivanko Petronski's "Punctured Net in a Burning Field," Emiko Daisuke's "Bleeding Centerback and the Shoes that Didn't Fit," and Abiku Kapoonga's "Year of the Nigerian Wolf, or A Simple Toothless Grin that Disguised the Mute Beneath." We found these with the intent to compare them, their ideas, their metaphors, their imagery, their voices, to long-form sentences we could gather in a handful of other books, all of them novels, all of them lengthy homages to something beautiful and brave, such works as Natalia Gallego's *The Case of the Four Missing Vaqueros*, Ira Khatri's *A Domestic Kind of Simple*, Mahommed Mahommed Nuandir's *Calico Days*, all these novels inclusive of characters bound to the realm and life of the sport, the first book about a kidnapped goalkeeper and a gun-toting statistician, the second about a woman's pursuit of an athleticism the men around her don't enjoy or simply can't fathom, and the last book about a James Bond-like spy/assassin-for-hire who keeps a day job as a high profile coach in the Saudi A League.

Olivia and I holed ourselves up in a second-floor meeting room, spread all seven books across an oval table. Central air conditioning seemed inept at keeping the room cool, and at times, it simmered in there. At one point, and perhaps it was the intimacy of a locked door, or the opportunity to lean into each other across a wide table without touching for stretches at a time, or the way we were able, regularly enough, to share a shorthand of commentary and directives, not the least of which was the erotic *Could you turn the page for us darling*, her seat inching closer by necessity, her legs within aromatic grazing, or, in the end, perhaps we could only fathom relieving ourselves of sweat with yet more sweat. In any case, the heat between us heightened a common tension into an unbearably taut spring, and we rushed into the janitor's closet, conveniently accessible from within the room, and we pressed into each other's hips between a vacuum cleaner and a set of brooms, her nipples shivering, shaking, against my unbuttoned shirt.

When we finished, her breath against mine ricocheted down our bellies, past our hips, and I leaned over to pick up our underwear, to help her raise hers past her knees. In the conference room, after I closed the janitor's closet door behind us, a bespectacled student worker entered as curious as she seemed lost, though she didn't hesitate to ask about a commotion in the room, about a rattling she felt she heard from inside our room, and an apology that she opened the door without knocking. She said she'd been worried. She said she'd heard stories of what students do when they're alone to do with each other what they can. Olivia told the girl not to worry, that we were only there exploring the words we could, feeling our way down avenues of mind and heart that we could manage before we left for the day, and I figured it was as much euphemism as assurances to the poor girl. Olivia's glance at me confirmed as much, and when the girl left, nodding and rather shy, Olivia turned to me and asked if I'd noticed the girl's legs, which I hadn't, and if I'd seen the girl's hips, which I hadn't, or if I'd noticed the girl's cheekbones, which I barely gleaned awaiting her reactions to Olivia's descriptions of what we'd been doing, to which Olivia replied that she didn't believe me and that she would hear of no such thing, Because did you notice how beautiful that girl was, followed by, And can you imagine how stunning that bookish girl will be one day.

Our assessment of the poems were made up of margin notes, mostly in notebooks Olivia brought for the occasion, because having re-written each poem on the available space at the heart of every page we used, what was left but the edges in which to annotate a guess at the imagery ("reminds me of Nolasco's critique of feminist aesthetics") or a guess at the allusion ("Rivas's approach to voice and autofiction, perhaps?") or an assessment of the cultural references ("likely adapting the idea of the flaneur to the suburbs") or an assessment of the repetition ("how many times must she repeat this new word *joyworthy*").

After an hour, largely in silence, before and after the heat of the moment in the closet, and occasionally in soft conversation about sound, voice, and the shape of a work, we did exactly what we'd set out to do, that is determine the efficacy of each poem as determined by our impressions of its intentions as determined by what we knew of the collection in which it was included and the writer's oeuvre as we understood it, and, of course, for how it embodied the essence of the sport, as we determined its nature to be, including but not limited to the athletic thrill through elongated moments of explored footwork, collaborative approaches to goal, counter-strikes like an opposing, contradictory response of form and momentum, and a notion of an unpacking scene, a series of touches that made for both tangible expectation and a sense of mystery, and to both allude to, if not satisfy, some end goal.

Admittedly, there was a lot to hold, but it was so much more fun than it sounds.

Olivia concluded that Daisuke's and Kapoonga's lyrics most satisfied our attribute checklist, primarily because of the poems' personal natures, zoomed in as they were on an individual player's moment, though I remained skeptical of Daisuke's third stanza:

> crouching firstly then hopping coals, his toes
> crushed leather fastened two sizes small, seething
> grass oceans burn and when he fell, conches shells
> and worms, slithering over stones in mouse holed
> soil, covered cleats in mud and stringed blood

which seemed to me a bit digressive, losing me in a seashore and porous earth analogy that never earned its comparative meanings. The initial two stanzas (of six) earned my trust because its focus appeared clear, that is, a scene, so to speak, of forward Mitsuzoka Honda tiptoeing at midfield because he appeared to be in pain after he'd put on his defensemen's smaller and thinner cleats prior to the game, Honda playing a large portion of the match in those much tighter shoes, whether by mistake or as the result of a prank no one, as of this writing, had yet solved the history of that on-field mishap. He seemed to find himself incapable of sideways field adjustments for incoming passes, most steps feeling incredibly painful procedures in those too-cramped laces, and so Honda actually idled for most of the game. Naturally, Daisuke presented an unfortunate, befuddled Honda in the early part of the poem, a player prepared (almost heroically, at that!) to fight through unspeakable frustration for the sake of his teammates. But Daisuke erred in every subsequent stanza, I would argue, transforming Honda into a bumbling striker, stumbling like a too-dumb man unaware of his quickly growing deformities and not, for example, as a tragic kind of hero, which, because we're dealing in poetry here, Daisuke should at the very least have decided to do, and though I can understand Daisuke's attempt at humor, he stopped two blocks short of funny for me, and what had begun as an ode ultimately became a mishmash of wavering purposes.

Contrasted to Daisuke's collapse, Kapoonga's "Year of the Nigerian Wolf…" uses concision to cut your heart open, to deeply embed image and meaning into the reader's psyche. To say it briefly (though I couldn't possibly sum it shorter than the poem's very text!), Kapoonga, a notable sketch artist in his own right, struggling four years in Manhattan freelancing for three local dailies drawing the Sunday comic strips *Bushwick Tourist Bus*, *Rouge Herring Blues*, and *The Unemployment Line*, uses couplets before each of two drawings, the texts serving like unorthodox metaphysical captions inviting readers onto the field and repelling them all at once into some airy landscape just over the scoreboard. Olivia concluded that this poem, for her, embodied its muse soccer match better than any poem we'd read that afternoon, and I couldn't have more certainly agreed, even though I was unable at times to wholly categorize or define the characteristics of Kapoonga's poem. Generally, when I get this way about anything, I succumb to elementary tactics, namely, I throw words around until something sticks. *This feels real—I can* touch *this imagery—The text and sketches correlate without being redundant—This turn of phrase just feels good.* I don't even know why I wrote any margin notes, to be honest, almost futilely trying to understand and classify and describe, and, consequently, my words outnumbered Olivia's on my sheet to an embarrassing extent, her notes more than just a gift of clarity—they were a gift *to* clarity. *The stutter works here—Shooting across the field like a ball—Feels sensual in its syntax and verb choice.* Compiling our notes, I could summarize that in its misleading lack of ambition, Kapoonga's textual-visual pairing jumped off the page like a bomb, primarily from its play on the unexpected, but more probably because one could almost feel Kapoonga's notoriously modest monotone (regardless of italic emphasis) reciting every word to you,

Twenty-Something girls tossed their half-drunk beers
onto the *Niger* bench, and Head Coach Richards

responded *furiously* by grabbing the ball—*in play*—
from his midfielder and kicking it just over the girls' *noses*

and then culminating in what I can only describe as both a feeling of a feeling and the experience of spectating-competing, this interplay between the action on the field and the action off it, that moment when the passes between players becomes an exchange of aesthetic with the fans, and Kapoonga's visual transformation, of both the sketch and the text, is an accomplishment of both narrative restraint and implicit movement.

Best known for his incomprehensible and *near impossible* solitude amid *a twenty-two man game*, midfielder Ma-kailoo, two minutes

later, raced end to end and scored a near *logarithmic* shot from the *left corner,*
and celebrated by hand signing to the girls, "The next round is *on me.*"

The poem met our criteria, and even with extensive margin notes, we couldn't really explain completely how, and though I (we) admit Kapoonga's textual-visual pairing may not jump off the page like a bomb to everyone, it did to us, and the juxtapositions were an application of both unbound form and tonal tempering, leaving a rather large shadow of both the sport and the art form in its wake.

Consequently, it was easy to turn our attention to the prose in our hands, having satisfied at least a moment in which poetry didn't just get its fair shake, in which we didn't just arrive at a kind of representation of the sport in a poem, but we acquired the most fitting poem we could find and came to understand it as completely as our intellect allowed. Turning our attention, however, took on quite a weight. Quite soon, even the marvel of Kapoonga's work felt *very* limited in scope and capture, a rather incomplete embodiment as we read through and read with those beautiful long prose sentences. Kapoonga's simplicity merits praise, but when we arrive to Gallego's *Four Missing Vaqueros*, and even Nuandir's *Calico Days*, the *real* reading begins. Our purpose was to find a poem that could embody its muse soccer match better than a fiction prose excerpt, and the fact is that we have Gallego's culminating words to his novel's Chapter Eleven engrained in us since first sight:

> Sheriff Horacio's Chilean mustache seemed a firm fixed beast on the field's sideline, a thick bushel not even shivering when, amid the Patagonian seven o'clock breeze, his country's third-string goalkeeper, Ronaldo Redondo, a tough though vertically challenged man at 1.09 meters, standing in for kidnapped first- and second-string goalkeepers, Bananero Francisco and Guillermo Pedántico, allowed his 11th goal of the match, a liner well beyond his diving hands, and after Uruguayan striker, Bobby Pacheco, screamed and hurled his shirt and cartwheeled and removed his shorts to satisfy the extent of his celebrating ego, he triumphantly ran up to and stung his middle finger at Sheriff Horacio, who had all the while been rocking in his chair just out of bounds at midfield, tapping the rifle on his lap and waiting for the radioed signal to shoot Pacheco between the eyes, the word imminent from his deputies, who, at that moment, were raiding Pacheco's compound on a tip that both kidnapped goalkeepers had been captive there seven weeks, chained to a broken radiator and forced to watch

videotaped highlights of Pacheco's European league exploits on
an old VCR with no tracking knob to clarify the moving image

Olivia wasn't initially convinced of my lauding Gallego's work, which she
called *merely acceptable*. It's true that once I zeroed in on personal preference,
on acquired taste, on bias of a not insignificant order, I got rather impatient
collectively assessing the novel and, admittedly, a little insufferable. The turns
in that sentence. The approaches and misdirections and run-arounds. The
appositives that amplify the central thread and could be distracting but which
feel both interactive and representative of the momentum on a soccer pitch.
Driving and stuttering and accelerating and luring into a kind of lull before a
series of strikes which might initially be off mark or blocked but nonetheless
create a routine in which the footballer aggressively pursues an end one hopes
arrives but is never guaranteed. And then the payoff, the sudden shift to end
the sentence that at once feels like an obstacle the next series of sentences
must overcome. A goal, or the hope of one, to chase another goal, or the hope
of one, straight to conclusion, whether it ends in heartbreak, diffusion, love,
or the antithesis of all this.

Olivia admitted that she didn't *want* so quickly to buy into the "illusion"
that the first prose sample we studied at length, however great it was, as there
as there were a couple others we rather quickly put aside, could settle the
argument, Yes the poetry samples we've found might not match up in one or
another esteemed opinion but can this really be the heart of the matter and
the heart of a conclusion Boli.

I understood her reluctance. I understood her need to keep comparing.
I sighed, of course, as anyone would after five hours in the library, but I understood her need to keep reaching for a best fit comparison, not just a best fit
model. We weren't exactly marking points for or against so that either she or
I, like opposing sides of a debate, would account for the claims we'd present,
the substantiating evidence we'd include, and the arguments we'd complete in
the process. That would require addition, but we were embroiled, instead, in a
math of accumulation, a tally, simply, of ideas shared and sentences completed,
of words that could add to the meaning of other words and sustain the breath
of an exploration, arriving hopefully to a discovery of other discoveries, and
so, yes, we gave into another scour, and we followed our earlier protocol of an
online search followed by a library data set match followed by a grabbing of a
volume or two from the shelves.

It was in the process that we arrived to Mariano Quetletlao, the Ecuadorian-born émigré to Glasgow, and his book *Musings of a Jesuit with No Attention Span*. How we could have missed *Musings* during that first go-around feels both reasonable and unforgivable, that mixed sentiment one often gets when they feel they've overlooked something so wonderful that also lamentably gets overlooked, to the point of being discarded, by a popular culture of its time and place. Quetletlao's first book of poems in his adopted Irish English is an ode-riddled collection of sport. I say "riddled" because to label something a collection presupposes connective tissue, but a form such as this almost demands a proclamation, and we don't get that here. We get, instead, generally speaking, praises for competition in golf and cricket and rugby and the beautiful game, and though its pacing and lauding vary, something like a futbolian lore amasses as the pages wear on, such that even when the poems are exclusively about stumps and scrums and putts, the verses and the appearance of verses identify an intensity that drives up field and down with a sideways dribble that leaves us looking left after the ball has already been double-tapped right, as if, by both happenstance and purpose, the collection uses the other sports as a means to drive its point home about the most beautiful of games. Add to this Olivia's handling of the book, turning pages with a delicate ease that flips the pages without tearing, helping them ring with a fragility that all but ages you as you read, and *Musings* emerges as an artifact that belongs to history as to the palm of one's hand, an object both out of time and with no place that can claim it as its own.

And we both had to laugh at how many of the pages appeared to have stuck together after what we only imagined was disuse, not necessarily fingerprint grease or some wayward drop of coffee. It felt almost too fitting that somewhere near the middle of the collection, there were two pages that, in fact, seemed glued together in their upper corners. It mattered that Olivia pried them apart as gently as she did because when she did, she opened the view to a trilogy of poems that would extend to four pages in total, the second poem in the series initially reading like an unassuming hallway painting in a dentist's office, something that at a glance one glazes over. But when one stops, when one pauses to pay attention, something happens to both the body and the mind. It's a single-stanza poem, more emblematic of 1970s California Renaissance verse than the culturally ambiguous post-millennial Scotland, and, yet, there it was—the humblest of poems whose title, "The Dirt that Collects and Pleases," appears just below the previous poem that ends at the top of the page, a poem that reads as more than a just run-on verse lineated for the sake of layout and content, but also because its (dis)continuous homage to the most beautiful of beautiful games models the game itself, a free form start-stop-start-and-go movement that brings to mind the works of Brazilian Flavia Sousa and Samoan Kalei Ioane:

> pigeons
> dart'd
> into the cheap
> seats
> the wom'n by
> me hurl'd hands
> hurl'd her hands and scream'd for
> my leg I says please
> don't
> dry cleaning's
> for the rich and
> the old man he
> fell ov'r his seat into
> mine he'd
> saw numb'r 12's heel
> shine
> just ov'r the moon
> moments
> 'fore Babel
> reach'd heav'n and
> erupt'd in-
> to a discordant one-note
> melody
> goal—
> they shout it loud and then
> goal—
> they shout it to
> the goats that
> bleat by god

The absence of punctuation rings like an unnameable definition of truth, one that blends in it the echoes of what is not true only because it can't be touched. The broken lines, an interruption of nouns and prepositions and people and screams, reflects the collection's title, musings like episodic interactions, observations, and digressions. When the pages fluttered after the overhead air conditioning kicked on, Olivia let a silence slip between us, and then she read the poem aloud, in that soft but affirming way she reads everything, raspy and as if her tongue had been born coated in red wine, a certain graininess to her lisp that awakens the spirit inside her in the presence of a good book.

After the reading, her eyes moistened, sweat blended with sunlight and a cold spell, and my voice, when I offered to grab us poké bowls from the food truck on the corner, couldn't match the raw aggression in her voice, one that both demanded time to ease out and its own space in which to do so. She smiled, nonetheless, and though she was hungry, she said that she didn't mind waiting, I know I've entertained the joy of this for too long, I understand you love, So if we're going to eat I want to be done with this Boli, And so I suppose the question we have to answer my love is are we finished with this, I don't think we're far from it Boli.

And, as with all things, she was right, both about our ability to use our craving as a tool to sharpen the intellect and that what we needed, what would finally end this approach of ours, was a final piece of prose, one last assessment of breathlessness and fiction that would clarify, if not once and for all at least until the next academic year, that a long sentence can capture the tone and tenor of the most beautiful of most beautiful games better than a poem attempting to do the same.

The sun did as it usually does in late June, linger further than you'd expect it to without breaking the day, like an arched back that bends without collapsing, a bridge that sways to extremes if only to remind you of its permanence. There was a sunroof in the room, which I took for granted until the sun, at an angle, poured only a sliver of its light onto the table. Olivia sighed over her hands, and then she yawned, her grin like a sage's when they know how the night comes and how it all ends, I haven't been timekeeping but I have some idea, I said to her, and she said, Isn't that every experience of full play when full play is a joy.

She watched me from across the table, which I know because I watched her just the same, for which notebook she would pick to rewrite the text from the last example and, I can only assume, for which book *I* would pick to be that example. We watched each other with a snicker in the air, perhaps something of a challenge to see who would turn away first and who would be the slowest to admit that loss. I didn't take long to do so, and I smiled through the admission.

I had two remaining books from which to choose, and so I reached for the one closest to her. The book, Ayanna Geunzel's *Hermione's Hand*, had accumulated dings on its hard cover. As thick as the book was, its corners seemed to wear their bruises well, curled but not cut, flattened but not creased, as if the text had not only gifted a toughness to its shell but also an agility to every bang, a response to wherever its readers would stuff or toss it, whether across a room or into a backpack, behind the couch or under a coffee table. I'd been familiar with the novel already, read its review last year when the paperback came out, and because critics can be beasts with no den mothers to warm them, the author's work, the emotional appeal in every overwrought sentence, seemed to be reduced to a disingenuous, cold technique that "went fishing," according to one reviewer in *The Narrative Call*, "instead of just letting the text stay where it should have always stayed, understated or never stated at all." I thought it was relatively unfair, but I also understood the frustration.

Practically every page in the novel bore no indentation, just blocks and blocks of prose, most of which posed extensive forays into those thoughts we never share, those identities we hold dear but can't wrap a story around, those insecurities that mar us when we let aggression sit with us for too long, Here's page seventy-two my love, and I handed Olivia the opened book. I'm sure my eyes lamented the end of this moment, not because we wouldn't enjoy more like it, but because every one of these small delusions, as Olivia calls them, seems to cement something unnameable between us, an inch closer to something if only that much nearer to the chasm between always and never, and in that moment, a weary breath left me just as she started to read the page aloud. She cleared her throat and said, Are you tired of my voice Boli, The sigh was a different kind of release my love, Good, she said, in a half-smile and with a half-sunset across her face, the streak of sky, partially lit and partially undone, as if it had found in her a body it could lay a field on, one end marked by solitude and the other in a busyness of the mind, two extremes that, at any moment, could turn on each other and set a whole game into motion, such that a net couldn't hold and not a perimeter line could contain, precisely because the field of play has always been, will always be, sound and sweat and speed and insatiable movement, the kind that you can only anticipate in dreams, even when the sod gets chopped up and the mud tears away the traction. When Olivia read our last reading of the day, it felt almost like a final kick, a shot hurled into an ordinary moon, gone wide but no less thrilling, through which the dark revealed itself to be more than just depth, to be, also, simple and warm, to be a shout in the company of strangers, an eagerness satisfied by the memory of our hearts racing, of our best attempts to articulate something bigger than ourselves on the page and on the pitch, that which is both fundamentally personal and inevitably public, and so we imagine how, as Geunzel writes,

> Hermione had done her best, but walking through the lobby, one of straight faces and suits and cleaning men mopping marble, left her no recourse but to reconsider everything endlessly, from her introductory handshake to the way she pressed the elevator button going down when she left, knowing wholly the critical eyes that beset her at every point during her job interview, a judgmental gaze that began, of course, the moment she walked through the marketing company's double glass doors and approached the welcome desk, where first the advertising agency's receptionist greeted her and then proceeded to lead her into the waiting room and said, Any seat is fine, Thank you, Someone will be in here shortly, Thank you, Please don't touch the magazines, Oh yes of course, And don't eat the candy, Ah yes okay, and then the company's Creative Director, who stepped into the waiting room holding a sandwich in one hand, a napkin in the other, I hope you don't mind, No of course not, We have concurrent projects in process developing twenty-five second television spots for soccer cleats and I'm literally swallowing sandwiches and a salad while rearranging the screen layout on a single frame, That sounds exciting, Honey you don't have to impress me, Excuse me, Listen and keep the optimism to a minimum in the interview room and you'll do just fine, and so Hermione nodded, slowly, as if to demonstrate an understated skepticism that tried not to betray her distrust of petty workplace oligarchies, and as he led her to the interview room, the company's Montaigne Board Room, a suite so impressive its window view of the ocean paled in comparison to the individually molded overhanging lamps shining sharp orange lighting that made for both easy reading and minimal shading across the floor, and once in the board room, Hermione greeted those whom she assumed were chief officers of the firm but who, throughout the interview, remained nameless to her,

not to mention the fact they merely extended their hands without
standing when Hermione entered the room and extended hers,
something of a cold and consistent, and rather corporate, if you ask
me, attention to formality, one that emerged during the interview
as an insistence to interrupt Hermione's every answer, Yes actually I
did play collegiate soccer at—, Honey the particulars aren't important. We'd wanted to confirm only your familiarity with the sport's
equipment products generally and of course our company products
specifically, Yes of course well in my previous position at Golden
Kick Innovations I organized and managed extensive regional cus-
tomer surveys based on—, So then the answer's yes, Excuse me,
Honey are you familiar with our products, Yes of course, Great then
next item, an ugly routine, really, a scathing transcript, one whose
blunt demeaning tone emanated off the page like campfire brush,
and after Hermione had returned home, dropped her suitcase by
the door plopped on the couch and decided to stare soothingly
through the open living room window, she mentally recreated the
entire interview, as if its replay on the bus ride home hadn't been
enough, this time recalling the two stone-faced female executives,
a certain Odetta Partridge and Bella Gestape, and then searching
for their available digital information online, including photographs
of the women on the company's primary site, both piercing Hermione's mobile screen with knifing gazes, as stiff as their breathing
embodiments had been, and after Hermione surfaced from her
temporarily anaesthetizing pity, she rose from the couch, her eyebrows bitter by necessity, and she strode to her drafting desk, where
she kept a handwritten chart tracking her job application process
upon which, of twenty-two resumes distributed, seven companies
called for interviews, and of those seven, three interviews, including
this latest one at Goalpost Gears, had happened and proven flops,
and not because the previous two had confirmed their choosing
someone else for the position, but because Hermione had relied
on her procedural familiarity to know, the corporate hiring firing
structure a breed so homogenous as to mock the animal instinct to
hurl fire and run at the wind, and so Hermione reached for her loose
ball under the drafting desk, stretching her toes until she could
press against the ball and roll it her way, and then she massaged

her bare left foot over the top curve, something of a lover's habit to trace contour and stitched skins at a moment's notice, and then, beyond a conscious thought, she reared her leg back and rammed her foot's arch squarely, pop air and boom, and she fired the ball into her kitchen, rattling the wall sink and cupboard doors, not to mention shaking her stacked dishes, because if the expressionless stench of our economy's executive branch had snuck up and scored thrice, Hermione would return the offensive spurt with at least one broken stove, if only to prove that no three-nil mark would ever go uncontested, so just as long as there remained something to kick.

T H
R E E
A L A R
M F I R E

Three Alarm Fire

POETICS OF A BROKEN CONVERSATION

It feels like this. Just like this. When the whole world screams prompted by only the byte of a soundless letter, it *always* feels like this.

There's a tragedy. A mass shooting, an earthquake, a mass shooting, a police betrayal, a mass shooting. As Americans, we have our inclinations.

You hear the news from a friend and then you explore it, and its details pass through trains of conversation, and you're not alone. You know people touched by the thing, though you don't know them well, but that isn't the point, so you take a walk to clear your head because you're trying to find the point, and you rub your eyes again as the traffic rolls by and the apartment buildings across the street linger like stones and the world just goes on.

Waiting on the corner, you stuff your hands into your pockets to keep them from twitching, as everybody around you, as they wait for the light to change and the *Walk* sign to appear, walk to where they're going like they've made promises. About getting to places on time. About keeping to themselves to get there. About bringing meaning into the world without fighting it.

And you, too. You've made a promise to *yourself*. To get where you're going. To keep to yourself. To keep your eyes on the road and stay off social media.

Promises, though, aren't easy. How do you even hold to them, anyway, if there's nothing to touch.

So, you pull out your cell phone. You unlock the screen. You find the app that tells you what the world is thinking, what's *really* at stake and where your investments should be. The app takes a minute to pop open. Your phone is slow. In the meanwhile, the Ubers motor on like they don't need proof of life, and the apartment buildings puff their chests like they don't need to be ashamed of their congestion, and students from the high school nearby walk in packs but like they're circling lambs to protect them.

The red light takes forever, so you start scrolling through the feed. It isn't long before you come across one and then two and then a lot of posts that people keep posting about the tragedy. So many words about what happened, who did what and *why* it happened and why it *shouldn't* have happened and where it happened, people replying with opinions, so many opinions. Some responses begging clarity and others with some tacit questions, like *Can you morons get the details right before you start spreading rumors* and *Why is this world such a fucked up place* and *How do we know these weren't just actors faking a shooting* and *But do we really have the full story.*

These are the posts that interest you because they're not wrong. It's been long enough, and you're sure people should have gotten the particulars all lined up by now, but so many responses are stuck in that muddy middle with words like *This was so horrible* and *Politicians are shit and whatever* and *Guns are a fucking disaster, bro* and *America, amirite* and *How is every time worse than we could ever have imagined* and *What is happening to our world*, and all of it, *all* of it, right next to the likes of *Stop tying your balls in knots and get over it already* and *There's nothing new under the sun so how don't we know this isn't the matrix* and *Yeah, sure, but what like does it mean for me* and *You're right, my brother in christ, this shit ain't got nothing to do with me.* Opinions bleed into each other like fog smothering treetops, like it's all just vapor between you and the next person, all of you butting heads in an open field because nobody can see two feet in front of them, speed picking up and your only choices, go breathless finding your way north or hurl your body to the ground to keep from outright dying—both choices are only bruises waiting to add up, so you look up from your phone, again, and you take a deep damn breath to be okay with the buses stalling the intersection and drivers shouting out their window and the some of the office buildings in the distance rising over everything like indifferent bullies.

This *world*, man, you tell yourself, dragging out that middle like only you can. Like you're the only one who can walk without bumping into people and leave this whole place whenever you want.

The comment threads have so much left to tell you, so you scroll, scroll, scroll, and these responses, one into the next into them all until answers learn how to keep pace with their provocations, conversations hurdling over other conversations, everyone convinced they can manage exchanges without the natural constraints of a tongue, because lord knows it's faster to process anxiety through bone and skin than past teeth and lips.

Thumbs. Your kingdom—your kingdom for a pair of fast-typing thumbs.

You scroll because you're sure that there's something you can post and somewhere you can post it, where you can offer real feelings that bring comfort to other people's real feelings, bring reason—*real* reason—to the conversation. You're pretty sure everybody needs you to post *something* because how else to keep them from stumbling into each other and into themselves, to keep them from replacing a tragedy of dead children with a tragedy of unpasteurized ideas. Everyone needs you—*you*—to keep from overwhelming the dead and turning the tragedy into just another blasphemy, something that evaporates after people have proven it wrong. But *damn* if you're not finding where to type what you need to type, what posts and comments need your thoughts the most, and, looking up again, it's time to cross the street, to make a decision, the pedestrians, the storefronts, the honking, all of it flickering at the world like camera flash turning the world into poses. People walk past you like you're not even there, the brick walls standing there like they're just bored of you.

At the corner across the street, you scroll, you keep scrolling, until you fix your attention to just the right words—the post that *really* makes you feel—*What an awful human disaster that could have been prevented if we'd only had the will to do something to prevent it and the will to will ourselves to care*, and you give it a heart, wishing you could give it a *real* big heart, the kind of *Like* that lets everybody know you have the biggest heart. But then you read someone's reply to that original post, *But there are so many tragedies every day though so what makes this one so goddamn different*, and you feel like it's insulting the feelings of the first but like it's also getting to its own kind of truth, so you give this post a *Like*, too, though you're not exactly sure if this diminishes your real feelings or affirms them passively. And then you realize that there's something wrong with the comment mill on this one because some weird replies start coming up like *Shut up about all these stupid fake tragedies about these stupid fake school* and then like *Stuff happens every day and so what so please get a life, losers* followed by *Who fucking goes to community college anyway and who just fucking sits there getting shot* and *The fucking media and all their sob stories like what is even real anymore* and *Yeah how do we even know it was even real* and *Yeah this is just hype and Hollywood actors and what's next a PSA about global warming from some dipshit Hollywood actors*, and just awful stuff, people's feelings procreating with other feelings in a festival of feelings, mutations abound, deformities guaranteed.

You shake the phone. You look up, and you're at the next corner, the traffic crossing lanes to get around a double-parked delivery truck, curtains and blinds in the open apartment windows batting around like you're standing on a pier saluting the ship as it steers into the ocean. All of it despite the iceberg we're all just pretending isn't there.

You cross the street, and the comment mill gets worse, but you keep up because damn them for thinking you wouldn't, so you work up the nerve to type *How can you be so disrespectful.*

You're confident that whoever uses social media and participates on a comment thread understands the façade of the medium, that within contained boxes to type and a constrained volume of text to use, there's always context beyond the font, an applicable ethos that we, indeed, must presume a compassionate meaning behind the words. After all, we simply don't have the space to explain it all, and we simply don't have the time to articulate the reasoning behind the reasoning, and you're pretty certain that everyone operates under the same rules, and you're fairly certain these aren't just *your* rules, and that *you* are always faithful to your rules.

You can't believe it when other people's comments start talking back to yours. You shake your head at everyone's habit to scream, and you reread your comment to be sure you didn't mean what the responses to yours seem to think that you meant, and you reread it again because the comments back at you are getting so wild, like *What's wrong with you, you stupid crybaby* and *Who died and made you chancellor of the fucking internet, asshole* and *Violence is violence and you're never going to stop what's in somebody's head and heart to go do so why don't you just go and die or whatever and leave us alone.*

You don't mean to get loud at the next intersection, but you do. You yell right into your phone, like Are these fucking people for *real*. Right at a red light. Right next to a father with his son and a woman with her backpack, all of whom turn to look at you and then at your phone, and they seem to know what is and isn't up with the situation, but you don't confirm a damn thing. You nod at the adults even though they ask you nothing, and then the light turns green. You walk ahead. You're just trying to keep up with the comments as they suggest that the victims of this most recent tragedy are just playing dead and that the cameras are everywhere and everybody wants to be on camera and so all the media is doing is making up the stories to sell newspapers and that it's all just about the money, that capitalism is all just about the money.

You keep walking, but you don't thumb back at the internet right away. The sidewalk starts to descend, and you don't want to trip over a crack in the cement. As the traffic eases and the buildings chop into smaller heights, you move faster. Your arms start swinging in order to control your tempo, and you skip over a tree trunk breaking the sidewalk like a seismic shift pushing earth into the sky.

You're already walking in a neighborhood when you realize you've probably been walking in a neighborhood for at least two blocks. You're fairly certain you're almost where you need to be. Just two more streets to go according to your calculations.

You have a job to do.

The front gates. The front yard toys. The passing curbside mailboxes. The comment threads. It all needs you. It's *all* absurd. Tragedy carries you up and down the street, from wall to wall like a cornered mouse, and when gutters congested in leaves and errant shopping bags, all stranded by the last rainfall, start passing by you one by one, garbage starts sticking to the bottom of your shoes, and you have to kick a few things away to keep from slipping.

So many words you find are just garbage sticking to the bottom of people's shoes, and you have a job to do, and you're almost there.

The comments keep rolling in, of course, stuff like *Death is all around us* and *This must be great for ratings* and *Can't everybody see that all we need is freedom.* And just when you think it couldn't get worse, the next intersection meets you with ivy cascading over a retaining wall, and just like comments, the vines pour over the top and you wonder how much longer the game can run, and whether or not the score is too wild for everyone to believe you're still playing the same sport, or even that you're really on the same team together. And then you notice the numbers on the houses, and you're just three addresses down, and you have a job to do, and so just as long as that is true, the clock keeps looking forward to the next word.

Finally, when you've arrived where you need to be, you turn on your live feed. The phone falls out of your hand, but it doesn't matter because no one tunes into anything right away. You pick up the phone and dust off the screen and introduce yourself. It's all formality, but the world has never been lost over too much etiquette. You introduce the house you're standing in front of. You tell whoever's tuned in about the presence of a grieving family inside that house. You point to the hedges, to the fence, to the garage. To the trash and recycling and compost bins. To the uncut grass. You wonder aloud about how grief distracts us from basic chores, about how everything falls by the wayside when we feel too much pain. How even sleeping can be hard to do. You touch the shrubs. The dandelions at the gate. You affirm the acreage and the house number and the latch to get in, the basic information that this kind of situation demands. You tell your growing viewership that you're just trying to collaborate with them, that you're just trying to create a living demonstration that honors the family, a testament to the kinds of things we all need at a time like this. Connection. Intersection. Participation. And you're just trying to explain what the tragedy really means to us all. And in that vein, you have to offer a disclaimer, that you're not sure if you can deliver on the promise to interview the family, that they have not returned your phone calls or your emails, and you point the phone back at yourself so that the family's porch frames your face. You give your viewers that that's-how-life-goes kind of face. You make the effort to sigh as users tuning in keep adding up.

And then you exhale before telling everyone that it's time to take a closer look.

You push open the wobbly front gate. You identify the losses that all the families have faced. The daughters, sons, fathers, mothers, providers, lovers, friends, dear friends, companions. Standing on the gravel path, you confirm how families like these don't need ridicule, that trespassing into their mourning would be a disgrace, that opening their front door would be criminal, that whosoever tarnishes this family's name on social media only lays their own bodies to shame.

You ask your audience if they can hear it, the sounds just inside the front door, seeping through the natural crevices in the house. You kneel by the door. You place your phone's speaker and voice receiver against the wood. You point the camera back at yourself and you confirm it all in a whisper. The family inside is sobbing, a crying depth so profound only wolves moan more wildly, especially when they can no longer find the moon to tell them where to go. This, you tell everyone, is no fiction. This, you say, begs us to be faithful to the truth. Tragedy, you tell your live feed audience, is always clearer as a question than an answer.

You point the live feed away from you to capture the curtains and the blinds and the doormat smothered in unopened mail. You point to the chimney smoke and the vehicles in the driveway. A jogger passes by and you explain to your social media viewership that one always finds people for whom the world goes on, for whom the world continues in sweat and sore knees. You posit that perhaps the density of a neighborhood's runners identifies a ratio one extrapolates to make a statement about the people who've been spared, that fraction of a population unaffected by tragedy, something like three in every four or four in five or five in six or some other particular that feels meaningful and smart. All tragedies, whether mass shootings or earthquakes or mass shootings or police betrayals or mass shootings, bring meaning, and as Americans, we have our inclinations to search for meaning, and after every time, we have fewer and fewer places to hide.

You shut down the live feed. You tap off because you need a breath. Exhaustive work collaborates with extensive reprieves as strongly as with anything else, but right then the jogger that had earlier passed the house circles back. She stops to check her time and sideways glances as if more than just measuring her pulse. She leans over her knees as if stretching her hamstrings, and then she coughs and spits onto the curb, and then she calls out to you. You hold the family's unrolled newspaper as you wave. She approaches the wobbly gate and looks up and down the street and shouts for you to tell her your name. You nod. It occurs to you that not everyone is trained in good intentions, that we don't all receive manuals of discernment. And you don't know why but your heart jumps a palpitation. You clear your throat and nudge your way out of yourself by starting down the porch steps. You want her to believe your legs can sway easily into any kind of question. After all, no one asks for explanations from someone who knows how to adapt to their surroundings and fit and belong.

You have not invaded this family's privacy. Their information is all over social media anyway. No one loses their youngest child in a mass shooting without television reporters obsessing on the whereabouts of everybody and all their crying. All you really wanted was to capture this house, record its face, acknowledge its pain to teach other people sympathy. We can all be steered to pity. Intentions are all we can ever have.

The jogger reminds you that the onus is on you, and she demands to see a lanyard or a badge or a driver's license or something. Prove you're not a spy, she says. Prove you're with the press, she says. Prove you're not a troll, she says. Always these questions. Always people think that the internet is full of crazy people and crazy ideas and crazy situations.

You tell her that you can provide what you need to provide, but that you don't know what will or won't assure someone, and so words and movements are always an experiment. Surely the jogger will see that you're one of the good ones. That you've brought good intentions. And so you tell the jogger that you're not there to bother the family because at a time like death every good neighbor extends just the necessary hand and nothing more. And what makes you such a good neighbor, she says, and you're not sure how much to approach her third question. Anything beyond two makes for an interrogation, and the sun is already blaring strong enough to make the whole world feel like an inquisition. Tone is a weapon, and because it can just as easily cut through time and through bodies, you tell the jogger that you're not there to disturb anyone, But do you know them, she says, and you ask her if that kind of certainty doesn't just get in the way, Then why are you here, she says, and you tell her that this family shouldn't be bothered, But do you know them, she says, and so you ask her why any of that should stop somebody from being moved, which is when you notice that the adjacent neighbor is out on his front porch, halfway down his steps, a light, long-sleeved shirt billowing over his loose pants, and you don't know why, but you start to wonder how far personal spaces extend, and whether or not breaking them down is a process with instructions not everybody gets a manual for.

The jogger tells you to leave, and you try to tell her you're there to help, but then she tells you that you're not a real neighbor, but you try to tell her that helping hands are all different, but then she says that neighbors don't keep people away at the butt of gun, which surprises you because nobody has opened up any debate about what is and is not a tragedy, and so you start to wonder why she can't see that you can only work with what you have, that you can only bring your good intentions. But then she brings the world on you when she asks you if you have a gun, and your eyes shoot open, perhaps uncontrollably, which you hope isn't the case, and in that process, you realize you don't answer her, and because hesitations can be their own kind of weapon, without one, the jogger pulls her phone off a bicep strap and unlocks her screen.

You can only imagine who she plans to call, and quickly, but you hope not too quickly, you reach into your back pocket and pull out your notebook. You tell her you're at the house to account for last details, something of a ritual that local newspapers process to confirm timelines and names and the states of everybody's souls. You shake the coiled pages hoping its flapping travels across the lawn, and you don't know how much of it has before she tells you that she doesn't know what to do and so she's going to call the police, which alarms you because when you look around you, there isn't a tragedy you can measure, and so you throw your palms up. You raise both your hands to demonstrate just how empty you've always been.

One foot at a time, you make sure not to trip on a gravel stone or over the weeds. As the impasse plays out, the neighbors across the street and to the left step onto their deck and the neighbor across the street and to the right gets to the sidewalk and the neighbor next door makes his way to his gate.

On the sidewalk, the jogger shuts the wobbly gate behind you, and even though no one's fired a gun, your skin bristles at a tempo in the air made worse by the gate's clamoring lock. You have a tendency to mumble to yourself when no one appears to be listening to you, and it's then that you realize how hard it is to control a habit. It takes all the fire in your body to cool down.

The jogger crosses her arms, and you tell her that your car is way up the road but that you'll leave for it now, and she says that she wants to walk you there, but then you tell her that you're not afraid to go alone, to which she says that fear doesn't have a direction when the world is as crazy as it is.

You see then the neighbors at their gates, all the way down the block. Couples. Singles. Strangers. Dogs. A plague whose only name is running talk, and though not everybody has a conversation, rumors have been known to travel without any wind. There's the story everyone sees and the story everyone makes up, and oceans can't always tell the difference.

Which is why you stop abruptly to reach into your back pocket because you want your phone to capture the street of stories, too, to combat these people's stories with your own story because that's the momentum that long ago set us asea. And it happens so quickly because it happens just like it feels, and it feels like your skin gets stretched and pulled off your bones, and you don't know what to call what happens next except that the elements of the broken conversation you were counting all fall out of order, and clarity stings you in the breaths that you start to lose because, evidently, you, too, are the reason neighbors can't reconcile what they have seen with what they are feeling.

First the jogger barrels into you like she's pushing through you and your only defense to hurl her aside surprises you because you can't believe somebody can feel so sturdy and at the same time so light. And then the next door neighbor rams you, and you stumble trying to wiggle out, but the shuffling puts you on the cement beneath him, where he shouts into the sky that you have a gun, that you've come bearing no intentions at all, and so you fight with open palms so the world can see how sick it can be when it doesn't want to see. You're in it thick, and you throw your hands around, but information fixes nothing and the heat gets hotter and you scream that you have good intentions because what else are you going to do.

You swing at the man's neck and chest, and you scream about the mistakes they're all making. No one listens and how can they when everybody screeches to get it away, shrieks for someone to take it away, kicks your side ribs to poke it away, jabs your hips because somebody keeps yelling that they're all going to die if they don't grab it away. And you try hollering that you're sorry for whatever you're sorry about, for whatever sorry means, about your intentions and that you only wanted to correct the record, to live feed and inform and alleviate the tension that exists in the world, but high noon is a plague, and everyone is always holstering a gun even when they're not. And when the neighbors let up for a moment, you try to tell them that you can't breathe, but someone sits on you hard and the coughing gets in the way of everything you can hear and everything you want to add. The weight of it like a poison of bad opinions that run into each other until no one can discern anymore one hand from another. And then you hear the shot. The one you're pretty sure they've been wanting to hear all along. The one that they couldn't have cleared their heads without. And then the world goes dark.

THE INSTITUTE OF JOY

In 1988, to see Humberto Pacheco in his homeless man's attire, overgrown coat sleeves and no undershirt, a rope tightening his waistband, the knot hovering in the shadow of his opened zipper, is to confuse the abandoned basement where he slept, and the purpose the larger building had formerly embodied, with the ever-deepening well of destitution it had become. Beer bottles rested by Humberto's feet. Scattered plywood and splintered wooden beams littered the basement floor otherwise covered in dust.

Forty years earlier, the Pacheco family had presented a novel idea to the mayor. Felipe Pacheco, Humberto's father, envisioned a two-story building where the sad could cry, where the happy could laugh, and where greying shades abiding the full emotional spectrum could intersect and analyze each other's lives, such that, in crossed perspectives and endless chatter, the attending world could meet in the middle, fuse into a pragmatic joy neither extravagant nor naïve, neither arrogant nor self-deprecating.

Felipe's brand of enduring passionate pestering of city officials, in signed petitions and visitations and greeting cards signed *Your beaming friend!*, sealed the first successful step in the formation of the center. After receiving as a gift a particularly tasty chunk of domestic honeyed ham, the mayor granted Doctor Pacheco an audience.

One afternoon, accompanied by municipal lawyers, the mayor assessed Doctor Pacheco's meticulously sketched schematics for the building and his detailed surveys of best practices and therapeutic methods, And so do you consider this a mission of yours Doctor, Mr. Mayor wholism is not uncommon in swaths of tribal lands not yet succumbed to the bottle, And why do you wish to incorporate the municipality into your plans, Because the building Your Honor would necessitate full community support to function properly and effectively, But why now Doctor and how does it benefit this community whose support you crave, Your Honor without work and with few looming prospects the community would benefit from exchanged perspectives minimizing hopelessness and criminal enterprise, I'm just not sure why you insist Doctor that our tax base should erect something for which there isn't a problem, Not yet Your Honor, Excuse me Doctor, Exasperation isn't *yet* a problem but left to simmer on its own without preemptive address can ultimately cost the city excessive wage-hours policing and fighting fires and detentions that should never have been, I'm just not understanding Doctor why this matters at all if clearly our sidewalks aren't muddy and there isn't a single picket sign even in homes, But we don't know that Your Honor, Excuse me Doctor, We don't really know the desperation that our people are either capable of or covertly begun, Is that a threat Doctor, By no means Your Honor, Because that sounded like a threat Doctor, Nothing of the sort Your Honor you must believe me, This office will stand up and stand down threats from all borders and peoples Doctor, Absolutely Your Honor and you'll receive none from me.

Funding sources and building team under contract, The Mayor's Institute of Wellness and Joy was up and running by 1947. The Institute rode the memory of antebellum rations into a postwar excitement in which the words, both *wellness* and *joy*, immediately adopted an anticommunist allusion. The words also lent the new building an air like that of a community nerve center from which both steady gazes and ambient, curtailed smiles were able to radiate from the building like coupled plagues, Your Honor We have thus far been a wild success, Your first annual report Doctor appears rather impressive, With six soothing rooms upstairs and three lounges on this floor and a large open contemplative space in the basement Your Honor only the emotional stars will be our limit, Did you say scars Doctor, No Your Honor I said stars, Scars you say Doctor, No Your Honor I meant the stars.

Felipe Pacheco served, expectedly, as The Institute's first managing director. By 1952 when the doctor's only son, Humberto, was born, The Institute had blossomed into a daily breathing space for anyone ailing with stoic lips and drooping eyes, for everyone whose egos had been drilled into the ground by nagging bosses. Doctor Pacheco had even grown comfortable with opening his living room for weekend overflows twice a month, permitting out-patient exchanges under his chandelier. This, unfortunately, left Mrs. Pacheco often horribly confused, as she bore witness to patient exchanges, thinking to herself once why a woman so beautiful and elated and agitated, and who should have been restrained by chains, would so rabidly converse with a man so morose that he belonged under permanent therapeutic supervision for possible suicide.

In any case, a husband's dream is a husband's dream. However, and unfortunately for Mrs. Pacheco, the most extreme case of transformation in those early years of The Institute happened in Doctor Pacheco's own home.

And it was this that finally convinced him, because the comfort of homely scents seemed to stabilize everyone's gazes, and in light of The Institute's increasingly bustling schedule of patients, that an annex was needed, one that looked and smelled and flowed like being home for the holidays.

And so, the incident of extreme transformation happened in the winter of 1958, when a woman who'd been despondent upon arrival became so animated, the renewed feeling in her hands convinced her she could climb the doctor's backyard oak, only to pause frightened two-thirds up and start sobbing uncontrollably because she'd lost sight of her shoes. Conversely, the man she'd been sharing a conversation with had arrived rosy-cheeked and ecstatic and absurdly happy only to become so melancholic by three o'clock that he went missing for thirty minutes and Mrs. Pacheco screeched upon finding him in the kitchen, and then she kicked him unconscious just so she could pull his head from the oven without his restraint, What are you doing Elena, Felipe the man's ears were smoking, But you could have simply encouraged him to slither out, Felipe the man was hardly listening to me, Oh Elena I have a method to these things, And it seems sometimes even our best intentions wind up baked or inhaling gas, Oh Elena he was already having a hard go of things, Then I'm sure his newly bruised forehead will only be at home in the gloominess.

In the election turnovers of its first decade and a half, The Institute had slowly lost all municipal support. Several mayors and city council members came and went, and city commissioners gradually lost all attachment to the gentlemen's agreements of earlier administrations. The waned formal encouragement, and scheduled termination of financial sponsorship by year-end 1963, left Doctor Pacheco with little choice but to pursue private endowments.

His first two applications that season were denied. But, as luck would have it, a local banking executive had sat on both selection committees. This independent woman banker soon approached Doctor Pacheco with an administrative arrangement that offered the good doctor a way to continue his project unabated, And so what do you say Doctor, Would you mind if I think it over, Of course Doctor I'm just not sure what's to think over, It's just that I'm not sure a boutique of medicines and medical supplies in the lobby would benefit my patients and I'm hesitant to grant a board of trustees and members with no medical experience even a third of executive privilege, You mustn't worry Doctor because having a board of trustees is simply old hat nowadays for any growing organization, I would still like several days to think it over,

Absolutely Doctor and please remember that not only is my investment team thoroughly excited by the prospects of joining your project we are also a highly coveted commodity, Excuse me, Nothing more Doctor but please take your time and think things through, Excuse me but did you just say I'm competing for your attentions, You mustn't worry Doctor because having a board of trustees is simply necessary nowadays for any growing organization.

Rebranded simply The Institute of Joy in 1964, after its first long-term foundational contract and the inevitable contraction that followed, the center experienced something of a second birth. Even though the annex home Doctor Pacheco had envisioned as a crowning therapeutic innovation was turned into a boutique medicine and medical supplies shop, its basement a temporary stock warehouse for items before shelf life, the remaining group rooms continued their usual ambience.

True, the furniture had begun to reflect its age. And, true, the walls begged for new paint. However, a new cycle of patients arrived with a better formal understanding of words, and many immediately caught on to The Institute's sudden omission of the noun and in group exercises, And the *wellness* Doctor, Excuse me, Should we no longer be *well* Doctor, Of course you must we must all be, Then why reduce our experience to *joy*, My dear boy these are only formalities of the bureaucratic kind, But Doctor everyone here is insisting all they want is happiness, My dear boy any brute can be satisfied through fleeting satiation but it takes more so much more to be well, I see Doctor, On you go then for balance and even keel.

However, by 1971, even the patients that had remained from The Institute's earlier era no longer recalled first generation incentives and whole names. In short, they'd succumbed to executive formality, and by 1974, as part of higher annual dues, The Institute required all patients to monthly purchase medications that, to their knowledge, offered supplemental nutritional value for their meals. And even though some had begun to complain the following year of crystallized urine and consistently harder fecal matter, the board of trustees released a statement ensuring all patients that medical studies had already proven, without a shadow of a doubt, nutritional supplements remain effective so just as long as one's diet followed federal government daily intake recommendations.

And, so, per popular patient request, the annex medicine and medical supplies boutique began stocking and selling meal plans which soon became mandatory for all new patients, existing patients rolling over into the program so just as long as they agreed to contractually bind themselves to three more years' residency at The Institute.

In the meanwhile, Doctor Pacheco had grown increasingly frustrated with his patients' reliance on ingestions, as opposed to exorcisms of pains and words, for the emotional leveling he insisted they all strive for, But Doctor every option taken together feels very good and very energizing, Yes my dear girl but one mustn't forget that learning how to both laugh and cry is a base goal of this program, Yes Doctor but doesn't it make sense we've all come to you for joy, Wellness and joy my dear girl wellness and joy and though we might fluctuate above and below it's that center line that matters, Yes Doctor but you yourself have named this place The Institute of Joy, My dear girl one mustn't fall prey to a bureaucracy of titles, Yes Doctor but me I've signed up for The Institute of Joy and I love The Institute of Joy.

By 1982, having sold his private practice, opening his schedule for father-son collaborations, emerging therapist Doctor Humberto Pacheco joined The Institute of Joy and immediately lent his modernizing hand. In conjunction with the board of trustees, and according to its guidance, Humberto secured sponsorship from a pharmaceuticals company for new carpeting and flooring, and in exchange The Institute agreed to carry solely that company's brand of diarrhetic and incontinence products in the annex boutique. Additionally, Humberto agreed to partnership with another pharmaceuticals company, bound to contract for four years, in which that company would foot The Institute's utility bills in exchange for carrying only that company's nutritional supplements and all variety of skin products in the boutique. Lastly, Humberto trademarked the center's name and then sold its copyright, under agreement he and his father could use it for their single center on only that single plot of land for as long as the younger shall live, to a third pharmaceuticals company that agreed also to refurbish, repaint, and repair the building in order to update The Institute's façade so to match its neighbors' contemporary exterior décor.

The senior, ever the pragmatist for executive control, remained skeptical of his son's renovation and modernization projects. The junior, ever the ambitious one, assured his father that such organizational shifts have been old hat for small businesses for years.

In any case, tragedy, which to some extent had been approaching the surface for years, emerged finally in 1985, and for Humberto, the road's sudden profusion of glass showed him that regardless of where he'd started or thought to put his feet, one arduous step after the next would follow him until time inevitably taught him that both laughing and crying were really, as his father had attempted to reveal time and again, the best way to ensure one's ready momentum if life so chose to try you, to shift either both left and/or right, this way back and/or that way and forward.

First, the elder Doctor Pacheco passed away via sudden complication of the heart. All the doctor could tell Mrs. Pacheco, who died three months later, and Humberto was that Felipe, having always circulated around median blood pressure, too quickly dipped in that department, and his sudden change of heart left him without the strength to recover from his two heart attacks in the span of a single week.

As aforementioned, Mrs. Pacheco also passed on. Humberto and his father had already been training staff for months, and so Humberto did not question leaving others temporarily in charge of The Institute of Joy.

In the month that followed his mother's funeral, Humberto had not remained as privy as he should have to The Institute's contractual handlings. As it turned out, in the span of the previous year, the pharmaceuticals company owning The Institute's conceptual copyright, had purchased the other two pharmaceuticals companies with which The Institute partnered in sponsorship and sales. In the paperwork mayhem that accompanied the mergers, the holding company reportedly mixed up and misplaced sponsorship files and took to believing that The Institute's copyright licensing arrangement with the Pacheco family had expired on December 31st, 1986, and so the holding company immediately set their legal team into restitution mode, and within two months, the holding company had drafted a cease and desist letter for the Pacheco family, attempting to legally block them from using "The Institute of Joy" as the center's name.

Because the paperwork never made it into Humberto's hands, and the clerical staff on site returned the form signed but without checking a box for this or that copyright option, the day after Humberto's return proved to be his most hideous swing between laughing and crying, shouting all the same during each and throwing his desk phone across the lobby to assert, once and for all, that his father had clearly forgotten to embed *Grief* in the center's first moniker, *The Mayor's Institute for Grief, Wellness, and Joy*.

And then the sheriff's office bolted the center's doors shut, with patients still inside, in order to carry out the pharmaceuticals company's filed lien on the property. In the raucous following, because patients had only just arrived and still suffered from antecedent pendulum peak points, everyone's first register after the sheriff left was concern, and then many throttled into panic, and though Humberto had yet to shatter composure, his patients did. The more anxious ones started walking circles, or back-and-forth lines, muttering to themselves hoping to themselves pulling at their roots until someone pulled another's hair, and when one patient went to another's defense, the cycle continued until a drunk pub brawl erupted in a second floor meeting space, and in fits, a patient shattered the window just before another lost his footing and stumbled into a third until both persons fell onto the pavement below, dying, and one fracturing his face.

Beyond that, hope lay smashed on the sidewalk. Patients ran through halls and stairwells, room to room. One started a fire in the basement bathroom and a second, numbed and thoughtless, tossed paper into the flames, and then suddenly, because the annex and main Institute basement were one and the same, an explosion rocked the foundation. Perhaps vials and pulverized chemicals fed the growing blaze until everything boomed, and then the first floor blew out, and everyone leapt through now empty window frames, Humberto hurling himself onto the curb, and then he wrapped his face in a jacket and braced himself for some second boom.

TOMORROW EVERYONE LIVES

I *have* to believe that you can come back from the dead. That you can climb out of a grave and pick up the broken pieces and glue them back or pray they stick when you try to stand. I have to *believe* it's already happened. That it's not just a story. I have to believe that angels in real life showed up and tapped Jesus on the shoulder and said, Come on We gotta go.

I have to believe that Jesus opened his eyes and looked around, shocked, and that he tapped his chest to remember a heart rhythm he'd forgotten, and then that he got all, Who the hell are you, to the angels.

One of the angels would have walked to the edge of the tomb and pulled a half-smoked cigarette out of his wings. Angels are timeless, you know, and then the angel addicted to smoking would have got all, Can you believe this fool, to the other angel.

That other angel would have pulled Jesus to his feet and said, It's okay we got you, and then Jesus would have felt the weight in his knees, the thump in his heart again, the sonic beat that makes all things go, and then he would have just started crying. Some mix of happy tears and sad ones and disbelieving ones and just really awful ones, the memory of everything washing over him like a gale wind pushing its way through a crack in the stone wall, and he'd have said, Nobody's ever said that to me.

The angel who helped him to his feet would have been taken aback by that, and he would have asked, What do you mean, and Jesus would have said, That thing you just said Nobody's ever said to me that they got my back.

The angel puffing his cigarette on the other side of the tomb would have rolled his eyes and said, Go on already Get outta here and take him with you, and the other angel would have been like, And what are *you* gonna do.

The inhaling-puff-puff angel would have gone all, I'll just be here finishing my cigarette, and the other angel, by then holding Jesus's hand, would have asked, What if somebody sees you, and the exhaling-puff-puff angel would have said, I'll just tell them what happened.

He would have snorted, Like they'd believe me.

I just killed two more people. You don't have to believe I've never done this to anyone who wasn't already aiming to kill *me*, but it was in an elevator this time. My body did its *thing*, where it expands to fill a space and hardens as it presses into the walls. That thing where the skin becomes scales like bulletproof diamonds interlocking to keep out everybody else's shit. The doctor who gave me all the experimental injections said my skin was like titanium with a shade of grey he's never seen. He said it when he was arguing with one of the guards after the guard got all, I don't want to reach for the kid when he's like this, and the doctor in charge answered back, Can you just grab the boy before he starts screaming again, and the guard shouted back, But every time he cries his body does that thing where it puffs up and everybody near him dies.

I don't remember much more after that, not after the guard leapt at me and plugged a needle into my chest like he was stabbing a shark that had eaten his family.

I didn't feel like a predator then. I'm trying, especially after everything that's happened, not to feel like one now.

The two dead people on the floor, I—I didn't come into the building for *them*. When I got into the elevator, I hit the top floor button on the panel. Button thirty-two. I was supposed to ride straight up because that's how it happens in the movies. Fast, you know. Cut shot to the elevator doors closing. Cut shot to the ding before the elevator doors open. And then cut shot to the hallway in front of you. The guards and soldiers and hitmen aiming all their guns at you. Some of them nervous. Some of them firm and sweating but holding onto their triggers like the sun clinging to its place in the cosmos. Outsized, but never guaranteed. And then cut shot back to you. The glimmer on your face. The eyes that refuse to cry. And then you whisper to yourself, For you mamá, and then—and then just hell. All fire.

I didn't mean to kill *these* people, though. They hadn't come into the elevator on the second floor gunning for me. One of them had actually had a hard time getting inside in the first place. He came in pushing and then tugging a cart. The birthday cake on top of it swayed a little too much after he rolled the wheels over the entrance, and so he had to dive to steady the base layer. Even I thought the whole thing was going to topple.

He sighed after he settled the cake, and then he scratched an itch on his nose with his shoulder, and when he stood up again, he wiped sweat off his forehead and then found some frosting on his thumb. He almost licked it off before remembering something. I could tell by the look in his eye that whatever thought had prompted not licking the frosting off his thumb had been something serious.

In any case, he nervously tried to ease the frosting back into place between the bottom two layers of the cake, but he ended up just blurring a whole streak of frosting, and then he whispered something like, Ugh I hate you Karen.

And then on cue, somebody named Karen walked into the elevator, and the guy got all, Oh hey Karen you made it, and the woman got all, I hope you didn't lick the cake Don.

Karen tapped her forehead like she was calling Don an idiot. Don quickly pulled blue frosting off his receded hairline and wiped it, as if on instinct, onto the back of his pants, like he'd been used to soiling himself in the name of somebody else. In the name of somebody in charge.

And then Karen turned to *me*. Not with the same condescension. At least I don't think so. People usually save that kind of look for somebody they know. Instead, Karen eyed me up and down like she was both trying to be subtle and like she was thirsty. Women have a funny way of doing that. Taking all of you in like they think you don't know that they're doing it. I'm not *very* tall, but I still get that look a lot for any number of reasons. Sometimes, I think, just for the bruises on my forehead and hands, though always from the grown-ups. Adults seem to have this glancing game down. Like they're always trying to find a body to grab or get into or like they want to just imagine what it'd be like to weave any number of bodies together.

Or like they're just itching to turn somebody in.

And maybe it was the logo on the back wall that had me tense already. The Defenders of Eviction United, Inc.—the D.E.U., company logo with a lion in a suit and bowtie, its paws suspended midair like a hairy, toothy Buddha, a wink in its eye, all of it encircled in a bold, gold halo. All of it like the lion was trying to tell you that it knew how to make money but also how to keep that money a secret.

Maybe I was already tense from the gel in my hair. There was too much of it. I'd told Stephanie as she was putting it on me that she was putting on too much, but she insisted that my hair was too wild. That it was prone to sticking up in a swoop that sometimes made me look handsome but sometimes made me look like a clown who hadn't tried hard enough to brush his hair.

Or maybe I was just tense because I'd seen this script before. I'd lived it. When somebody decides to ogle you like they're looking for cracks, they're *going* to find them. I wasn't wearing the right company badge. Stephanie and I had tried to get creative, laminating a company-standard rectangle with a stenciled black and white logo and a fake barcode and a touched-up grayscale ID photo and a fake name. For this journey into vengeance, Stephanie made up the name Mario Jean Munro for me. She tried to make me feel better about it when she told me, Just act like you're not from the United States, and I told her, We're not *from* the fucking United States Stephanie, and then she said, Then pretend like you're from Europe or something, and then I got offended, I said, What's wrong with being American Stephanie.

She grabbed me by the collar and pulled me to her lips and gritted through her teeth, and she said, Stop pretending like these people here think we're American too.

I swatted her hands away and told her I'll never care what these people think. That America's too big to let these northerners take the identity away from the rest of us. In any case, I said, I'm bulletproof now and *they* made *me* that way.

They're the monsters, I said, making other monsters in their image.

Sometimes, I want to forget I ever said that.

In the elevator, Karen cleared her throat and pressed button five just as we started riding the elevator up again. Maybe she thought I'd hear her clearing her throat and be stirred into something. Like maybe she thought I'd register what almost sounded like a guttural choke and then decide to chime in and say, Hello ma'am How are you My name is Carlos Echevarria de las Nieves What's *your* name. She clearly thought something because she rolled her eyes at Don and then glanced at me and then cleared her throat again.

North American subtlety can be so passive aggressive.

I checked the button on my suit jacket. Made sure they couldn't see a lot of the tuxedo shirt underneath. I'd only stolen it an hour ago and we didn't have time to run back to the motel and iron it. My cufflinks rattled when I tried to smooth my hands back into my pockets, and Karen did *not* clear her throat this time when she got all, Excuse me young man but are you going to a wedding.

I knew it. I'd told Stephanie that the cufflinks were a touch too much. Like somebody was going to notice how big they were and probably think I'd just come back from a funeral—but a wedding? Makes sense, I guess. Revealing yourself completely to somebody can feel maybe like its own kind of death.

I didn't want to tell Karen too much so I just said, There's a corporate event on the thirty-second floor ma'am that the company I work for is catering this afternoon.

I nailed it. At least I thought I did. Karen nodded, and then she glanced at Don, and then she glanced at the elevator panel, and then she cleared her throat again. I didn't realize anything was wrong until Karen started tapping the door open button after the monitor dinged the number four. Freight elevators can take forever. Don shook his head crazy-like, but Karen turned to me anyway and said, I don't know where you got that company badge young man.

She said, It doesn't make sense that a caterer would have a company badge at all now does it.

She said, You didn't go to the lobby to get your visitor's pass did you.

And then she said, Open goddammit Open already.

The building had already been attacked a few times. Rioters the month before. Protestors occupied the lobby the month before that. A lot of people, it seemed, didn't like the idea of a company that built, maintained, and secured warehouses where immigrant children and their parents stayed locked up. A lot of people, it seemed, but not enough. It's not like anything had happened to this building. It's not like anything had happened to the warehouses.

I wouldn't even have been able to make it in here if it hadn't been for Stephanie. She got the experimental injections, too, but her body reacted different. She started disappearing and being able to walk through walls after like the twenty-fourth or twenty-fifth injection. But, like me, only after the injections *and* after weeks and weeks of just crying until you didn't know how to cry anymore.

After we escaped and had already been a few days on the run, we figured out she could also disappear into people's bodies. Control them. But it took her a while to master that one. At first she stayed so long inside people's bodies that she had to jump out exhausted when she felt herself running out of breath. Then it became a timing issue. One time she tried to muscle through the breathlessness but stayed in there so long that she re-materialized inside the person, and then, well—he just blew up.

In the elevator, Karen kept mouthing something about needing to get out. The monitor finally dinged five, and she got all, Don call security when you get to the emergency phone down the hall, and Don got all, *Stop* it Karen, and Karen got all, Would you just follow an order without *fucking* it up Don, and then Don said, It's *him* Karen, and then Karen said, Speak *up* Don, It's *him* Karen, It's *who* Don, It's the kid from the *news* Karen.

And then Karen looked at me as if for the first time. Acknowledging me without the satisfaction her authority in the building had probably gotten her used to. Recognizing me with a pause in her eyes. Recognizing me with the recognition that this was all likely going to end just one way.

I thought I saw her gulp. The elevator stopped, and maybe she saw me gulp, too. And then I closed my eyes. I let my body do what it does now. What it can do now even when I can't feel the brokenness in my heart anymore.

The breath.

The release.

The expansion.

It used to happen only when I screamed. Only when I didn't know how else to respond to the pain in my chest that remembered my mother's hand when she tried to grab me before they dragged her out of our shared detention cell. That remembered the pain in my arms when they slapped me and tossed me against a hallway wall outside this other detention cell door that some guard had opened up as he was trying to zip up his pants and all I could see in the room's shadow was my mother's shoes and her pants at her ankles. That remembered the pain in my head after a morning of just banging it against a wall, just banging it so many times hoping I could forget our house, forget my dad, forget my sister, and forget the train and the desert and the line that becomes a river that can *not* possibly be a boundary between anything because both sides of the border are just a shared road to hell—that remembered my throbbing migraines after the first set of experimental injections, after which the guard had said, You're doing a lot to help us out kid.

He had tried to explain in detail about what he'd meant by that until the guard pulling me by my other arm stopped him and said, Don't tell the kid anything, and then the first guard got all, Well it's true isn't it, and the second guard got all, So *what* if it's true, and then the first guard said, The kid's gonna die in here anyway so maybe it's just the right thing to do to be honest, and then the second guard said, He's a wetback and he probably doesn't even understand you He doesn't even speak American.

And then the ringing in my ear had started like somebody was trying to bury a knife in it. The two guards had gone on about a sickness. About a virus in the country, in the only country that ever seems to matter in these stories. About some disease that had been really bad at some point just recently but that wasn't so bad anymore. Something about the vaccines they'd developed that hadn't worked but that seemed like they could have still been good for something. So why not try them out on the immigrant kids. Just a whole cocktail of that stuff to see what happens. It's science, right. A question, hypothesis, and testing. Observing the kids until they go green in the face and they can prove something, say something about what's happening to their bodies, about how much their lives can mean when their lives are numbers on a chart.

Or until their green faces turn blue and then pale and they just get buried behind the warehouse when their hearts break.

I can remember all of it now without crying anymore.

I can remember all of it now so nobody hears me screaming anymore.

The elevator doors rattle open. The fifth-floor landing is empty. I am my own size again, and the elevator walls are dirty. The floor, too. Part of the carpet's got cake mushed in. There's guck everywhere. Orange and purple. A whole cocktail of red and blue and broken white bones. There's no more Don. And no more Karen.

When anyone's ever asked me, I always tell them the same thing. I'm only ever just the size I am. I don't go into specifics. Like that sometimes I'm really narrow like angel spaghetti but also flat like paper. Like that sometimes I'm a balloon bigger than a car, my skin thick and head huge, like a cannonball with hair and pimples and fingernails. I don't tell anybody any of that. I prefer the line Stephanie taught me. *I'm only ever just the size I am.* So I don't blame people for looking at me like they think I'm lying. Like I'm only sharing part of the story.

The elevator doors close again. There's never any time to talk when you got to keep moving. But if you want to hear the whole thing, I guess you can stick around. We can hang out together until the guns start booming on the top floor. Until we make it through the bullets and explosions and we're inside the boardroom and we meet the people around the boardroom table. The people with answers, with plans, with means. The people with stories that sound like lies. The people that like to say, Hey it's just business. *Good* business, this business of bodies and cages and children.

Eventually, the elevator will have a last stop. Until then, it's a long ride up.

All Apologies

THE WAY IT ENDS

I want to start by confessing that I don't know how to stop and that I don't know how much to dim the lamp or how far to open the curtains—that I don't know how to stand apart from it all. A streetlight can flicker, and I can almost smell the sidewalk if I let the thought of everyone's shoes and the steps they take slither up and into me. If I imagine their toes, tips, and heels that rub into the cushions again and again, soft to avoid a squeal and just strong enough to make the cement burn. A thought can be a gut check coming into place and coming sooner than anyone expects, and because the pillow knows where to exhale, my eyes sink into the fluff there. My cheeks rub into the covers and my hands press into me and I don't pull them off and my free knuckles almost punch the mattress. The bed always—*always*—remembers how long it takes me to get to where I need to go and how much coming matters in this endless repetition of a night, and the mattress—*especially* the mattress—remembers every hair on me when my nostrils flare and my lips part, hanging dry just above the linen, and I lick it all, my teeth and mouth, if only to feel, again, the lengths I've taken to be alone. And then I've finished, and I stretch my tongue to the cloth almost like a reflex, but I pull it back, and then I exhale like a motherfucker over the stitching. The air over my face like the fog of an animal that's crept to me. Curious about what leaves me breathless. Fascinated by how I start crying sometimes and how it can all feel so lonely.

Maybe I should worry that I do what I do with the window open. That I touch myself thinking that nobody can hear me touching myself, though maybe I want them to—maybe I *need* them to. Like I don't really want separation or some kind of distance from anyone. A third-floor apartment doesn't stand far above the buzz anyway. Not with its bedroom and bathroom lights on. Not with its hard floors that ricochet sound like a handball court. Not when I can smell the breeze that every passing windshield pushes up. I'm over it all, but I'm not—I *know* I'm not—over any of it.

My heart pounds sometimes, but it never surfaces. Third floor apartments have this self-centered way of knowing that you're going to feel more trapped in them than eager to skip down the stairs onto the road. And why would you need to leave when just the shuffling on the street, just the sound of the world absorbed in its own rituals, can touch you like the flip of a fresh newspaper? A newness every time it catches you sleeping. And I'm talking about *all the melodies below*, the echoes coming so sharp at you that they cling, they stick, they tattoo you like moths you swat onto the wall but can never rub off. Like the doorbell jingle of the pharmacy downstairs, a ring so clear that the chime above the front door might as well be a mirror. And like the old hinge of the jewelry store's front door, that diamond shop on the corner whose finesse falls apart when you hear, at the end of each day, the bars coming down to lock the night away. And like the laughter when somebody leaves the Cuban bakery next door, the smell of bread and nicotine blending into some proverb about what goes into your mouth and what comes out, about the fires that can burn when different worlds mix.

And then there's Theo, who'd always told me—*always*—that the brush of every person's sole could sometimes ring like the hush of a partner asking you to stop talking so they can feel the world that thrums in the sheets. Who used to love waxing poetic about the world and its whispers and the world and its bedside manners that don't always know how to ease the nerves you carry when you can't sleep.

I still feel his fingers, between mine, around mine. His hands like a car that could lead me down highways a map hadn't carved yet. I didn't wear a ring long enough before he died, and it would have been fun to have eventually—ultimately—tapped our diamonds together in a clasp just walking down the street, even in a movie theater before the title card appeared, even as we sat across each other at a restaurant table. If we would have just made it to the wedding, even if it had been a lazy wedding with bad dancing and homegrown flowers and cheap Party City decorations, how different this whole story could have been, this story about days that keep repeating because somebody took a gun to the minute hand. And I'm not saying that Theo was some kind of clock that kept the days beating for me. I can measure my own time, thank you. I don't need lovers for that. But we never got a chance to test the full scale of a promise, even if it would eventually shatter like a stray car into a storefront. There's only this now. There's only *now* now, these days that keep repeating to keep replaying all that happened.

So I sit up. With time spent—a *lot* of time—on my side, on my back, sitting up helps. I can't just keep touching myself. My hands feel caught between my thighs, so I pull the blanket out from under me. I pull out a wedgie, too. The glow from the neon signs across the street flickers across the ceiling. One bird and then a few more disrupt the light stream. There's always *something* interrupting the view. My sister tells me as much all the time, and she tells me, too, that I have to eat, that I can't keep pretending like my stomachache isn't also to blame by now, that something is always going to fuck up what should have been, and that if I'm just going to be lying here, You have to fucking eat Sonya, she says. You have to get the fuck out of bed, she says.

I'm thinner now, my underwear looser, but if Theo were alive, he wouldn't have said anything about it. He would have lied, saying that all he was seeing was the feeling that bridged the heart to the kind of desire that revved all things into motion. Like he would have just said, *Baby, how come you don't change, and how come I love these hips even more today*. He used to graze one side or both in passing when I knew something about them had shifted, as if to comfort me through progressions across the song of my body, and especially because I wear change like a wild coat. He could always see the tension that had to be tamed. Stress never knows what it wants to do with my body. Make it wider. Narrow it. Leave it alone. All these conditions, and everything in between, falling onto my lap like a dog barking for attention and promising nothing in return but more demands.

Theo used to flirt all the time. In voicemails. In notes on the counter by the fridge. In text messages. *Honey I pulled the blanket over your hips last night just so. Honey last night I fell asleep massaging your thighs.* I used to fold those slips of paper or pull out my phone and read those messages at work. *All* the time. I used to *love* reading that kind of shit at work *all* the time. On breaks. At lunch. In the elevator between patient room check-ins on different floors. One time, tired as whatnot, I exhaled loudly outside the room of a post-op follow-up, and I then unlocked my phone and read Theo's most recent message, and, afterward, I had to force on a straight face so that I could walk into the room and tell the patient I was seeing that there wasn't anything wrong with them, that the scans came back all clear, that the pain in their side was maybe just a phantom, and that they didn't have an ulcer or an appendix problem or cancer or anything. That all they had was a bad imagination. Of course, all I really told them was that the clinic had to charge them a co-pay for their worries on the way out, and I said what I could say while stuck with Theo's words on my mind, messages like *Your legs look good in scrubs, baby.* Messages like *Your body temperature getting warmer yet, baby?* and like *You on your way home feeling the wind on your neck yet, baby?* Sometimes, too, our messages had a way of going from sensual to grocery lists in just two lines, like he'd text, *I miss you*, and I'd text back, *I know you do*, and he'd text, *I want to take your shirt off the minute you shut the front door*, he'd text, and I'd text, *Don't forget to pick up bleach wipes and eggs at Target on your way home.*

My shirt's looser now, like how it should be when the world and the warmth of what you thought you knew is gone. I don't hate myself, it's just that my body rings different now. Like the way my knees chap at night now, like the way my shoulders slack when I don't wear a shirt now and like the lamplight that seems to spread apart the veins and bones on my feet. Maybe it was always like that, but I'm only paying attention now because I don't always know how to keep my hands off me anymore, off the dry and wet, off my hair and heat. Shadows tickle like a special kind of pleasure when the weather chills, too. It's been warmer for a while now so that just a degree difference can raise hairs, and two degrees—even just *two* degrees—and I go reaching for socks and sweatpants in the drawer.

Theo's phone is always right here, too, on the pillow, and so close that I can touch it mid-thought, mid-want. I talk right into it sometimes, just whispers of incomplete affection. Of letting go. Of what he let go of. Touching myself comes easy with it on, so I keep it charged, just to be staring at it and then start feeling my way into some kind of nostalgia. About his hands. His legs. His waist. All of him. A lot of time like this, with the nearness and the reflexes and the impulses and the pulsating, and it's not like the feelings go hand in hand so easy like that, but with his old phone on his old pillow, the same pillow that used to catch the back of his neck after a few drinks or after he came home smelling like the company he'd shared or after he'd sweat through his shirt after sweating me, the feelings, the urges, come fast sometimes. His phone always sinking into the pillow and my hands always sinking into things that shouldn't make sense anymore. The heat of the screen like it radiates his face.

The last wallpaper he'd saved on his phone was a selfie of us, our grins pressing into each other while sitting on a train, two tired smiles I'm always lingering over, lingering with, my imagination stoned by that image like the impression on the pillow the phone is always leaving behind, like the carpeted spot in a living room after years of a bookshelf standing on it. That much story, recorded and preserved and tattooed on and in a machine, can disappear when the machine does, so why not tap the screen now and again and often to keep it alive and looking back at me with a world, a time before collapse, salvaged every time the phone lights up.

Before he died, I used to browse his pictures all the time. He used to love the ordinariness of his drives or walks or rides on the bus, taking pictures of people's shoes and coffee mugs and mailboxes and graffiti and coat zippers pulled to somebody's chin, always on his commute to work, from work. When he texted me to show me his pictures, even the captions would echo the wonder of commonplace things. *You'll never believe how this train today smells completely like this woman's hazelnut coffee creamer,* he'd text. *Baby you will never believe the things caught under this guy's boots,* he'd text. *Honey I wish you were here right now cuz this joker next to me has Prince blasting through headphones like they want this whole train to break into a flash mob,* he'd text. And then later his eyes would shiver when he told me about it all over dinner, swiping across pictures with greasy fingers.

And he was always like that. Wanting your attention. Your *complete* attention. Always searching for it, needing it, insecure without it. But the thing that nobody tells you about attention is that it can start to beg you to start looking for more, and it seems like his body just couldn't contain that urge, that push, to touch something—some*one*—when wanting their attention turned into wanting more than just their attention. And nobody teaches you, until it's too late, that that kind of excitement, that *that* kind of energy and anxiety, can circulate through your body until it becomes an addiction. Attention slowly turning to vice. Vice becoming a mole that you can't remove. The mole begging to be touched until that touch becomes indistinguishable from a need and then that need nags you like a second hand begging you to jump to the next minute. I never worried back then that I wasn't doing enough, or that I wasn't enough, but now—the *now* right now—is a different story. I toggle through memories sometimes like they're countless grains of sand and I'm digging, clawing, through them, to try to find water. And sometimes it rains in the desert, but even then it's only a passing cloud, and the world dries up again, fast, and sometimes something grows from it and sometimes nothing does, and I spin through all those feelings, at every hour every night, and the only thing that helps me sometimes—many times—the only thing that lets me down in a different kind of way is the air that spins above me when I touch myself, when I *really* dig into things. Masturbation, when you can't sleep, is the comfort that can't always keep on giving because it doesn't always know how to, even when it's always tempting you to ask something more from it.

Of all people, too, it had to be my best friend. Of all *fucking* people, it had to be a *fucking* cliché. And if I think about it too long, I start to reason into forgiveness, logic like a journey that wants a resolution it can't blame anyone for, not the people who broke those relationships or the institutions that compel us to lose ourselves to impulse and the impulses that lose themselves to the moment.

I can't count anymore the number of times Nell didn't say anything when she could have, the occasions she had to tell me about what had happened and what was going on. But instead it was all *Theo doesn't seem to like it when you kiss him in public* and *Are you sure Theo likes it when you rest your chin on his shoulder at dinner like that* and *I don't know but it seemed like Theo's face turned all wrong when you pressed in from behind and entwined your fingers in his*, and whatever else she'd noticed in larger company. Like her eyes felt bad for me, too. Like what she wanted to say was that the craft of a feeling was exhibitionism coming from me. Like the expressions in my body amounted to more performance than reflection, every movement in me offered more show than grace. But it's not like I used to French kiss his throat, like I couldn't control where I set my hands or where I thrust my hips. I just enjoyed him—the way anyone would enjoy a lover's company in the company of other people. But then there was this woman, and I don't know when she turned, who used to tell me that his face maybe stiffened when I leaned in or that it seemed to freeze like he wanted to tell me something. And I don't know that anything she said came in a rate worth measuring then, only that I can elaborate on it all now like the volume of her criticism had come loud, like I should have recognized then the picture I know now to have been true.

Theo's phone smiles when I turn off the light, like the way he used to when he left for work. Like all the texts he used to send me from the bus station or from the front steps at his ad agency job before stepping into the building. Like *Baby, I'll be home early today and I'll cook* or like *Baby, I'll be home late tonight but I'll have flowers*. The kind of stuff that could shape a history as it unspooled at the cusp of every day.

But now I scream into the phone sometimes. I pick it up when I can't sleep, and I hold it to my chin, like my teeth could bite it or like my lips could part with a lamentation that mattered. Me and this thing, alone, even as messages for Theo keep coming through and lighting up the screen. Buddhists believe it's the hearing that dies last, as if the auditory nature of the body wants some final directions home, and so monks chant for weeks after one of them passes, offering the soul a rhythm of instructions to navigate the airy spaces between here and the everywhere that follows. Theo's phone, meanwhile, keeps dinging, text messages coming through like they don't know how to shut off the night. And I should be muting them, but what if notifications, when we don't cut off the line, replace the humming that drives the soul home. Nothing seems to let the dead rest anyway. People calling on Theo with their own lamentations and condolences like *We're here for you, Theo,* and *We're marching the streets for you, man,* and *We won't stop fighting for you, ever,* and *We miss you every day* and *#FightThePower* and *Injustice on one is injustice on all,* like every death amounts to more than the truths it leads to and even when you hope no one dies alone, who, in the end, ever really dies in the company of a love that won't leave them dry.

And there she was, in the end, in a place that didn't belong to her and occupying a space of time so short that it could have amounted to nothing if it had only been given more time.

The pictures on Theo's phone can be a bedtime story when I linger with them, some of them to keep up you at night, some of them so ordinary like he had only ever ambitioned to accept the reality before him. Close-ups of soft edges. The hemming of a sweater. The back of a sneaker. The leather of his work satchel, he hated it when I called it a satchel, even if there was nothing else to call a brown, manageably square bag with a strap that fell across his chest and cargo enough for a notebook and a laptop. He told me once *We're not in the eighteenth century anymore, baby, just call it a bag,* and I raised my brows at him, answering back *I know what era in human history we're in, I'm holding you with a free hand, aren't I.* Criticize the language of a shared experience all you want, but the words we exchange and the gestures of a body that ring like a proposition can't just hide from a world always watching.

Sometimes I press the phone between my thighs, just above my knees, and I hold it there. I cry because it can't get me off. I cry because I don't want it to turn me on. I cry because there's no one left to scream at and no one left to help me reconcile lost things. Sometimes I press the phone to my chest, the sternum, onto that patch of birthmarks Theo used to graze and right onto the skin where he rested his head after proposing to me on the waterfront. I want to believe that our bodies were always each other's, even if only *mainly,* but I don't want to say *Fuck you, Nell* and *Fuck you, Theo* because screaming gets old, and urging for something from the dead gets old. Dead passions age everything, and I don't know that I have answers, only that I have a problem, this need to flip through pictures and video on Theo's old phone, again and again, to trace the momentum that got us here and to try uncovering a path that could have brought him home, a past that had him walking through our front door, with or without a confession and apology.

I don't like it that I have to stop my fingernails from clawing into my ankles. I don't like it that I have to keep my hands busy after an orgasm. I can't believe I have it in me to hurl one pillow after the next into the closet until the cushions pile into a bed and I can walk right into it and shut the sliding door behind me, or that in the thick of the worst of it, I can throw the phone across the room when I'm done swiping pictures, videos, making my way through faces that, by and large, seem to cut off the time I want to spend understanding anything, or that I can beat the phone into the carpet or hammer it back into the pillow. The screen never seems to break, even when the video—*the* video—spins at me, *re*-spinning every time I tap the eastward triangle, and I've been at this a long time, hitting play again even after I've already hit play a hundred times, hitting play because it only makes sense to call it all a hit, a strike you can aim or an overplayed spectacle that you've seen, the whole world has seen, too many times.

And it goes like this, Theo's final video on his phone starting when Nell laughs. She's always laughed, maybe she's still laughing, almost emphatically, at some anecdote about Theo's boss or his commute. Right as her laugh ends, she touches his forearm, a light touch she turns into a temporary graze, up to the nook of his elbow and then over the hill of his bicep, and then she glides her fingerprints back to his wrist and knuckle, and then she points up. She tells him there's marinara sauce on his cheek. She feels that patch of his skin, too, as if not so subtly exploring what she can before she gets told to stop or before anyone can tell her *No!*, and then she reaches for his shirt and tells him his buttons have come undone. You're sloppy, she says, licking her lips like she's sealing the sight of him in her mouth.

He holds the phone up as he drives. Light traffic on a thoroughfare lined with thinned branches and overburdened trash cans. Not a lot of people filling the sidewalks. Nell laughs again as if her voice could comfort even the sunset, and who knows how many they had already enjoyed.

There's video time and then there's unnerving time, and I know what happens, what always happens, when the two accrue tension like twins feeding off the same mother.

Almost twenty-five seconds in, Theo turns the phone on himself and offers a choked balloon face. The only "funny" face he's got, and then he says, Let's pull over somewhere I'm about to blow, and then Nell says something off screen like, Don't be taking away my job now baby, or something like that, and he laughs trying to tell her it's that he has to go to the bathroom, and when he turns the phone back to her, there she sits, blushing, trying to keep a straight face. He tells her, he teases her, that she owned that meeting they just had. That she owned all those execs in that room staring at her, transfixed by the bright of her, the methods on her, the straits and curves on her. That she owned all those projected revenue and market share stats, and that she can own him whenever she wants.

She surprises him when she grabs the wheel and tells him the light's changed. He drops the phone and shouts after it, and then in that fake Theo way, he laughs that he's got marinara sauce on his pants, too. Carelessness can be a habit, but to be surprised about what comes next when you've already seen it can lead to an addiction, of shock, of a rattling to the core, of a numbing that can't stay numb unless you keep injecting yourself with the same images.

The video sound muffles for a bit, the image a shadow of Theo's pant leg, his foot on the brake, and I think Theo and Nell trade quips, and then I think I hear them kissing. There's honking, and then there's Theo pretending to yell at the driver behind him. And I like to imagine he'd been drinking, that I could blame his stupidity on two or more pints of beer and too much talking and a phone he couldn't put down. Combinations can knit themselves into blankets that can suffocate you in your sleep, and then I hear them diffuse an argument by trying to get ahead of the moment outside the car, Please get the hazard lights on baby, I got it Nell, We're just stopped here, I know that, And I don't think anybody behind us knows what we're doing, I can find the phone Nell.

I still jump when I hear the tapped glass. When the light skips off the floor of the car and I can see where the phone fell. When the aura of the flashlight beam lingers over the seat, and I can see, finally, the extent of the camera angle and the shadow on the driver's window.

It's Nell that finally grabs the phone, even as the police officer commands her to keep still, to stop moving, to show her face. It's Nell that sets the phone on the middle console where it faces the window, and I hate that the sunlight ricocheting off the tress frames the officer's face when he scratches his cheek, Is that off, It's off officer, Don't dare move again, I won't officer.

Some auras in the world go misplaced or stolen or should have stayed home where vanity can be contained. I hate it that my hands shake after how often I've seen this video, even this part of the video, and when my sister knocks on the bedroom door to make sure I'm okay, I hate it that I don't know how to tell her that I don't know how to hate anymore and that I don't know how to say that we all have to contend with a world where the miracle is just another morning and that I don't know that I can say as much any better than anyone who's been through the fire like this.

I can hear the hazard lights flickering, Is everything okay officer.

I think it's Nell who clears her throat first, and her hands, clasped like a prayer, gesture all over the place. I think she actually wants to point at something as she talks. I know I'd certainly want to point at something in that situation, like the officer's inability to expand the moment into a lifetime. But some of us only know how to bury anxiety in a prayer. Even when we don't believe in god.

Nell tries explaining to the officer that she and Theo are on their way home after a work function, and, goodness, does she apologize, I'm sorry officer we were just looking for my phone that fell, she said, I'm sorry miss but I wasn't talking to you, he said, I'm sorry officer but I just want to help, she said, I'm sorry miss but your friend here shouldn't have to need any help, he said, I'm sorry officer but I'm just trying to stay out of the way, she said, Then you need to be sorry a lot more quietly and stay out of the way, he said.

Why did you have to snicker, Theo.

Theo says something like *I'm sorry officer* but which, even if you didn't know Theo, sounded very like a *What the fuck do* you *want asshole*, which I used to tell him, often enough, to temper, to disguise, that it wasn't any reason for anyone to do a goddamn thing but that there were people everywhere who wanted to use it as fodder for *every* goddamn thing. And I don't know if that was it. I don't know if that small tone was all that drove the man's senses through a busted storefront like a car run astray. But the officer went there, for whatever reason, for every reason, that was no reason at all *and* all at once every pointed thing for him, and it was all, Can you step out of the car please sir, I'm sorry officer but why, I need you to step out of the car immediately sir, Just get out of the fucking car Theo, Back off Nell, Keep your hands down Theo, This is *my* car, Sonya you have to stop watching that video Sonya, Tell mom I'll be right out, You have to come out of that room Sonya, I'm not hungry right now, I understand you'll have weekends like this Sonya, Please I'll be right—, I'm getting the bedroom key Sonya.

I don't hit pause because how else would I ever get to see Nell throw her body away for the sake of anybody else's. I watch the video straight through because how else would I get to see Theo's face tilt to the rhythm of an evening again. How else would I get to see the last *No* he would ever say, spelled across his eyes before he fired his last word into the air, before the last face Theo would ever see, that face and all its history spelled across the air, fired his own loud *No* back into the car.

SYG

There's no responding. Not when The Father appeals like that. To one's necessary ties to family. And on a phone call at work, no less. But also why did The Son even pick up his phone. Especially after it read "The Dude" on the screen. Because there are few reasons The Father would call as The Son ended his workday. And of those reasons, only one that keeps repeating. And so here we are. The clock at well after five-thirty. The twelfth-floor office half-empty. A few old-timers still in their seats and most young-timers off to wherever, far from these cubicles set up like a maze that a lab mouse would just find pointless. Not even a challenge. Only confusing as to why anyone would willingly pretend to lose themselves to the rhythm of a stale carpet and gray walls. Confused why anyone would revisit this maze at all. Day in. Day out.

Leaning back in his chair, the phone cupped at his ear, The Son pauses. He runs his hands through his hair. He even slaps his cheek. Lightly but with a strength as if to feel the palm dig into his skin. And then he leans further back in his chair. Far enough to peek down both sides of the aisle between cubicle sections. To make sure that everyone who uses the corridor to leave has already left, Are you listening, says The Father, What else would I be doing, says The Son.

We need you at your grandmother's birthday party tonight, says The Father, I have plans, says The Son, Is it a date, It's hanging out with someone is what it is, I'll save you the mystery, What's that supposed to mean, You have a full-time job in an expensive city, And what, You'll always find someone else to *hang out* with, the words coming off The Father's lips as if intimacy, real intimacy, were just a fiction, stories people tell each other with air quotes and winks.

The Son coughs into his fist. Away from the phone. Cutting a sigh short before it echoes into the receiver, So just come on, says The Father, I don't know dad, says The Son, Family first am I right, But *why* is it always family first dad.

Always the guilt. So vital to maintaining a family. *Family* defined as more than just the parents and the children, but also *all* the nuclear families of a bloodline two generations back, and *all* the individuals who share the burden of having married into the family, and *all* the children of their children, lives so far removed from the tension of who migrated first to the United States and who came second and what it all means. The family's history like the idea of a nation itself, merely a story we tell ourselves about why being together feels better than being apart. A story, of course, with regular doses of guilt, the *But your grandmother would be disappointed* variety or *Your aunts would disappointed* kind or *Do you really want to be a disappointment* rendition, Just come, says The Father, It's never just *stop by* and it's always *stay forever why don't you*, says The Son, You get it then, says The Father, a man so woven into the family's larger knot that he no longer sees how to untie himself from it, or is no longer able to recognize that he can, or perhaps he simply doesn't want to. All this, The Son thinks, as he restrains another sigh on the phone, another grunt that might very well have wanted to be a groan.

What do you have left to do at work, says The Father, I have to print some schematics I'm taking home for the weekend, says The Son, Will you have time for all that, I always have time for things I *plan* for dad, The Son unsure if the word *plan* would bait The Father into an argument but also hoping it could, at the very least that it could sit there with the kind of tension that an argument can be had but should it.

Just lean into it, says The Father, a platitude that sets a fire to the notion of a *plan*.

The Father lights a cigarette. The Son can hear it from his end of the call. The Father very likely in his usual spot at the living room window and very likely exhaling so his eyes dim, so his heart feels softer, so his hands feel lighter and his apartment, as small as it might feel, expands, even only in spirit, for as long as the cigarette holds steady and lit.

So who's the girl, says The Father, I met her when I was out for drinks with some friends last week, says The Son, Which day last week, When you last asked me to cancel my plans and we argued, That was a good argument we had, We've had practice, You're used to it by now and you're leaning into it, It's like laundry at this point dad, And how often did we teach you to do laundry, Every other day dad, And every other day you make it work.

A good argument. Lean in. Make it work. The intangible nature of language makes songs of unexpected refrains.

The Father takes another drag that carries a silence towing its own reprieve, and on his end, The Son glances around the cubicle farm where very little stirs beyond the overhead vents keeping the temperature steady, Are you still on the line, says The Father, You called my landline, says The Son, What's that supposed to mean, I'm not losing a call connection on a *landline* dad.

As with all friction on the verge of burning what we haul, the repeating nature of the request to cancel plans, to fight about what matters most and how adults can or don't make their way through relationships and friendships on their terms—the simmering experience has always felt like an out-of-body one to The Son. As if this always happens to a character in some story, in some fiction that can turn the seemingly arbitrary repetition into a lesson that changes what the next iteration means, I'll have a plate ready for you when you arrive, says The Father, I look like a fool with people sometimes dad, Everyone has a debt to their family, Why do you always treat it like something owed, It's a duty we have, Why do you treat it like a job we have to work at, Because it's work to maintain these things, Why do you treat this stuff like a thankless gesture no one even gets recognized for, Please just stop focusing on my words, What else do we have dad.

The Son pauses, almost venturing to apologize. Words, in the end, can also sever the things we want to work our way through, We just celebrated the old lady this morning, says The Son, Today's party is for everyone who can't show up tomorrow, says The Father, Why can't we just exclude people like normal families, Because it's not how your grandmother wants to celebrate her seventieth birthday, Why do these things always feel like a surprise, I'll warn you next time we do something last minute, Please stop laughing dad.

The Son clicks *Print* on the computer. The machine starts churning pages, and The Son exhales, staring at the electronica of melodies. Saying yes, even when he knows he *has* to say yes, never feels like the last time he's going to have to say yes. Birthday parties. Graduation parties. Got-a-medal-at-karate parties. Dance recital afterparties. Checked-out-of-the-hospital parties. A big family compels, it seems, constant celebrations to prove that the glue that binds them has cemented it all.

The printer sits by the stacked file folders adjacent to the *In/Out* box by the cubicle wall right next to the convex mirror angled toward the corridor between cubicles so that The Son can see everyone approaching his desk before anyone can surprise him. The Son leans back in his chair anyway to check the status of the corridor between cubicles, as if he doesn't trust the mirror and what it shows, as if the status quo can change abruptly to mess up even the change to the change of plans he's undergoing, How do you always do that, says The Son, Do what, says The Father, Funnel your needs until they become everyone else's too, You get better at it with age, Didn't you ever want to feel apart from everybody, Maybe, So it's really never bothered you, I don't know that I've ever wanted more than what I've needed, What's so wrong with that feeling, It can leave you breathless and always unsatisfied I guess, Do you really think that, I don't think that I'm ready to have a philosophical argument about it is what I'm definitely sure of.

In that moment, the printer completes its job, shaking the desk as the toner cartridge resets to the center of the spool. The Son grabs the stack and rifles through them, briefly making sure that the pages are numbered correctly and ordered appropriately. Outside, some pigeons approach the office windows and then avoid the glass in a glide. A construction crane in the distance appears to be both moving and hanging completely still. And inside the cubicle farm, The Son shuts his eyes, tight, and then he braces the back of his neck after he settles the print-outs on the desk, I'll go, he says, You can keep on with your plans after we eat, says The Father, I don't know that I will, Your plans are important to you though aren't they, Not enough to know how to make them important to everyone else I guess.

~~~~~

On the bus ride into the family neighborhood, you press the back of your hair into the headrest. You settle your elbow on the metal window frame and rest your chin in your palm.

Along the river, the freeway overlooks the ferry traffic and the scheduled tugboats that pull barges of garbage and coal upstream. The surface of the water reflects it all, even the monstrosities across the river. The city's office buildings are all about their windows. Their menial tasks inside made important by the glimmer. As if those professions would be meaningless, exaggerated, even comical, were they to appear anywhere else on earth.

The bus passes alongside bunched homes which turn into bunched apartment buildings and tightly packed bakeries and florists and diners. Each marked by a distinct flag as if every proprietor wanted to colonize some concrete plot the only way they knew how. With an immigrant's hodgepodge of pride and nostalgia and survival and volume.

You reach into your pocket for your phone to shut off its ringer. A moment later, it vibrates. You take a peek at the screen, confirm the calling number, and then hang up. Picking up would mean you'd have to explain all this, and there's no point answering a young woman's question about *So what time will you be here?* when all you can say, if there's anything you can say at all, is *As soon as I can* or *I'm not sure right now* or *I'm just going to try my best to have the energy to come out.* It'll sound too ridiculous, you think, to articulate the whole story, and you're not going to text back *My family added another birthday celebration for my grandmother for tonight because certain family members won't be able to come to tomorrow's originally scheduled birthday dinner, but me—I'm somehow expected to attend both* because you fear not getting anywhere that matters. You need to send something, though but just imagining having to type all that out revives your lower back pain. That pang, if you're honest with yourself, has always been one of those not-so-subtle reminders that you don't *lean in* to changes very well and you don't just *make it work* when you have to and that you can't even explain anymore what family looks like and what it's supposed to mean. In the end, you text *Call back soon. Will try to be there by 8. I hope.*

You start to think that you have to be a better persuader. That you have to learn how to better reason through and out of *obligation.* That word, like attraction, more a matter of perception than objective reality. More like a disagreeable tradition that determines parameters of action, reaction, and the mountains we climb to be able to escape it all. Like some enforceable habit maintained by guilt. And the energy to consider all this, you think, is the drain that leaves you empty, the tug-of-war that feels useless not only because you've fought in it for so long, but also because it all feels like warring yourself. The opposite, really, of *leaning in* and *making it work.* And then you realize that you really are quite logistician about this, it feeling like so much of a lighter burden if you can imagine it happening to someone who carries the burden with you. Someone just like you.

Any attempt to exit the family party, even if it is pre-arranged between you and your father, will almost certainly be met with *So where are you going now?* which would inevitably morph into *Wait, what for again?* which would ultimately become *But we only just ate* and then transition into *But we haven't even stopped dancing yet* and then ease almost seamlessly into *But have you even said hello to your grandmother's cousin's stepbrother across the living room, oh, wait, they're in the bathroom, you must stick around to say hello to them* which, if you hadn't become exhausted enough, would follow smoothly into *Are you sure you want to leave?* and *Are you really sure you want to leave?* and *So you really want to go, huh?* And in the heart of the battering, you know you just won't have the muscle, or even the desire, to stand your ground.

And, besides, who wants to go out after all that anyway. You'll be mentally exhausted. You won't have the energy to even hold a smile, to even seem interested in listening, flirting, bantering, and the whole lot of what it takes to hold someone's attention and be sure to let them know they hold yours.

The bus passes the gas station ten blocks away from the stop to your grandmother's apartment. The bus rocking in that familiar way that a public utility moves through the world. Grounded and sometimes grinding the curb as if jarring the world awake to make sure it still feels attached. It's always surprising how on this narrow, winding two-lane, two-way road the bus doesn't just rip off every side view mirror it passes. How the bus doesn't just *lean into* its route but also *makes* the finesse of it all *just work*.

The bus approaches every stop steadily. Every stop two blocks apart though barely marked always with someone there. Eyes like tired cold sores. Prominent and trying to avoid anyone's stares as they board. They just get on and find a seat like they know, like *you* know, that the world is a market and we're all just window shopping. Eye contact is permission, so nobody gives anyone a thing. And the cycle repeats. The grind of the bus slowing down. The crank of the brake. The swoosh of the open door. The thump of a stranger's shoes up the steps. The ratchet of the closed door. The deflation of the brakes. The moaning of the bus moving again.

Across the water, trees line the city's riverfront. Some of its buildings slant north as if pointing to a preference of class. The sides of some buildings contoured like a canyon, impenetrable and fixed. And perhaps this is why the errant, taller, straighter buildings emerge from the steel forest as if proud of the attention. Like roosters nodding at you, chins angled high, eyes cast down, understanding that you've come to accept your place in the world, well below theirs. The wind whipping against the windows of the bus, fast approaching your stop, with a certain shame or some other feeling you can't name yet, a feeling that circles the traffic and zigzags the clouds, cawing to remind you that you've given up. And how that feeling arrives and where its roots take hold seems to tailor-make the family experience, the immigrant experience, everyone avoiding the fear of feeling lonely by fabricating every possible occasion to be together, with no one having made the distinction yet, the contrast, between feeling lonely and feeling at ease feeling alone.

~~~~~

My cousin opens the door to the party and hands me his half-drunk beer, and then he scoots me inside so he can close the door, What's-her-face five doors down has been complaining about the noise, he says.

He peeks down the hallway to make sure that the old lady that always nags about our parties hasn't been standing outside her front door, arms crossed and staring, cursing under her breath and snorting like a dragon ready to pull the fire alarm to end it all. Or maybe ready with a phone in her hand to call the cops. Finding nothing, my cousin tucks back into the apartment and gestures to the windows on the other side of the living room, Let's hit up our usual spot at the margins, he says.

As I start to make my way, I catch my dad's eyes from across the apartment. Him in his usual spot by the fridge, keeping busy ready to hand out water, soda, and ice cubes to anyone with an empty cup in their hand. Keeping busy at parties seems to be his efficient way to keep time moving, how he avoids any questions directed at *him*. My mother dying last year hasn't been easy on anybody, and too many family members have, in all the months since, almost overemphasized the loss we all share, as if wanting to anticipate my dad's and my sadness by dramatizing their own, as if pain were a theater best staged perpetually, the curtains always open. Embellished mourning operates like a barometer, lament, generally speaking, unable to achieve its fullest self if it isn't also constantly being compared to somebody else's lament. Better to ham it up, I guess, even with an honest foundation, than to underachieve it.

I'm not complaining, though, not about the continuing condolences. Not the phone calls and meal trains and text messages and drop-bys. It's helped, especially those early days when I moved back in with my dad in January. But temporary has become longer, and phasing back to my place in the City has gone tepidly. At first I thought I'd be in a rush to get back to myself. But when that imposed date between he and I came, I postponed moving my toiletries and shoes back, I delayed moving my bedding and shirts back. The return to solitary life, one could say, has felt like a bus ride. Bumpy, slow, with soft regressions when I hit the brakes.

The two of us is all we've got, in the end. My mother's half-dozen miscarriages meant my parents stopped trying to offer me even an imperfect companion by high school, my father and I making do with only each other in her absence. One could say, then, that I've practiced *alone* for a while now, such that even a heavy subtraction leaves you able to *lean into* the moments, so just as long as everybody else, that is, lets you *make it work* how *you* need to make it work. I think about all this as I nod at my dad from afar, and he raises his glass, likely just tap water, though he also has a penchant for flat Sprite.

Through the living room, I follow our usual third-generation, family party entry protocol. General hellos to everybody at once, navigating the aisle between couches that face each other, broken up momentarily by the oval glass coffee table that has been owned now by four households and which gets moved on like a dog everybody thinks can fit into their family unit but which inevitably becomes something you hide in the bedroom until somebody else takes it upon themselves to try making the thing compatible to them. And then I have to circumvent the dining table blocking the hallway to the bedrooms because who needs a pass-through space when you must fit an extra, round table close enough to both the entertainment center and the hallway to the bathroom. And after the table, I have to scoot past chairs lined along the far wall where the windows don't just hang exposed by open blinds but are also raised wide open, with fans in each corner of the apartment helping to circulate air blowing into what essentially amounts to a multi-purpose room, one that functions as kitchenette, dining room, living room, and spare bedroom, all, lamentably, without air conditioning.

My cousin and I find our place at the window closest to the fire alarm, where he'd left a ready, unopened drink on the sill, It was either going to be mine or it was going to be yours, he says.

He raises the can, and we tap aluminum edges. I don't, at first, hear what he says, what we might be toasting to. Sounds at a family party come at you from an interconnected network of speakers and screens that hit you at odd angles, each set at their own volumes. My uncles usually wire everyone's place for celebration, and that means a central television mounted in a visible corner of the room, wired or WiFi-ed into at least one sound bar and at least three speakers set along the tops of walls, sometimes in series and sometimes, like scattered clouds after a rainfall, in whatever arrangement felt instinctual when the sweat of mounting the television got them completely exhausted, Did you have to cancel your plans too, my cousin says, I may or may not have someone waiting to meet me in the City later, I tell him, and eventually my hearing adjusts to the overwhelming mixture of it all, the ear like a sifter thrown into the mix and forced to settle in after ingredients have been distinguished. An engine purring after a clunky start.

Like an automated machine, too, my aunt makes her way through the crowd and hands my cousin and I our own plates of cake, the celebration moving through its pleasantries fast, or skipping some altogether, We didn't even sing happy birthday to her yet, my cousin says, and his mother, as familiar as anyone with the rifling through of duty and autonomy, shrugs and then smiles and then kisses me on the cheek and tells me I'm too thin.

I can see my uncle with the pack of cigarettes in his hand itching to raise the volume on the YouTube channel streaming some kind of song whose title I won't recall until he shoots up the volume so that even families four blocks away can hear it and sing along, I'll tell you right now, I say to my cousin, I'm not staying long enough to hear it.

He raises his eyebrows at me, like I've said that line. before, like we've both said it—like we've all said it before. How we all feel about each other feeling like something of an inheritance that blends into this imperfect bind we all want to call love.

My grandmother, whose smile widens almost facetiously with every other word from her sister, offers me a side glance, a nod. She bites her bottom lip to emphasize the attention she gives to every other word from her niece and from her sister's husband, who has, until now, maintained that nobody ever listens to him, that nobody in this family cares about people who come into this family.

My cousin and I admit as much to each other every now again, but also the chatter everywhere, at once repelling and warm, can't help but entrench us all, no matter how much we fight it, into some covering that holds your hands. It makes a certain kind of easy, though not completely easy, and then my cousin starts to rail on about his job, about what it should feel like to command a fifth-grade classroom versus how it actually feels like, about his girlfriend already talking about what next year will look like for them even as this year hasn't yet hit its summer stride, And that's a lot of pressure, he says.

Like yeah let's get married but also let me get through a second year of teaching before I know for sure this is how I want to earn my health insurance, he says.

They had to push back their last dinner date, he says, But she's used to it and she does the same shit to me too, he says.

She got a big family too, he says, An impossible family and I'm not even sure they like me.

It's been five months between them, and I don't know how to imagine right now being there, in that same emotional space, where tomorrow doesn't feel like a strip of paper that can't just be torn off by a storm.

And what about you, he says, suggesting I have a dating life worth talking about. Nothing, I tell him.

I've had nights out and mornings I haven't regretted, I tell him.

There's really not a lot to say about it, I tell him, Who are you meeting later, he says, Someone new, I tell him, Does she get it, he says, I don't know, I tell him.

I don't imagine she will, I tell him.

He shrugs, taps his beer can to mine again, and a breeze seems to thread the room tight, spinning into the apartment with an oily pavement smell, an overfull curbside trash bin smell, a sweat-off-a-kid's-back-riding-a-skate-board smell, a-live-wire-somewhere-down-the-street-giving-off-sparks kind of smell. The perfumes of a neighborhood don't tickle anymore after they become so familiar, but one carries the scent everywhere. At least it feels that way. Like the look when you arrive anywhere that isn't home is knowing, pitying look.

My dad joins us, chewing on his own bite of cake. You two always together, he says. You two keep helping each other pull through all this, he says.

My cousin pulls out a couple cigars from his shirt's breast pocket, lumps in the cloth I hadn't paid attention to until they disappear, I've been meaning to give these to you both, he says.

My dad nods, and I know what the glimmer in his eyes means, so I take my cousin's gift and slip them into my dad's shirt pocket to hold for later. And you two, my cousin says, Making your way through it all with only the slightest almost unnoticeable indication that you don't know what the fuck you're doing.

My dad's grin almost keeps him from chewing, but then he swallows with the help of the drink in his hand, and then he tells us that the garbage bag needs taking out. A knowing look as gestures to the bin by the fridge.

Make sure to grab it on your way out, he says.

I must watch him confused because he sets his plate on the sill and grabs my shoulder, Please take out the trash as you leave to get back into the City, and he hands me a MetroCard from his pocket. He asks me to refill it for him on my way back home.

~~~~~

The Son reaches for a napkin at the edge of the bar, and he wipes the young woman's bottom lip with it. Careful not to press. Careful only to graze and then put the napkin back on the counter by her drink. She laughs, saying he missed, and she points to the spot on her chin again as if offering permission to run his eyes across the contours there, unexpectedly, unexpectedly playful. They seem to watch each other for the next move or word. He arrived an hour later than originally planned, so this moment, as long as it went on, felt like a redemptive lateness.

Here, she says, smiling, and so he dabs the ends of her lips again, smiling, too, but not the kind of smile obvious about what it wants or about what it was eager to know more about. Just the kind of smile that helps him focus. On her cheekbones with its lines and soft almost unnoticeable hairs, all coalescing into a curve like the nose of a plane.

The Son enjoys this part. The reading part. The language in the pauses and general demeanor of a woman part. The pages of her whole self that sometimes open and turn from one to the next, sometimes quickly, sometimes gently, but always revealing a plot turn, a new idea about the world, an interpretation about the world in a smile or twitch. Everything like it can inform him about how and why she eyes a room the way she does or pronounces words the way she does or paces her thoughts the way she does. We are all, thinks The Son, a complicated root system. Foundations that branch out in every direction and connect us to each other and keep the world moving.

He thinks to himself, too, to correct his posture. To remember to sit upright. To try to forget that he isn't entirely exhausted and that he doesn't have to hunch on the stool, and so he tries his best to straighten his back, subtly, no sudden jerks, to remember, in other words, that he can be present to both his needs and the needs of perception. That he can also remember to appear how he is, fully present at the bar counter of a lounge on 6th Street and Avenue A with a woman he only met a week ago over drinks with friends, or, as he wouldn't tell The Father, at a magazine party that his friend had invited him to where he'd also had a few cigarettes and drags of better things—a woman who'd initially introduced herself as, My friends call me the hardest working legal aide in Brooklyn which might or might not mean I don't go out much, and then immediately rolled her eyes at the compliment. As if she was both feigning modesty and feigning that she could appreciate a compliment and simultaneously accept its limitations. At that first encounter between them, especially after her wit, he wanted to introduce himself as the hardest working schematics drafter at the most mid-level of engineering companies, but he wanted to give the impression that he might be competitive, which he wasn't really. And he hadn't wanted to lead on that he couldn't formulate his own jokes, which he really wasn't known for anyway. So he just said in that moment, I know a thing or two about working hard. He wanted to add that he might or might not always be pulled in so many different directions that he might or might not go out much himself. That he spent too much time at work or caught in a whirlwind of family and obligations and perceptions. But he definitely didn't follow through on that. Instead, he asked her what had brought her to the party, and the conversation went on from there.

At the lounge on 6th Street and Avenue A, with its warehouse interior design, the exposed plumbing, vents, and gas pipes, the grated ceiling, the maroon curtains that hang like banners in regular intervals from light fixtures, the world is a far cry from the busy, almost long-ago chatter of a family apartment congested in a family's stories.

Behind the bar, the basketball game airs on the wall-mounted television. The volume just high enough to catch sneakers squealing and the commentators almost dully going on about plays and stats. Occasionally, The Son and the woman take turns glancing at the game. Though, it seems to The Son, just to enjoy the idea of a distraction, not to be consumed by it. As if latching their attention onto something else for a spurt can relieve someone of having to carry someone else's attention so consistently. As if to remind oneself that reprieves in moments like these, moments of good tension waiting for, waiting through, someone else's gestures and words, don't just feel good, they feel essential. Like pausing to walk every so often during a long run. Like taking a moment to look at your phone waiting for the line at Starbucks to get moving again.

And so they bake in each other's company. Their feet almost touching. Their hands resting on the counter inches from the other's. Their knees almost pressing into the counter wall. And each of these descriptions coming with its own suggestions. Like humidity before a rainfall. Breeze through an open doorway after you've walked somebody home.

When the silence breaks, the young woman turns her stool completely to The Son. With a smile that hints at nothing more than attention but which seems to warm the air between them. The woman asks about who had texted

The Son, shortly after he arrived, and The Son said that the text message had come from his dad, that the Father had wanted to know how The Son had made it to the bar, And how *did* you make it, the young woman says, her eyes facing him more squarely. He smiles, reading, hoping to read, *wanting* to read, in that question, in *everything* she says, a clue that she wanted to invite him to say more, ask more, see more. The Son says, I arrived just fine, and then he adds, I was looking forward to getting here I guess you could say, to which he adds, And excited to end the night *and* start the night on a chair right next to you is something else you could say.

A whole room can float sometimes when answers become invitations and those invitations open a whole new set of questions that want to be answered.

The woman asks, too, if The Son and The Father are close, Because you seem to be close, she says, knowing nothing more, The Son thinks, beyond the impression of a single text message on an August night. The Son says, It's just me and him now so yeah we check up on each other, and then he adds, More than most fathers and sons I guess, to which he adds, A lot I guess, and he has to stop himself from saying more. As if by adding another caveat or any number of them, he's apologizing for the circumstances that not long ago prompted the communication and the closeness and the steadiness of it all. This word, closeness, in the echo off the young woman's lips, taking on, in The Son's mind, something resembling a condition. Like something that needed scans and an explanation. Like solitude and loss mixed with need that, once blended, can't be extricated from each other.

When the woman asks about The Son's mother, softly, almost *too* softly, as if caught between wanting to know and hesitating to want to know, she takes another sip of her drink. She starts sipping, in fact, before completing the question. Something in the move, The Son thinks, that changes the air between them, that seems to understand the context evident in the *just* part of the *me and him* part of what he'd already said, which is probably why she says, I'm sorry, and The Son just nods, leaving that pertinent elaboration unspoken. I shouldn't have asked, she adds. I'm sorry, she says again, and The Son says, That's fine You're all right It's okay, as if they both need the relief of releasing the apology into the never-world of a good *nevermind*.

And, yet, The Son does end up saying more. Obligation can feel like that sometimes. Like an interjection that disrupts the peace. Like a silence that needs filling even when only one person reads its emptiness. Obligation, when habitualized to the extent The Son has, encroaches into every conversation, and so he says something like, She passed away last year, and he continues, as if hoping to prevent another apology, Around Christmas she had an accident and it was all unexpected, but he makes it more explicit to avoid in the thought of another apology, But we're good now, he says.

We're all good now, he says again.

The woman nods, smiles, no differently than before but also, yes, a little differently than before, and when she turns back to the television, she also shifts in her body a little differently than before, using the basketball game like it's meant to be used. A ready-made diversion amidst the volume and chatter and shuffling of feet at a bar with a single aisle between the front door and the back lounge area full of tables and couches.

And then the next thing that happens, who knows *how* it happens. It just does, and strangely, at that, because it feels a bit familiar. First punches like first dates. You're in a comfortable daze until you're not. Time passing like a false comfort.

You started to believe you were pulling it off, you think to yourself. This delicate dance of being there for everyone else *and* for yourself. You communicated clearly. Picked up every phone call and answered every text message. You met everything asked of you and—*and*—went out for a chance to enjoy a night out with someone else. You *leaned into* everything, you think to yourself, even if initially reluctantly, and you *made it all work.*

But then that fucking punch. Out of nowhere. And it happens fast, and you start to consider, in that strange moment falling, that speed has no direction and, therefore, no acceleration, and that perhaps these small wisdoms have always been right. That you can't really be there for everyone else *and* yourself and that obligation and self-preservation are incompatible intentions. Like the spokes that eventually pop off the wheel of a bike you want to ride steadily into a fruitful life are your self-awareness, your situational awareness, your center of gravity, your ability to read others and the moment you're in, and you miss something. Like someone gunning for you on the periphery and punching you off the stool at a bar.

As you're about to hit the floor, you get the flashing thought that whatever the hell has just happened, or has just started happening, has happened in spite of you *and* because of you. Like everything you have control over and nothing you have control of have been stirring together all day like opposing ions of unequal power until untended friction meets a spark and something breaks open the fabric of time, the chemical reaction in your skull something more than just the back of your head hitting a stool leg, your shoulder hitting the floor, your nose hitting the counter wall.

And a faster replay of the moment goes like this. A jab like a bullet to the back of your neck, which if it had landed two inches higher would have knocked you out cold, pops you off the stool. Your arms stop your mouth from slamming the bar top, and then you tumble into other people's legs and stir up a commotion that becomes a watchful silence after you roll for a bit and jump back onto your feet.

You react the way you do because you always do. Quick. With a readiness that almost anticipates something worse. Like that time when your father called you at work and told you how your mother had avoided getting hit by a speeding driver when she opened her car door only to trip and hit her face on the curb, and not another breath passes before you shut your computer down and got your coat on and started running down the aisle between cubicles to the elevators. Like when you got to the hospital and you met your father in the lobby after having stopped at home first, showing up with two overnight bags and takeout dinner. Like when, that very next moment, his eyes narrated a whole story as he choked back his heavy breathing to tell you that the prognosis didn't look good and that the family needs to be there, like right away, and your hands seemed to register almost immediately that you had to pick up your phone and make some phone calls. To your grandmothers and aunts. To your cousins. To the family that could frustrate you every moment together precisely because their demands for together can feel so intense. But it was them, *all* of them, that received those phone calls and knew what to do, who always know what to do, when tension comes down the line and something has to happen before you have the time to think about what has to happen next.

You have that in you. The impulse so deeply embedded that you don't even register scrambling to your feet. A straight push-up off the floor, and then you pivot to meet whatever kind of accuser this is. A mid-size dude with a lump in his throat. You brace for another impact and an armful of him when he gives you exactly the cliché you'd imagined. A white dude, nervous and red in the eyes, who rushes you. His shoulder into your stomach, and you wrap him up. Turn and twist him. Pull him down and work him into a hold you don't need to reason through because you've already done everything you need to that day. You lean into what you have to. You make it work. You wrestle each other across the floor like you're maneuvering a current, the waves and ripples bruising your ribs and jaw, until you get a lock on his shoulder to try shoving it from its socket, but his instincts seem to kick in and he kicks you in the chest, and so you hurl punches and land them where you can. Scrambles are breathless.

When heavy arms grip you whole and pull you, you don't know where you are until you see the clarity of the parting sea. Bar-goers up the aisle to the front door clearing a path for you like a man getting dragged swiftly through booking at a police station. Soon enough, the bouncer tosses you onto the crowded sidewalk and, after you, the guy who punched you and, after him, the young woman you met up with that night. Two bouncers hold position between you and the dude, and a third bouncer keeps watch at the front door.

You steady yourself at a *No Parking* sign, the other dude at a streetlight. You recognize the bus stop where you hopped off, having transferred to above-ground transportation when you got off at the 1st Avenue subway stop, and all for this. You wipe your chin dry and the sweat off your brow, and you rub the back of your head like you're trying to find blood that never materializes.

The woman seems to want to cry, but she holds steady between fumes and an outright scream, looking at the guy and then looking away, and then glancing at you but with something like an apology hanging in the stare she doesn't hold long.

She doesn't scream when she tells the guy, What do you think you're doing here, and the guy seems to restrain a growl when he says, So who is this guy, to which she says, That's none of your business anymore, to which he says, Like hell it isn't.

And they linger there, in some silence of past lovers. In some silence, it seems, of lopsided endings, Your friends are never very far away are they, she says, What do you care, he says, Because somebody needs to take you home, she says, I'm going to stay here as long as I want to, he says, As long as I need to, he says, No you're not, she says.

How she holds her sneer, how she keeps her hands clasped and her feet shoulder-width apart, you think, makes her look like an out-and-out statue holding pity for congregants at a church. Though maybe that's no analogy at all, you think, because saints hold stories that sometimes impose, sometimes get in the way, of any real kind of experience, certainly any human one, So this is the guy who takes my place, he says, You have no fucking right, she says, I have *all* the fucking right, he says, Go home, she says, You're always going to choose dirty is what he is, he says, Fuck you, she says, Fucking Spanish guys is gonna be just a phase you fuck yourself out of and come crying back to me, he says, He probably doesn't have a fucking green card, he says, He probably just picked any old white chick out of a hat, he says.

The fight is yours and it isn't at all, and this is where you walk away. Not convincingly, though, only just like an amble around the corner, a scoot even, a drag into the shadow of a one-way street and off the well-lit avenue. And right before turning the corner, you hear something about papers, about language and countries and continents, and about going back wherever it is clichés go back to. And you don't stick around to extend the fight. You don't stick around because it all feels so old. So fucking old. Talking points about the countries you all have to go back to polluting the street like atomic waste. Long half-lives and even longer wakes, ripples that stretch everything until not even the echoes dim to silence.

I barely get to sit on the bottom step of a squat apartment building stoop when she catches up to me, and I don't think she even had to run. I didn't hear any steps behind me, just the usual traffic that comes with a Friday night. Group talk about where to go next. Honking at a red light, even after it only just turned green, everyone everywhere barely mustering the trust in anyone else to move at their own pace.

I barely get to touch the concrete when she starts with her *I'm sorry*, an apology like she has any more control of the world than I do, like she could even pretend to have any power to stem its impulses and cut off its tides. It was no confident *sorry*, though, so not like she actually believes she deserves to carry even a fraction of a fraction of the blame. And she does it again, I'm sorry, confusing maybe my silence for an anger that did actually blame her, a silence that had actually registered her first *sorry* and dared to expect more from it. Like some reimbursement or reparation.

But I tell her it's fine, I tell her it's all right, but I don't know what I want from even the railing my hand clings to, from even the separation I thought I wanted when I started the long walk here. Less than half a block from 1st Avenue feels like solitude just hangs there laughing. Like the thought of being alone just waves at you, taunting you like a red cape, and rushing to it bears only the ghost of a comfort I can't rest my head on.

She sits next to me and clasps her hands and doesn't turn her eyes my way. We just sit there overlooking the landscape of an ocean of cars, poorly parked or double-parked and just waiting for someone to come swipe off a sideview mirror or two. She pulls out her phone like she's checking the time or checking for messages, though I suspect the gesture was more to fill the air with movement, with shuffling and the shadow of a sound, than with purpose.

I don't know that my voice carries even the semblance of believability when I tell her she doesn't have to stick around. That she can just head home if she wants to. Especially when all she does is nod, when she follows up my suggestions by clearing her throat and then saying, I understand. But she doesn't move, and I don't move, and then she says, Or maybe I don't get it so I don't know, and we linger like that for a bit. Like who can expect more of an answer than that, in a moment like that, when neither of us knows what kind of answer can get us to end the night right there. I take a deep breath even as her breathing goes on unadorned, and the pause feels like a good, jumbled *whatthefuckism*, a kind of hesitation that feels like a shrug that feels like it can't spell what to do next or even point to possibilities that would even make sense.

And then my phone rings. Caught in the spell of things, I barely react. Caught between massaging my ribs and tending to my shoulder, I don't know that I want to reach into my side pocket, having already felt a jolt when I swung my arms walking. When it stops ringing, she offers to grab the phone for me the next time it rings, I'm sure it will again, she says, I don't even know how to respond to that, I say, I'm sure it's your dad, she says, I'm sure it was, I say.

My neck still stings hot and my chest bubbles when I inhale. My eyes seem to buzz, and the breaths that leave me scrape my throat on the way out. It's embarrassing, maybe, all that heat just funneled into and through me, and all I did was throw myself like blinding white into a fight. Can I give you a hug, she says, Please don't, I say, and she continues to sit there with me, cupping her phone and tapping it, passing it between hands.

I don't know why, in this moment, I replay the moments after my mother's accident. What I did when my father called, when I arrived to the hospital, when I called everyone who needed calling. Information mattered then. Knowing everything matters to me always, and it matters now, but I don't know that I'll be satisfied with anything she says, and I don't know she'll know that I want to be satisfied with everything she can possibly say. When my mother died, I became the relay point for every bit of news that needed bouncing from one person to the next. But on this stoop, what's even the diagnosis. What's even the accident I can point to and say *This is why the back of my neck tripped into that dude's fist.*

I don't even check the number when the phone rings again. I just ask her to reach into my pocket, tap the call on, and hold the phone to my ear. And she does, and gently, too, like someone still trying to apologize.

I muster a good, Hey, when the call starts, and I can hear my dad breathing, likely measuring his own hello, Are you all right, he says, suspecting, maybe, that the crack in my voice means that the mood has changed, I'm home, he says, And you don't have to join me at home tonight if you don't want to, he adds.

Checking in with each other this past almost-year has felt like permission. Like I can be okay being okay with the next thing I want to do, even if it is apart from him, You alright, he says, I'm fine, I say, I just want to call to apologize, he says, What for, I say, For dragging you anywhere today, It's okay, It's not, I want to make sure you're doing okay too, Your mother would have wanted something better for us, We're leaning into it right, I guess we are, he says, We're making our way through, I say, We can always get better at it, he says.

I hang up, and then she slides her hand off the phone as I slide my hands to pick up the slack. When she stands up, she says, I'll take a cab home, and she adds, I'm sorry about everything, and I tell her, No, I say, *I'm* sorry about everything. She does me the favor of letting the numbness sit there before almost retaliating for the sympathy I want to feel publicly for everything that just went down, Why are *you* apologizing, she says, I don't know, I say, I'd prefer if we just didn't say anything else, she says, Excuse me, I say, I'm sorry I just don't know how to go home right now which is what I think you need, You don't have to tell me what I need right now, I'm sorry, And please stop apologizing, I'm sorry, Please.

The recurring soundtrack of the city fills the next bit. Cars rolling over loose manholes. Window air conditioning units turning on and clanking off. Footsteps jumping off curbs and skipping down steps, You'll be okay, she says, I don't need any comforting either, I say, and I don't want to cut her off, I don't *mean* to cut her off, but I don't know how else to catch my tone before it gets ahead of me, so I apologize, again, for the last time, as if to bring a final measure to the penitence part, to a night of absolutions gone wrong, Tonight's all been one bad foot hasn't it, she says, It has, I say, and she nods. And then she looks down the street. I follow her eyes to where no cab appears, but she doesn't start walking up to 1st Avenue like I know she'll need to do in order to catch a ride home. Instead, she keeps her footing by the rail, and I keep my place on the bottom step, and we hang there, our spots there like craters. Once formed, the trenches might take millennia to blend back into the landscape from which they emerged.

DROWN

My first mistake that night was to drive into the Holland Tunnel the wrong way.

10:34pm should have made me think twice about that right turn. Not the time, per se, just the general lateness, how over-eager I was, how the steady traffic of trucks along the waterfront crossing the river to hit the interstate for a day's drive before sunrise made for the kind of barrier even a planet couldn't flip off.

Not a hundred feet from us, maybe not even fifty, an oncoming truck blared its horn when it saw me. Its headlights gawking at us, its cab might as well have been a sun aiming right for us, and I hit the brakes. Hard. Full stop. And then I shifted into reverse faster than someone's guts after a shot too much of whiskey.

It's true what they say. You notice *everything* the moment you near dying. We'd just crossed the threshold into the tunnel. The tone after the first few wall lights went from warm to cold. The double white lines looked like a fresh coat of paint. And the plumbing pipes running along opposing corners the length of the tunnel into Tribeca just seemed off. Not just that the copper pipes weren't even straight anymore or the U-bolts that pinned them to the ceiling seemed like they'd started to sag, but also like someone had pinned them differently to their situations. One interconnected series of pipes looked like it hung inches further from its wall than the interconnected series of pipes along the opposite wall. I know it might be stupid to think about all that, to think you remember all that, to think it matters to consider it now, but attention to that much detail makes you pause. Detail overdrive in one place, and like, you run out of headspace to consider the details in some other place.

Reversing, I pulled the steering wheel hard right, so much so that my left hand slipped, so much so that I had to swing hard back left to keep from crashing into or grazing the stone wall. I was lucky, *we* were lucky, there was a shoulder outside the mouth of the tunnel to just sit on and keep my foot off the pedal.

That truck, though. It's honking like a bomb. The blast almost stopped my heart. Weird, though, too, that I felt like a hero right after feeling like a fool, saving us after almost killing us. Both feelings, I'd say, are as lies as lies get.

But let's rewind a minute. Because it's not like I wasn't paying *any* attention.

Selena and I had been on a date. Her skin and collarbone and hips and chest, you notice all these things at seventeen. We'd touched each other all over our bodies in the movie theatre. We'd held hands walking out. We'd kissed, too, after dinner at the cheap Mediterranean place in the mall, and she'd taken her shoes off to touch toes under the table. I wore sandals because it was almost summer and my feet get so sweaty in shoes starting in, like, May, and I didn't want to go sloshing around everywhere while she looked good looking that good.

And what else are we going do after all that but drive, and maybe too long, too, cruising past red lights and stop signs, under streetlamps so bright that we might as well have been interrogated by police with the wheels rolling. We even coasted along downtown's emptied buildings, through the strip of upscale hotels between downtown and the interstate, and I know what you're thinking, but we were kids. She was smart and horny, and I was smart and horny, and seventeen is, in the end, just seventeen, and so we started playing with each other just driving around. My free hand where she let it go, her busy hand where I needed it to go, and that's all we were doing, pieces of us heating up and flaring big and just plain old wet in the most beautiful of ways.

And, sure, I was distracted, and maybe I wasn't paying any *real* attention, but, yeah, I wasn't giving the road *all* my attention, and at that right turn, I didn't notice the *No Right Turn* sign, and right then, she pulled my hand somehow further into her and then squeezed my thigh, and she even rotated my fingertips in the thick of it, and I pressed in and up and high, and, yes, I turned to read the expression on her face. In her eyes. To see what we'd managed to do together in the dark.

And then just as soon as all that, nothing in front of us but bright and brightening lights shook me all kinds of loose. Something like an eternal horn blast. The oncoming truck and its churning engine wailing to keep from derailing everything. Us. It. The tunnel's exit mouth.

But let's rewind a minute, because it's not like that night hadn't been building up in my head for a while.

Selena and I had known each other a long time, since first day first year of high school, the teacher taking attendance and us two one after the other on the roll, and when I didn't initially answer to my name—I hadn't even heard it—she intuitively elbowed me from her desk across the aisle to ask if it'd been me, and I answered in a daze, What, and then she said, I said is the teacher calling your *name*, What do you mean, Is your name stupid or is your name Hector, It's Hector, Then stop being stupid and raise your hand Hector. She straight up air-quoted "stupid" like she'd intended a capital *S*, some actual name against all will and reason.

As far as I could tell, we'd hooked up with enough people over the four years that followed, and she had one serious relationship in that time, which I was never been able to tell when it started, and I had one serious relationship in that time, too, a relationship that ended in ways I can't even pinpoint. It just happened. I started calling that old girlfriend less, she started calling me less, and then I saw her kiss somebody else on the lips in the cafeteria as we all left lunch, and later on that same day, some senior pulled me into the girls' locker room to tell me that she'd heard all about our breakup, something even *I* hadn't heard about yet, and then she told me that our bodies could do the rest of the talking on a bench there.

So, yeah, I finally asked Selena out our last year in school. Last month of the last semester. June can be a great time to ask somebody out. If it doesn't work out, hey, no worries, I've got college or work and they've got college or work, and everybody's busy. If it doesn't not work out, then you spend the days counting the minutes in which you fear the other person might let you down or you might let the other person down, and every day it gets warmer. Every day the temperature messes with your head. Not to mention, I was the oldest child in a family living in an apartment where somehow everybody was always so busy. Mom with work. Dad with work. Younger sister working to save money for her camping trip. Little brother working to save money to travel with his soccer club. If there's one thing immigrants don't mind, it's putting their noses down and fearlessly driving into too much work, and, eventually, you realize you've been no role model at all—like at *all*, or at least not like them. Nobody ever looked to *me* for advice, and nobody ever looked to *me* for help, and I might as well have accidentally made a wrong turn the wrong way into the Holland Tunnel because surviving meant, at least, I'd have a story to tell, something like, If I have any advice for you it's that you shouldn't be getting hot heavy with a date in the car while you're driving around town, or something like, At least wait until you're parked somewhere.

When I asked Selena out, at first she hesitated. I didn't take it personally because it made sense. Because why would anyone say *Yes* right away when your on-and-off lab partner of a few years in high school asks you out. Really, all we'd done together is dissected a frog, observed amoeba under a microscope, made printing errors with our analysis reports, paid too much money for a tri-fold cardboard, and repeat the cycle, and we weren't even in the same room writing the reports we submitted. Digital life. It's valuable for precisely what it should be valued for. Attraction at a distance.

Anyway, hesitating was likely the only thing she could have done. Eventually, though, right there after a moment of silence, she said some kind of *yes*. She said, Let me think about it, and after school, in the parking lot, we passed each other outside on the sidewalk, and she said some other version of *yes*. She said, Sure, and then she said, I trust you as far as I could shove you, but okay.

I nodded. I said, Okay, like I wasn't sure if the sun had risen on something or if the day had just set on something worse.

Just don't make it boring, she said.

Outside the Holland Tunnel, I tore my hands off the steering wheel where I'd put them. I don't know that I could have told anyone then what happens to your brain when it's toggling between fainting and screaming and can't decide on either, but I can point, now, to the kind of situation where it's likely to happen.

I pressed my hands into my chest and brought them to my neck. My fingertips like they wanted a pulse. Like they wanted to scrape bone or just hold blood. When Selena grabbed my right hand, she almost crushed it. She probably just wanted to measure her racing heart against mine to test whether the adage had always been true. That people sharing a near-death experience share more than just the memory of it. Their bodies, too, overlap in this symbolic space between panic and desire.

She grazed the stubble under my chin. Her touch loosening something inside me. I wanted to say something like *Sorry*, but I shut my mouth because I found myself inching closer to a space between *I can explain this* and *It wasn't my fault*. Even in that moment, I couldn't stand myself for the impulse to *not* just apologize, so I just nodded like I wasn't absolutely clueless about what came next. Moving meant certainty and starting the engine again could skip over the beats I didn't know how to keep, so I turned the key in the ignition.

Selena asked me what I thought I was doing when I grabbed the back of her headrest, and I said, Getting into a k-turn and getting the hell out of here, and she said, Wait, and I said, For what, and she said, Just take a breath, and I said, I'm good I just want to go, and just then a police officer flashed his lights as he pulled up behind us.

I caught her eyes turning from the rear window back to me.

I wanted to argue in that moment. I wanted to slap the steering wheel. I wanted to lean my face into the dashboard lights to make sure nothing was wrong with the car, but all I said was, Dude sure likes riding another car's ass, which did nothing to help me calm down.

The cop had stopped ten feet closer than I wished he would have. The cop got out of the car a lot faster and smoother than I wished he would have.

I reached for Selena's hand, but instead of clasping my hand back, she just patted it. This, like, polite tap-tap I didn't know what to make of. It was the kind of tap-tap my mother gives my father when he does something capital-S stupid, so I pretended like Selena had done anything *but* that. I pretended in my head that she'd instead hooked her arm into mine and then that she'd started massaging my shoulder and then that she'd accepted to mutually curl her fingers into mine, and all this to pretend to drown, even if for only a second, in the comfort of a touch that could help me forget about the possibility of a ticket, of a DUI, of an arrest, of a beating.

The tunnel regurgitated one car at a time at such a clip it was anybody's guess if the world ever slept. As the officer approached my window, I switched from high beams to low, without a clue as to how they got from low to high in the first place and without a clue as to why I didn't just shut the lights off entirely. It was like my wrists were too fragile to make that last turn on the tab even happen. Like my hands went stuck in this impossibly catastrophic freeze.

Selena lowered her window and then reached over to lower mine, this freeze in the absence of knowing how to center myself in the right now. She even reached for my wallet in my pocket and for the insurance card in the glove compartment, and I said, Okay, like I'd given her permission to dress my body before it went in a coffin.

In the end, too, who else would I have given that permission to. This girl who enjoyed 12th grade pre-calc enough to tutor me and eventually let me copy the homework. This girl who could synthesize stuff from AP History and AP Bio and contemplate thoughts about trouble, about the world, about the trouble the world was in, not to mention intersectional things that make for less trouble and even better solutions. And then there was me—too hung up sometimes on the difference between "solve for x" and "explain your answer," between the state of the world and the state of a world's lies, and I was still too afraid to make anything personal and, worse, to steady my field of vision long enough to understand some of the things right in front of me.

In any case, I took a deep breath. Before the officer arrived to my window, I said, I drove the wrong way into interstate traffic and almost killed us and it was almost an accident and I just wasn't paying attention *God* I wasn't any paying attention, and saying it felt like I'd wanted somebody else to say it all for me when the time came. I said it all like I didn't know if I'd meant it as a question or an affirmation. Like I didn't know how to trust what I knew and didn't.

Yes, she said, Say all of that.

Except the part about you not paying any attention, she added, Omit that part.

The police officer tapped his flashlight on the side view mirror. He shone his flashlight on my lap. He leaned down and asked for my documentation, and at first I froze because who the hell carries a passport when they aren't flying, and then he poked the light beam onto Selena's lap and then he smirked as he told us to wait while he checked our details back in his car.

Goddamn fields of vision. I hadn't even noticed Selena give him all the papers. All I could notice was how he eyed her like a bear spotting an RV full of food.

I looked at Selena and she pursed her lips so tight that her nostrils almost flared into balloons. She didn't take any breaths that weren't worth wasting, and she seemed to be inhaling at such a steady clip, she sat there defining *necessary cool* in ways most of us couldn't have even imitated. I reached for and pulled the hem of her skirt back to her knees, but she immediately slapped my hand away, and then she told me to glue my fingers to the steering wheel before Mr. Peeping Tom came back, And certainly before I lose my taste for anything but the sight of my own house tonight.

When he returned, the officer asked us where we thought we were going with such shit-poor directions. His pregnant pause after the question like a dare. Like even if I'd tried answering, not a word could have satisfied him. He asked us why nobody likes to face the right way anymore. You people, he said, like he'd had too much practice generalizing the idea of youth and the idea of strangers. He even went on to ask why people were always looking to go places they didn't understand, and he kept on like that, waxing some kind of pigsty poetics that, whether it made sense to anyone or not, certainly re-molded that moment to suit his own image. And then he stood tall again, peered both ways down the road like he didn't care for an answer or even if I'd given one at all, like even if I'd tried, it would have been an extended wasted time in more ways than one. And then he smacked his lips and leaned back into the open window, I'm letting you off with a warning, he said. So park somewhere else off the road to do whatever it is you people do, he added, cocking a nod at Selena again, where he let his eyes linger for longer than I thought men were supposed to let that happen.

What a feeling that was. The anxiety that you couldn't do shit in the breath of a bigger man with a gun and disenchanted cologne. The kind of feeling that made you feel horrible for being someone who wanted something, who wanted the same thing as that other kind of man who could turn wanting into an active crime scene—and even worse for being someone who somebody else wanted badly enough to risk putting the whole world on notice for it, wanted something with a bad kind of wanting that cut their heart open ready to tear something out of you just to get it. Even after the officer walked away, I couldn't shake my hands loose of the feeling enough to move the car. The man's utility belt with all its angles and jutting handles swaying. The leather and the clips. The holster and his handcuffs. All of it shaking like he wanted to be seen.

The tunnel regurgitated one car at a time at such a clip it was anybody's guess if the world ever hesitated long enough to catch its breath. Tires rolling. Cars whirring. The officer deciding to shout into all of that to tell us to follow him out. I barely heard him, and then his roof lights went on. The red and blue spun. His siren wailed twice. It halted the next car out of the tunnel, and my shoulders tightened like an insecure machine. Selena, again, took her wherewithal to grab the stick and shift us into movement. Are we okay, she said, Are *you*, I said, Stop pretending like we're going to be in this long enough for you to know the half of it, she said, firmly, without hesitation, into that threshold between disaster and tomorrow. She went on, too, after I'd started driving, talking low but clearly, securely, about aggression, about manners, about the things in people's eyes that people, And by people I mean men, she said, think that they're always so good at but are always so terrible at hiding.

We drove around a lot after that. Through the edge of Jersey City. The awkward traffic triangles and the acute turns. Through Hoboken. The abrupt pavement changes and the acute turns. Sticking to speed limits. Slow around double-parked cars. Coming up to road signs and lights at an easy pace to keep from making the tires squeal, and maybe I thought we both wanted to be alone, together-alone, in that part of the night where things feel still but aren't, well after 11pm, where staying alert means thinking to yourself to keep your eyes open.

We eventually found a spot by a shuttered seafood restaurant and a burnt-down bank, both on a gravel jetty along the Hudson overlooking the city and with a lot between the buildings that was just dirt and grass.

I thought for a minute that maybe Selena stayed quiet because she wanted to ask me to take her home, to just drop her off somewhere. Instead, she lowered her window all the way, and I lowered mine all the way, and along the river, water splashed against the rocks and the moss. Even in supposed silence, there was a comforting lack of it, and maybe it was *me* who'd wanted to take us home. Her back to her parents and me back to mine. She asked me if I was feeling okay. I said I was. I asked her the same question. She fired back the same answer.

I remembered the time when we were in lab alone once, and she'd wanted me to teach her how to dance. She didn't like to, but did it when she had to, and it was going to be her cousin's birthday that weekend, and she hated to move in those kinds of ways, as much as she hated to not *know* how to do it, so every family party seemed like a compromise between smiling through condescension and faking it to avoid being patronized, and so she'd said to me, Just brush me up on the stuff because I'm not here to pretend I enjoy the intimacy of the stuff.

So I tried, more than happy to do it, really. We pushed our stools aside in the empty classroom. I held my hand out and she grabbed it, and when we started moving together, she imitated my basic steps. That's all we ever got to that day. The easy stuff. I warned her about the steps I didn't know. I held her waist and elevated her arm. I told her I could teach her about different positions. I could teach her strength. I told her that learning didn't so much mean attention as it meant pattern. But I was nobody to be teaching either, really, least of all teaching somebody who could have taught me everything I needed to know about patience and tension, lies and the questions that didn't need asking.

Her body moved that day with a certain toughness, a sturdiness, that radiated from her rib cage like an electrical pulse. A centeredness that always seemed to lead even when she didn't mean to. Her knees, too, bent with a strictness that gave her ankles and calves definition. She moved, essentially, like she did at every track and field warmup. As if every stretch mattered, every stride an actual attempt to win, every flex meaningless if not for winning. She carried discipline at seventeen like a soldier, and when I nudged her close, she held firm to a form that kept her distance, her elbows steady, bending only so much.

In the gravel lot, too, she kept her hands clasped on her lap, her head leaning on the doorframe and her ankles crossed. I kept the battery running and turned the radio on low. I didn't lean my chair back, so I simply hugged myself, the soft breeze not cool enough to make me uncomfortable, just cool enough to remind me, especially vital in the context of the night, that I'd had a body that shook in the face of anxiety and attraction, conversation and silence, I want to go home but not yet, she said, Absolutely, I said, That shit wasn't anybody's fault, It was *my* fault, Don't do that, What am I doing, Pretending like I need you to be some kind of hero.

Commercials on a radio station compel the worst kinds of silences, too, amping you into a kind of energy that expects something, that expects to build into something, even if that something is the kind of feeling that refuses something outright with a kind of aggressive *no*, Just don't apologize please, Yeah, Let's just sit here and with some better music please.

She reached over and changed the station, putting us through a stream of jumbled sounds, of hard beats and then no beats and then pop songs and then jazz and then DJ chatter and then commercials and more commercials. When she stopped at the folk music station, nylon string guitars and the cajóns and the harmonies, the gravity of the humming engine pulled me into a different kind of attention, and she said, I don't want to talk about the cop okay, and I said, Yeah yeah of course, but not like I'd meant it, only like I'd *wanted* to mean it. Like I'd wanted to hide precisely how much I'd expected to be in that headspace with her, readying myself for it since we parked, steadying myself to hear her scream, maybe, to hear her cry, maybe.

But she didn't. She just gazed out onto the water, sighed occasionally through the open window, pointed out some lights across the river, The flickering like its own kind of statement, she said, Like nothing here or anywhere ever knows how to stop thinking and moving and feeling and so it all just keeps moving because it's better than stopping.

I didn't want to pretend then, like I don't want to pretend now, that I knew how to pass the time. Before she told me to take her home, she changed the music station a few more times, and she changed the position of her hands even more, and she said things like, I've never seen anyone drive with barely their fingers on the wheel like that, and, I don't think I realized before tonight how almost nothing changes between one town and the next out here, and, Who knows who we're going to be a year from now, and my responses didn't vary much, from, Yeah, and, I know, and, I can't imagine, the empty stuff, the stuff that can come out of your mouth and help you float on a silence to keep you from drowning in it.

THEREVIEWSAREIN

The Reviews Are In

REVIEW OF PABLO JUAN PABLO'S WRITE-IN: THE MAKING OF *SITTING DOWN*

Pablo Juan Pablo is maybe the most explicit writer of our time. After eleven books and dozens of awards, he's turned the craft of writing into the art of being a writer, slowly, of course, and more generally in this most recent quarter of a career. Therefore, publicizing his press release online to announce that he'd be opening his study for staging, inspection, and critique, yet again, didn't come as a surprise. The man has slowly been transforming the writing process into the kind of drama his literary antecedents had never imagined possible. To actually invite the reading public to watch him do what he does, at his desk, in a dimly lit room, with a coffee to one side of his laptop and a notebook on the other, might fill so many others with dread or impatience. But for Juan Pablo, critics from as far as Springfield, TX, scrambled to his doorstep to fill his study, all so he could embody the process, so everyone present could witness the act, will, and metaphysics of this thing we call writing.

Juan Pablo's most recent two novels, *The Bourbon Conspiracy* and *Incognito in Río*, were a creative test of and preparation for process as theater. During the creation of the former book, he'd invited his neighbors into his study to watch him write. He'd asked them to make themselves at home. He'd offered them tea, coffee, and Danishes, and even a bucket of cigarettes, cartons available upon entry. Thereafter, for all intents and purposes, Juan Pablo disappeared into the text. He typed and scribbled into his notebook when his thoughts demanded, standing up on occasion to ponder the screen or the room or even himself. He might have written, likely, with his audience in mind, while also treating their presence like figments on a canvas that turned the whole world to mirage, an approach to writing that considered both the culture prepared to receive his work and everyone's complete absence from the landscape of his mind, a feat that every writer has to manage, whether they admit to it or not, that of turning us all into ghosts precisely to be able to write about us.

As Juan Pablo noted in an interview with the *Dutchess New Ledger*,

"I don't think my neighbors knew what I'd invited them for. Some seemed to want conversation, uncomfortably, at times, trying to start a banter, though I never replied. Some even repeated a question or two, some going so far as to add bland commentary about the weather or about my interior décor. I didn't care very much to meet anyone's eyes. I just wanted them to watch, and it took many of them a while to catch on, if they caught on at all."

After the first spectacle, the reviews started rolling in. First from Portland's *Paris & Prose* and then from Miami's *The Sunday Edition* and then from likes of *The Sun* and *The Guardian*. And the most intimate review, two weeks to the day of that first performance, came from Molly Suh-Chase, a culture reporter for the *Newton Constitution Journal*, who chimed in with what has become the emblematic description of that first performance:

"A writer in America has decided to open their process to judgment, believing, perhaps, that he can reveal everything that goes into writing a book, as if the presence of both himself and the spectator, like an awful tennis match, somehow validates the very little that happens and the hours we spend watching."

Suh-Chase has lived four doors down from Juan Pablo for almost two years and has found him emotionally distant though not unkind. She once said of him, in an interview about the review she wrote of his performance, that "he's not always able to read the room," and to illustrate she used as an example a community hubbub that happened when Juan Pablo decided to rally his neighbors to host a book club for some of *his* unpublished works, a gesture he later apologized for, informing his nearest neighbors that writing groups are not only hard to come by but that they are also hard to put up with, seeing as writers have so many different schedules and too many writers have such competing opinions about other writers' character choices, sentence structures, metaphor splices, adverb accounting, plot hemming, narrator rigidity, crot tension, and any number of literary terms that writers, artists by default, invent if only to assure themselves they have the power to invent anything at all.

Suh-Chase, though, in a stroke of compassion, considers Juan Pablo's self-centered book club a formative experience for him, the idea like a predecessor initiative to eventually inviting people into his home to watch him write. As she continues in her article,

> "In inviting us to watch him edit the final proof of his tenth novel, he wanted, maybe, a punctuation for the process, something that could make the pain of a lonely labor feel shared. Exhibitionists, after all, need reluctant participants to propel them, a will that earns them the power to be more willful. I can call his performance bored or brave, outcome-unspecific or a failed misdirection, but I would have to interrogate myself in so doing. Critics often don't know how to name what appears to be outside the bounds of a structured publication process, struggling at times with insisting that a writer must always ambition to be part of the canon, forgetting that this continent has quite a long history of writers who've told the canon to go to hell, if only to end up, with time on their side, squarely inside it."

The following year, for his second attempt to model craft as performance, Juan Pablo marketed the spectacle with the description "The Task of Drafting the Final Pages of My Eleventh Novel," a book later to be titled *Incognito in Río*, what turned out to be the story of an undercover journalist infiltrating a criminal network of publishers. Attending this second performance piece was the *Holmes-Rockford Times* book critic Gayle Hass, and in her review, she criticized the author for succumbing to celebrity and using this new trajectory as an excuse to render the writing process more about showmanship than product. As she writes,

> "First, he charges readers inflated prices, and then one has to sign up for unsolicited email advertising from his editors, and then one encounters a revamped studio with pull-away curtains and graded audience seating, and then one is expected, in the face of all that, to observe him drafting the end of his book, which turned out to be the protagonist riding a cab across the Manhattan Bridge and into the literal sunset peeking over the skyline, and we were all

somehow supposed to pretend that the scene wasn't melodramatic. But I just couldn't fake it, though I was also in some uncomfortable tension of my own: I didn't want to laugh even outside his house because laughing would only have condoned this experiment with craft, would have only demonstrated even a tangential entertainment value."

Hass, however, later in her review, also attempts to contextualize the literary times in which we live, reflective as they are of a drive more and more writers have to eagerly embody their craft beyond the page, to write a book so that it compels somebody to adapt it to television or into a movie, to write with more than just the writing in mind, and it's in this light that Hass ultimately praises Juan Pablo for the gall to own the dramatization of his own work and for the guts to dramatize more than just the end product, to dare to adapt the process itself, irrespective of whether or not its content is adaptable at all, a courage to produce a staging that refuses to rely on the machinations of studio and production and which can elevate the author's intentions to the same level as an audience's appreciation for the story between the covers.

Echoing Hass's sentiment, Che Mendoza in Seattle's *Popular Examiner* writes more succinctly, "Juan Pablo, taking dramatization into his own hands, has complicated the nature of adaptation, one that might now have to consider, and comment upon, the process by which the source text has been created, a move, I'm sure, that will not sit well with critics whose living depends on the creative maneuvers to transition a text from page to something more."

Perhaps echoing the discomfort others might feel around what he's done, Juan Pablo has increasingly turned down more interviews than he's accepted, choosing to protect, as he has said, "the integrity of the work and the story, *my* story, *the* story, that informs the work." In publishing beyond his mother tongue, the writer has already had to make concessions of form and structure in order to fit American English language conventions that don't, as he has previously confessed, always fit with the output of his mind. He has been quoted as fearing the initial compulsion to perform the act of writing, suggesting in the first interview he ever gave, to Bob Modoff at *The Sunday Phonograph*, "My stomach turned even after I made the decision to produce these small performances, and I didn't know if I would be able to continue mapping what I do, from language to language and one part of my brain to the other, without slipping here and there, as I've done for the better part of two decades, with mistakes both off the page and in the way I write, often sounding out the words I need and the words I'm looking for before anything gets typed, before a live studio audience."

Working through these initial feelings to preserve himself, then, seems to add weight to what critics have called his "determination to do this," because to choose to welcome people into his studio to watch him craft viable thoughts and makeshift ideas might have felt, based on Juan Pablo's own reflections, like ripe opportunity for criticism beyond the text, the kind of criticism that could claw body, blood, and soul if it ever got to the point of interrogating the writer's perspective, history, and humanity.

But luckily, I don't find evidence that it has, and I, for one, am thankful that, as the writer stated in that *Sunday Phonograph* interview, he "just had to do it."

The audacity seems to have begun, as things usually do, with a challenge to the act of making meaning and language, the very process of that construction, one that is constantly under pressure, constantly in the cooker of an ever-present watchfulness. The destination society for immigrants can feel like an overwhelming, constant, almost omnipotent gaze, and so if home, work, clothing, and general subsistence are products of constant negotiation and flexibility, then why not bring that interrogation to the very act of expression, why not question how and why we produce the language we do. If the physical part of our lives is fair game for manipulation, as is the case for any immigrant that moves anywhere, then it matters to make *all* parts of our lives that compliant, if only to retake control over those parts that we don't choose to be provisional or scarce. Or, as Juan Pablo once said in a televised interview with Phillip Neimann, the producer and host of Continental Public Television's *Craft Hour with Phillip Neimann,*

> "American English sentences, even before you set them to paper, carry a certain expectation to them, a way of processing the world that feels, even in their arrangements of clauses and punctuation, far too linear in their progress, like their tension is only allowed to increase from beginning to end and like you can't be playful with a sonic fluctuation before getting to the period, and that approach can feel ahistorical, limited by the past because one's craft can't expressly learn from it, not to mention that I can't always get down with that kind of system, with the burden of having to repeat the system until you fit into it."

Generally speaking, of course, Juan Pablo has been known to reject the various systems of his career, not the least of which has been the romance of publishing itself, the false allure of the *big* publisher, preferring the tangibility of a local publisher wherever he's lived, in so many cases leaving big money on that pretentiously big table, as well as the attention that comes with the announcement of that kind of negotiation. Even this approach has developed imperfectly, however, and so Juan Pablo has had to occasionally adjust his own rebellions, systems everywhere coming with their own demands and their own constraints, every revolution, inevitably, requiring flexibility to meet the nuances of their day. In this view, these not-so-small performances of his, this approach to literary endeavor, have had to adapt language to fit this new craft, as such creating a new vocabulary in the process, something that reshapes both the product of the page and the exhibition at the heart of this review.

And, so, we arrive, finally, to what this review is about: Juan Pablo's third performance in as many years, the process of writing in his writing studio available for anyone to see. As far as genre goes, one could fit these performances into the increasingly visual trend of framing one's stories, preparing them for market and reception before a reader gets their hand on a book. The writer has always been the occupant of the seat behind the words, of course, but a writer has also increasingly been the focus of the attention their publication receives, the one posing with their book on the shelf, the one grinning with their readers at an event, the one prioritizing a glimpse of themselves over a glimpse of the book. In this context, Juan Pablo's performance is only the next theatrical step, whether or not he's explicitly defined it as such, the writer as more than persona: the writer as actor. And just like any staged drama, every new rendition leaves the next closer to intentional, and *this* is what we might call *craft*, this word I've used so loosely thus far: craft as the repetition of one's messy habits until they become a process we recognize and repeat, even with revisions, until we get closer to our own resemblance in this thing we do, this thing of arrangement and subject and action and life.

For this third iteration of Juan Pablo's a private-writing-process-as-public-drama, he scheduled a string of performances across a weekend. For my part, I attended the Sunday matinee, and I arrived with that figurative eyeglass-and-shovel to unearth the meaning and man behind the work, to discern the motivation that has propelled him to repeat what was almost a failure at first into what has become a *not*-such-a-failure.

On Juan Pablo's website, for this run of exhibitions, the description of each performance has appeared only moments before showtime, and Juan Pablo's decision for the Sunday matinee was to draft a portion of Chapter 4 of his twelfth novel, one very much still in-progress, tentatively titled *Sitting Down*.

What the novel is about remains to be seen, but from what I was able to glimpse of his pages from where I stood, with the help of another audience member's long-range eyewear, the book has writers as protagonists and features the writer's parents with their undue burdens, the writers' friends with their strange intimacy habits, and outright strangers with happenstance encounters that compel something emotionally offensive enough to move the plot forward.

When I first walked into Juan Pablo's performance space, the studio was standing room only. The seated audience sat four rows deep, six seats wide, the wall between Juan Pablo's office and living room was torn down and left tastefully disrepaired, to which I mean that some modernist, and I'm sure it was one, had painted the edges of the exposed sheetrock to resemble the rocky texture of a desert amphitheater. The chairs had been imported from a shuttered independent theatre in Mexico City, the stamp "hecho en jalisco" stained into the armrests, though not originally, as the insignia appears to have been a more recent addition, likely a craft choice by Juan Pablo to offer the studio a certain displacement. Alongside the recess lighting and the aged indoor wood shutters and a replica of David's bust on a fiberglass Doric column in the corner by the printer, the room bore the impression of a place that didn't *want* to know where it was. Along the walls, too, there were alternating vertical postures of bookshelves and brown curtains, and the audience that hadn't arrived before the rush, but insisted nevertheless to endure the humidity, stood in clusters along the perimeter, and I formed part of this gathering in the crowd. On top of all this, six overhead fans spun to make sure no one fainted, which left something like sighing echoes from wall to wall, lots of deep breathing making for a kind of symphony of the curious as the lights dimmed and the show began.

Critics have noted that in previous performances, Juan Pablo's long preoccupations with similes, sometimes deleting the word "like" only to reinstate it moments later, were sometimes the most intense portions of his show. Friday's performance, for example, as Paulo Tomás wrote in his review for the Los Angeles Writers Association blog,

"Juan Pablo's tinkering here and there with language became so tense, at one point lingering on a pun for so long, that a woman in the front row almost fainted from the anger, so impassioned as she was, fuming from her eyes, that the woman's wife had to embrace the woman tightly, so tightly, and assure her, 'He's going to replace that introductory clause, Pam, with a straight subject-verb-predicate approach. I'm sure of it. Just you wait, Pam. Just you wait.'"

In the Sunday matinee I attended, there were certainly some harumphs and even *hmms* from the audience members, to the point where I borrowed my neighbor's binoculars to get a close enough look at the screen to witness why the buzz had started to rise. The most pressing tension, it seemed, had to do with the extent of a sentence, at one point, near the bottom of the second page he drafted that afternoon, choosing to combine what had originally been three short sentences into a single cohesive one, in the process adding clause after clause complicating the prose, interrupting the protagonist's interiority in a store with childhood memories of the character's mother, something about baking chocolate cake and the nurture of a family oven. In its own nuanced plot, the original three-sentence structure became a half-page meandering through action and memory, and then Juan Pablo chopped up the sentence into many shorter ones, nine in all, akin to something like a writer's literary violence not only shredding point of view but also the fabric of a story, the comings and goings of language like its own kind of process. Juan Pablo lingered on these lines for almost twenty minutes, rejoining the sentences in unexpected combinations and then dividing them up again, and the audience *ahh*-ed and *hmm*-ed, nods of approval sprinkled everywhere like confetti, slanted faces and eyes unsure of what was happening and generally all of us trying to come to terms with all those small movements that happen in this, one writer's solitary orchestra of choices.

I felt the tension in the air, certainly, but no more than I would my own, which is to say I knew a thing or two about writing processes, generally speaking, and so I perceived what I perceived as a cousin understanding another cousin's pain and pensiveness. But the tension might have been a bit much for those of us unfamiliar enough with the heart of the literary endeavor.

I couldn't tell when it started, but a good number in the crowd had begun working through that tension, and perhaps even their anxieties, with cigarettes. Enough of us had taken up Juan Pablo's invitation to smoke, in the studio's congestion, no less, and more notably very few people coughed and almost nobody walked out. I occasionally had to wave away a cloud of smoke approaching my face, but I didn't realize I'd resigned to enduring the discomfort of it all until I caught myself shooing away a puff and returning my gaze, diligently, to Juan Pablo at his desk. My eyes might have been reddening or drying, but I'll venture to say I didn't care. Not that I *actually* didn't care, but more that I hadn't consciously registered what distractions I had or had not cared about, itself a testament to my own willingness to participate in Juan Pablo's performance. I looked around plenty, of course, and I couldn't help but think that the whole lot of us had been goaded into our own pretentious exhibition, some reproduction of posture in which an audience appraises art the way an artist might want to be appraised, with the smell of tobacco in the air and grunts of approval from afar. I can't say for sure that this was Juan Pablo's intention, but I also can't say for sure it wasn't. All I can do is acknowledge, now, that the writer must have wanted a response like what he got, this whole literary moment like a satire of the process, established to be critical of itself and its readership and for what the art and the art's production appeared to be compelling us to do, perhaps like a commentary on the nature of group assemblage, on the nature of a human being's inability to excuse themself from a herd.

And I argue for all this because if Juan Pablo had not wanted some echo like this from us observing his performance then he would not have attached selfie sticks to the edge of his desk and to his seat's backrest. His phones were both going off, flash and all, every few minutes, auto-posting the pictures almost immediately onto a social media thread that viewers from around the world could follow. I, myself, was not following the online documentation, but many people around me were, and they seemed to be engaged in this *Did you see it? / Did you see that?* back-and-forth, simultaneously attending to both the in-person phenomenon and the live feed, and with quite the rage, too. I overheard one person say something to another about Juan Pablo's choice of imagery for the protagonist's apartment, explicit criticism, specifically, of how the uncleaned dishes in the sink were described as "the remnants of a war she had recently waged and wanted no part of," to which the audience member said, elbowing her partner to the left, "Why do writers have to use so many metaphors about war. Only war can really be war, am I right?" after which she proceeded to type that exact comment into Juan Pablo's social media live feed, and when the audience member started receiving hearts and likes to her comment, she elbowed her partner again to tell him, "You see, did you see that, Dave? I got everybody's wheels turning."

A reprieve in the action, a downturn in the performance's plot, came when Juan Pablo spent a minute or two formatting his page numbers, and then another few minutes removing or altering the indentation of a handful of paragraphs, and then a couple minutes combining them and then rearranging larger paragraphs into smaller paragraphs, and then another minute or two checking his print preview options and altering the orientation of the page.

The most notable structural moment of the afternoon came at approximately 2:15 p.m., after an hour of Juan Pablo doing any number of things, though primarily sifting through previously written pages to add or delete, rather unevenly, to paragraphs and sentences here and there as he scrolled up and down his pages, at one point returning to Chapter 3, copying and pasting a few lines here and there and stopping to consider changes in verb tense and then rereading a sentence or two aloud to himself to contemplate the potential shifts in tone. After this reverie of small revisions, the moment came for him to stand up. Nobody knows, can ever know, if this was scheduled as part of the writing. It happened and it shocked many of us, but no one more than the woman in the middle of the first row. She screamed, "No!" shouting as if at all of us and not at Juan Pablo directly, her tone resigning to the performance as something she could impact but never change, and she grunted probably on account of that feeling, though never angry or frustrated, only like she wanted to be audible, like someone half-cognizant of carrying the emotional labor of herself and others. I never caught her name. For all intents and purposes, she might as well have been our Pam, our very own Pam in the first row, pressing a hand to her chest and then running her free hand through her hair and embodying a dramatic shift in the audience as a whole, a radical transformation of demeanor that extended to the far corners of Juan Pablo's expanded studio.

Having gotten to his feet, he circled his chair, and he seemed to anticipate the room rising as he paced around the seat, because he suddenly walked away from his desk in some kind of cool self-possessed stride, a man caught up in both the pull of his will and the direction of his bones. It was, if I might be so bold, as if Moses had just emerged with his tablets from Sinai but gone straight to Pharaoh with them, not exactly a scandal but with the general perception of *this-is-not-what-people-of-manners-do* kind of feeling, with members of the first row shouting, members of the second row telling the rest to quiet down, members of the third row telling everybody else to sit down, and members of the fourth row telling us all that they'd *paid* for their tickets *goddammit*, that they spent *good money for this show.*

And then, as if he couldn't have compelled more from us, an almost-hell broke loose when Juan Pablo came into the stands. The whole first row stood up, shakily, clumsily, spilling their drinks, most of them climbing over their chairs into the row behind them. The whole second row stood to make room, everything rattled, and perhaps because Juan Pablo remained self-possessed, perhaps because the seeming-improvisation felt orchestrated, the commotion went from disruption to an easy wildness, to a controlled chaos, as one person shook the floor dust off their jacket and another grabbed the shoulders of those closest to her to steady herself and another crouched as if anticipating that he'd have to catch someone slipping, something like the good nature in all of us giving rise to collective stability.

Juan Pablo, though, in the end, only stopped at that first row. He settled his foot onto one chair. He settled his elbow onto his right knee. He became, as if to punctuate the whole show, his own kind of monument, a literary thinker carved from the marble of his own skin, statuesque not because *one* person had explicitly carved him but because *everyone* had, literary history and every last one of us in that studio. I don't want to belabor the moment longer, as I neither want to aggrandize it all or excuse the melodrama of the show's culmination, which I'm not sure anyone realized had arrived until it just simply did. What marked that finish line, too, very tangibly and unexpectedly, was that woman in the first row, our own makeshift kind of Pam, when her giggle turned into a cackle, and she crouched there staring at Juan Pablo until he looked up and took a deep breath to compose himself.

Who knows where in the novel Juan Pablo had stopped. Perhaps, like with any good work, the words had suddenly turned on him and so he decided, in order to seize control again, that what he needed most in the world was us, our attention, our absorption, fixed to the way his shirt fluttered in the fans' breeze and to the small twitches on his face and to the way he stepped back onto his own two feet and, finally and for the first time, gazed around the room as if to return the observation to each and every person present. And then he nodded, ever so slightly, as if to appreciate the endeavor that we hadn't realized, and perhaps *he* hadn't realized, had been a joint crescendo to conclusion.

The applause couldn't have been louder or more singular, as if it had been compelled on queue. He bowed. His chest rose and fell as he started to wave at all of us, and when he finally smiled, his eyes seemed to be fixed on a spot behind me, and though I knew, logically, that he wasn't looking at me, I turned around anyway to confirm as much, to find the presence of something else behind me, actually. There, hanging on the wall, its bottom edge crossing behind my neck, was the portrait of a door that opened unto another door and which opened unto another door into perpetuity, a metaphor, if any there could have been, of Juan Pablo's whole enterprise, this act of the act of writing.

When I turned back to look at him, my eyes fixed on the way Juan Pablo's shoulders ebbed and flowed with his breathing, the whole studio transformed by the clapping and the hollering, a confirmation that in the best of creative spaces, something like a circadian rhythm exists that can turn the very act of being creative and witnessing creativity into a dream you don't know how to wake yourself from, existence reproducing until both the embodiment and its shadow create a new kind of craft.

As the applause faded, Juan Pablo returned to his workstation and lowered his screen, his left hand, for a spell, lingering over the edge of his desk, seemingly reaching for everything at once. When he finally settled his hand down, he shut off his laptop with his free hand, remaining in that standing position as if all or part of him didn't know how to stop, as if he couldn't fake even the illusion of pausing to write. The process itself, I've been told, is like an addiction, such that when one finally pulls back, one must come to terms with how one's emotional and cellular chemistry has changed, returning to the world demanding a relinquishing of power, of one's body, of one's ability to recognize wisdom, of one's ability to make anything possible.

I have been told that writing changes you, that too much time spent with it alters a sense of self until that version of you with your hands over the keys begins to exert its will over you in every other part of your life. That Juan Pablo has continued to reveal that part of himself so intensely for his readers, even if the most recent effort to draft an entire novel in front of us fails to produce any novel at all, should situate the writer into his own kind of literary canon, whether or not we ever decide to put him into *the* literary canon. To suggest that he knows how *to carve* a space for himself feels too rudimentary for these performances, as *to carve* implies a more minor action and the kind of toolset Juan Pablo simply isn't working with. To suggest, however, that he has *designed* a space for himself implies not only a much more modern appreciation of our cultural moment but one that considers, yes, carving what's right here and there with one's own hands, *and* it considers a plan that has been strategically created, the process for a process that no one sees but the grand designer of their place in the world. It's this imagery I am left sitting with, not only in terms of what Juan Pablo has done and will continue to do in and for his work but also in light of what I am doing in the space I create for myself, this space of reviewing elements of the world that matter, if only because I have made them matter for the sensory world. We are all inventing ourselves, in these and similar spaces, whether or not we acknowledge we have a path at all. Strategy isn't about knowing a plan; it's about designing one after acknowledging that your life has discovered and followed a direction of its own free will and intuition with the senses that have made something of themselves and you until you become wise enough to define what they've built, like a monarch butterfly who knows when it's time, without ever having seen its country of hope, to unmoor from the garden they have called home for too long and set off for something they believe will be there, at some place somewhere called *the end*, the smells of it all becoming more than just imaginary the closer their wings shed the horizon and the view of it becoming more than just illusion the clearer their eyes begin to realize that everything they have seen, every piece and fabric of the world behind them, when compiled and reconstituted, have been exactly the thing they have always been aiming to be.

"VIGNETTES, REGRETS, AND NOT-SO-STYLISH SILHOUETTES":

SALVADOR PLASCENCIA'S REVIEW OF JUAN CARLOS REYES'S COLLECTION OF FICTION, *THREE ALARM FIRE*

When you picture a story, it's usually because words string a light show that you can touch. A subject precedes a verb that precedes everything else, like the timeline of a holiday meal. You begin with the chips and then the appetizers and then the alcohol and then the rest of the night somehow follows the rhythm of its own misfortunes.

I picked up Juan Carlos Reyes's *Three Alarm Fire* at the recommendation of a few friends, all of whom were too pressed for time to tell me what they actually thought about the collection. One hung up before finishing the sentence, "What can I say about the book but…" Another friend left their copy duct taped to my door while I was out on a walk in the park, as usual, worrying about the things that needed worrying about, and that friend had pasted a sticky-note to the book binding that read, "I have a feeling that this book…" When finally a third friend contorted a copy of the book, stuffing it into my mailbox, I had to do something with one or all three copies, so I proceeded to read them all, one after the next, as anyone who worries about being a terrible friend would, just in case—god forbid—one of your friends comes to inspect the book and realizes, as they flip through it, that you haven't touched a single page.

Every sentence in a good book, if you're a writer with some luck, bears the power of a narrator to press love and resentment so closely together that a reader believes that the narrator really believes in the language and luster that dance up and down the page, and perhaps Reyes's collection of fiction does that. Perhaps, too, it does not. I worry sometimes about the things I commit to, whether opinion or a fact, both of which, if we're honest with ourselves, have become a matter of perspective.

In any case, if you're a writer with any luck, you can suggest with everything between the covers that you not only want a relationship with the reader but also need one, badly, and you're willing to risk it all, self and self-doubt included, just to get it. And I can imagine that those dear friends of mine who could not finish their sentences on the phone or on sticky-notes had meant to say precisely this, something like, "What can I say about the book but that every fiction collection, no matter whose anxieties produce it, desperately desires to offer a contact point so a reader can have some kind of touching moment with themself," or perhaps something like, "I have a feeling that this book, like so many collections of fiction before it, does this accumulation effect from fiction to fiction, like a small shuffle of concerns that, for example, rack up on a shower hook like a bunch of bath towels that, once all perched on a single hanger, eventually bring everything down with them, including the bathroom door."

As any book critic will tell you, thou shalt not open a book between the hours of 1pm and 3pm. Siestas are important, and you need time to let the coffee grinds settle well into the boiled water before serving yourself a cup. The best reading hour is just before dinner, after two pastries and a cup of tea, as there's no better time than when the sun begins to slip behind the trees to identify story arrangements, assess narrative structures, imagine a different formatting to the white space, have an opinion about font choices for page numbers, snicker at who makes the acknowledgements page and who's left out, and research the writer, artist, or philosopher behind the epigraph. Writers, in the end, are all liars, and one can never take for granted that anyone said what a book purports them to have said. ● ● •

Reyes's narrators feel like oddities, people who speak to feel heard, move to see themselves in action, cry to identify the reasons people live and die, and scream because amidst all the pain, the world can tell us something about who we are when our voices echo in the wind. The wilderness, I've been told, sits at such a distance away that we can bury the dead there and never find them, leave those stories there that don't work so no one reads them. When I opened Reyes's collection, I proceeded from one word to the next, to every next page as recommended, numbered as the pages were in Helvetica 9 pt. font, a generous type but not as gracious as Book Antiqua. I continued attentively from one fiction to the next, which demanded sacrifice, particularly in the face of

all I do, namely, writing and evenings with my girlfriend and commuting to work with my girlfriend and holding down multiple teaching positions to contribute to a shared apartment with my girlfriend. I should mention that I always wear socks. My girlfriend keeps the apartment at such a temperature that natural air, the warm or boiling air, at times, feels like a stranger.

As any book critic worth their time will tell you, you draft your initial thoughts about a book and then reconsider that you're wrong, completely wrong, and then go get a drink of water or take a shower because, as it turns out, you might also be wrong about being wrong.

At times, the narrators in Reyes's collection seemed to be begging, and the urgency of it all left me drained, and I didn't know what to make of the dead energy, because my white blood cell count might have decreased after the first page or perhaps I simply couldn't get enough sleep after moving too far past the first page. In any case, I had to give my friend, the writer Elizabeth Acevedo, author of *Poet X* and other rebellions, a call to share what had been happening to me, the kind of mystery only a writer of her reputation could appreciate, and she said, "When I read this book, Reyes's collection felt like an anthology of the holiest of losses, first one life and then the next and then an unfinished love and then you're immersed in a headspace where you can't even trust the path you're on, unknowing which emotion comes next or which one feels like you can reliably blame for outpacing all the others. Perhaps, too, I'd started to hallucinate after making it far past the first page, like I couldn't trust my reflection in the mirror. Anyway, I gotta run, but thanks for the coffee," and she started to stash her notebook back into her satchel. Elizabeth had left me waiting thirty minutes before her arrival, and then she decided to leave after finishing her croissant. She said she'd pay me back, in cash, for the latté, too, but when she first couldn't find her wallet and then she couldn't find her phone, she seemed convinced she'd dropped it on the freeway between her apartment and the coffee shop.

I was able to convince Elizabeth to stay a bit longer by telling her that I wouldn't hold a grudge, at least not until her tab with me got over $100, under the guise that I would pay for another cup if she earned the value in conversation. She pursed her lips when she nodded, and then she said to me, "I know you like to process aloud, and these ruminations of yours remind me of what someone once told me reminded him of Rigoberto Gonzalez's creative process. You know who I'm talking about, the author of *Mariposa Boy* and so many external review letters for other people's tenure applications. Academia, am I right? In any case, neither of us can really be Rigoberto Gonzalez, which is sad, of course, but no more sad than, well..." and then Elizabeth gestured to the empty cup on the table before her.

She likes to feel the power of a name-drop, and she also likes to stay dehydrated, so the flick of her wrist could have meant anything in between.

Reyes's *Three Alarm Fire* opens up with a triptych of stories that interrogate the role of men in an era of both empowerment and responsibility, which, arguably, should have been the role of men and menfolk and the male-identified in every goddamn human era of all of the human history of eras. But, also, we examine the complex system of witness, what it means to witness, how witness distinguishes itself from interventionist, and what it looks like to walk beside the women, womenfolk, female-identified, and every survivor in the process of removing victim from their name.

Later, when we arrive to the triptych of violence, the subset of fictions for which the whole collection is named, we arrive at the line drawn, at the path pathed, at the trajectory of fictions trajected and led to, and it appears we have been goaded there through patience and a cyclic kind of lulling. A woman whose fiancée was gunned down by police, who, in some extreme emotional weathering, makes love to his cell phone. She re-watches the shooting he recorded on his phone, and when Reyes's narrator says, "A thought can be a gut check coming into place and coming sooner than I expect, and when the pillow knows where to exhale, my eyes sink," one can reasonably assume that Reyes either knows pain or knows what it sounds like when someone closes the door on you.

■ ■ ■   In another story, the narrator initially comes across as sympathetic, trying to process another school shooting with the help of his cell phone. He walks through the city with running commentary telling us about one of many families who've experienced the tragedy personally. And then he shows up on a doorstep, the family's doorstep, and he unlocks his phone and turns on his social media live feed, all in the second person, and we suddenly become complicit in something we did not sign up for. "You introduce the house you're standing in front of. You confirm the presence of a grieving family inside the house. ... But you have to confirm that you can't deliver on the promise to interview the family. After all, they haven't returned your phone calls or your emails." There's a big emotional leap in just the first three stories, much less the first thirteen, so much so that I threw the book against the wall after the first eight dozen pages. I didn't know what else to do with my hands. On the carpet, the binding looked like caulk masking flaws in the living room trimming. The bookmark, which traveled half the distance, looked like a discarded sock, something you tear off as you run into the shower after a tussle in the mud or a swamp or a back alley. I didn't know at first whether I'd murdered the book, so I leaned forward to assess the damage, lamplight reflecting off the pages as if the book had drawn its own chalk outline.

I have these visions sometimes of someone who surprises me as I sit at my desk working. They tap me on the shoulder, tell me that I've run out of coffee, and then swivel me in the chair and hold a creamer out to me. It's frightening.

My friend, the writer Juliana Delgado Lopera, author of *Fiebre Tropical* and other misdemeanors, once said to me, "Sal, this coffee is terrible. Where have you taken me?" We had only just arrived together to a classic Salvadorean restaurant on the outskirts of Los Angeles. I had heard they were coming to town, and so I had my publicist contact their publicist who then put us in touch with their editor who in turn said that they had no more contact with Juliana than we had, and so she directed us to their social media profiles, and after various stages of indirect messaging, we concluded that Juliana had been at a nondescript motel for too long without effective caffeine, and so we agreed to meet.

As they sat across the table, they nibbled on their muffin. I devoured my first and had proceeded directly into all but ingesting the second, when, during my third or fourth bite, Delgado Lopera pulled their sunglasses over their eyes and continued, "But back to this collection by Reyes, which feels like it's regularly on point and also regularly makes the point twice but also masks the point in layers of language, como torta de tres leches pero, a la vez, mas como torta de tantas leches que solamente un fuego separará los niveles grasa. But, as I was clarifying, those elements of life beneath the whispers we get to hear are what this collection exposes us to, and I must add that when I finished the book, so serendipitously, I had to confirm to my publicist who confirmed with my editor that it was okay for them to pass you my social media handle, which you could have found on your own, but I'm not here to judge. At any rate, si no se puede saborear el cafecito asi de negro, por que tomarlo."

I reminded Juliana that I have never heard them once call anything the *language of layers*, and, if anything, the term feels remarkably similar to something Gloria Anzaldua once said when she was interviewed for the *Paris*

Review, to which Juliana said, "Gloria Anzaldua was never interviewed by the *Paris Review*, my friend," to which I responded, "Well, god*damn*," to which Juliana responded, equally exhausted with the world of publishing, "A fucking tragedy, my man."

There are stories in Reyes's collection, fictions that are not always stories and some that are, but I don't know that we're supposed to prefer one term over another. All I know is that Venn diagrams can become a habit, an addiction, really, if one is not careful. We are, after all, embittered by the norms of modern publishing where one thing must be this and another must be that and there are overlapping ideologies where nothing can be named for fear of disturbing the market, and the parameters of who gets to define themselves and who is defined before anyone opens their pages is constantly changing. And all I know is that this book seems to exist to test me, because, for example, I once, in the course of reading this book, had to wring a damp towel over my fevered head and spend the afternoon on bed rest. I couldn't even turn on a podcast. I couldn't even raise my window, largely because the frames had been painted shut, and the only thing that permitted heat into the room were the very old, very frail, panes.

But the fiction I really want to talk about, which my friend, the writer Carribean Fragoza, author of *Eat the Mouth That Feeds You* and other revolutions, also wanted to talk about when, over coffee in Alameda, she said to me, "Sal, I'm never going to ████ your text messages again if you keep bringing me to places that brew espresso that tastes like paper filters, so if you'd like to keep this train of thought going, this one that has you quite obsessed about a ████ collection that might pass the smell test of original creation but very little else, then we're going to have to start meeting somewhere else, perhaps somewhere Cuban, or somewhere Guatemalan, or somewhere that models itself after a country that actually grows coffee beans or where sugar is so plentiful it has to be cut from rooftops and stairwells like mold, and perhaps, too, we can meet closer to sunset when the hills glimmer enough to keep me distracted looking outside the window should your brazen excitement get too carried away to fully enjoy you and this (she points to the table) and us (she points to the book in my hands and herself), but where was I," to which I responded, "Yes, of course, I believe you'll love that place in Glendale that offers complimentary tortillas with every meal, and I believe you had just mentioned getting into the story of the kid and his powers and the unfinished business of eager violence," to which she responded, "Yes, of course, immigration, tragedy, and a murder, the kinds of correlation that telegraph through a dense, fascinating fog made of knives and points of interest," to which I responded, "And don't forget the family dynamic, the strangers that abet, the aides that betray, the point of no return that leaves us breathless, and the coldness, the utter frigidity, of a vengeance that doesn't even know how to name itself," to which she responded, "There were a lot of words in that contemplation, and you're already forgetting the white people in the story who, once named, cease to exist," to which I responded, "I want a biscuit," to which she responded, "Sal, we're in a Dominican restaurant, and we're not in London, and I thought you had more taste than that," to which I responded, "I understand, but all this talk of language and opportunity, and what would it matter if we reverse imperialize for a change," to which she responded, "We can also just ask the server to bring us some water and maybe just a cup of fire to get the taste of this awful latte out of our mouths," to which I responded, "You really did have a rough ride of emotions through this collection, didn't you," and she responded, "I did, Sal. I did."

I told Carribean that the intensity and urgency of the story reminded me of Piri Tomas, of his downright fire of a sound, a flame of a voice, an emblazoned trill of an utterance that once heard could not be shaken, to which she responded, "But also not like Piri at all, Sal, because, if we're honest, there was one Piri, singular and inimitable, barely replicable by Piri himself, an artist who couldn't even repeat himself, and he certainly spent the better part of a life trying," which sent me into a spiral of sorts, a silence between us that I might have initiated or I might have only just mirrored after it settled on the table. I was stuck there. Carribean, this thrill of a human, had seemingly found the trajectory I had missed, this appreciation for the sounds and shapes of this collection that never once wanted to repeat themselves but only wanted, like a comedian whose act centers seemingly disparate jokes into a cohesive narrative of resistance and redemption, to center the experience of a rebellion from one point to the next, from A to Z.

After glances around the room, this beautiful friend of a friend, or rather, friend of a friend's friend, Caribbean smiled, rather half-politely, and then she took a phone call, though I never actually heard the phone ring. She nodded quite vigorously, holding the earpiece to her face, and she said, "You don't say," and, "Wow, now *that's* an emergency," and when she hung up, or perhaps only when she tapped a screen that had already been locked, or perhaps after she simply just cupped the phone between her palms, she said to me that she just heard about an act of God that she must very urgently attend to, repeating that word, *urgently*, and then *urgent*, over-pronouncing the *r* and then the *t*,

"And I should go immediately to validate my parking, you understand, don't you Sal." When she repeated *urgent* again, she did so in air quotes, which startled me but also led me to believe she wanted me to be in on the joke with her, but I was stuck in that place, like the least readerly of readers, feeling like I didn't know which feeling to get to.

I'll confess that reading emails confuses me, especially in the middle of a book. I might answer them sometimes in the voice of a character, like a narrator unwilling to let their plots go, like a voice that wants to sustain itself because there's simply far too much to share about who ██████████. And all of this leads me to believe that you simply can't read this collection in the middle of a separate activity, like a phone call or a writing sprint or a time-sensitive freelance gig that has you writing about ██████████ and repurposing freight containers for *Architectural Digest*. The mix-and-match process of it all might leave you confused, might leave you displaced, and might even leave you embarrassed, to the point where you begin to obfuscate the most mundane parts of yourself and your word choices, the language you once ██ ██████████ with, become objects of timidity.

Reyes, the author of this collection, emails me so many times a week, that I only really have time to respond to four or five of his three dozen any given Monday-through-Friday spread. Every persuasive effort, now a dozen weeks running, essentially amounts to the plea of his first message, "I offer you this manuscript in the hopes that you will be able to offer a back cover blurb ahead of its publication." Attentive to pleasantries, surely, but I never did put two and two together, and I should have. It's been *his* deliveries of the book I've received, his hands that have grazed my front door and my mailbox, and how each of my friends, writers, all of them, have only flattered my trains of thought, my small obsessions with this book, instead of stating the obvious, the fact that they had *not* read this collection before I had and that they had *not* even heard of it before I asked them about it and that they flatly knew nothing about it. Writers—liars—the whole lot of them. How readily they've bantered about its contents, its narrative ventures, its narrators whose only pursuit of life has been a pursuit of sound, of voice, of an intensity that has wanted nothing more than open ears to hear them urge themselves into existence, into that blood between heart and lung where words can choke you and purpose can make your skin crawl.

And each of my friends eventually confirmed it, that they had not advanced me a copy of this collection, that they were, in fact, only amusing me and my fixation for this book, for its fictions, for its points of view, for its narrators whose daring ability to let us see them as completely as they were hoping to see themselves. When I respond to the author of this book, I tell him that I will only be able to write this review, and that it scares me to offer that he can do whatever he wants with it after submission.

██████████ completing that most recent sentence, an email pings on my laptop, one in which the ████████████████████████████████████ ██████████ review, a clear reference to these narrators as 'daring' and 'intense,' this collection made more valuable by the general assessment that you have read every page and assessed every edge." I have to consider at this point that I'm being watched. I pull my blinds apart to peer between them. I eye into the peephole to make sure no one's pressed their ear to my front door. My front yard is indistinguishable from any other, not a chair, gnome, or flamingo in sight. But I have to consider that Reyes has found me, though I don't imagine he can see it all, certainly nothing under ████████████████, beneath which I can be honest. For example, I can suggest that Reyes's narrators might feel unfinished in their definitions of self and that this review, as yet unfinished, can be honest about Reyes's uncanny ability to prophecy social dilemmas and tribulations and ills, those public cuts and bruises his narrators confess to so potently for a reader that we all but internalize the pain, compelled to carry it for these voices, and so you can imagine my surprise when in his email dated today, he writes, "Thank you so much for your kind words declaring my ability to anticipate the cultural tribulations of our age and making them explicit in the fictions of our time and the prose of our era, and etc., etc.,…," because *what—the—hell.*

I know I should stop before the lines between us blur and where who begins where no longer feels like a joke we can distinguish, and so I'll say it now before I don't get the chance, that *Three Alarm Fire* is a collection that arrives ██
██
██
██
██
██
██
██
████████████████████████████ and I don't want to say

more. To say that the collection didn't bring me to tears, I would be lying. To say that this book didn't also at times make me reconsider my place in the world, I would be lying.

Frailty, I have learned, can wear your body like a blanket, coming to you like a friend and staying by you like a tiger pretending to be asleep, an animal that, once stirred, can burn like the sun. Whoever has the nerve to heed this, I beg you not to overlook yourself, to be mindful of where you end and where the author's presence at your doorstep begins, Stop that Sal, Excuse me, I said stop that, I knew it, I'm done with games Sal, Then be done and tell me, Tell you what Sal, Why me, You must know Sal, Why choose me to write this review, You said it yourself Sal *that of all things we read and of those writers whose words we see, none of it ever leaves us*, So you've *read* me, We've read *each other* now Sal, That doesn't make us one and the same, And yet *none of this influence will ever leave us*, At least quote me correctly if you want to keep doing it, I haven't chosen you any more than the things we read choose us to expand themselves into the living world, But the me on this page is only a composite of the me you imagine and the literary world you imagine holds us both, And I'm no less than that same composite, So why me, Why *not* you, Stop that, Stop what, Stop throwing my question back at me, As Urayoán Noel author of *Transversal* and other disruptions once said *We have the things people tell us we are and the things we think we aren't and I'm most interested in the contradictions that emerge when I imagine all the many ideas I've cobbled together to become the person I imagine I want to be*, Urayoán never said that, I wouldn't be one to judge what is and isn't fiction Sal, So what now then, We finish this Sal, Then can I be left to it, We have to end this Sal.

I assume then that this is the complicated state of the craft of fiction, an economy where, if we're not careful, we become each other, we absorb each other, particularly if the game is to understand what we do within and beyond those communities we call ours and that call us theirs. When we type up what we do, on the fly or premeditated, we're only really bringing to bear the history of our attachments to language upon every word we mime, and so why not simply spell it out. Why not simply, There you go Sal, Stop that, Don't stop now Sal—why not simply clarify for all time the company you want to keep and the mirror images you look into when you write.

REVIEW OF A LAST ACT: THE WESTIN BETHEL CHURCH AND THE LATHAM CEMETERY PROTEST

A cemetery autumn is usually the Westin Bethel moment. As September turns into October, the leaves start weaning from their trees. The world busies itself with new school years and youth sports and new fashion, jackets and scarves and wool socks. And we all start to become entrenched in that familiar, perpetual exhaustion. Westin Bethel feels at home in these weeks that turn breezes into winds and drizzle into frequent rain—these seasons of ups and downs, of tempests and sunrises, of floods and receding waters, that have toughened the band like jerky drying in salt and heat.

At the concert venue, the bus driver is the first to disembark, and he lights a cigarette by the door where he glances at the burial stones. He tries to keep from yawning, his grimace like even his facial expressions have bored him. When he squints, shielding his eyes from the morning sun, he scans the landscape as if trying to read the names on the gravestones but also like someone trying to translate ancient scrolls with a preference for simply getting the job done. Soon afterward, all nine band members file off the bus to their own coughs and shivers. Their lead singer calls them all to the bus's headlights, where they hook their arms together and where the *Colonel George E. Latham Cemetery* sign frames their huddle like they're all mannequins in a storefront window. Up for sale. Up for consumption.

The lead singer asks if anyone might want to lead the rest in prayer, but nobody speaks up, and the driver from across the grass says, "For fuck's sake the show's about to start," pointing to the lead car of a caravan of funeral procession vehicles just down the road. And so the lead singer volunteers himself. "Dear God," he begins, and I lose track of the remaining bit, filled, in part, with a "bless this moment" and a "we invite you in" and a "may our message carry." Their half-dim eyes, their nervous faces, are obvious, even the way the percussionists tap their hips feels like they're just trying to get through the prayer, like they're all privately hoping no one comes to see them perform. It's eight-thirty in the morning, and the briskness of the occasionally tumbling leaf lends the moment an air of dusk, an eleventh-hour vibe that, contrary to most ticking bombs, carries no threat at all.

The rock historian, Samúel Björn, speaking of the great Icelandic band The Unbloomed Flowers, once wrote, "At the twilight of a band's career, one can see the dimmed breaths around the musicians that comprise the group, an energy that barely inflates a balloon much less a stadium." Björn, of course, was referring to The Unbloomed Flowers front man Magnús Jonsson who had always believed that his band carried a hopeful message for the downtrodden. Jonsson's eagerness, however, came tied to the misconception that the Earth was flat, and though the lyrics never directly testified to his beliefs, Jonsson's anecdotes between songs regularly did.

Initially, his interactions with the audiences were testy. Shouts from the stands like "Just get to the music, science man!" and "Your balls are flat, too, bro!" invited a tension the band seemed eager to argue with. But as the years wore on, the band's schtick got old, and fans would hold up signs at shows like "Do you *even* believe you anymore?" and "What Goes Around Comes Around, morons," the latter referring both to the reality of a round world and the joke that the band's unwavering position ultimately fed into the music falling flat.

It seems that Westin Bethel, too, has arrived to such a crossroad. There was a time when Westin Bethel's front man, Pastor Reynard Pepper, felt free to go off script, just shout at the audience oddities like "Bless these liberals, lord, for they'll be frying in hell," and the audience would respond with a "Fuck off, Mr. Seasoning" and a "Get back to the music, dip shit," just as hard and just as angry. It used to be, too, that Pastor Pepper would hear clapbacks like "Go to hell, church man" and "How far deep is Jesus up inside you, bruh," whenever he scolded the audience, whenever he asked accusingly how many of them had "accepted Jesus as your lord and savior" and "You're nothing without letting him come inside you."

But things have changed for Pepper and Westin Bethel. Audiences over the past year have begun returning his antics by just holding up signs. "God don't discriminate, dude!" "You sure do love what people do in their bedrooms, bro!" "What are you hiding, church man." Even as late as February, Pastor Pepper would harangue audiences with suggestive gyrations and hand gestures to provoke them all, but no one would even offer a sigh, responding instead like pedestrians observing a hawker outside a restaurant. A head shake. A polite shrug. Walking away.

At Latham Cemetery, the band's huddle falls away, one member after the next scattering. There's a practiced kind of loneliness to their slumped shoulders, not unlike the willows and October maples slouching around us. Taking full stock of a venue means seeing even the gravel and patches of weed for what they are, bare spots of earth where the momentum drags and nothing grazes. For the music to matter, the stage landscape has to matter to the band first. They have to envision the emotional possibility of stone and mud, in the concrete and grass. Slight variations in all these can alter how audiences receive the music and so, by default, must alter the way a band delivers their sound, and the band has to recognize that their coordination begins with a true relationship to the nature of the stage.

But Westin Bethel arrives to venues now like differences in function and form don't matter. One critic, for example, has remarked upon the band's recent pre-show rehearsals, how singers move through vocal tuning more and more quickly without considering the direction of the winds, how the string instrument musicians barely pause anymore to tune their strings to account for the rustling leaves, how the brass musicians no longer grease the key levers on their horns or clean out their mouthpieces. As Kenny Hwang, long-time writer for *Tower Sounds* magazine, has said, "Any good look at a band begins with how their mannerisms reveal what they might want from each other and what they might want from the world." Hwang specifically references this April's Pittsburgh show where Pastor Pepper told everyone watching that "god hates them, yes sir" and that "god wants a man to stay a man-man," these comments sandwiched between the band's notorious "The Straights of Paradise" and their overly nuanced cover of "Amazing Grace," but the words grunted too closely to the microphone caused the speakers to blast a hiss, one that echoed across the auditorium and seemed to leave Pepper confused about the very microphone in his hands.

It used to be that Pastor Pepper could build a full-throttle spray of damnations, especially in venues like street fairs, youth basketball games, and farmer's markets. He would hit audiences with his "You're all going to hell, doobie-doo" and "The devil's got you in his throes, wabba-doo-wah!" But, as Hwang noted about the Pittsburgh show not six months ago, the band has undergone a monstrous decay of form, a hemorrhaging of energy from one show into the next as if they've been treating performances like tearing sheets off a calendar. Something that has to happen, with barely the energy to dress properly for them. The anxiety that once fueled them, the ego that once energized them, gone.

At Latham Cemetery, the bus driver unloads instruments and lines them up in rows on the grass, dust clouds kicking up like mist on a cold day. The band stands around exchanging glances, afraid, perhaps, to consider the passing time. The trombonist, the first to reach for his case, fidgets with the latch, and when it finally opens, his eyes don't so much pop as sink, as if what emerges carries the weight of the glare that meets him. The French horn player mounts his case onto his shoulder and pauses mid-stride back to his bandmates, as if skeptical about the direction forward. And when the pianist grabs his keyboard with his right hand and his keyboard stand with his left, he seems unsure about his footing, unaware, maybe, that his elbows jut like a soldier's at the precipice of an invasion, ready but scared.

It's these gestures ahead of a performance that rock and jazz theorist Lorenzo Jay once called "the somberness of anticipation," and he defines it as

> "the band's grand air of battle. In the full language of
> their posture, one can tell whether the band wants to
> be there or whether its members don't know how much
> longer they can keep getting up in the morning."

The band's faces, encumbered by the baritone of morning dew, seem to drop when the driver posts the song list on the bus window, which leads one member and then the rest to feign testing their instruments, almost nervously, the trees like a discordant accompaniment as the sounds get going. The percussionists bop their tambourine and cajón, and the choral section initiates their octaves—a humming in C major that transitions into D minor—and Pastor Pepper tells the banjoist to just get going already. Scales help musicians understand the world as a range of spectrums which, much like language, comprise qualities and quantities that bleed into each other with only subtle definitions to distinguish them. But when musicians fail to heed the messaging in the scales that train them, "That very same artist," Chilean sonic architecturalist Diyana Silva tells us,

> "fails to recognize the impact of her craft on the world, even the world's impact on her own craft, the latter of which, if she's listening, will help her recognize what is most true and most profound about her work, such that she can then approach her creative process with an explicit affinity to the spirit of the world around us, and particularly to the stories the world might be telling us about who we really are."

When a few minutes into the band's arousal of the senses, Pastor Pepper tells everyone to gather by the gravel, it's like he doesn't trust the moment's idiosyncrasy. Haphazard musical arrangement, what some call loosening your body as you refamiliarize yourself with your instrument, helps bring our intentions to the surface and to prepare to receive the music. And yet Pastor Pepper rushes his bandmates forward to just jump into their first number, "Come on now, Faithful, Come on now, Obedient Do-Gooders," as if he can't help himself but to resist, to *refuse*, collective meditation and organic musical tinkering. As if volume and quick action can keep those insecure reminders of one's fragility and vulnerability far, far away.

Westin Bethel is in that career phase where they'd prefer to lie to themselves that their history can carry over into every next performance, the animosity and rage of past shows bearing down on new ones. But the band wears more wrinkles around the lips, chalkier skin on their hands, and age is no armor against criticism, just as youth offers no balm for arrogance. Their voices, on a good day now, can barely tune to A minor or even B♭, unable at times to shift smoothly into thirds and fifths, to hit the notes of their more common lyrical obsessions, namely, *gay* in F♯, *hell* in C♯, *fire* and *flames* in D.

We certainly carry our past wherever we go, but our performative past alone doesn't inform the present. Times change, the world moves on, and audiences beg us to accept them as equals in the creative process, which points to preparation and the effort to understand, *really* understand, where you are and what you bring. As Italian musical theorist, Carlotto Duicci, remarks in *Vocal Treachery: the Animalism and Instincts of Performance,*

> "[all] musical groups must stagger onto the stage with the past and present of those songs they have made and remade *squarely on their shoulders,* like a tattoo for all to see. They must be ready, upon that grand stage, *to make visible the effort it took to work through and master their craft to the extent they have,* every next performance like a new story to share, every next show bearing the signatures of all the performances before it while at once arriving to its own unique destination. But if a musician can no longer find the key that connects the soul of their work to the soul of their times, then it's likely they no longer believe the premise with which they began—they no longer find their message essential, important, or even true."

Westin Bethel has become a ritual with no history, exposing once and for all that the nature of their persuasion might never have had any power to persuade.

The band's primary mission has always been to condemn same sex marriage, and so when the band members fan out across the road leading into Latham Cemetery, as the funeral procession slowly enters the cemetery drive, Pastor Pepper steps ahead of the others and inhales deeply, shoulders barely rising to meet the occasion.

He shakes his head as if to wake himself up, a shivering that extends to his feet, and then he raises his hand, intending more than a lazy wave but really just looking haggard. He raises his palm to try to stop the caravan of cars, and about half the band members behind Pepper steel themselves to be as unbudging, most of them juggling, to varying degrees of failure, their instruments along with some antagonizing gestures. One sign that reads "God Has Laws, Y'all" slips out of the trombonist's hand and into the mud. The French horn player has to tuck a sign reading "No Gay Man to Man" under his arm and then presses it into his waistband just to keep from doubling over into the mud.

As in earlier performances, Pastor Pepper works himself into humming their most often performed song, "No Room for Doom," as the chorus chimes in with its baritones and the soprano section works to alleviate the tension on every second beat. When the driver in the lead car exits his vehicle, Pastor Pepper slams on the hood and barks for every "Heathen menace / of hypocrisy and sinful crevice" to "March on back / March on back / oh, yeaaa-e-eahhh / to that Isle of Lost Isles / Gomorrah and God's hammer / for now and all time / oh, yeaaa-e-eahhh/ *all* time, *aaaa-aaall tiiiiiiiiiiiime.*"

But his barking feels almost forced. The action is there. The grunt is there. The facial expressions are there. But it all just feels like the specter of intention. He sighs to keep from running out of breath. His lips shiver as he sings. He takes big gulps of nothing again and again as if trying to unearth the power to pretend like he has any power at all. Even when he steps sideways away from the car, his heels drag. He can't even muster the strength to pick up his feet.

The refrain, "March on back / March on back to your backbreak crack," has always been the song's twist where monosyllables become multisyllabic, holding onto their climax until the strings culminate the melody before the next verse. But on this occasion, even the driver who'd stepped out of the lead car seems to restrain a yawn, and then he checks his watch, holding steady with a soft gaze as Pepper continues with the band's opening number. Even the older woman in the passenger seat of the car simply crosses her arms, her stare aimed at the road ahead as if the band weren't even there. An elderly couple in the backseat takes deep breaths and then raise their automatic windows, the soft buzzing of the rising panes like the static on a radio dial when one's distance to the station tower gets too far.

When the band then proceeds into its second song, Pastor Pepper steps further away from the car, carrying his harmony in G. The driver, meanwhile, looks over his suit buttons, tidies the lapel and its crease. He coughs into his fist and then nods at the cars behind him. Meanwhile, Pastor Pepper seems to be losing himself in a beat of his own choosing as the musicians behind him struggle to slow down or speed up or keep to whatever fluctuating pace Pepper's shakiness compels. After more than two minutes of what feels like concerted aggravation among band members, during which the caravan's lead driver returns to his seat, clicks on his seat belt, turns the car engine back on, Westin Bethel's percussionists seem to want to throw their hands up.

The sopranos are the first to unsurely get off the road, the baritones next to trickle off, though the band continues playing. But without the power of a swelling harmony, the remaining musicians hold whatever rhythm the winds dictate, looking like lost seagulls when no one throws them food.

Music critic Joanne Gaye once defined "a band's last grasp, in her collected interviews *Reaching for a National Sound*, as any

> "last-ditch attempt to recreate some kind of encore, or at least to distinguish some end only they have seen and felt, and it publicly steeps the group in some dazed and confused morality, a brutal unveiling of just how far their creativity has gone bloated with ego."

In other words, without a narrative of grace, primarily for oneself and for the limited nature of simply being human, a band risks believing itself the arbiters of all content, of all craft, perhaps as a defense mechanism against the awareness of their own futility. As psychoanalyst Gregor Brumman wrote in *Grace and the Psychopathy of the Empty Tin Can* (1972),

> "perhaps the greatest fear of all performers is that audiences forget them, that audiences themselves become objects of fear—that understanding the mass before them, and therefore comfortably performing for them, becomes easier when they feel like audience members are all the same, every listener desiring the same thing."

On this October 15th, the funeral procession is here to bury First Lieutenant Deshaun Lorenzo Peaux and Lieutenant Junior Andrés Romario Gonzalo, and the caravan begins to move again when the Minister at the top of the hill waves at them to continue their drive to him. The Minister, waiting approximately a click away from the gate, by the ceremony's setup and seats, points to the parking spaces near him. The lead driver keeps his hand on the car horn, perhaps as a just-in-case gesture, but restrains himself from honking at Pastor Pepper as the lead singer finally steps off the road. Remaining members of Westin Bethel follow suit and move aside, and no one from the caravan lowers their windows or so much as bats an eye at the band. For this performance, the band doesn't even get to intermission before its audience cuts them off with inattention, with the staying power of silence. After all, the band is only noise now, and on this afternoon, the more important remembrance is that of one man and one man, who had once been engaged, having served their country simultaneously abroad, but who are now being laid to rest, their bodies lying in caskets near the top of the hill overlooking the cemetery plot.

As with us all, these men once had a birth and a life, and now at the end of it all, they are being celebrated for how much they have been loved as much for how much they loved, commemorated by friends, families, and acquaintances, many of whom file out of their vehicles after parking as close to the couple's burial grounds as they can. The road, itself like a recently traced desert road, gleams with fresh gravel. The mud, pushed to the side, might inevitably return to the road. It will take months to do so.

It's impossible to distinguish the couple's parents from the rest of the elders who congregate around the flowers set up on easels by the caskets. Between the wreaths sits a table of small portraits of Peaux and Gonzalo, pictures of them individually and of them together, smiling into the camera or looking off into the distance. Their expressions range from playful to thoughtful, somber to happy. The photographs sit arranged from left to right spanning decades, from childhood into semi-formed adulthood, from an individual story into the narrative of a shared love, a continuity that illustrates how we navigate from self-awareness into a story that overlaps with and complements someone else's, a story now woven into a relationship no more fragile and no more flawed than anyone else's. The soldiers' names hang printed on banners clinging to trees that feel almost rooted for the purpose, the landscape lending the men's lives a kind of symmetrical language.

As a means of firmly centering their final experience, each veteran's military portrait sits on the ground leaning against their respective caskets, lower than eye level. Their lives of service, in the end, have become a footnote in a life of discovery and affection. Westin Bethel's insistence, therefore, to foreground these men's sexuality and military deaths in their music contradicts the couple's expressions in every posted photograph, their prime etched into eternity and standing just feet from their permanent place in the earth. Their portraits will later be buried with them, recollections of a life returned to the earth that inevitably hold onto the memories of us all like a parent welcoming a child home.

When later in the day I interview the Minister, she tells me that upon receiving the family's request to officiate the funeral service, she'd believed, and warned the family as much, that Westin Bethel would likely be making an appearance, some of the band's shows, the Minister tells me, springing up like weeds after heavy rain. As a result, the Minister has set up her makeshift altar to the left of the caskets, preferring to decenter herself in her own performances, but near enough to the road that she could step between the band and the family should the moment arrive. The Minister had also instructed the funeral director to slant the chairs so the guests' gaze would face the caskets, the road out of view entirely should the guests need it to be. "This would not necessarily have guaranteed tranquility," Minister Saralee Ulloa says. "But having experience with bands of the sort in my own musical past, I know the type. I know the hype they arrive with and the energy that drives them."

Minister Ulloa used to be in a band herself, with an entirely distinct modus operandi, called Jericho's Wall. At first, she says, they didn't carry any particular mission beyond the craft of making music and the melodies that funnel thoughts into verse. But as industry trends steered the group into a more popular bias, "like musicians back in the day embracing flannel even when flannel did not suit them," she muses, she found herself increasingly at odds with her old band's lead singer and co-founder. He might not have been any kind of Pastor Pepper, but Minister Ulloa explicitly recalls a moment where Jericho's Wall's co-founder challenged the other original members to decide what social issue they could muster an argument for, what they could build their music around, what they could position themselves at the center of. "As if the world needed yet another band to be critical of a world that might have started to finally feel a little more interconnected," she says.

The ensuing debates amongst Jericho's Wall's band members about whether that position would be anti-communist or anti-abortionist, anti-climate or anti-PETA, seemed to distract, in Minister Ulloa's mind, from the core principle of any art, "which is to be a space of radical generosity and welcome, a true and beautiful funnel for patience and grace."

"But there was no budging the band from this adopted approach, not with our lead singer being so adamant about adopting something to argue for at the exclusion of all else, everyone else," she says. And so Minister Ulloa ventured out on her own before disillusion got the best of her creative process.

Her solo musical career offered its turbulence, too, however. A solo artist, for example, has a smaller network of producers and collaborators with which to write songs, with which to produce and master recordings. A solo musician also can't split the costs of touring the way a band can, having to muster sometimes two or three simultaneous jobs just to earn the means to make and exhibit her work. And being a woman in the industry comes with its own unmistakable complications, not the least of which is having to work twice as hard to be taken seriously. For example, when passing her demo around, she was second-guessed by a number of people about why she isn't in a band, why she didn't defend this or that point of view, why she didn't wear doctrinal positions on her sleeve like an ugly tattoo.

The trade-offs, however, have also been unmistakable. She alone chooses who she opens for, the venues she plays in, the festivals she joins. She can also take as long as she needs in her process, allowing for "the spirit," as she understands it, to work its way into her songwriting, her production, her shows.

And, yet, despite her insistence at independence, she still keeps a regular slot in her calendar for studio time with members of Jericho's Wall, or any other musicians or bands, for that matter, that she feels inspired to join.

> "I'll schedule regular studio time with everyone, to visit with them, see how they're doing, see for myself how much I've changed, how much I haven't, how far I've yet to go, and to generally see where everybody's hearts might be, what pain their souls might be holding on to. I'll always leave that place in my heart open to them, not because I don't believe I can't make it on my own. I can. I have. But because I like that check-in. Maybe we can build into some kind of magic still. Maybe, too, we'll never get there together. I keep back and nothing's really changed since I went on my own. Some of the band still want to feel nostalgic for some musical recipe that we never had. Some don't speak up to fact check everyone else when conversations and stubbornness get the best of some of us in the studio. And, yeah, every time I spend time with them, I feel a little bit alone in their company, not because I'm any voice of reason. I'm not. I can't pretend to harbor some truth about the world that no one else has ever arrived to. I voice what I think I'm seeing, what I think can be true, and then just try to listen, however imperfectly. And I'll always be coming back to check in on everyone, even if it means carving a weekly time to do so. But I'll always go back out on my own if it's not working. I'm not going to romanticize a story that just isn't there if it isn't."

At Latham Cemetery, once the family, relatives, and friends of First Lieutenant Peaux and Lieutenant Junior Gonzalo have taken their seats, Minister Ulloa announces the title of her first song, "To the Courage of Binding Love for Self and Others," an airy number that begins with muted guitar strumming and then transitions into explicit beat-making on the pickguard to accompany her gravely falsetto. When Minister Ulloa starts singing, there's a timbre to her voice at once earnest and operatic. To tall it folksy would be limiting. To call it pop-rock would feel incomplete. The catchiest verse, the one that begins "There was a time when the word and the breath did meet" and ends with "And where does that leave us but to measure the tremor beneath our feet," transitions into an instrumental bridge in which her humming echoes hauntingly between the trees, at once encircling the proceedings in a warmth I don't think I initially expected, the melancholy in her lyrics like a familiar embrace that inevitably shares something with us without telling us what to do or what to feel about it.

Her intention, in the brief set she has, is to frame the moment. As with all matters of respect and reverence, Minister Ulloa addresses the soldiers by their complete names, an improvised chant during her first outro that embraces their correct pronunciations, as well as an announcement of their birth dates and their deceased dates, as if days, months, and years were more than just gifts from the reverberations that bind us but also proof that it's time itself that names us, that testifies to who we've been and to the people we might have become.

As with all things about the war they fought, Minister Ulloa does not mention its particulars, its ends or its means, the geographies of its impact or how many years, how so very many years, it has taken from us as a nation. Instead, the minister waxes poetic about the moods she discerns in the pictures of Peaux and Gonzalo, the love in their faces, the joy in their smiles and the mountains of energy that continue to bear fruit.

Westin Bethel follows the caravan only as far as approximately a hundred yards away, stopping, it appears, when Minister Ulloa completes her third and final song and looks up to find them there, at a distance and hesitant to come any closer. I don't think she knowingly raised her gaze to meet theirs, only that eye contact, firm and poised and aware of itself, can halt an army.

After the reverberation of her strings fades, Minister Ulloa puts her guitar on its stand and asks everyone to bow their heads in prayer, all the while maintaining eye contact with Pastor Pepper. She seems to glare at him in the silence, a breeze like a lion with no need to argue. Reason, at its purest, is indistinguishable from compassion, and though Ulloa and Pepper may be cut from similar cloths, their visions of history do not overlap. You could say one of their perspectives feels like a betrayal of the other, and the other like a warning, a "Do Not Enter" sign, that doesn't need volume to carry a melody. Minister Ulloa tells me later that in the story of the prodigal son, no one ever pays attention to the lessons learned by studying the brother who stayed, the one who gets angry when the lost brother returns from his bout of loneliness, having preferred a life lived apart—that no one pays attention to the supposedly good brother, the rule-following one, who, in the end, prefers to stay outside the party rather than the celebrate the return of his brother, choosing to stew alone.

"That's what happens to people so insistent on following real and perceived rules," says Minister Ulloa. "They prefer to keep a private hell for themselves rather than relinquish an inch of their pride to anyone who learns what genuine love might mean in practice, or at least a different kind of practice, and what love looks like in the face of, and in spite of, all those real and perceived rules."

When she begins her prayer, Minister Ulloa shuts her eyes and gets into the portions of your average Christian prayer, stuff like "Bless this moment" and "We invite you in" and "May our message carry." Except that Minister Ulloa's words do not reference some apocalypse or sexuality, and she makes no explicit mention of genitals or how any variety of person might enjoy another's intimate presence in the world. She also does not pause to single anyone out or steer anyone to antagonize anyone else. Instead, she carries a much more beautiful melody, words that articulate a longing and a deep sort of love in *this* life, and her song rings in the kind of language that speaks of memories that draw us together, that offer a clear path to each other.

She considers the soul of her god, the spirit that joins us in the here and now, in this space between two pillars that upholds the history of all our names. When she concludes, before she invites the parents of both men to center stage, she asks every guest to look upon the sun, to consider its warmth, its heat, its ability to touch us despite the distance. She says that sometimes just looking up reminds her of a narrative longer than time, of a story larger than the obstacles imposed upon the living and the dead. And then Minister Ulloa starts humming, talking about a life that once made cannot be erased, to which the men's families respond with a "Hear, hear." Minister Ulloa sings for everyone about the power of redemption that halts the floods and helps us cry those healing cries that we all need from time to time, and the men's families respond with an "Amen." And when Minister Ulloa ends her ad hoc arousal of the senses, her improvised moment of spirit, she asks us all to breathe, deeply, and everyone responds almost in unison, inhaling with an echo like a storm making landfall and then exhaling with the calm of ebbs returning to the ocean, with a peace knowing that the work of eternity, as all work should be, is ours to shoulder together.

A
S U
U M M
E R S L Y
N C H I N G

A Summer's Lynching

"A crowd isn't interested in fine points of authorship.
A crowd has no intellect, only passions."

—J. M. Coetzee, *The Master of Petersburg*

"Draw the city: dark and dense, a knot that can't be untied."

—Daniel Alarcón, *Lost City Radio*

"It seemed to us that the buildings were about to melt in the
flame of that weird day. It was a day of pestilential moonlight, a
day of upheavals, a day of gunfire, a day of suicide, a day of death,
a day of collapse, a day of rejection, and a day to end all days."

—Muhammad Khudayyir, *Basrayatha*

LOOP ONE: THE CITY

When a story is retold, hues lighten. Shades darken. Words become an amalgamation of things that should have happened. When a story is retold, people become larger than the places they've been, and unexpected shouts become intentional screams until no one remembers who it was that covered their ears first. Such is the case with this story.

Where it happened is not important. Suffice to say it happened and that it happened somewhere you know. After all, it most certainly happened in a place on Earth where highways bleed congestion and hospitals are rooted in mud and neighbors insist that they've consoled each other, mothers and fathers and the childless, alike, until the very next day when, without irony, everyone shuts their doors upon hearing someone in tears.

Who this story is about is also unimportant. Suffice to say that it's about these people here. Suffice to say that it might also be about you. About what you think of these people and how they scamper when the sun goes down and how they mistake windows for the portraits they encase and how, most importantly, you feel when they forget your name, when they forget your story, and when they take both name and story to test the old adage *Should you dare appropriate someone's story, you may as well erase them*. It's what people do, after all, and it's what I will do.

Who tells this story is also unimportant. But because you must know, because too many of us will keep from turning the page if they don't find a face in which to place the voice of the unwavering sun, I have to grant you at least some clarity. To be certain, *I* will tell this story. To be certain, everyone here will be telling it, too. I am them, I am *all* of them, and I will tell it the way they told each other and then told me so that I can tell you. There are many of them, and so there will be many of me. I will judge them because they have judged each other, and I will stand above them because they have overwhelmed each other. After all, there will always be places on Earth where elevated things happen, where things we don't understand will unfold and upset us, where things unearth and where names rise and fall and where few people will even call each other by their proper names, where voices sprinkle across pavement and seep into cracks, and where stories are codified in the song of humming air conditioning vents and whistling manhole covers, flooded gutters and freshly opened soda cans, aging Camaros and nagging door bells, store-light gnats and encaged dogs, pigeons smothering pavement with their shadow-selves and ten-year-olds littering sidewalks, and near endless repair projects that just feign renovations of a city without ever improving it.

There will always be places on Earth where something happens that feels like nothing and where nothing happens that feels like everything. And so this story will ebb and flow and ebb and flow and ebb and flow again. You'll see the story, and then you'll see it repeat, but keep yourself at a healthy distance from these people and you'll experience a flat ride. No. You're going to have to get into the stairwell, feel the aging walls there, the chipped windows, the rusty banisters, all of which threaten to keep us encaged if no one among you braves the day with us, braves the foul musty air in the basement with us.

LOOP TWO: THE BOILER ROOM

Old Lady Echohawk was the first to open the boiler room door and find Isidrio Rafael hanging by a noose from a plumbing pipe in the basement. She saw his face, his cold lips, and her hands quivered. She walked behind him, almost touched him. She circled him and snapped her hand back when she realized his arms weren't just pretending to hang without a sway. She moaned into her fist, to keep from coughing, to keep from falling, and then she rubbed her eyes, and she backed away cupping her nose, the stench obvious, finally, from the stain down the back of his pants. The man's posthumous defecation ridden down to his calves, his ankles.

Bearing first witness all but broke her. She hobbled out of the basement where we saw her stumble down the sidewalk and into the building. Dazed, she tugged almost savagely at the old metal banister up the steps to the building's second entrance. At the top of the stairs, she fell back against the cold foyer door. She turned, confused, to the plate of apartment buzzers, her sight a blur as she searched for her buzzer, the twelfth. But she ended up pressing wrong one after wrong one, her nose and lips against the plate, trying their best to read number and silence, and with each press of an apartment buzzer, Old Lady Echohawk moaned into the intercom, Hello Georgia, and when no one responded, she hollered, *Hello* Georgia, and when she feared herself too loud, she whispered and then gasped into the intercom, The dead are a *mess* Georgia. She kept buzzing wrong buzzer after wrong one until finally someone, the wrong someone, replied, Who is this, The dead are dying

Georgia, Who is this, Do I have the wrong number, I demand to know who this is, Oh Georgia I've buzzed the wrong one.

Old Lady Echohawk all but grazed the whole wall, pressing six and then seven mistaken buttons, and she kept on and on with desperations that interrupted family meals, talking, panting, about the sight of a young man and his wrung neck and the military uniform that wore him like a closet hanger. Even when no one responded on the intercom, she rattled on about the ribbons and medals that had hung from his collar but which had slipped and fallen to the floor by the time she'd opened the boiler room door. And when finally she pressed buzzer twelve, the fifth buzzer down the second column from the left, that familiar flat melody echoed through intercom static, Mother, Georgia, Mother is that you, Georgia the boys are crying in the lot, Mother what's wrong, Georgia, Mother what's happened, Georgia the heat is a disease, Mother I'm buzzing you in, The news Georgia the news, Mother slow down, The basement is swamped in flies Georgia and a man just hung there like a buffalo hunted down for sport and a picture.

The paramedics arrived shortly after six o'clock and, by then, Old Lady Echohawk had been replaced in the basement by all of us as we were, clueless about the happenstance of hanging men. Everyone shuffled about, the cement floors of the basement hallway riddled with chipping paint bits, the basement ceiling a maze of pipes and conduits and broken red and yellow wires. We stood beneath and inside an anatomy of unnerving reins and toiled-over cords that, if nothing else, served as incontrovertible proof that municipal property safety inspectors had visited the building and were either careless with their concerns or downright truant in their professional responsibilities.

Paramedics on scene had been told nothing, more mystery than medical fact, dispatch leaving uncertain, for example, whether or not there were dead on site. All they were told was the location, a building on the corner of Mystic and Pyre, two blocks south of The Avenue of Innuendos. Upon arrival, they lifted Isidrio Rafael off the noose, pushed his face through the loop, pressed his chin and nose off the rope, and then laid him flat on the concrete floor, his body as thick, as distressing, as a crack running through the foundation of the building.

On scene, the paramedics really only required a proclamation of death. But because due course has always been our most elusive thief, they had to follow procedure. They attempted to restart the man's heart because one of them had noticed upon inspection his lukewarm wrists. The paramedics did what they had to as quickly as they could do, and after they pressed the electromagnetic conductors to either side of Isidrio's rib cage, they set hand towels across their shoulders and steadied their arms.

Too many of us crowded the boiler room archway entrance, pressing into each other to see the man's face, his ankles, his feet, all those portions of a person that run gray when the last of all ends arrives. But the paramedics pulled his hemming low and his sleeves over his knuckles, flipped his collar up to shield neck and chin and jaw, concealing one piece at a time from us as if we, *we*, had arrived to claw something from *him*. The paramedics circled the man, walking to this side of his body and then the other, following protocol to charge the battery which, as with all things, only needed time to get fired up. One paramedic knelt and pulled up Isidrio's shirt, revealing, because he had to, the lumps at his chest, the bruises at his ribs, the cuts at his side. The second paramedic tuned a dial on the battery and pressed several buttons until a hum rose, Everyone stand back. An electrode pad into Isidrio's chest and another into his hip, his body jumped, pumping twice midair and in one concerted motion.

Isidrio's body returned to its lame sprawl, and the first paramedic slapped Isidrio's chest, and then he arched Isidrio's neck and then he hunched over him, breathed into his mouth fifteen times. Exhausted after the last wind, he laid Isidrio's head down and wiped his own chin dry and then announced to the waiting audience standing rapt for explanations, for definitions, for a reason for why the man's scars seemed so heavy and why they seemed pour out of him, Ladies and gentlemen, said the paramedic, This man is dead.

Murmurs followed. Paces agitated. Old Lady Echohawk, who'd returned to the basement with her grandson, asked the boy to turn and push his way out, And hold me Oliver don't you dare not hold me.

They managed their way through the basement hallway, haze smothering their faces. Her wheezing restrained a frustration that almost coughed over all of us, until she was able to find an open space under the light, her lungs unloading a hock of phlegm, age and awful things going hand in hand like gasoline and a match. In tandem, Old Lady Echohawk and her grandson pushed past shoes and crevices in the concrete, the young man holding his grandmother's elbow, pulling her by the wrist, You shouldn't have wanted to come back anymore, Oliver I needed to show you, You can't complain about the smell and then return to the smell grandmother, Summer is what it is grandson, Please don't waste your energy grandmother, A time for us all to heave our heaviest sighs.

Down the hall and through two more thresholds, the basement door opened onto the sidewalk. Old Lady Echohawk and Oliver pushed through the crowd. They marched into the building front doors and upstairs and into the foyer, past the secondary entrance held unlocked for everyone coming in and out. Oliver kicked aside leaflets and misaddressed envelopes scattered by the mad rush to the basement, a whirlwind hour when stacked telephone books and coupon booklets in the lobby turned to shreds. Coupled with the walls that stood red and peeling, everything looked like the regurgitated remains of a parade.

Four stories up, his feet fell like anchors when Oliver unlocked the apartment door, and everything that Old Lady Echohawk had considered at each step up spilled out of her like an involuntary slap, Everyone in this awful building just killed a man.

Georgia, who'd met her mother and son at the door, grabbed her mother's arm as the old woman leaned, and then Georgia told them both that she just got off the phone with the police, and they have to stay out of the lobby for their own peace of mind, That basement door should have been chained Georgia, This awful thing would have happened all the same mother, People fray and people die Georgia, All I'm saying mother is that people will always do what they're committed to do.

Old Lady Echohawk walked ahead and into the bathroom, and Oliver shut the front door behind them, locked it in three places, including a peg he stepped on and pushed into the floor.

Georgia led her mother to the kitchen sink to wash her hands and then walked her to the kitchen window, to the flowery soft loveseat she goes to at least twice a day, after dinner and after the memory of a heart ache. The chair had never been one to sway, but the tension in the old woman's eyes shone like it could shake the room. Georgia had taken a rag from the sink to give to her mother, as if control were just a matter of cleanliness when the world took to spinning, but Old Lady Echohawk had to be prompted to taking it, Georgia ultimately stuffing the rag into her mother's hands as the old woman looked lost like the wind banging bricks to escape the alley outside the window.

Oliver brought his grandmother a glass of water, which he settled on the sill by her knees. He brushed her shoulders as he left, walking up to the living room threshold to find his place in the sight between rooms, What's wrong

Oliver, Sunset is coloring the floor mother, Go back to your own apartment Oliver, I'm not leaving either of you, We'll be okay Oliver.

Patience accompanied the coffee table, couches and pictures all pushed to one side of the television shelf. Oliver glanced at the open window that faced the street, the brushing cars, the swirling air, the evening heat that echoed a commotion all too familiar but which no one had expected to multiply, Were you able to tell everyone to leave at least, The paramedics were making a show of it when we left mother, This city confines people Georgia, I'm aware of your fears mother, I want you to get out of this city Oliver before you can't, Yes grandmother.

Old Lady Echohawk tried to swivel in the seat, but it didn't budge, This thing is broken Georgia, How many times have I told you that it isn't a rocking chair mother.

The old woman made to stand, a slow thing, planting her feet on the floor and then pushing herself up, Please mother, I hate to sit at a time like this Georgia, Did nobody listen to you when you told them to leave Oliver, I'm only the landlord's son mother I'm not the landlord.

Georgia reached over to the window to bring it down, to almost shut it to keep her mother from stumbling to her end.

At the refrigerator door, Georgia tried to convince her mother to eat, but the old woman refused, Had you never had a conversation with the man Georgia, I collect rent mother and I pay the mortgage on the building, Your father did not teach you to be absentminded Georgia, My father also refused to sell the building when it was actually worth something, We have land Georgia we have property and we have our values, And I had my own life before having to move back here to tend to it all mother, You were also divorced Georgia, And making a living for myself and Oliver just fine, And what ancestor before you could say that they had a life *and* a deed they could be proud of Georgia, This is not the time for that kind of conversation mother.

Oliver, at nineteen, seemed to know enough to keep himself accessible to the living room and foyer, to the bathroom and the first aid kit in the pantry, halfway between his mother's apartment's front door and her bedroom windows where the world of a building's worries confronted the world clawing to know what it feels like to have seen a dead man come and go, I saw a the boy Georgia, He won't be anyone's problem anymore mother, That isn't the point Georgia, What do you think we should do next Oliver, I don't know, Maybe go into the man's apartment before the police do, Don't you dare interrupt the history of things Georgia, The police have their procedures mother and I'm going to have to let them in at some point, And so rightfully we should have our own procedures don't you think our own process and our own uncrossable lines, If it's not in the rental agreement mother then it's meaningless and I can't keep out the law, That's who we are then isn't it, Please stop it with the morality mother, Nothing but new colonizers to replace the old colonizers.

Georgia sighed over the sink, a new rag in hand. She slapped it against the ceramic and left it in the basin, and then she grabbed a cup and opened the tap, and after she had a big gulp of water, she turned around to meet her mother and son, as well as herself, in their accumulating questions of what business to attend to next, never addressing, of course, that in the account of one's life, we can also live and die by choosing to let the world take its own course without us imposing, without us having to imagine that anything around us needs us at all, You didn't you see what I saw Georgia, What you both witnessed was enough for me mother, The man's suit was ironed and it was pressed and it was clean Georgia, You've already told us all about his military garb mother, And for what Georgia, That's a question only you can answer, Because it's important to acknowledge that what we die in is how we want to be remembered.

Old Lady Echohawk nodded, like an addiction she couldn't kick, as if always looking to punctuate everything she said before and after she said it because she didn't trust herself, because who would, to always have all the right words and all the right explanations that combined them all into a story people could trust, You should be ashamed Georgia, I understand where you're coming from mother but this is not the time, We should *all* be ashamed Georgia, Oliver do you know who we can ask to help us sort through the man's things before the police ask to. Oliver, however, was transfixed by his grandmother, his gaze lost in her mumbling descriptions of the young man's jawline, his handsome eyes, his hanging lips that might have once smiled like a banner clinging to the rafters, He could have been a man of passion Georgia, Oliver did you hear me, Or a man full of shame Georgia, Oliver, Or a man whose story broke him because he could never escape the memory of the passions that drive us to war and then drive us to shame Georgia.

Old Lady Echohawk looked up at her daughter, and then she started fidgeting with her fingernails, Not everyone has the privilege to live a life for something that isn't their own survival Georgia, and then the old woman turned to feigning to pick her fingernails clean, I don't have to answer that mother, This was our fault too Georgia, Don't do that mother, Do what Georgia raise an important question, You're framing the question like you're interrogating the intention to doubt it, Well I don't think people are who they are or do what they do without a whole world around them to compel them to be and do it, You're complicating something that isn't about us mother, I'm declaring our affinity for humanity Georgia, You're making this about you and me mother when it has nothing to do with you and me.

The old woman sighed over the window, her breath fogging the pane over the handle, her breath carrying into the alley as if demons could be expelled from us with just nudge and not, as in most cases, by sacrificing the best of us, I didn't raise you to be pitiless Georgia, Why are we arguing mother, Because you refuse to know the story of a man you never knew, And that is my right mother, Who are we if not each other's anchors Georgia, Mother the man was a veteran and he had likely seen and done things none of us could have healed from or been healed by, Then hate him Georgia, I don't hate him mother, Well if you don't love him then there's no in-between Georgia, That's ridiculous mother, We don't just raise our heroes to watch them die Georgia, In this country we do precisely that mother we convince each other that we can be anything we want to be and then we actively keep each other from being any of it.

Old Lady Echohawk pursed her lips, scratched and adjusted them as if molding a smile and then letting it go, her sneer watching itself in the window as if measuring what words she could trust and what words she couldn't, When I was young Georgia I don't know that we would have treated a neighbor like this, Don't do that mother don't glamorize your pretentions about the past, It's true Georgia, The only difference between your childhood and Oliver's is that we all lived the same complications but you all denied they were even there, Men who went to war used to have purpose Georgia and they used to have hope, War is a hopeless thing mother and something we're all tired of fighting, Men were men Georgia and they never brought the war back home, My father brought everything back with him mother, Leave your father out of this, My father hung some kind of flag in every room just to tell us what we should be thankful for even as he mumbled in his sleep every obscenity of what he needed to be forgiven for, Your father needed meaning Georgia, And you once said he once tried to kill himself with his own belt, But he failed Georgia and he healed Georgia and I helped him Georgia I didn't just let him go, He drank himself into liver failure mother, You just don't understand Georgia, I do mother, Imagine Georgia tying your soul to intentions and stories and nations and nothing, I understand that whatever guilt you're processing mother is only partially to do with the man downstairs.

The old woman's voice cracked as if trying to get another word in, but she kept her lips still and she straightened her back, The man couldn't have been older than Oliver Georgia, He probably wasn't mother, His suit was clean Georgia pressed and ironed, So he probably wanted to leave an impression didn't he mother, I don't know that anyone knew him Georgia, Loneliness has this awful way of keeping us all apart mother, Men in uniform deserve our respect Georgia, But they do not own my reverence mother, You're mincing hairs Georgia, I'm being honest mother.

Georgia glanced and nodded at Oliver, and immediately the boy left for her bedroom, for her closet, as if having already exchanged glances and instructions, what to do and what could be happening in a building they never had any control of, they were both tired of the silence and resigned to the process, to the fact that it was them, and only them, mother and son, who retained the responsibility, after all was said and done, to make the decisions that could clean up a mess and, if they weren't careful, the decisions that staged an opportunity for any mess to unfold in the first place, Why do we always do this to each other Georgia, You were never the reason my father drank himself senseless mother, I could have helped more, My father hung himself by a noose of a different kind and it wasn't your fault, You don't know anything Georgia, I know everything you've ever told me mother and what you've told me has been a lot, So it's my fault now that I've always needed someone to talk to, None of it was your fault, You don't know *anything* Georgia, Every man's story is his own story to share or keep to himself mother and my father didn't choose to share much of it with anyone, Leave it alone Georgia, I would if I could but you've never let me and it's always just been us mother, It's always just been me Georgia, It's been *us* mother, I'm tired Georgia, I know you are mother.

Imposed narratives can feel like half a nightmare, the half of it embodied by congestion and movement, by the feeling that even with a kitchen table and a cabinet where the microwave took up all the space, everyone always sat or stood anywhere else, even by the fridge that encroached into the walkway between foyer and living room, even by the oven that could never warn you when it stood too hot to touch.

The night had become a spectacle, a conversation of few options and even fewer ways to navigate the tension, and all because the end of all things will loosen the senses and never repair them, remind us we live in cities with painful constrictions and isolating, cramped spaces, silences so overwhelming that they will never know how to welcome us home.

Old Lady Echohawk crossed her arms and leaned back in the chair. She slouched. She sighed. And when Oliver called from the bedroom, about having grabbed towels and sheets, a pillow and a hat, she looked up at Georgia as if pleading for someone to raise the volume of her voice, even if, after her gazed dipped back to the window, she really didn't want anything more to say. Oliver said, too, that all he could think to reach for were the things that could help with dust and footsteps, help to mask whatever people might do in the man's apartment, But is there anything else I haven't thought of, There's nothing Oliver, What's that mother, There's nothing Oliver.

When Oliver returned to the kitchen, a bag slung over his shoulders and towels under his arms, his mother handed him a box of crackers, You haven't had any dinner tonight, It's barely night mother, What's that supposed to mean, There's still time to fill up, Be careful you don't give the rumors down there any more legs than they already have Oliver, I can't imagine they don't already have wings to fly mother, Just don't encourage anymore hearsay. He nodded, and then he left the kitchen, the bustling and commotion in the building coming into the apartment as soon as he opened the front door.

Old Lady Echohawk scowled at the pigeons that lingered on a wire outside the window, and then for the first time that evening, she let her eyes slump, let her stare turn soft, let her cheekbones rest. She closed her eyes and said, That poor boy dangled like a joke with its eyes shut Georgia, I wish you hadn't been the first one downstairs mother, and then Georgia came over to her mother and rested her hands on her shoulder, Someone always seems to be sacrificed in times like these Georgia.

The landlord, peering over her mother at the darkened alley walls, rested her forehead on her mother's head and ran her hands down her mother's arms. In kind, Old Lady Echohawk buried her fingers in her daughter's hair, grazing the top and sides of it like a consolation for being made to live in times such as these. Times like now and always. Times with no forgiveness.

LOOP THREE: THE APARTMENT

When we stare at the faces that have fallen around us, we stare into the houses no one saw crumbling until they become a disaster. Until they become a stench. Sometimes we move toward each other in this life. Sometimes we only help each other when we lose our ability to touch, when there's no opportunity anymore to meet anyone's eyes. It's these moments when it's easy to dig into each other's past, if only to pretend we can measure how high and deep the damage has always been.

When the knock came at apartment four, the four Brothers Valdez living inside roamed to the door. They'd been leaning that evening at their windowsill overlooking the street. Staring at the sudden wash of headlights and sirens, at the sudden congestion of murmurs and hawkers selling ice cream and drivers trying to bust open the traffic.

The Oldest Brother swung open the door and the others huddled up behind him. The Shortest Brother looked almost bored in the hallway light that streamed into the foyer. The Tallest Brother rubbed his eyes as if trying to stay awake. The Youngest got onto his toes to lean over everyone to get a look at who was at the door. And all four seemed both too calm and too prepared, as if they'd already accepted the call for volunteers to go into the dead man's apartment even before it came. And then it did, from the Near Stranger at the door, a young man they'd occasionally see when they each came home from work, a young man they'd sometimes nod at or sometimes wave to but had never shared a word with.

And the call seemed clear enough, at least at first listen, My mother and I need someone to go through the dead man's door and see what there is to see.

All four Brothers Valdez threw up their hands before it was even clear what they had to be looking for, and so the Near Stranger said, You can put your hands down, and the Oldest Brother asked why, and the Near Stranger in the doorway said, Because I'm not asking which of you want to go, Then what are you asking, I'm asking *all* of you to go.

The Oldest Brother started with his nod, then the Shortest Brother, and then the rest. All four Brothers Valdez seemed to know that they knew where the dead man's apartment was, but the Near Stranger needed to confirm anyway, Do you remember where you last saw him go into, We don't remember so much as know, What is that supposed to mean, The apartment above ours seems to have been quiet all night, And—, And it's the only part of the building that doesn't seem to be moving.

The Near Stranger nodded, as if assuring them, as if approving of them, but with a tilt to his face, a tilt that suspected that the four Brothers Valdez, the same as every conversation swirling that evening, seemed to have arrived at their conclusions by hear nothing and seeing nothing, that is, by just assuming that doing nothing meant a scene had to have happened, a crime had to have been committed, if only because neglect had become its own reason to believe that the worst of things was afoot, the worst of all things had come and gone.

Lost in so many thoughts, especially the *why*s and *how*s of what to tell the Brothers Valdez and why it mattered to say it, the Near Stranger snapped out of it by snapping his fingers, which also seemed to bring the Brothers Valdez alive again, and then the Near Stranger turned over what he had in his hands. A blanket and a sheet. A towel and a flashlight. But the Near Stranger offered no action steps, which did not stop the Youngest Brother from saying, We accept the responsibility willfully sir, to which the Near Stranger said, Just clean up the apartment and see what you see, to which the Oldest Brothers said, We'll open every door we see sir, Discreetly please, and then the Shortest Brother said, I'd like to close them all back sir, Discreetly please, and then the Youngest Brother said, I don't know that we'll stay that long sir, As long as you leave discreetly please so I hope you're starting to get the point.

The Near Stranger offered the Brothers Valdez a broom and a dust pan, too, as well as a screwdriver, a paper towel roll, and a spray bottle, and when the Shortest Brother asked if what they had was enough, the Near Stranger said, I'm giving you quite a lot, Which suggests that there's a lot we'll have to do, Just don't be so eager to do it, We promise not to move as much as a mouse per your instructions, And don't be too eager to do even that, So then you want us to do something between nothing and less, Just remember to keep an eye out for something or other about why the man did this, And it's too upsetting, Answers are answers my friends, But what if he didn't do this alone sir.

The Near Stranger, arrested by the question, exhaled in the doorway, like he could have provoked thunder if egged on. Honking on the street leaked into the lobby and crawled up the stairs, and it seemed like everybody wanted everybody else out of the way, Why would you think he didn't do this alone, Why does anyone do anything alone sir, I'm not asking you to dig through his stuff to erase his privacy, But opening his door is the invasion that spells it all out, Just keep your eyes open, Should we be looking for labels sir, Please stop calling me sir, Labels always suggest important things and small boxes always suggest something valuable, I trust you to tell nobody but me anything when you get out of there, So you want us to keep secrets, I want you to know what it means to protect a good man's soul.

The instructions seemed like broad appeals to scour floors, inspect walls, graze and measure surfaces, scan corners and check for absences, and who knows what else. When nothing else has a language to describe the next step up, the next step up might as well be a complete erasure of everything seen and unseen, the kind of fray nobody wants any part of.

They all looked at each other, which seemed to worry the Near Stranger, so he avoided eye contact and scanned the Brothers Valdez's foyer for signs that he should leave, for signs that anything else would have just complicated the next look between them. And the Brothers Valdez watched the Near Stranger scanning everything and them, a kind of stalemate that almost ridiculed the nothing between them, seeing as so much, so very much, can be shouted under a silence when the silence itself feels only temporary. The Near Stranger seemed to take this very stale mate as the invitation he needed, so he started to turn away, but then he looked over his shoulder like he didn't believe anything, especially the ends of things, could arrive so easily without interruptions, I'm trusting you all, We'll do our best sir, The whole building is trusting you, As long as there's nothing more specific we need to know, You have your instincts, Which means what sir, Intuition helps to make everything particular doesn't it.

The Oldest Brother coughed as if to speak up, but the Near Stranger had to explicitly invite him to say it, What more do you need, We don't have a map of his apartment sir, Are you afraid to go inside, We haven't discussed that yet, Then are you worried about what the walls will say, Brick and mortar never tell us the full story sir, Well you have your compulsions then, And we'll do what we know how to do and what we know we can do, And you can figure out the rest when you find yourselves in the middle of it all.

The Brothers Valdez watched the Near Stranger leave for the stairwell and then turn back around, again, as if the Brothers Valdez had been too hesitant to move or too reluctant to ask another question, and the gaze between them felt almost dangerous, the silence between them almost goading. But then something slipped to the floor alongside the Near Stranger's eyes, and he stepped into his apartment across the hall from the Brothers Valdez and then shut his door slowly, his eyes glued to the men as the peep hole and keyhole eventually replaced his full body and form, his dull nerves and motives.

Everything in hand, the Brothers Valdez crept into the hallway, Grab the key, If I knew where you left it. When the Shortest Brother returned, having gone to the kitchen and scoured the wall where the refrigerator stood, they locked the door behind them.

They stumbled into a march, locked in step, up the stairs, one story up and one story out of sight until it wasn't. Their thoughts in whispers or just above low as they stood in front of the dead man's apartment, their hair tossed around like rags in some endless dryer, Should we look through his books, Maybe, What about his desks, If he has any, And what about his drawers, Seems reasonable, And we have to be discreet, How often do have to repeat that.

Everything seemed larger than it was, the red walls a bit taller, the brown floor a bit longer, and the Oldest Brother assessed the dead man's keyhole for evidence it hadn't been shaken loose, until, with clammy palms, he turned the knob.

The door swung open. Its hinges creaked and the doorway unveiled nothing but shadow beyond it, a pitch made darker by the corridor light that settled into the apartment like a turtle at high tide. Immovable. Permanent. There was a brown table against the foyer's far wall, its single chair tucked beneath. There was a portrait of a man at a table, hung on the wall by an envelope holder. And there were light fixtures attached to opposing walls with a single switch by the bathroom doorway, and when the Oldest Brother flipped it, the overhead and wall lamps sprung on like a tall, cloudy explosion in the desert, But we're here to keep our eyes open, We remember big brother, We're here to scan everything and touch nothing, There are some things that can be helped big brother, And what is that supposed to mean, That there are also some things that simply can't.

The Shortest Brother was the first at the kitchen threshold, prepared, as it was, to judge it all, the living and the dead, to steel himself into conclusions even the barest of exposures could offer, This apartment has been left to itself for quite some time, The man is dead brother, And it appears the man has seen orderly conduct, We know enough to know the man had been a soldier, And there's what we will see that won't be unseen, We're barely in the apartment brother.

The Tallest Brother reached over the Shortest Brother and turned on the kitchen light. There were no chairs. The only thing moving was the second hand on the clock over the stove. The sink held no dishes, and the refrigerator stood like a narrow beast squeezing itself between the oven and the radiator. The narrow cabinet where a table should have been glimmered like a trophy case, and when the Oldest Brother pressed his nose to the glass, his shadow brought the medals encased there into focus, It's a shrine brothers, We can't assume the man had a religion, It certainly seems he put his trust into things, Belief and trust are two different things, Belief and trust are the same thing when you live your life by them.

The Oldest Brother encouraged them to abide by the guiding rule of the human jungle, to agree to disagree. The Oldest Brother opened the cabinet and rubbed his finger on the shelf, There's no dust on the flag here, Why are you touching that, I'm impressed by the cleanliness, It's all façade brother, We can't say anything for sure, Mother would have encouraged us to disagree more, Well mother isn't here is she, She'd tell us to obsess over all the right things, Well mother left us ten years ago didn't she, She'd tell us that her absence hasn't mattered as much as the power her absence has given us, She left without a note or a forwarding address, I want to go home big brother, We're here for a mission and conclusions and you're right, What am I right about, I've already touched too much.

The Tallest Brother had slipped into the spare bedroom by the front door as the others had gone to the kitchen, and when he called to them from some twenty, twenty-five away, he reminded them all that keeping their voices down was paramount, All good and fine but what do you have to report from the spare room, That everything is covered in plastic, You see then, See what, The man's cleanliness was paramount, I'm telling you brother that it's all a façade, There's a mattress without a bed frame in here and two dressers and a mirror on the wall and there isn't a speck of dust on the blinds, The man had found no ground on earth, What makes you say that, Only those who live to leave find no comfort in the recoverable mess of using things, Will you all please keep your voices down.

The Tallest Brother reached the kitchen and immediately opened the pantry. He *hmmm*-ed and *huh*-ed scanning up and down the shelves, and when the Youngest pulled up a chair, dragging its leg across the floor, the Shortest Brother reached for the Youngest Brother's shoulders and almost tossed him off the chair, What is wrong with you, I miss mother sometimes, Loss is what it is, Which is what, Inevitable and distributed across the world as evenly as the best of things, Then why haven't we caught up with the best of things yet, Because cities crowd us all into boxes making the best of things hard to catch as they're raining to the ground.

The Youngest Brother never seemed to never have these questions, the same questions, as if repetition hadn't just become habitual but also a comfort, the rejoinders between the Brothers Valdez like the glue that bound them, their shared loss something of a stain they could hide in their apartment simply by not talking to anyone, simply by keeping to themselves in the company of so much congestion and even in the face of so much collective desperation, isolation, and, Cities are awful things brother, Do you remember what mother's note said, That we should remember to always keep the dishes dry and the table clear and that we weren't to come looking for her, She wrote that she hated the city, And yet she still left us here, And she wrote that cities were a microcosm of all humanity, Mother was a coward, And she wrote that it's that violence grows and we're all at our worst, And like all things sitting at some extreme little brother the city also becomes the very place for redemption.

Loss, shared this thoroughly among neighbors, never becomes the story that binds anyone, Was there anything out of place in the spare bedroom brother, Nothing, And the bathroom brother, Only a striped towel on the floor and striped towels on the hook behind the door, Were they wrinkled, They were crisp, This man was all façade, Probably why no one could break through to him, Who would know to even try brother, Patriotism is just a shield against all advancement, Patriotism is like a band-aid on skin over broken ribs, War turns us all against ourselves, What is that supposed to mean, That when you bring it home there's no helping anyone.

The kitchen light shone brightest on the walking path between foyer and living room, extending in a skewed rectangle of shine from kitchen to main bedroom. The door was locked, initials written above it. The Oldest Brother, who'd arrived to the bedroom door first, rubbed his palms over a label across the top of the door frame, as if the dead man had left an enchanted inscription one could recite to walk inside. But the Oldest Brother smelled his hands and then told the remaining Brothers Valdez that it was time for a decision.

He removed the screwdriver from his pants pocket, but the Youngest grabbed his brother's shoulder before the Oldest jammed the Phillips head into the door jamb, Have you seen the room we're in brother, I have to focus little one, There isn't any furniture in the room, Then I would say the man didn't have a barracks to speak of, And there isn't so much as a fingerprint on the lamp stands or even the fixtures, Then I would say it's all the more reason to keep going little one.

But the Oldest Brother sighed anyway, and he gave in to the Youngest Brother's concerns, and when he looked across the room, he could feel his brothers' breathing, sense the beating tires on the street, attest to the isolation in the pigeons steady on the highwires that congregated over the pavement, and he could identify, at least *feel* like he could see, the words that arrived and like he could put them somewhere and that where he was putting them had nothing to do with the room, We have to go inside, It's been all façade until now big brother, Which means it may not be once we open this door, Things have been going smoothly big brother, Which means it may not be anymore once we open this door.

The Oldest Brother stepped forward and positioned himself alone in front of the bedroom door. He hesitated to jam the screwdriver into the lock and instead shook the doorknob to make sure they couldn't just break in with permission. He assessed the doorframe, its rigor, its hinges, its paint. He wrapped his hand in the rag that the Near Stranger had given him, and then he firmly positioned the screwdriver into the keyhole. With the large book, he hammered away at the butt end. Hard. Two times. A third. The walls shook, and the sound of a crack seemed to want to squeeze from the brass, and when the Oldest Brother paused, he acknowledged to his brothers that he wouldn't be surprised if maybe the door had just been waiting to be asked, but that if he hammered any harder, especially in succession, he'd call too much attention to them and this place, What do you mean, Like who breaks into each other's homes like this, We were asked to be here big brother, But like why did we come to say yes, Because we always say yes if only to be left alone, But like maybe I'm tired of just being the four of us, But it's the four us who survive because it's just the four of us, And it's the four of us who are the four of us because who else can be trusted, Because imagine being asked to enter this man's home without any consent and one day someone else enters ours without any consent, And are we sure we want to stay that alone, We're sure big brother, And are we sure we can't trust each other, We're sure big brother, I'll always go where we all can agree to go, We're sure of it big brother, It's only right big brother, But are you sure we can call ourselves a neighbor if we're only so interested in him now but now that the man has left us completely my brothers.

The four Brothers Valdez, the heat among them bringing them closer and still wrenching them apart, were islands in the wake of the Oldest Brother's big bangs. The Shortest Brother acknowledged that it felt like the whole building had trembled, the Tallest Brother saying that he'd heard the light fixtures rattle, and the Youngest Brother saying that he wanted to go back home, You've already said all that young one, Times don't change big brother, I'm the one who taught *you* that little one, Taught me what, That history repeats itself because it's always turning around the same sun little one.

The Oldest Brother jammed the screwdriver into the lock, tired of waiting any longer, and he hammered hard, Go at it big brother, and he hammered harder, Go big brother, and he hammered the hardest bang yet, Take it away big brother, and then the brass knob split open. The Oldest Brother sprayed water into the exposure and then dried the surrounding frame with a paper towel, and then he hammered again, one last time, as if releasing the metal from its own responsibility, and the knob fell off entirely.

Parts rattled on the living room floor.

The dead man's bedroom door swung open.

Inside, the air hung congested in wood shavings and shed hair and the smell of salt as if someone had kicked up the desert. The Brothers Valdez shielded their eyes from the streetlight shine that pierced into the room.

Composition books lay sprawled on a desk between two windows. Loose leaf papers lay shuffled beneath the desk, pens and pencils sprinkled around the chair that had been pushed out. A lamp lay spilled over envelopes, its bulb still on.

The Oldest Brother asked the rest if they could see their hands in front of their face, and they all responded that even the visions of themselves were just a blur.

The mattress lay bare, jagged coils jutting from the cushion, sheets and pillows rolled against the wall, books, so many books, stacked as if unable to find a peace but at the bottom of a dead man's mind, Are you all seeing this.

Skeletal dressers abutted the windows, drawers tossed concave all the way to the bedside. White paint peeled off the walls, the ceiling over the mattress patched up with cardboard, duct tape, plywood. The room appeared before the doorway like the portrait of a sandstorm from which time had been stripped and heat had eradicated even the rain, and when the Shortest Brother stepped forward before the others, he stepped over more than just an armful of rope and more than just shreds of twine, Are you all seeing *this*.

The Tallest Brother reached up and stripped a cobweb off the light fixture that had been tugged from its place in the ceiling, and when his hand came down, he didn't mean to hold it up to his brothers, but he did, because his fingers had come down with a short piece of rope, and even he was surprised by the look of a mistake, by the look of a tear that seemed to take intention, and even practice, to come undone.

And it was then that a combination lock came into visual relief for all of them, all seeing it almost simultaneously, a small case at the center of the bed. They looked at each other, walked up to the mattress, and leaned over the comforter. The Oldest Brother sat at the bed's edge, and he peered at the others, a look inviting them, and they took turns settling down, the metal container between them as if its edges pointed to cardinal directions and the shadow of a spying world.

The Oldest Brother reached for his screwdriver again, wishing he'd had a flat head to stick into the secondary keyhole on the back of the lock, but no matter. He inserted and hammered violently, and he kept at it, three times, two times, four more times, and then twice more and then what he thought would be one last time, except that he didn't need the thirteenth bang. The combination lock, made heavy by the weight of its body, slid open, unclicked from its responsibility to uphold any privacy, and when the Oldest Brother removed the lock entirely from the latch, and the lid popped off, and pictures sprayed across the bed, the four Brothers Valdez suddenly caught between looking around at each other and unsure if they should be taking the leap to look into the dead man's soul, pictures, as they'd become, a window into the best and worst of us, the surfaces that don't want to reveal the cracks until they do, until they tell you everything you need to know because there's no escaping the view, the clear view, into another person's eyes.

The Brothers Valdez leaned in, their noses pressed into the prints. When the Oldest Brother asked if they should arrange the pictures, the Shortest Brother asked what order they were imagining, to which the Tallest Brother questioned whether something in the pictures wasn't looking back at them and they shouldn't shut their eyes, to which the Youngest Brother said he just wanted to leave, go home, go back to wherever it was that made them feel safe, even if feeling safe was just an unreliable place they imagined to be true when it just wasn't, We're not in a welcoming story right now my brothers.

Every picture was a picture of a man that did not exist. Every picture with a face, just a single face, punched through or cut out or burned up, just straight missing, an abscess in every picture that was no longer a face at all but a disappearance, and a desperate one, where not even the person's beard had been spared and where just a neck had been left, as if the decapitation had been both brutal and quick, and as with all things in the apartment until they arrived to the bedroom, necessary and neat.

The pictures, like the worst of movies, seemed as animated as the dreams we can't see because in them we're never allowed to speak. Soldiers in uniform. Dogs next to charred vehicles. Explosions caught midflame. Soldiers in masks with cigarette lights and no smiles. Soldiers hosting faraway gazes, maybe even latched to memories that couldn't soften a harsh desert no matter how forgiving the roads had been. The soldiers in these pictures seemed to care about one another or at least feign an intimacy that the threat of a looming accident or murder could nurture. In one picture, someone was leaning into the cut-out face as if to catch a whisper. In another picture, someone seemed to be crooning to the punched-through face, chin high and a sunset framing the hills in the distance. In yet another picture, someone seemed to be pressing her cheek to the cheek of the face that had been burned out of the picture. The feeling in every erasure like a rage stuck in permanent in-between-ness, one that makes prayers impossible to get anywhere they were intended to go.

The Tallest Brother said it was time to get out, Now. The Shortest Brother said that he might need the most help, I'm not sure I can look away. The Youngest Brother stood and slouched to the bedroom door, I don't want to be here anymore. And the Oldest Brother remained on the bed shaking his head, confused as to whether what they'd found was everything or nothing at all, We're in a pristine apartment that didn't want to disclose the room it didn't want us to find big brother, What were you expecting big brother, An explanation maybe, Well we have a story to tell if we can ever be allowed to tell it, But it's no explanation, A story has an ending and it has a beginning and if what you want is an explanation big brother you're not going to get it.

The Tallest Brother rested his hand on the Oldest Brother's shoulder, I honor the feeling big brother, Please don't patronize me, But a hero with no faces is just as good as a hero with a thousand, And what is that supposed to mean, He's just a story now, I'm feeling sick right now, We're a part of it now and there's no getting out.

The Oldest Brother shrugged off his brother's hand, seeing, like we all did long after that night, that rolling the boulder away and unveiling the body makes us responsible, too, if not to repeat the story then to take pains to try to get it, to try to put words to it, even if the only lesson learned is that what we imagine we see and don't in each other, who we are in our losses and shortcomings, frailties and tragedies, all we really recognize, in the end, are interchangeable faces that could be holding each other's burdens but don't.

As if avoiding a poison that threatened to smother their lungs, the Oldest Brother stood up and egged his brothers to leave everything as it was and everything as they had made it. Once outside the bedroom, the Oldest slammed the door shut and jammed the screwdriver into the door frame through the doorknob hole, and then he stuffed the hole with the rolled book and rag and then he sprayed a handful of paper towels and wadded them into the hole. He looked around one last time, and then he emphasized to his brothers they hadn't seen anything worth sharing, nothing the police won't find later. That they couldn't be responsible for the stories they didn't repeat, and that there was no way to repeat a story covered in so much must, so much poor lighting.

LOOP FOUR: THE AMBULANCE

The next part happened quickly. So quickly, in fact, that to this day, no one knows who had the pen or who'd taken it upon themself to extract the man's name from all formalities that would have rendered him legitimately dead and, in turn, legitimately having lived.

As night closed in, flies and dust and all but the hanging man's shoes left the basement as the paramedics carted his limp body up the steps and onto the sidewalk. It was hot, but squeezing past us, children reaching for the dead man's feet and hands and grabbing the gurney and men waving cigarettes to explain that they only wanted to see the dead man's face, just made it all hotter. Simmering had long been an evening effect as we'd arrived to dusk, those last prayers, before boiling. After the paramedics slammed the back compartment doors shut, night all but officially closed on the body. After slamming the driver's and passenger's doors shut, the Paramedics all but sealed themselves away from ever retrieving whatever, if anything important, had happened in the boiler room.

At the steering wheel, Paramedic No.1 buckled herself in. There were dozens of us around the ambulance. We didn't share any particular arrangement, or rather we were consumed in something like the haphazard walk of the dead, lingering around the truck, circling it as if waiting for decay, as if listening for signs of a beating heart we all knew had already begun drying. When she turned the ignition, a random someone's keys clanked the hood.

Someone else's hands slapped the company sign on the side of the truck. Meanwhile, someone else's boot kicked the back tires, and still another person's purse slapped the passenger door. The Paramedics looked at one another. A pebble hit one of the side view mirrors.

Paramedic No.1 eased off the brake. The headlights actually thickened the otherwise loose density, perhaps because a thud and a slap and a kick that had echoed into the front compartment had threatened to turn the dozen or so of us into so much more. Paramedic No. 1 paused over the steering wheel, Are you okay, I am.

She refused to meet anyone's eyes, all of us, it seemed, beaming with a premonition that terrorizes in shouts and blown windows and anonymously so, embedding an obsession to know who's looking in and who's wanting out.

When phlegm crashed into the windshield, the Paramedics ducked, and after they glanced each other's way, Paramedic No. 1 honked four times, The first to know that I still could, she said later, The last to know the first three weren't a hallucination of the ears and the mind, she clarified later.

Behind the loose crowd, a police car emerged to clear the way. Its siren blared in some unidentifiable rhythm, a song with nothing on beat. The ambulance staggered forward, offering measured howls of its own, maneuvering carefully to the corner and around double-parked cars that had already been ticketed but which were nevertheless still narrowing the mouth of the street. Coupled with every one of us holding random positions on the pavement, the Paramedics seemed to be navigating the most misleading of mazes, because if two dozen had ever promised to become two hundred, this was certainly one of those nights.

Windows open and lights flashing mute, the officer honked his horn, sirens telling what had to be said and his left hand's tapping a baton on the roof saying all the rest as the ambulance passed. Paramedic No. 1 acknowledged the officer, and the officer returned her nod with a last tap. Paramedic No. 2, meanwhile, looked back, straining his neck as if to throw his blind spot open to whatever moonlight he could reach, They're not following us, Did you think they were going to yell at us, I'm not sure, Did you think there were going to be more, I really don't know what there was going to be.

On the road, the dim lights passed by, a laundromat, a hardware shop, a pharmacy, storefronts streaking in smudges overworked and old. Paramedic No. 2 grabbed the clipboard. He attempted to glean information from the document stack, those formalized necessities that are usually no bother and utterly replaceable. He flipped through them, page two, empty lines accounting for time, page three, the hour they arrived and attempted to revive the man. He grabbed the radio to phone dispatch. The response was static-ridden, and so he recounted the most pressing details that he firmly controlled, talking calculated and cold into the mouthpiece. Before dispatch signed off, its operator instructed the Paramedics to take the body to the hospital morgue where the coroner's office, caught between shifts, would retrieve it, And assign the body a number, What number do you want us to use, Follow protocol, But we don't share the coroner's protocol, Then all we can hope for is *a* protocol.

Beyond the truck, the road, the tires, the lights. The Paramedics shared untimed breaths, smothered as they both were by the air conditioner that had already made their skins fragile and ripe for cracking. Paramedic No. 2 returned to the clipboard as if mentally annotating a wound he didn't realize still needed scabbing, and he impatiently flipped through several more pages. Everything fair on the first page. Nothing on pages two and three.

And then there was page four. Paramedic No. 2 flipped back to the first page. There was nothing listed for the dead man's name. When he flipped back to the fourth page, a second position for the dead man's name also did not have the dead man's name. Instead, what had been registered in place of it was a much, much longer and looser association of words that resembled interruptions often shouted in place of names in very public places, This is all wrong, What do you mean, We don't have a name, Who filled it out, I'm not sure, What do we have instead, A very long sentence, I don't understand, I don't think it matters that we don't.

Lifeless in the back, the dead man's body rattled, even as it lay strapped, its chest inflated, a choppy, misplaced book bulging in the shirt's breast pocket, What are we going to do about the number we assign, What do you mean, Don't we have to base it on his name, That isn't here or there anymore, What is all that exactly, I'm flipping through pages here and it seems like everyone else's name on here instead of his, I don't understand, I'll just read it to you. Paramedic No. 2 almost laughed, It looks like we'll have to make up an assigned number, Are you sure we should, Even if I think it's bad protocol it's still a protocol.

A curtain between front and back compartments wavered over their shoulders, This really is laughable, What's it like, It's like fiction, No one deserves that kind of treatment, But it's just a number, But aren't we all just numbers, I guess, If we're not a specific number then we're no number at all,

But we have our orders, But even when they don't make sense, Especially when they don't make sense.

In place of the dead man's name, there sat only words, several deeply drawn breaths covering formal documentation that should have otherwise accounted for essentials delineating the man's death, information that should have completed a certificate registering the man's end but which instead would never be paired with his birth certificate to complete the story, and because lines do not exist with only one certain point, we now have what we have.

The nature of the sentences on pages four and five and six and seven was such that it squeezed between the typeset text and in between the lines otherwise left blank for legitimate things to be written upon them. The sentences wound down the right margin of page four until they emerged on later pages along both margins, left and then right, until too much of everything that did not matter bled over the fine print and across the bottoms of pages and over those places reserved for the measurements that make for who we are, because formality, in the end, just doesn't have places to understand the kind of persons we were or the shapes of people we wanted to be or the shadows of persons we never were.

Along the way, someone, whoever, had decided to muse upon the fact that *I'm not sure I've ever seen this man but I'll pass the clipboard on to someone who has oh wait I'm sorry there's no one here who fits the criteria of a colleague or friend or family which I hope you don't read as condescending or sarcastic in any way even though I've been accused of as much in other places it's only that there's no one here I can reliably pass this clipboard to who can say for certain that this is that or those are these.* And as the writing rushed through spaces for address of passing or nearest location of death, someone else, most likely someone else, continued far too eagerly *because I didn't expect to find him when I came home and all I know for sure is that of the two basement apartments I live in the one on the right and it was from my place in the kitchen that I did not hear a single pipe bend or grow weighty with a dead man's neck and it wasn't until a commotion had already made its way to the boiler that I knew anything about anything so please don't hold it against me and please don't return to haunt me with a lawyer I wouldn't know what to do either biologically or emotionally or anything at all so you must believe me I didn't know what had happened or what was going on until someone pounded my door and told me that the basement was far too hot to hold this many people.* Whoever had attempted to complete the portion of known diagnoses was equally ill-fitted to the task, instead using the open space to introduce herself, or himself, to clarify for state and municipal readers that *hello I must say up front that I am not the original person who began this document and in my attempts to discover who no one else can tell me with any certainty but because a certain pattern has begun I can hardly be the one to interrupt the string of things which is to say we must all everyone here must vouch for what this man looks like and because no one before has clarified for you I will do my best to describe his broad shoes gone slack his straight nose skewed right his sturdy hands gone white his deep-set eyes gone cold his plump chin thinned by the heat and his back pockets hanging so bunched that it seems the man's defecations could not wait to bunch up to his waist and also his collar have I mentioned his collar it seemed so loose around his neck that it actually pointed back in a cloth crisp cloth arrow as if it could not forget its past but please forgive these final musings as I cannot erase what has already been imprinted in ink,* Maybe there's a number for anonymous patients, You mean the anonymous dead, What might the protocol be for that, I'm sure there's something everyone uses, Then there couldn't possibly be a rule we'd threaten to break.

In the back compartment, the dead man's breast pocket popped open. The book inside peeked over the stitching like a groundhog suspicious that the changing seasons were all really just theatre. After a bump, the book splayed open to some unfamiliar title, like it wanted as much attention for its literary merit as for the formal documentation filed this day with the municipal Commissioner of Death and Reservations. The book's pages flapped open with numbers that were each coupled with a name. That is, because the book had thickened to two hundred pages, there were two hundred different names registered along the full stack of corners, which, by way of plot, tallied the book's most prevalent obsessions and years of solitude. In the book, an insomnia had compelled the main character to realize that, after scratching the outline of his face in the bedroom mirror during a scene on page one hundred and forty-four, there emerged a nervousness in him as he tried to recall all those wars that he could not remember well. He had, in the end, fought in too many to count, volunteering for each one because he could not pronounce his name without also mimicking the sound of a gun. And so he concluded that if he could forget his name without anyone around him to remind of what it had been, then it was probably because there had never been anything about him that had ever been real or his, whence he found, after a soliloquy in his bathroom, that he was nothing but a character in someone else's book, employed by hands persistent about destroying his present because the past had been shot to hell, and it took him well into the epilogue to muster the courage to scold the book's narrator, which ultimately proved ineffective because mercy, like all of life's most illuminating books, is often nowhere to be found when one most needs it, Would you please rewrite me, I cannot and so you must be patient, But can you answer me this, I will try, Am I someone important, I don't know, Tell me something, About what, About me, I will say that what you are is true whether or not you ever again pick up a gun, Thank you, For what, For telling me something like that, Then there it is, But one more question, Certainly, Am I known to anyone but myself, I can't say for sure, Then I'm all alone, We'll work on that, But this story is already written, It certainly has been, Well that isn't fair, But stories are stories and they should be written, But that isn't fair, And there's nothing I can do about that soldier, Can you leave me an open ending at least, I can't, Can I live to feel past this war, You won't, But aren't you in charge of all this, When it comes to war soldier rules will always be rules.

From the back compartment, all kinds of things rattled, all sounds welding into a single shape that only made sense in the clashing voices of that night.

On page five of the formal documentation, whoever had taken charge had decided to proudly add a certain telling of events aware of itself being uninformed but nonetheless expert about whom and where things had gone wrong for us because *to whomever will read this I apologize on all our behalf for our helplessness and being less than helpful though you mustn't judge us nor revisit this after all this man was clearly fond of the spectacle he was leaving a telling story all its own as men of no quality at all are usually the most comfortable with spectacles gone public because they don't understand the public they're shouting to much less whatever memory we don't have or refused to have of him.* In the page footer, impressed so firmly the pen bore holes in the middle of words, whoever it was all but argued that *I'd like to add that this all feels so threatening, as if somehow you have been threatened by our place and find now comfort in nothing, and so we'll demand that you read between the lines that, like this man, will find meaning in the floors between and beneath us, and because there's a message more menacing than the uncertainty of the war we all find and will always find ourselves in the history of the damned*, We should at least list what we can as some reasonable cause here, I would call these people enough probable cause, I didn't notice but was there anything about his clothes, He was wearing a uniform, Then we should describe an honorable cause, Is it that important to you, If he won't have a name then we can agree truth is only a shadow, But everyone's body will at some point decompose, Yes but documentation is sometimes the only legacy we can leave.

The Paramedics glanced at each other. They turned to the road before them without a nod. They didn't need one.

Stopped at a red light and almost where they needed to be, Paramedic No. 2 settled the clipboard on the dashboard and left for the back compartment. As the ambulance slowed, he reached for the floor, picked up the open book that had slipped off the dead man's chest, and started flipping through it when he was interrupted by Paramedic No. 1 setting the parking brake. When Paramedic No. 2 stood up and steadied himself, he set all things down for time immemorial when he zipped up the bag and then opened the back compartment doors, where Paramedic No. 1 met him and then shouted for help carting an unnumbered man to where he'd always be forgotten.

LOOP FIVE: THE POWER COMPANY

The Power Company has always offered inconsistent messages when appearing to repair burst high voltage wires and transformers. Sometimes they post warnings when they work with overhead cables. Sometimes they don't. On days they remember, traffic backs up, honks and insults shower the road, and the heat becomes too much to bear standing still. On days repair crews forget their traffic cones and signs, people will unknowingly pass under disjointed wires, sometimes firing off, and they'll growl at repair crews, like dogs, a snappiness that bites when unexpected sparks scare the shit out of everyone.

By seven o'clock that night, the pavement really was a mess. The electricity had gone out for one whole side of the street, and hundreds of us streamed onto the sidewalk. The curb ran amok with feet and people in and around cars, ignitions running, radios chiming, air conditioners whirring. When Power Company repair crews finally arrived, they honked their way down the block. After they parked, Foreman Freedman tried to get people off the road, trying to direct them, telling his workers to hold up rerouting signs for the neighborhood people to shoo away, but even cones didn't matter, did they. People knocked them over intentionally or not, and they tore through caution tape hanging between car bumpers, and they spilled almost all orange warning flags set up on the road. Sometimes even the living danger of electrocution means nothing to people, especially when a hanging of unnatural currents is enough to drive us into the dark and out of our apartments, enough to set the whole street buzzing.

Foreman Freedman was some kind of man. Stout. Loud. Nervous. So very nervous. He and his crew seemed to quickly assess the power lines, because he pointed to the truck and then pointed to one of his guys and then pulled on his hair, like he was trying to brush it back with his fingers but like he could only tug on the pressure of it all, a rider steering a horse by its mane but forgetting that you can't just turn a cold, you can't just guide, with your anxiety. Though we can all be prone to it, do what we can to toggle our thoughts loose, Foreman Freedman screamed at one guy to point the power bulb, Up at that pole there, and then he told his other guy to get to the control levers behind the passenger seat, and then he climbed into the bucket. He shouted, Up man up, and as the motor hummed, the bucket rose above us, Foreman Freedman holding onto the safety cord that strapped him to the metal arm, which he seemed to be pulling hard, his forearms bulging, his whole body like hawsers struggling to keep a ferry moored.

He raised his hand at the height he wanted, and the bucket jerked still when Foreman Freedman arrived at the accomplice of it all, at the culprit that had stripped all the power. He yelled down to his guys as he pointed to a blown joint and a burnt transformer bushing, And don't mess with the levers anymore please. He stood back, the distance between himself and the live wires, as with all impulses gone wrong, seemingly not enough.

The Foreman quickly sent his men down two blocks to estimate the cable length to string through, as it appeared a second transformer down street was also smoking and the whole line needed to be replaced at least one transformer's length back from each one that had gone out. When his crew returned, they confirmed the fumes and that they would need approximately three hundred feet. Back down to street level, he directed his guys to shut down the transformers on both opposing corners of the block, I don't any more wired energy to be pulsating down this street, and then he scanned the street, the crowd, the whole city, it felt like, that seemed to be caught under the wires like an untapped power grid ready to escalate and blow.

Foreman Freedman radioed the power company equipment yard with a report about the power gone across a landscape of low-lying buildings and a tricky situation, and at first the necessary response was nothing extraordinary, We need a cable truck, Did you say a truck, You heard me right and two new bushings from the yard and more pedestrian cones and we need so much more caution tape. But then the yard operator returned to the line with the usual lack of pleasantries. Well shit, What's wrong, Our cable trucks are all assigned out now right now, How soon can I get one on sight, Maybe before the next shift, We have four more hours until the next shift, You'll have it when I tell you we have it Freedman.

The Foreman tossed his radio into the repair van and slammed the driver side door, We're waiting, Where do we wait Foreman, Right here, This doesn't feel safe though Foreman, It took us long enough to squeeze through the crowd so we're not backing out now, There are more ways than one Foreman for the world to act like a hot wire uncoiled by the tension, I don't want to hear it, But we all feel the same way Foreman, It took us long enough to squeeze through the crowd to get here and I don't want to run into anybody else if we don't have to. The crowd had only just started to swell when they first attempted to pull into the street, and the driver had become distracted by his cell phone that rang as he made the left turn. His friend, a jittery paramedic, asked him to be careful, so goddamn careful, of what had been going down and to keep his eyes open and to keep from talking to anyone on the street, And don't let anyone write anything down on your forms, the paramedic friend had said, Don't let anyone get their hands on anything you might later need. And because the phone call had distracted him, he only almost ran over a child chasing the truck too close to the front tires, and it had been the Foreman who screamed to keep from swerving too far right.

Foreman Freedman ordered his crew to prepare, regardless, for the cable truck's arrival, whenever that might be, from whichever main road it might come from, which meant clearing the road of the elderly and animals first, followed by children and expecting mothers and then everyone else, should they prove themselves to be any fool who hadn't followed either of the first two groups back into their apartments. But everywhere they directed people, either down the sidewalk or across the street, we just weren't listening, not all of us or many or at least not with any clarity of intention. And Foreman Freedman lingered behind the truck as his crew tried replacing cones back upright, tried tying ends of the striped caution tape, tried holding up signs like *This Way* and *Not That Way*, but the crowd had become so dense it was almost impossible to maneuver neatly. Foreman Freedman even grew tired of responding to his crew, and he waved them all away when they came over to appeal to him, Please stop asking, But even the old guy in a wheelchair won't get back on the curb, What do you want me to do, You're the boss Foreman, Correction I'm a guide, You're my supervisor Foreman, We both get checks signed by the same people so I'm nobody's boss even if you do have to do what I tell you.

And people just hung out there, really, leaning on cars, sitting on their hoods, radio music playing with their engines running and their doors open, children shouting at each other to keep off their new shoes, fathers hurling napkins from kitchen windows, mothers tossing spare rags from fire escapes, the lot of it as if the street had become a delusion that needed tidying, an energy that needed revving up.

Foreman Freedman caught some of the falling debris to wipe his forehead, so many thoughts swirling, so regularly now pulling off his baseball cap to brush back his hair only to replace the hat on his head and repeat the anxiety of it all every few minutes. A member of his work crew pointed to the building stoop, and the Foreman soon ordered everybody off the street and way from the truck, the busted wire and the burnt transformer bushing like dead weights just hanging over everything, Move cautiously, Yes sir, And don't agitate the zoo, Yes sir.

A grocer had set up a cooler on the steps, though he wasn't the only vendor who'd mobbed the building stoop in makeshift racks of potato chips and cookies. One grocer had even carted popsicles in a wagon, another grocer with oranges and bananas in boxes by the crosswalk, another grocer with flares and emergency snap-on lights by the entrance to the basement where the whole night had started, the whole scene absent of a portable generator but still loaded with potential, the kind of potent opportunity where anyone, just about anyone, could wiggle a makeshift light and turn the street into a stampede.

Shuffling and shoving their way back to the van, Foreman Freedman and his crew had managed to gather at least one thing beyond cool, humid water bottles they pressed to their foreheads and necks, I've read these kinds of things in books, I didn't know you read Foreman, My family is full of enough illiterate bastards thank you very much, What do you read Foreman, Mysteries and detective books and stuff with the kind of vision for the world that simply can't be imitated by the world.

Foreman Freedman's crew stayed close, so very close, afraid, it seemed, to hover too far from the bear that could claw the worst of things away, that kind of man that no matter how often his arms shoulders jerked or how often his neck twitched, no involuntary movement of his body could soften the ground beneath him, These kinds of stories never end well, So are the rumors of the dead man true Foreman, When you read enough things about the world you start to believe that they're telling the truth, But aren't some stories lies sir, They're all lies so you can never believe that someone just took their life because they were just sick, But taking one's life Foreman is all about being sick, It's about who cares and who doesn't and it's about a world never enough for the kind of people who feel too much.

Every next moment, Foreman Freedman shook, not violently but with no warning, and when a crew member reminded him to take his medication, at first he told everyone he was fine, and then he angrily reached into his pocket for a small bottle, and then he didn't care to count how many pills he poured into his palm, and then he didn't care for the water in his hand when he struggled to swallow it all, I'm telling you, he said, How many times do we have to hear that this or that wanted out of all of this until we realize that all of this wasn't made for anyone, and then he grunted, almost growled, as if to release the visions of everything crawling to his mouth.

Every few minutes, too, he coughed like he was also trying to restrain a choking laugh, but his eyes seemed to make certain that he found nothing funny, that night or any night, watching everything, looking across everything, as if expecting to have to study it all even as he had already concluded everything he needed to know, I don't hate anything, he said, But I don't want to hear anything more about a world that's already proven it doesn't know how to receive anyone in it.

Even if the cable truck did arrive, its girth would never have let it snake through the crowd. It would have taken more of the night than Foreman Freedman wanted to relent just to get the cable and the bushings into place. He was stuck, and he knew it, and you could tell by the sweat he kept wiping off his cheek. The collar of his shirt was soon enough so wet it threatened to soak him just standing there.

It was only a matter of time before he ordered his crew onto the roof of the work truck, into its bay or on top of the bins, all four like men and women that didn't only prefer to be told what to do but that also wouldn't do a thing until they were told to do it.

The view from the truck was like standing on the lighting platform of a concert. Even if there were visible pockets of bare pavement, it was all so scattered that it might as well have amounted to nothing, the crowd, as crowds always seemed, like an immutable sight that would never be repeated anywhere, could never be repeated ever again.

Time passed. Foreman Freedman's wax poetica went on, ran on, shot off, in sequence and sporadically, like sparks from a live wire, its protective coating stripped through and bare in so many spots that you couldn't deem them random. His *There's an author by the name of* and *I've read so many titles that look at the world as it's become and not how it can be* and *The wisdom books talk about this kind of night* all bleeding into one another, assessing it all, judging it all, even subtly, even tongue-in-cheek, and the cable truck—it was nowhere to be seen. The power company's equipment yard hadn't radioed with updates and the substation operator hadn't radioed with news about how far the outage had gone, about which repair vehicles had been sent where, about how long the grid would be partially undone. Foreman Freedman sat cross-legged on the truck's roof, his crew flanking him, their boots hanging over the ledge or rattling the windows, all of them like disciples waiting for instruction, for some truth about the legitimate and the illegitimate world that they might have guessed at on their own but which needed an authoritative voice, some authority over them, that could both sign their time card and let them know how well or how poorly their time had been used.

And time certainly passed, more of it, so much of it, and the street seemed to pass into some new dimension, like staring into the extent of the desert and becoming the singularity that marks one horizon after the next, undulating, shivering, riding the air and its thirst into the next nothing.

Foreman Freedman grabbed a crew member's sweat rag, glared at it and said he didn't care, and then he said that when there wasn't any order to follow, you watched over it until you knew where to go, and then he leaned over the ledge to yell at anyone leaning on the truck to get off, to stop leering at the truck, to get off the pavement, And soon, because the cable truck would be arriving and if anybody wanted their power back, they'd have to sprawl across the road or get off it.

On the sidewalk, there was a hole in the crowd, like a makeshift pond that collects after a storm. Scattered people, like winter fishing boats, crossed the open space, pensive, talking, in tears. News always spreads the way it can, slowly, softly, and even in scandalous affairs, subtly because no one ever wants to get caught too excited to share what isn't theirs or too timid and appearing afraid of words, because they're always only words, rolling off their tongue. But after news has traveled for some time, whispers become reckless, and the words themselves, irrespective of what they actually say, can become the things that cut, the very things that propel us into anger or worse, And why or how it happened that somebody started pounding on the side of the truck while crying, nobody could really say, only that it caught Foreman Freedman visibly surprised, and before he yelled at the man to back off, two others and then three others started crying and pounding on the truck. And Foreman Freedman did not hold back. Get off you tyrants, and, Enough with all of you, and, Someone has to call the police, and, Order you fools order the police will call all of you to order.

When nobody backed away, the Foreman took to banging on the truck's ceiling, obliterating the plastic water bottle in his hand in the process, Excuse me, shouting, Hello there, and, I know you hear me, and trying to reach for each person's fist, their shoulders, their elbows, but nothing, not the thumps of, Stop it, made anyone stop, I will call the police on all of you, They're not budging sir, If you make me do it I will most certainly do it, No one is listening sir, I will most certainly be the one to make sure you never get back whatever power you thought you had I will most certainly be the one to make that happen.

Bleary noses looked at him. Wet lips and chins looked him over. The handful who'd thumped on the truck stepped back, but no one walked away, and the commotion and his shouting only brought more people to encircle the truck, which had already been surrounded by people, though it's one thing to sit in the middle of things and another thing entirely to sit at the center of it all.

Foreman Freedman's brow, his eyes, his gaze, the way his expressions tried to balance the weight of an anger with hesitant direction and the heaviness of the faces around him that wanted to spill over that reluctance, all of it like he didn't know how to keep his own footing on the truck, and so he sat down. He'd rendered something from it all, like a painter, even a storyteller, with fractions of an image that don't come together until the connectivity stills you, and so there they were, What just happened sir, They're still now but just staring at us sir, What kind of hive did you prod sir, I want to get out of here sir.

As if from the very air nobody trusted, an older woman started passing through the crown, jotting things into a notepad, the page to her nose, her pen pressing down like it had been carving its own rendering from ash and lead, Can I get a statement sir, Excuse me, Are you a foreman of some kind, A foreman for the power company's overhead electrical unit, And can I get your impressions about what happened, But who are you, A freelancer, What kind of freelancer, One who writes and comes to a judgment of things, So you have no objectivity, Objectivity is a lie sir, Please don't call me sir, Would you prefer foreman, I would prefer to say nothing.

The Freelancer considered Foreman Freedman and then the people around the truck, all of whom, at least those among the most aggressive, had started to back away into the larger crowd, as if by simply having someone there, someone whose job purported to be stories and points of view, interrogations and the conclusions we arrive to when it's our job to mine them even from scratch, the pressure could eased, the tension could erode—as if simply having someone there whose role it was to communicate to the world all that was there and that would be lost, at least for now, could help everyone settle at least a little further back from the truck, without one's eyes completely off it, I couldn't help but overhear you, What did you overhear, Something about what should have been seen before it happened, I don't know that I said that, I wrote it all down, I don't know that you did, I most certainly did, I want to see your notebook, You will do no such thing, Give it here now, And I also overheard you say something about all the things that had been there plain as day that everyone should have seen coming but which nobody did, I said give that notebook here now, And something about what was always going to happen to someone somewhere that this kind of thing the tragedies of hurt men will become a tragedy for us all because hurt people hurt people and that it's in our world's nature to look away from whatever doesn't pertain to us because whatever does pertain to us must be clear as day and plain as paper.

Foreman Freedman and the Freelancer watched each other, both considering the scope of the other one's heft and who it was they stood beside. In such moments, perceptions become unknowable when nobody spells anything explicitly across an open space, What exactly do you write for, I write for a blog, And what exactly does that mean, If you don't know then you don't know.

Who knows if there might be a dozen stages like this, their street, too, caught in some awful kind of theater, with words that paw at each other or swing expecting to land because bearing anything alone, especially bearing witness, becomes simply impossible.

When the police finally arrived, they started, like a slow roll of fire, barring people from leaving the intersection, building a barrier of words and barricades before a wall of uncertain people could begin to protest. Gnats in the streetlamp made for shadowy monsters across the tops of everyone's heads, and the blinking police lights looked like airport beams telling everything, fear and whisper, alike, where to land, where to park, and where to keep still lest someone have to come over and detain you.

And then the journalists arrived, the paid ones, with pictures snapping and cameras rolling, and first one reporter ran to an officer at the barrier to ask about what had happened to cause these people to run out onto the street and then another reporter found a police offer to ask what could possibly be wrong with these people. But not even the third or fourth reporter jumped to ask anyone behind the barrier, and so it really began, A hanging man you say, Yes ma'am a hanging man, Officer would you say the man was a threat, The situation doesn't call for an official statement at this time, But would you say the man's decision intended to shake us all out of ourselves, We can't attest to a motivation without an official statement at this time, But would you say the man's insistence to make the statement he did proved enough to rattle us to the core, We can't say for sure who's to blame here but we will find those persons soon and find them we will.

Before long, some police officers started smoking, and clouds hanging like alarming cells ahead of a storm lingered over everything, so much so that Foreman Freedman had to waved the smoke and errant ashes away, and he ordered his crew inside the truck, Now, But sir, Now.

They managed sure enough to pull open the doors and get inside, but inside they were pinched. The cabin had been set to fit four, and here they were, the five of them, Close the windows please, But it's hot in here sir, I'm telling you to close the window.

But the truck had been turned off, and the keys weren't in the driver's pockets, and so the orchestra of murmurs and shouting slivered into the truck's cabin playing whatever song about the aftermath of a summer's hanging and blaming the Foreman and his crew for raising the temperature, blaming them for bringing on the reporters and calling the police, But I'd barely gotten the operator on the line, They don't care sir, And all I could manage to say was that the people were here scared and that the people here were violent, That appeared to be enough sir, Well then this place is a mess, This place is a *disheveled* mess sir, And I'm glad I did what I did, This place is going to come crashing down sir, And it's me and don't you forget it that it's me who finally started to bring this place to its knees.

LOOP SIX: THE CLOSET

The fifth-floor hallway light flickered all night. Regularly, it spilled a deep shadow across every front door and mat. The flutter dimmed the commotion outside that attempted, like a venom searching unprotected pathways into our veins, to invade a room, toss open a curtain, overturn a bedroom, reveal every stashed secret, messily and without distinction.

The hallway tiles lay cracked everywhere. They'd been static without spreading for so long it seemed their shattering was intentional design, a building's roiled nerves waiting, threatening, to one day sever a quiet summer evening. An especially wide crack ran like a center line down the hallway. Webs of cracks also jutted from the bottom of the concrete wall, evenly spaced, offering character, movement, a story, like dozens of moths under a country veranda.

That night, every fifth-floor tenant had shut their doors tight. Whereas confusion hurled most everyone else onto the street, the same kept these tenants home. The third floor beneath them, two stories below, had boxed away a deep moan, one that never again found its listing in a phone book. But because none of us knew why it happened or how many names exactly were lost, and almost no one asked the right questions, the street showered uncertainty, and all the fifth-floor tenants felt a crack in disbelieving shakes they couldn't unfeel.

One old man clamored that everyone beneath them had started searching for something worse than awful, and then he slammed his door. A jingle rang ominously over his knob. A young couple in the neighboring apartment stuttered that something beneath them had leapt from a window, etched itself into the concrete and pavement, and then they eased their door closed. They pulled a chain tight, dropped an iron bar across the entrance, padlocked it to the wall. A family of three across the hall stood quietly at their open doorway until a police blare implied they were better off locked away. Bathroom, bedroom, or closet pantry, it doesn't matter to any of us. And we shut ourselves in, pushed the dining room table and living room couch against the front door, trying, though it doesn't really matter why, to exile the night as if to another country.

The last tenants on the floor, a family of five, insisted to stay above the ghosts, Away from things that won't let you sleep, Yes mother. Dad had initially told everyone to bunker down beside the bedroom dresser, pillows and sheets on the rug, the television and radio unplugged. Mom had made sandwiches, wrapped them in napkins, the little she could do in the rush she felt she needed to be in. As everyone snacked, as the first hour dragged on, she impressed a wisdom that arrives when stuck in the shadows, Echoes will startle awake only the ugly things girls, Yes mother, And soft steps you don't count give things you can't see permission to join us, Yes mother.

After they'd waited long enough, for what, exactly, even Mom was unsure of, Dad moved everyone into the living room, where he built a sofa cushion fort, leaving a slight opening for the air conditioner to circulate a closeness he and Mom had wanted to navigate without having to say why. But soon everyone was hungry again, and the family moved into the kitchen, and as Mom toasted a tortilla and eggs over the stove, Dad and his three daughters sat huddled by the sink, the cupboard lamp on, the ceiling fan spinning, Mom glancing regularly at the front door as if ready to measure the degrees it had swung open, if at all.

Eventually, the family ate their late evening meal at the kitchen table, every girl in her seat, Mom and Dad taking from their plates while standing up. After tossing the scraps and settling the dishes in the sink, Mom said she wanted to open the front door, to at least start discerning the grumbles, Our family Domingo has nothing to hide. She insisted she could open the door without even letting anyone's secrets slither into the pantry, Nothing

Domingo not even legless whispers, Okay Soria, I promise Domingo not even the flies, Fine Soria open the door.

Dad slowly took his girls to the staircase, Mom lingering at the front door, concerned it would lock them out. The Oldest Daughter walked with her gaze stuck on the tiles, the Middle Daughter paced as if approaching a canyon, the Youngest complained about the heat. When Mom finally pulled up the rear, she told everyone she was prepared to yank them back, We're not going down the steps, Never Soria, So pick up your feet girls, Yes mother, In case we need to hurry into the closets, Yes mother.

Dad sat on the top step, his girls beside him, Mom beside them. They watched the open stairwell window, the adjacent building's bricks, pigeons on and off the ledge. After a few minutes, the Oldest Daughter excused herself to the bathroom, a few minutes later Mom and the Middle Daughter returned to the kitchen, and then later the Youngest was gone. After a while only Dad remained, a sentinel for everyone he couldn't see.

He passed the time nibbling grapes. He shuffled between sitting against the wall and then leaning against the banister rail, and then he braved to sit one step lower, daring to move near the story he seemed far too hesitant to join.

After the electricity collapsed across the street and harsh reality congested the summer heat, the Youngest Daughter rejoined Dad. She ran to him swinging a crackling plastic bag with her own grapes, plopped on the top step beside her father, Hi dad, Hi peach. She caught her breath, exhaled, and the wind seemed to scrape the stairwell window clean, innocence always adamant about tearing down walls where the glaring moonlight obstructs bridges between stories, Did you tell your mother you were coming, Yes dad, Don't eat the seeds honey, Yes dad.

Far below them, in the lobby, an argument between tenants erupted. It seemed a woman was yelling at a man until a younger man interrupted to yell at them both, and then someone alluded to things behind closed doors no one interrupts no matter how deeply they dig at their own grave, Will we be able to go downstairs tomorrow dad, I don't know honey, But you aren't fighting with me, I'm not honey, Then why are they fighting each other, It's not always so easy to say honey.

Dad heard something. He stiffened, tugged for a moment by someone on the street, a laugh that rang over everyone else's, a sob, a shout, a rush, What are they looking for dad, They're looking for the right kind of story honey, What kind of story is the right kind, One that's honest about having none of the right answers, Is it hard daddy, To do what honey, To be honest about the right answers, Sometimes it's really hard to say we just don't know.

Dad reached for his pocket, grazed the outside, made sure of his keys, his change. He reached over his Youngest Daughter's shoulder. She slid into his arm, Do they know, Do they know what honey, That it's okay not to know, They're busy fighting for the wrong things right now, What are the wrong things, Stories that try to be facts instead of hope, What does it matter, Stories give you the past honey so it's easy to see the future, Can you make everyone stop yelling, I can't honey, Why are there so many people around us, Because the alternative is to hide in a closet, Why, Because there are always things we'll raise fists for to make sure nobody sees.

She nodded, I don't care about stories, Don't say that honey, Mom says stories are lies, Mom likes to see more than she has to, I don't want to be like the people downstairs, Sometimes we can't help it honey.

Mom's shirt hung over her belt and fluttered when she called from the door, Where's Laura, She's in the living room, Where's Nora, She's in the bedroom I think, What do you mean, Or in the closet I think I know she's inside. Inside, somebody was moving furniture. Inside, legs and arms went limp in the dark.

After he closed the front door behind them, Dad hung the chain. He stomped on the clamp that dug into the floor, and he turned the knob that drove a bolt into the frame. Mom crouched to slide pots under the stove. Dad settled clean plates into the cupboard. The Youngest Daughter started helping her mother put necessities into an ice chest: milk, ketchup, cheese, onion. Dad reached over her to drop bananas into the bin. Through the open window, the commotion seemed no match for the wall-mounted clock over the table measuring echoes and burning the minutes with only a battery.

From somewhere no one saw coming, too many things fell and shook the floor, It's Nora, I'll go check, Go easy on her Domingo, I'll handle this calmly Soria.

Dad tripped over a dollhouse and two plastic water guns in the hallway after the living room. He pushed the guns aside and crouched to make sure he hadn't broken the chimney. At his bedroom, Dad slowly pushed open the door, peeked inside, and there she was, the Middle Daughter, standing over a toppled hanger and one of her father's suits and a seven-foot piece of rope, What were you doing, I wanted to try on a scarf, But neither of those things is a scarf. She shrugged, What have I told you about rummaging through our things, I just jumped and reached for something I thought it would be, But you can't do that honey, I just jumped reaching for something I thought I could see.

Dad left the door ajar and circled the bed. The moonlight shone faintly on the pillows. He crouched to pick up the suit, Here hold it by the hem, Yes dad, And here hold it softly at the sleeves, Yes dad. He insisted gentleness lest they startle something awake. He almost lost his balance but caught himself and his breath before his knee hit the floor, Thank you honey, And there was something else, It's okay honey, Dad I dropped two things but I don't see the second anymore, I'm not splitting hairs here honey.

Dad patted her on the head and leaned over to kiss her, and then Mom came in asking what everything had been. She stopped mid sentence, though, for reasons only her story of things had managed to piece together because even in the moonlight, the things that happened yesterday were apparent, Please go to the living room Nora.

The girl skirted around the room to leave and stumbled into the rope her father had attempted to deftly slip under the bed.

Mom closed the bedroom door behind her, She dropped the suit but it's fine, What is that, Trust me I didn't yell at her, The suit isn't the only goddamn thing in this room Domingo.

A pigeon leapt between banisters on the fire escape. A squirrel hopped wires running between windows and scurried across the ledge, Think about what you intend to say, This isn't the best light in which to see anything Soria, Be absolutely sure Domingo you know the order of things, I'm not sure what you think this looks like Soria, You know damn well Domingo we may not know the whole story up here but we absolutely surely know the most important part.

Sometimes secrets scurry into the bedroom before a marriage ever gets to hiding under the sheets, and even when they don't find their way completely to the door, their smells trail onto the pillows from faraway places where no one ever remembers other people's names, I've been meaning to throw that out, Where was that exactly, It's just trash, That's not what I'm asking, I don't know what you think I'm a part of Soria, Did you know what was going to happen, How could you say that, Why do you think I'm saying that, Somebody left a note by the mailboxes that they were looking for a piece of rope,

And so you sold the man a piece of rope, Yes I sold the man a long piece of rope what does it matter.

A quiet like a caged hog began stomping floorboards and ramming the walls, punching holes with a story too many of us wanted to stop repeating by the end of the night, Does anyone else know about this, I'm sure everyone saw the note, But do they know you gave it to him, Silence isn't a virtue in this place Soria, What does that mean, I'm sure if someone else had known we'd have been asked by now, Then we're going to have to hide it because we can't just throw it away right now, You're not going to convince me this was my fault, There was a note Domingo the man was all but asking someone to help him.

A plastic bag rolled across the neighboring rooftop. A gnat dove into the window and got caught in the screen, You're being unreasonable Soria, Get it out of our house, I'm not going public with it, I don't care if you hurl it from the roof just hide it, Where do you expect me to go, If that stays here then I'm going to start feeling as responsible as you, What that man did was his own problem Soria and his own fault, And it's yours too and you've covered my hands in the same blood you're too selfish to see is all over you too.

Mom yanked the suit from the bed and hung it up. Dad barely budged as she pushed him aside to grab the hanger, and as she walked out, the faint moonlight spilled onto the back of his hair, casting a shadow so thick onto the bed, his cheeks contrasted the discernible yellow blue orange and red behind him, everything bubbling with the vibrant, almost violent clamor of a dark rainbow.

LOOP SEVEN: THE CLERK'S OFFICE

Down the street, where Mystic intersects Avenue of the Invention, City Hall sits draped in tri-colored, densely woven, polyester curtains, each sheet knotted at its center like an hourglass. Six curtains hang across the street-side façade, ruffled effects as low as the first-story windows, lending the one-hundred-year-old building an elegance not seen since the World Wars gave it something to celebrate.

On either side of the wide front steps, the city's renowned former mayors stand in all their bronze glory. The right statue depicts a man so thick, the cube base on which he stands is five meters wide, and the buttons on the bronze jacket, in true form, struggle to withhold the man's belly. To the left of the steps, the statue portrays a man so thin, even in bronze form his bony neck radiates a frailty so palpable the statue fights tooth and nail, with its every pound, against the summer breeze to keep from tipping over. Doric columns at the top of the steps support the triangular arch over the front entrance, guarding city magistrates the way city magistrates ought to be guarded, screened from the menial concerns surrounding municipal buildings, pettiness addressing the late-running buses and the litter around the credit union and the ever increasing price of milk. Every day, letters arrive for the mayor, mostly from the city's tenements where every tenant, it seems, sees fit to complain about faulty television reception or the wobbly slides at the park or, more often than not, the multiplying strays, Mr. Mayor please round up and euthanize the dogs outside my kitchen window, Mr. Mayor please four howling bitches in heat crept into my yard and I haven't slept in weeks, Mr. Mayor please what in God's name is it you do all day.

And because mayors do this, neglect less offensive social ills, few if any dilemmas would ever be addressed, few if any public afflictions heard or attended to or much less considered, if it weren't for the night shift clerks in City Hall's basement offices. Reading the volume of letters is the solitary labor that fully engrosses the several clerks at the mayor's disposal. It is they who scour incoming letters to discern the readable from the blatantly illegible, the reasonable from the logistically nightmarish, either because potential solutions for the latter fall beyond some allotted budget or because political will is but a lousy, flimsy shit. It is these clerks who nightly scan envelopes for legitimate proper names, so as to cross reference addressers with the city's voter registry, because ever since there have been cities, there have been weak municipal policies that do not require city officials to care for anyone who has not also cared for them.

And because street chatter is beneath no one, listless urban commotion catches everyone's attention. In this respect, City Hall's basement clerks are no different, especially attuned to rumors because their positions require it. They're particularly suited to catch wind of hearsay because their office windows are always ajar during summer evening working hours, despite the air conditioner that runs on end to lend rhythm to the filing. And so it must be said, as surely dozens before us have, as if time offers only the binding to learn from but not the whole book, which explains an awful worship of aphorisms for impressionable repetition, as if wisdom were something to fuck at convenience then leave shivering in the cold like a whore, these basement clerks have always embodied what must be repeated here for structural sake, that the world cannot and would never function if not for the ridicule and labor of the lonely.

Clerk No.1, closest to the open window, suppressed a long yawn, pressing her left hand to her chest when she cleared her throat, I've had several letters about the broken radio antenna at the baseball field, I'm always proud of the things we can fix, It isn't every day we find them, But it's every day we strive.

Clerk No.2, in a desk across the aisle, nodded and opened another envelope. Clerk No.1 fit into her slippers and then aimed for the cabinets arranged alphabetically on the far wall. She opened cabinet "R" to file away a letter that animatedly suggested solutions for porous rooftops in public housing and a second letter that denounced the mayor's political stance on rummaging through old railroad yards. Filing in established categories requires subdivisions, which in this case meant a hanging folder each for *radio antennae*, *radioactivity*, and *field rabbits*, I'm getting coffee, Thank you I'd love some.

Clerk No.1 closed and locked the cabinet drawer. Heading toward the kitchen, she passed Clerk No.2's desk as he swiveled to meet her, You look nice today. Clerk No.1 stopped midstride and glanced down her front, We must remain professional, But there isn't a wrinkle, We're both professionals here, I don't expect less, We manage well enough, I juggle two clerical jobs to do it, And the help we receive is formally appreciated, Indeed it must be.

Clerk No.1 nodded, Coffee is on its way.

Clerk No.2 swiveled back into his duties. As Clerk No.1 left the room, foreign footsteps echoed from the open window. Clerk No.2 looked up, but beyond glancing to the sill, he didn't pause to consider whether the steps indicated a man or a woman, friend or foe, heels clicking with the purposefulness of a metronome, which for an eight o'clock summer night was peculiar but not unexpected, the night unbearably hot but still welcoming, if only because the day was gone and the moon, as opposed to the sun, never imposes a scrutinizing glare.

After four minutes, Clerk No.1 returned with two cups swirling in steam, Cream and no sugar, As always. Clerk No.2 nodded, but he also seemed distracted, and so Clerk No.1 lingered at his desk, half-expecting him to unprofessionally compliment her shoes, half expecting him to recognize she'd also returned with a handful of napkins, I don't get it, What's not to get, It's an envelope with no stamp. Clerk No. 1 held up the envelope, I don't understand, This must have been personal, Have you looked inside, I have not, You must know it's a passion that inspires hand-written messages and personal delivery, You mean like a feeling, Just look at the face.

Clerk No.2 brought the envelope to his eyes, It has only initials, Imagine the passion to be so curt, I don't follow, This letter in your hands doesn't expect a reply.

Clerk No.1 took the envelope and held it high so the overhead lights enlivened the edges. She turned it forward and back and sideways, This can't be more than eight words long, And is that a feeling, Like solitude and negligence and buried away, Does it permeate paper, I'm not sure, Then I'll file it for later review before the midnight shift is done.

Another set of footsteps with regular heels echoed into the room. Clerk No.1 returned to her desk unbothered, but Clerk No.2 stared at the grass just outside the sill. He got up and leapt onto an empty desk to look at the sidewalk. At first all he could discern was the grass, but he quickly turned right and saw a woman's full back as she walked past City Hall's front steps, a street light glimmering off her calves and brushed hair and light jacket. Suddenly beside him, Clerk No.1 had reached for the desk to keep it from wobbling, What are you doing, I don't know, Don't lie to me, It's just not the same thing when I can't make out what I'm feeling.

The Clerks remained still until the heels' echoes were gone, Are you counting something, It's the third person walking past our window in formal shoes, Must be something official, Or consequential.

Clerk No.2 returned to the floor and, for as long as it took to shatter distances, he half-stared at Clerk No.1 half-expecting her to understand his judgment, Clerk No.1 half-expecting him to prefer a reasonable corporate behavior. In their dignified silence, they returned to their desks, Clerk No.2 reluctantly gazing across the room from the copier to the stapler to the light switch to the phone books stacked by the door to the shelved binders of detailed legislative history codified by fiscal year. Until a fourth person walked past the open window with their shoes clicking loudly, and both Clerks popped out of their seats without consulting the schedule.

Outside, the Clerks leaned quickly over the sidewalk, leaning so far forward it seemed they wanted to both see and hear the stranger, the fourth person that had passed their open basement window, across and just down the street. The stranger walked a half block and then stopped at a line of us standing outside the public defender's office. The stranger must have exhaled from afar because the clerks could see the man's shoulders fall, his flustered lips searching for something above the lights, muttering to himself, twitchy fingers in his pockets, his eyes unstill and his feet stuttering on the concrete. From his inside jacket pocket, he pulled out a form creased from top to bottom, and then he bothered the woman ahead of him, as if to question her occupation there or simply ask her about the timing between coincidences and what, if anything, can be done about things before they actually occur, and the woman pointed to the building's double-glass doors, where a flickering yellow sign read *Guilt Services*, to which the man retorted with the inaudible but certain *Thank you*.

When the Clerks set their feet firmly beneath them, they gave each other puzzled looks, What are they doing, Sometimes people get insomnia, But on a summer night the same night, What does your gut say, I just said it, What does your intuition say, That we hear about things first, I was thinking the same thing, Of course you were, But I don't know what else to think.

Clerk No.1 walked to the curb. Clerk No.2 waited for her as he sipped his coffee, It could be any number of things, We would have heard about them, Maybe it's an immutable sordid mess, Nothing is incorrigible, Well it makes sense to start somewhere, But not so loosely, But we have to start somewhere, We need evidence first we need to hear things.

They looked down the street the other way. Almost immediately, they discerned the growing footsteps of a fifth stranger one block away, steadily approaching and emerging into the street light, a thickening shadow across the sidewalk, Something is wrong, Perhaps this person will stop, We have to make them stop, We can't just make them stop, At some point we have to ask questions and make people stop, But that would be rude and invasive, Nothing is rude and invasive if it's absolutely necessary.

The palm above Clerk No.1 shivered in the breeze, the clatter of its leaves like the cushioned promises of a pillow that strangers share. The Clerks stared at the approaching stranger, which, from the stranger's perspective, must have felt like the paralyzing stares of beggars waiting to shake their tin cans, inductions of unnecessary guilt obstructing the walking path, like a public spectacle that forces upon us a spirit to things we don't want, like vision, like sight in the face of frustration and earnestness and pain we prefer to shut off because those incidentals leave us uneasy and a little bit guilty and the City a complicated place of insufferable mistakes.

Clerk No.1 stepped forward to stop the stranger and Clerk No.2 stepped forward to reluctantly stop Clerk No.1, but to the stranger it all seemed like an avalanche about to barrel her in supplication, Please miss, Excuse me I must be going, Please miss we're municipal clerks in search of answers, But I must be going, We don't mean to stop you so rudely miss, We're curious about the nature of all this, Please excuse me I'm only looking to make it through, Why is everyone in that line, Excuse me but I must be going, Is the law a particularly crude thing tonight, What my colleague is trying to say is we don't understand the business of that line, Another person's business is none of my own now if you would please excuse me, But certainly you must see that everyone there appears to be in the same warm bath, Whether my problem is in some way related to their problem is not my problem, But what my colleague is trying to say miss, I can understand English just fine, All we want to know miss is why we have a line at all, if you would please excuse me.

The Clerks could suddenly hear the chatter down street, because they had unintentionally raised their voices in response to the stranger raising her voice in response to their rising voices and suddenly all three of them had become so self-aware of their own volume that their lips short-circuited amidst streetlights gone brighter and so they all just shut up completely to listen to the still, humid air.

The stranger exhaled, I'm sorry, Miss we work for the Department of Resentment and Reasonable Complaints, Then you must have heard about what happened, As night shift clerks it's our duty to be informed, Then you must know all about what's occurred, Our department makes no presumptions or promises miss, Then as usual the City knows nothing, Perhaps if we could hear it from you, I reserve my privilege not to ask or say a word, It's only the barest details we need, Well I cannot share, Miss it's only the bare essentials we need to know.

The stranger read over the Clerks' nametags, A man has been found hanged, Goodness has the coroner arrived, They have come and gone, Have the police been called, They have shown up in force, Has an account been certified, There are stories being accounted for, Then what is the problem, I would like to keep my head down but it seems the world has changed. The Clerks looked at each other. They looked at the stranger. The stranger looked at them. The moon emerged from behind the clouds and tugged on their breathing rippling everywhere, Was there someone involved, It's precisely the problem, Were you involved, You should see everyone else, Is there something to blame, Where do you start, As long as it's somewhere, But we all started here, And what's wrong with this place, It's no place for people, Miss please tell us who's guilty, It's not my responsibility to get everyone's story straight, Miss we must all bear our stories out so that we can see and hear from each other, But Clerk I am just not wired that way.

All three of them looked off, the Clerks to the pavement, the stranger into the concrete, Then can you tell us Miss what that line is for, It's there because it's clear now that we're all involved, Because you saw something and you did nothing, Because we saw nothing and we all did less, But it's not a crime to want to change or do better, But it's incorrigible dear Clerk when you did nothing and still want to do less, But we can always use moments like this to amend those same moments tomorrow, But I'm simply not wired that way Clerk so I'll have to gamble with unwritten laws.

The stranger adjusted her shoulder bag and started walking away. Surprised, Clerk No.1 jumped quickly in stride alongside her, even though the pacing was slow and their words never came. At the corner, the crosswalk ahead of them like a beckoning plank, Clerk No.1 reached for the stranger's hand but the stranger pulled away and crossed unafraid and assured.

The Clerks watched the stranger join the standing line. Clerk No.1 struggled with a knotted throat and stiff lips when Clerk No.2 tapped her shoulder. She nodded and they both turned back to their office. Hands in their pockets, Clerk No.1 suffered no hesitation, but Clerk No.2 had to bury his hands deeply just to keep from turning around and turning to salt.

Back in the basement filing office, Clerk No.2 sat at his desk. He picked up the envelope that had been personally delivered to the office and opened it half-heartedly, half-automated, half-expecting to feel it burst without feeling or consequence. Clerk No.2 slit open the flap, *I.R.* initialed across the envelope seal, unfolded the letter, and the story without details that had covered our night, the sidewalk and pavement with permanent shadows, suddenly echoed from wall to wall in a deep silent moan, and so to keep it from ricocheting back to his hands, Clerk No.2 gave it calmly to Clerk No.1 so she could read it and feel the same pitted emptiness that he, and we, would never stop feeling, even after the City finally called us to order, even after the City asked us to resign unto things that would never be allowed another suggestion or definition: *I kept calling but no one spoke and I kept fighting but no one fought back and I kept insisting that being here was just the same as being there because I could never find those right directions to take to get out and to the city to everyone here it doesn't seem important to anyone to know how to get out of places we find ourselves unfortunately in and so I'd rather be nowhere than just stuck in between these places that cram us and don't let us leave. Thank you for your time.*

LOOP EIGHT: THE CHURCH

There are sentiments that possess letters because they do not deliver themselves, intentions behind their ink because they do not write themselves. But this is no longer a mere complication of hurried words, scripted, as they often are, carefully, such that a thick, horizontal line across a *t* might suggest that the word was deeply felt, wholeheartedly meant to express more than just the word *city*, for example, but also the spirit of one, the loneliness of one, cities like an accrual of strangers more secure in the clamoring company of a frantic pace than in the temporal silence of a solitary tree.

And the anonymous letter sent to the Department of Resentment and Reasonable Complaints, by incorporating the word *city*, transformed the collective noun into a whole person, a personality, one that inhales deeply into the thick of building, one that exhales relieved into the torments of alley, and one that, when lying down to sleep, enfolds each and every person in something akin to an envelope, a sealed warm embrace, a grip that tightens as the night matures, until at last, come morning, we find ourselves surrounded by bars, encaged by scratched shivering windows and unceasing ambulance sirens and delivery trucks delivering, loudly running their engines so as to become, in the scope of this new nature, the barnyard boar, only with purpose and yet always sauntering about with a veiled threat of chaos, as if to say, This could be the night I crash into the corner storefront and shatter the glass.

At some point that night, Old Man Rose got tired of it all. Just exhausted. They'd tried shutting their first-floor window to keep out the noise, but the rumbling still crept in. They'd tried raising the volume on their television during the news, but the echoes of the hallway shuffles still snuck into the kitchen. And they'd even tried, on top of all that, to run the vacuum cleaner across the living room rug and in the couch cushions and then keep the vacuum running, but nothing—no combination of anything gave them any peace, and when they eventually left the apartment and joined the whole neighborhood on the sidewalk, hobble and all, their nerves worsened. They kept moving. From curb to pavement. Around vendors and trucks. Into and through circles of busybodies. And it was the same everywhere. No peace. Anywhere.

They'd spent the afternoon writing another letter to their daughter, their only child, the one who hadn't forgiven them yet for changing, for being something else, for being more, for being who'd they'd always been—for being who they'd always been but hadn't shown. But they hadn't mailed the letter, and Old Man Rose thought about all that, about one day sending the letter, perhaps one day later that week, as he pressed his hand into a car window, and then turned his back to it to lean. The occasional siren put a comma to something else that somebody in the crowd had shouted or gone on about. The occasional siren put a period to something else that somebody in the crowd had shouted to the police about. Old Man Rose took their inhaler from their pocket and took a puff in the face of all that murmuring and shouting, inhaling as deeply as they ever had, the summer air like a limp butterfly. Clinging with nowhere to go. Stale, heavy, and thick.

We all have instincts, especially ones that mislead us, and so we fall prey to cynicism when our instincts fail us and leave us stuck in some bout of sweat and discomfort. And we blame *ourselves* for putting ourselves in the most crowded of situations, when we land ourselves onto a busy sidewalk with no one we know, with no one who cares to know about who we are or what our problems might be, but with everyone who cares too much, obsesses too much, about the death of a man they never knew and who will never be known, but because we enjoy the stories we make for ourselves, the stories we can spin and change every time we tell them, we are where we are. On a street with so much loss. On the intersection of Mystic and Pyre with so much left to be said.

Old Man Rose took another puff of their inhaler, and then they scanned the street, eyes lingering so far right that they spun them around so completely and circled them back to where they started. Nervous. Alone. They almost choked on that second breath with a hack so unforgiving and unrepentant and nauseating that the commotion temporarily felt easy, at home, and then their eyes recovered and they saw the spread of faces for what they might have been, all of them believing that just because they couldn't understand what had happened, they must have all done something awful to make it happen.

Old Man Rose could only take so much of it, though, and after a few minutes of lingering down the street, his hand grazing the bricks of the building's exterior wall, they started snapping their fingers. Initially to build the momentum to catch their breath, but people are what they've always been. People always assume that what you do for yourself has, in some way, in some unseen way, everything to do with them, and so the people around Old Man Rose started parting the way for them after the fourth or fifth snap, and Old Man Rose did what they often do. Fall into the momentum of the world around them. It's so much easier to fall into place than to carve your own place, and so they followed the ready-made path. They walked through the parting of the sea of people, and when they arrived to an unpassable bank of people, Old Man Rose snapped their fingers again, and the people there did the same. They made a way, and even with a cane, Old Man Rose could move, as if the cane were both prop and propulsion, something akin to the loud farting roar of a sports car engine. But moving quickly and moving faster than the world expected could feel like the same thing even as they amounted to completely different things, and despite the rush on their lips, mumbling as they were to themself, The dead why we do we care so much about the dead, they moved slowly, deliberately, their raise high if only to remind themself that they had a direction and that direction was anywhere that pointed ahead.

Old Man Rose yelled at no one, despite the look on their face that seemed to want to yell at everyone. Even as they came up to a couple holding hands who didn't release them, Old Man Rose had gotten too much into rhythm, too much into the spirit of the times, into the spirit of the night, that compelled him to sit in the loneliness of all this and still find a way to move through it and keep going. And so they snapped their finger until they caught the couple's attention, until the couple looked at one another and looked confused, so confused, and until they unclasped their hands and then let each other go and Old Man Rose walked between them, taking turns to meet their eyes and look forward, all the while muttering, We deserve this don't we and why wouldn't we deserve this.

Old Man Rose and those old elbows of theirs, jutting out, swinging like violent sticks, and that wide of stance of theirs, that bowlegged walk of theirs, that hobble of theirs, that pointed nose of theirs, all of it making a crooked walk that somehow teetered on the brink of both collapse and a full sprint. That jerking, that neck twitch, that shoulder spasm, when Old Man Rose moved, they commanded attention, and when Old Man Rose looked at you, they commanded confusion, and then they arrived to the curb, and the forward momentum was too much to stop. They banged the billboard barricade with their cane, disconnected as it was to its adjacent piece. But the nearest police officer only turned to them, tilted his head, narrowing his eyes, and watched Old Man Rose as if a beggar had arrived to his door, someone incapable of changing the tide of a night. But Old Man Rose had come too far, from their apartment and down the stairs and down the sidewalk and across the street and down the block some and finally to the intersection of Mystic and Pyre. They had come too far.

Old Man Rose snapped their fingers, fast, thrice, a succession like they weren't only demanding something but waking up an impulse in the night that had gone on too long without a voice, and the snaps parted nothing except something in the view of Old Man Rose, who took to finally seeing the part between two adjacent strips of billboard barricade, and so they nudged the barriers just a bit further apart, needing barely a push, and then they stepped right onto the pavement as if called to it, pulled to it, like a demon exorcised from the body of a torn man.

There had never been such a sight. Those old jutting elbows. That wide-stride walk. That hobble. Old Man Rose emerged into the intersection, and the closest police officer ran for them, took their arm, tried to divert them back onto the sidewalk. Too suddenly, though, other members of the crowd formed a line behind them, and too suddenly there was no clear path back onto the sidewalk. The crowd very much crowding the billboard barricade and streaming onto the street, and Old Man Rose tried pulling their arm from the officer's hand, but the officer's grip hardened. Old Man Rose tugged harder, but the Police Officer couldn't have become sterner, Don't be nasty elder, We deserve this is what we do, That's enough now elder, There's no forgiveness for negligence is there, I need you to get back onto sidewalk elder, What kind of penance will ever be enough, I said stop all this elder, We need to confess ourselves is what we need is what we're always going to need, That's enough now elder.

But the neighbor who'd lined up behind Old Man Rose yelled at the police officer, and the police officer told the woman to back off, but the woman almost fell forward because the person behind her pushed forward because the person behind them had pushed forward every person on down the line had pushed their way onto the street and there was no turning back. And the officer let Old Man Rose go because the commotion had elevated the temperature at the intersection, and every officer on scene rushed to the crowd as it made its way across the avenue, the hunched elder up front with those old jutting elbows and that wide-stride stance and that hobble leading everybody's way, leading them, truly, absolutely, like a Moses lost to the obscenities of a broken night.

And there they were, Old Man Rose leading everyone across the intersection, muttering, We're to blame we're to blame, repeating it to no one as the officers lined up to the left and right of the line of people streaming across the avenue. Dozens followed. Dozens more waited to follow. The billboard barricade truly, absolutely, eroding like riverbank weeds hacked off in time by a stampede that won't end.

Old Man Rose reached the opposing curb with the hemming of their pants bunched up and their cuffs undone, and when they raised their shirt to dry their chin, their belly all but pleaded for a cold, dark room in which to hide. The second person in line caught Old Man Rose from falling as they fumbled to tuck their shirt back into their pants, and then the two walked arm in arm up the sidewalk, but there was no interrogation. No question and no perceived direction. Just some odd sense of trust, some unnameable faith that this flame gone wild, this three-alarm fire compelled by a hanging and fueled by lament, had a place to go, somewhere it wanted to end. And then Old Man Rose pointed to the church, to its stairs, to its banister, and the woman holding him said, Yes, and, Of course, but without a dawned realization in her tone, with more of a stalwart appreciation that times like these, times with no forgiveness and no comfort, could find solace in a building that had already made clear no such thing could ever be found.

At the church door, Old Man Rose grabbed the knockers, tapped the door, and then pushed into the metal, the knocks as if just wanting to sound the alarm to let the old priests inside the building know that the main hall, and every red candle flame in the foyer, was about to be lit up.

The Parish Priest had been cleaning the altar with a spray bottle and cloth as Old Man Rose and everyone behind him entered the foyer and then the sanctuary. The Priest wiped the marble in circles and paid the entrants mind only insomuch as he was thankful to have his silence broken. He sprayed the northeast corner of the altar and then wiped. He crouched at the altar's east side and sprayed the marble and then wiped. All the while, men, women, couples, children, classifiable only by their shirts or mustaches, filed into the pews beginning with the rear ones, and when the Parish Priest stood up to look around, people like raindrops into the church had become a stream, a dead waterfall suddenly shocked to meet an unexpected current of fish.

The Priest didn't seem unsettled by it, though. After all, if nothing else, God is a mystery even unto God, and so after he folded his cleaning cloth and picked up his pail, he made his way across the front of the church, to a side door that opened into a corridor which, in turn, led to a broom closet and the rectory. As he leaned back opening the door, his pail rattled as if to announce an opening bell. For the Parish Priest, cleaning God's house always presented one endless chore after another, though not always the company to do so. And on this night, as he sighed stepping into the corridor, he straightened his collar knowing all he could hope for was at least the will and posture to remain upright in a rain of words.

Old Man Rose had already been kneeling for four minutes when the Parish Priest entered the confessional. After he sat, Hello there, he buttoned his cuffs and then adjusted the stole over his shoulders, And what is your name child, Hello father. The Parish Priest leaned into the screen, Hello father, Hello there. Old Man Rose leaned close, Father I have sinned, Tell me my child, I have killed and I have seen and I have taken it all in and can't take it anymore to hold it all in.

The Parish Priest cleared his throat. He tilted his right cheek slightly back and then rested his elbow on the armrest, Talk to me child, A man died tonight father, And how are you involved, I killed him, What did you do child, It's everything you think of and more father, and then Old Man Rose elaborated, in a curtness that seemed to suggest they were saying it all while omitting everything, and they listed their transgressions of abject neglect and abandon and those deficient social graces that fail to notice those sad eyes beneath hats, And I have lived two floors beneath him two years father and I haven't heard him once speak to me through the stone and concrete or through the vents and Lord knows he probably tried and because I couldn't hear him cry

I should have tapped the walls until the taps radiated as high as they could go if only to confirm that the man was still treasuring life the way of dogs and automobiles but I didn't father I didn't do a damn thing to look after him father.

The Parish Priest scratched his nose. It had been a long, hot evening, and his sweaty shoulders had left his sleeves moist. When he clasped his hands, he leaned forward to the edge of his seat, How were you involved child, I destroyed the man father, But how were you directly involved, I killed the man father, and then Old Man Rose generalized a host of crimes with little choice and whose passions were born without choice, failures to recognize souls in common and bodies without touch or flame, and those derelictions of duty illustrating a waned awareness of a dying world, And I think I saw the man closing the basement door father but I can't recall for sure but what I think I can remember is that I saw his deep-set eyes drop and I think I saw them drop not just on one day but on many days father and I said nothing I didn't think of doing anything and all I can think is that I did nothing to chase him down the basement steps whether or not my legs would have allowed it and whether or not he'd left a straight path between us to watch him descend so that I could follow and whether or not I actually saw what I thought I saw and all of these things father.

The Parish Priest sat upright. He pressed the ends of his lips into a frown for reasons too frustrating to excite, What exactly happened, He was hanged father, Did you hang him or did you find him hanging, An irrelevant difference, There are no minor distinctions where we sit, We should have all been better father, But how didn't you stop him if you could have stopped him, Our silence father the world's silence it shuts us in and leaves us stiff and we're left incapable of doing what we should be doing, But you weren't the one to open the door to the basement were you, Why are you just mincing details father, And you weren't the one who knowingly offered the man the rope he used, But our blindness father it was our blindness that might as well have sold the man's soul to the devil or negotiated for a place in your god's heaven father, But you weren't the one to hang the rope or hang the man's neck, It was our closed doors father that nudged the man to do what he did and then locked him away, But you weren't the one to threaten or coerce him to comply to hang himself nor were you the man to tighten the knot.

Old Man Rose exhaled, Why are you interrogating me father, You're an innocent man before someone else's grave sin, But I'm confessing the world to you father and you don't seem to care, But words sir even in this place have got to be cleared for posterity's sake, Why are you getting so agitated father, Because murder is not a confession I can take lightly, It's we who have eyes father that must be born to use them. The Parish Priest clenched his fists as if to keep from choking the screen.

He removed his glasses. Wiped the lenses. Rubbed his eyes. The confessor bowed his head, the lumpy shadow behind them hanging on the soundproof wall as if it bore a hundred faces, You've painted a logic my child, And with it I've murdered a man, But I need you to understand that it wasn't your fault, You don't know that father, I know enough to know that I need you to rest your head and be okay tonight, And yet there are men among us who will never be okay again and will never get the chance to do so again.

The Parish Priest pressed his palms into his knees. In the dusty corner, ruffled strands of hair shivered from the breeze slipping beneath the door, Are you there father, Yes I'm here, Why did you go quiet, Because there are no two ways I can say this, In the beginning was the word father and you can always find your way to it, You've done nothing wrong, You have no clue father about how the world really works do you, I'll grant you that your act is or can be an act of a higher order but you did not want the man dead, But didn't we, Well did you want the man dead, I never gave him a second thought, There you have it then, But our faith will always rest upon those things we give thought to even if we can't touch them, Sure but don't be so moved to impulse by the stories you hear or the stories you think you're discerning, The truth burns doesn't it father, Stop that, You're not getting it father, Confessing our sins must be qualified by the rhetoric we use, Our sins father are as much those things we know better not to do as they are the things we fail to do, But those omissions aren't enough to fill a church, That neglect father has already stepped into its doors and congested everything you hold close, Listen to me once and for all when I say that you did not kill this man, And yet someone is still dead, And this is not your fault, It indeed is, You're being self-centered elder, And you're not thinking enough about others father.

Old Man Rose pulled their shirt down after sneezing into it, and they stood up. The Parish Priest got up and reached for the doorknob but it was stiff. When he finally stepped out, every last pew sat full and even the far walls offered only standing room to people still trickling inside.

Old Man Rose had hobbled slowly out of the confessional, and they hadn't gone far when the Parish Priest reached firmly for their shoulder. Old Man Rose turned around and faced the priest with eyes so red that they might as well have just exorcised their grief, I want us to be clear about this, Why do you have ears father if you refuse to hear.

Around them, whispers drowned the church. Candle fumes fogged the pew ends, It isn't just a notion father if the world agrees it's at fault for what it is. Along the wall, people waited their confessional turn, the line so long it wound to the back and poured outside, and then someone pressed a rope into the Priest's hands, a seven-foot stretch he took as if holding an empty collection plate, We need absolution father for all those things we could not do.

The Parish Priest felt it through his fingers, and no one could tell you why he suddenly started counting the knots, but he did, And how were *you* involved, The responsibility we bear is a rain that waters the seasons full, But you didn't tie this rope yourself, We all have our roles father, But did you tie this man to this or any other rope, Retrospection father is what separates us from the animals, But no one among you hung this rope, We did what we could not do and did not do what we should have done father, But no one among you tied the rope or a rope just like it or coerced the man into his gravest sin so let's be clear about this because it's only murder if you hung the man yourself to the end of his life and to a goddamn piece of pipe and rope.

The Parish Priest pulled his hair back. He looked down at the woman who'd handed him the rope and she stared back, no indication she'd cow or bend, the wrinkles beneath her eyes like shades of war paint. The Parish Priest said nothing, and when he looked down the aisle, Old Man Rose had grabbed the last backrest before the open church doors, and then they disappeared.

LOOP NINE: THE HIGH SCHOOL

We lose ourselves in moments and meaning sometimes. And when we do, we turn to newspapers and books and desks. We find that place where lectures are more than sermons and context is all the content we need, because we lose sight of the drawn shades, especially when the cords are so constantly pulled that spools jam and sunlight streams in angles so deviant they squander across the floor like concerned eyes. And where there is only moon, flipping the light switch reveals the exile we hope for when the evening heat rattles the real world inescapable. After all, from time to time, moments will rile themselves until they roll into each other, incident for incident, person from person, story to story, anxiety upon anxiety until we breathe a tangible fear we can't avoid, however much its stench is the word we hung ourselves, however much its punctuation is the tone we used to share it. It's in these moments that we reach for the nearest classroom doors, our childhoods, and welcome fresh immersions into hallways full of hanging artwork and essays and those lessons we should have learned, if only to remind ourselves we still have time to learn them before someone writes above our names *You have no place here* or *You have learned nothing here.*

The City's memorial high school was such a place as this. It was commemorated in nineteen forty-seven for a soldier who, having dedicated consecutive tours of duty to his country, returned home with only the most dismal news, that which no patriot wants to hear, that war, however inescapable, is worthless and horrendously expressionless. It is with this feeling in mind that the City asked the soldier in whose honor the high school was being opened not to attend the ceremony, to find himself absent and speechless, to others and to himself, so that the ribbons could be cut without incident and so that the incoming students could apply their learning without perspective and without the horrors of our fair world to fear, Because they have their whole lives ahead to see things for what they really are, argued one commissioner, Because in the time they have left let's hope they can avoid the difficult things of this world altogether, argued another.

Places ultimately become their beginnings, and classrooms always return to the foundations that dug them dry. It's in this spirit that on that night, we arrived to the City's memorial high school and returned to learn something from its walls.

For most of the evening, there had been a candle holder sitting somewhere between us, on a yellow curb congested with ankles and white socks. At some point, she pulled out her lighter and lit her candle, and she stared into its flame as if expecting from it another story, a lie among other flying violent lies. Instead, it just flickered in her hands, the commotion everywhere stirring the flame left and then blowing it right, but mostly annulling opposing tendencies and leaving the flame to simply shiver in place.

In its small way, the fume rose unto the overhanging power lines and rattled the pigeons. The rising smoke, swaying as it coiled higher, went all but unnoticed in a sight already clouded by so many cigarettes. When the Candle Holder stood up, she looked around, and those of us beside her arched back to keep from burning. We broke up groups and separated huddles to let her pass. Some of us leaned back and waved her past and pulled others out of the way so as to make sure wherever the Candle Holder aimed she'd get there without another tragedy to count.

As she walked, she didn't have to push. The sea parted, and some of us soon began to follow, our inclinations to procession something that for one reason or another seemed hungry for revelation. But as we followed, murmurs revealed only unintelligible guesses about where she was going, and it wasn't until she neared the far intersection that the Candle Holder finally looked unto the flagpole and the state's crossroads coat-of-arms. Without chains, the high school's front doors seemed welcoming, and because one of the doors had been left ajar, the candle holder led us right inside as if in mourning for the empty desks.

We flooded the stairs. As we approached the school, we held above us lighters and candles and cell phones and flashlights aimed into the summer sky like distress signals calling for the comfort of strangers. Inside the school, everyone's upstretched hands beamed in the darkness. The procession to the back of the school was like a march to celebrate lives too enormous to capture without a fire. No one flipped the hallway light switch, and where we intended to go only the Candle Holder knew. Though with a gaze affixed to her flame, after a while, where we went didn't seem to matter.

When she stopped at the end of the second hallway, the Candle Holder turned into a twelfth-grade classroom. Initially she stopped at its door. She lowered her candle waist high, looked left and then right, and then above the door and beyond it, measuring empty spaces and the gravity of everyone that had followed this far. Slowly, we congregated around her, filling up the hallway until she discerned a familiar window and stepped into the classroom. When we followed, the school seemed to exhale, a prayer that leveled the walls and began what essentially amounted to a wake.

We occupied desks, surrounded the teacher's station, and covered the bulletin boards and supply closets and computer stations beneath the windows. The classroom quickly became a pedestal to stoke a fire. Even when someone flipped the switch, the light in everyone's hands outshined the bulbs above us. And in the ever-present shuffling of feet and soft chatter about what would happen next and why anyone had ruined the world with tall perspectives and even taller stories, about wars and faceless men whose intentions we uncover only after their lives oblige to a penultimate call to arms, apologies began to ring from one end of the classroom to the other. People excused themselves for incidentally tapping each other's elbows or brusquely stepping on each other's feet or mistakenly swiveling and stumbling into each other's knees, unnecessary *I'm-sorrys* but also gracious offerings of faces and lips to read and unburden the natural charges repelling us, illustrating up close the whites of our teeth and the vulnerabilities hanging between them.

The Candle Holder remained quiet, and so the First Speechmaker beside her assumed his position, which happens from time to time, this human effort to keep the volume going, to keep the silence at bay, because why else would anyone find themselves in the company of anyone else.

The First Speechmaker reached for the closest desk and stepped onto the attached chair, first shaking its base to test its strength, briefly screeching its legs across the floor to budge his stage into position. The First Speechmaker's first words were nowhere near as piercing, however, and when he spoke, he spoke of the dead. He spoke of things undone by inaction and left unsaid by too much silence, but also things left untouched and misunderstood by endless talking, particularly when the talking addresses nothing one sees or hears. But in his glaring omission of names, in his galling decision to avoid saying the words *Isidrio* and *Rafael*, either in succession or discontinuously, he created something of a story co-opted instead of cooperated, a story that failed to include everyone in town and most importantly the dead man at the center of all this. As such, the First Speechmaker spoke with an unmistakable lack of resolve, creating a beginning that proceeded without understanding and which could not bring rest, an oration that wanted to be a public confession but could only really speak of a world writ large to blame, not specifically *their* world that needed to bear the brunt of this guilt, And so the shame we think we feel is just that a shame we think we *should* feel one that doesn't reflect our actual feeling which is that this moment is about that we already see when the sun goes down and what I mean is that it's about those things that can't amount to much because they're out of focus or they're out of sight so let's keep that in mind when we blame ourselves for something because yes we should be carrying the night but we should be carrying everything that this is night is about.

Few of us in the classroom nodded.

Waves of people had not stopped coming into the school. Everyone streamed into the building and stairwells and hallways emerging from the shadows on the road, recognizing, perhaps, that their reflections in the painted bricks upholding the walls and in the glass encasing medals and banners were, at heart, more than just the faces they saw in the mirror. On the steps, we'd supported each other up, and in the crowded doorways, our moisture was a beach of breathless whispers wondering why the hanging world always waits until no one can remember its face before it stirs our tongues. With footsteps echoing as far as the teachers' closets and as loudly as the three o'clock bell, and with the same handheld candles and lighters and cameras and flashlights hoisted above us, we filled all twelfth-grade classrooms and their desks and chairs until what emerged across an entire high school floor was that which had always seemed fit for this time and for this place. A dark prayer framed by flashes of light.

Soon a Second Speechmaker rose onto the teacher's desk. After absorbing the words that the First Speechmaker had left behind, this second speechmaker found her place by the attendance binder and undid, in the most direct way possible, all the processed words of the First Speechmaker. She spoke softly of iridescent voices that hadn't shut up since proceeding onto the street, of the ways everyone pushed each other into regressions, emphasizing their missteps and back-steps, Everything I'd have hoped was beneath us and wasn't part of us and frankly wasn't so alien to us that we would do better is unfortunately otherwise because what we should have done is to attest to someone's death in the same way we embraced his life: peacefully and with our mouths shut and with as much distance and distraction as necessary to proceed onto the next hour and into the next day while putting all this behind us where it belongs and where it should stay.

So many of us just crossed our arms. Still. Earnest to hear and see what hadn't made its way to the fore yet and earnest, too, for something that we didn't know would show up when we all showed up here. And exhaling heavily, the Second Speechmaker pressed her hand to her chest and stood, lamentably obvious, alone on the teacher's desk, and so she stepped down, and she did so with a disappointment on her face, and she looked around hoping for a validation that never, probably could never, find its way to the front of the classroom.

We had a vigil on our hands. That much had become evident from the First and Second Speechmakers' failed attempts at testimony, from their failure, from the selfishness we're sure they didn't mean but which they amounted to anyway, and so we didn't leave because we assumed their best was what they had offered even if their best was insufficient. Their best had only wanted to explain something rather than just acknowledge it. It wanted to move away from this all rather than sit with it and cry into and be okay with the messiness of it all.

And what would he have thought, that man whose neck had turned and whose face had that morning, before the tragedy, been just another face in an ocean of indiscernible agonies that could have remained as one of ours but decided to become a singular one, something that needed to express itself so desperately so that it could feel, finally, shared and not alone, though ultimately alone because we could not go, did not want to go, with him.

And so, yes, we needed more, and we needed someone to assume a third position, perhaps even one last position, in the room. And so by the time the Third Speechmaker stepped onto the milk crate in the corner of the classroom, our silence had turned into private grieving which had turned into an expectation. A flurry of coughs and sniffles and words like *Don't let me go* and *No, I don't want space right now* having filled the room and set the tone. And it was a long silence, and awkward, too, but aren't all silences simply something extraordinary at war with what we've come to expect, a loud world telling us to go mute. But the classroom had grown unsteady, too, and we'd thought about leaving and we started to question why we'd even come, and so something like an accidental collusion had made us start thinking about the door.

But then the Third Speechmaker finally stood up. On old plastic casting a holed shadow across the wall. Of all stages, something discarded. Something reused. But there she was. Small. Nervous. But honest about her size and about her anxiety and about all those things that, in the end, the world tells us we should never be honest about. Our frailties. Our humilities. All those things the world tells us to hide when the world tells us we're not enough. And she stepped off the milk crate, too, believing she wasn't tall enough, believing her echoes wouldn't travel, but she stepped back on it after adjusting it further back from everyone, and her young forehead couldn't poke above the faces, and so the rest of us knelt, not for any reason anyone could discern. After the first people up front did it, then the people behind them did it, and soon everyone had done it, and there she was. The Third Speechmaker. Looking around the classroom and nodding, her eyes alight but refusing to cry. The sight of the well that almost poured out was, in the end, enough to command everyone's attention, and her first words emerged with an unconventional pride, the kind of audacity that always seems to brush away, for its speaker and the waiting audience, any and all incentive to contest.

In the Third Speechmaker's speech, she began with her *I don't know*s, those disclaimers of youth that anticipate snarls and refutations of immaturity, and then she continued with her *maybe I don't mind*s, those brief assessments of inexperience that permit the most lavish of broken rules, and when she finally spoke of her *but you know what*s, there were nodding heads, all around us, as well as shuffling hands clapping or snapping or tapping their legs, the kinds of response that alleviates the pressure of every call.

And then she went on, urgent and clear, all heart and mind, and with a body that couldn't contain the sounds that at times even she seemed surprised to be making. And soon enough it seemed that our realizations culminated in the disbelief that this Third Speechmaker, the last of all voices the school should would hear that night, had been talking for far longer, and with far more authority, than anyone before her, and that she'd been accounting for, in her lists of things that she was most afraid of and in her running count of things that she remained most hopeful for, all our failures and all our aspirations and all those things that have ever left our throats tight and choking for more water, because when a people like these, those who collide with stories and evasions, affirmations and lies, Then what comes out of us are the ways we forget about each other in real life and the things we tell people about how much we'll love and remember each other only in the next life because it's so easy to pray about the dead and talk about the dead and it's always so hard and beyond us to do something about the living before their lives go away.

Clichés can be a tragedy, but there wasn't a dry eye in the room, and we had all grown mindful of our breathing and we had become sensitive to the ways one another's skin had begun to radiate a presence that could have blown the walls right open had we wanted, really wanted, to let the body do what the bodies does in the best of cases. Be itself. Breathe into itself.

One by one, everyone in the room came back into themselves, and we could see it in our eyes, our shoulders come alive, our hands at our faces wiping the moisture away, our faces turning to the door. Something about the way the Third Speechmaker cleared her throat after her last word, as if wringing the last cobweb from her teeth, that seemed to indicate an end to the proceedings, but also a revelation that this end was not *the* end, at least not for us, not for us in this room or anyone outside it. Something about the way she sighed after a moment seemed to punctuate the fact that we'd been holding hands during her speech. Something about the way she looked toward the door that veered our eyes there, too, assured, finally, that if nothing else we'd left a trace of ourselves behind in the room.

When the Third Speechmaker stepped off the milk crate, someone reached for her palms, and then he took her in his arms. This older gentleman held onto the girl so tightly her limbs seemed to hang happily limp, her eyes shut in a way that *soothing*, as a description, couldn't accommodate the warmth on her face. When together man and girl looked towards the door, a group there had already started parting the way for them, and as we all started filing out, the Candle Holder in the corner of the room closed her eyes and exhaled across her hands, blowing out the flame, and then she set the candle on the windowsill where it rattled as everyone's feet thumped and filled the coarse exodus with what should have been an easy march home.

LOOP TEN: THE LIBRARY

Silence inside a library always precipitates a clamor outside of it to where the sound of the whipping City banner frantic on its flagpole is as loud and screeching as the brakes on a passing bus. And because silence, emphasized by the intentional whispers, overwhelms everything from the carpet to the backroom shelves, the street's gutter echoes into the shuttered study rooms like a heartbeat, steady and necessary, reassuring readers their homes outside the walls are alive, a reliable rhythm but also a nerve-racking one if you're trying to read.

On this particular night, the chief librarian and her assistant had been sitting by the checkout stands a long time. It had been almost two hours since the library had seen its last reader, and in that time, the Chief Librarian and the Assistant Librarian had gone about the uninterrupted business of organizing magazines and atlases that had been scattered everywhere, adjoined tables offering continents upon which to sprawl dreams and pretend no one dies.

The staff had had so much time to clean up, in fact, that the Assistant Librarian was able to wipe every glass surface of fingerprints while the Chief Librarian wiped sweat and beverage stains off every table. Together they returned every chair to its place, realigned the reference shelves, reorganized the media binders, and processed every book checked in that day.

However, they both wanted to remain mindful of incoming people. The Chief Librarian, for one, had long ago made it a strict requirement to offer a smile or soft *Hello* to new patrons. And so throughout their cleaning, they regularly visited the circulation desk to be sure they weren't passing up the opportunity. But no one arrived, It has been a while Ms. Nikemi since we have gone this long without checking out a book, Which isn't to say Mr. Palomar that the City has suddenly gone hopeless, Yes but an enduring illiteracy of this magnitude is not good for anyone, Certainly Mr. Palomar the City has justifiable reasons for its seasons.

One more hour later, a studious man wearing a suit, tie loose and jacket unbuttoned, entered and forewent the Chief Librarian and her Assistant and proceeded to the stairwell. His patient walk contrasted his swinging arms, indicating he knew exactly where to find what he had come to find and that he'd memorized education's most important axiom, that rushed learning is worse than no learning at all, that if he could not pull open a book thoughtfully and carefully to keep its binding intact, his lot would be left just the same as if he had never touched a book at all.

On his way up the stairwell, the Studious Man trotted past one of the library's second-floor shelvers. The woman stopped midstride coming down the steps and looked back at the man trotting up, and then she turned, puzzled, to the Chief Librarian leaning at the circulation desk, herself watching the man as he disappeared into the midlevel stacks.

At the circulation desk, the second-floor shelver settled two volumes of Margot Bender's *History of Impetuous English* at the barcode scanner, and in contrast to her usual meticulousness, the Chief Librarian left the books unattended, It's been three hours has it not Ms. Nikemi, The moon is known for enduring cycles, The man seemed tired but also driven by obligation, Evening has an effect on all of us dear, Should I attend to his questions, He may leave here without any to ask, But Ms. Nikemi you've always taught us to—, You're right dear I will see to him myself.

Upstairs, the Chief Librarian found the Studious Man poring over four books at once. Three lay open on the table, and he held the fourth in his left hand. The Chief Librarian crept into the aisle immediately behind him to avoid detection, and then she watched him, unbeknownst to him, feigning duty by replacing fallen books. That the man might have caused the spill was not lost on her, and so as she replaced the books, she thumped their covers against metal braces, a passive aggressive castigation common to the trade.

Eventually, the Chief Librarian endured her own curiosity by focusing on a collection of summarized cases heard between nineteen forty-five and nineteen ninety by the Federal District Court of Newark, New Jersey. She got lost perusing one particular case heard in nineteen eighty-nine, a ruling in favor of a Hudson County plumber indicted for murder by neglect, having failed to respond to an elderly woman's cries as she pressed her plunger into the toilet, soaking herself to her hips in what were ultimately futile attempts to unclog the plumbing and which compelled simultaneous heart attacks and death by pneumonia for which the prosecution unsuccessfully tried to convict the plumber of fourth-degree manslaughter.

Suddenly the Studious Man plopped his book onto the table, and then he looked around.

He tossed his head back. He sighed. He rubbed his eyes and then he returned to books. When he leaned forward, however, his eyes seemed useless. He opened each book to the table of contents to gather structure, but then he stopped his progress to massage his temples. He tried focusing again, and so he rearranged the books, but then he just as quickly ran his fingers through his hair. He took one last deep breath and then leaned forward and searched for comparisons to argue impossibles and contrasts to gauge his chances, which is when the Chief Librarian cleared her throat behind him, Excuse me may I help, I think I'm looking for ghosts, As a librarian I specialize in the unseen, I'm hedging my bets on local jurisdictions, Might I suggest that the best way to arrange an argument is to think globally.

The man scratched his chin. The Chief Librarian smiled politely, Can I direct you to a shelf, I'm looking for a precedent in shame, The stacks are arranged alphabetically, I've pored over the usual culprits with no luck, May I suggest a synonym, Is language that replaceable, It seems the nature of things leaves us alone or replaceable or both at once.

The lawyer reached for the furthest book, I'm looking for guilt, Which legal code and what principle, I'm looking for the monetary equivalent of the word and feeling, In our database one can peruse texts thematically and by title, I'm looking for a contemporary ruling in which the sentiment is a working vindication of itself, A matter of guilt as defense against itself and with the authority to reduce or absolve a sentence, Exactly, Let's see what we can do.

He handed the Chief Librarian a book and pointed to the second paragraph on the open page illustrating a Chicago ruling making permissible in Federal Appeals an incorporation of meaningful shame to acquit a teacher charged with evading assignments in a pre-approved district textbook, But I need something at the initial trial stage, A precedent of initial ruling as an un-equivocal standard bearer, A decision by jury and with only a single count, And as you mentioned a financial component that dollarizes the immeasurable.

The Chief Librarian leaned against the shelf, One or two things come to mind, I have to file a defense in anticipation of charges the defense itself would bring, I think the best I can do is a case that draws the necessary par-allels without a decisive economic result, I have a number of clients and the vagueness should envelope them all, I believe this can work then, Then let's go with one and see where to go from there, Excuse me then I'm wanted in the basement stacks.

When the Chief Librarian returned from the vault, she placed on the table the third volume of *The Queen's Melbourne Hearings of Nineteen Eighty-Six*, which the City library had retained as a gift from Her Majesty's royal court on the crown's tour of coastal cities, bypassing, of course, the City al-together, but her majesty's High Court gifts were offered as gratitude to rest and gas stops in between, her Majesty seemingly intent on uncluttering her high court vaults, a treasury of historical references and miscellaneous royal educations where perhaps this more contemporary book found its way into a lost and replaceable pile, We're in luck, How so, There are places so thorough-ly steeped in guilt that their national identities are founded on the principle of accrued shame.

The Studious Man spent the next few minutes poring over paragraphs at a time, using available appendices to situate himself in the definitions he lacked, legal customs not his own, and alien court reporting shorthand. Meanwhile, the Chief Librarian sat opposite him at the table, studying his face, his hands, and the range of hypotheticals that could have been this law-yer's working case.

Reading to himself, the Studious Man's lips mimed decisions that might as well have been imagined, but as he leaned back in his chair, the printed claims and sworn testimony were at least, in themselves, validation he hadn't searched in vain, Pardon my interruption but what is this about, A man was found hanging by a noose from a plumbing pipe in a basement, Was it his basement, I've been told it belonged to too many people, Was this nearby, Exit the building and turn right, Am I following the avenue, I've been told there's a crowd waiting to touch their own shame, Why would anyone wait for such a thing to become concrete, I've been told nothing is ever real until it can be pushed aside or burned.

The Chief Librarian straightened her lap and leaned forward, What is everyone waiting for exactly, I believe they're expecting to be charged wholesale for complicit neglect, So the man was hanged then, Preliminary accounts confuse the hanging man for the hangman and someone no one saw, Then who is it you're supposed to defend, The narrative that living alone and on your own and comfortably isn't a completely awful thing, Does this set a precedent for our jurisdiction, Even at face value nothing is ever all that new, Then what is the extenuating circumstance everyone in defense is maintaining, That the best way to cope with the horror is to keep an older arrangement to things, And what order is this, A list of the way things have always been, And how have things always been, I've been told they were more private and less shameful for being so, And does everyone approach you willingly, Some feel it best, And everyone else, Some feel coerced.

And then the Studious Man stopped. He found something on a page and read through it once, and then read through it again, Miss what do you think, and then he elaborated for the Chief Librarian about a May 4th property dispute between a farmer and his provincial governor, where the plaintiff's lawyer latched onto the defendant's own words during cross-examination by focusing on a particular line of testimony in which the local roads inspector stated *Provincial rules are provincial rules but my condolences to the farmer*, and in the exchange that followed, the defendant's attorney culminated his case for amendment, Mr. Roads Inspector can you repeat that, Repeat what, What you just said, Provincial rules are provincial rules, The next part, My condolences to the farmer, And what did you say before that, That provincial rules are provincial rules, And then, My condolences to the farmer, And so you see Your Honor the *but* that the roads inspector has stated overturns the jurisdiction's provincial rules, I object, Overruled, Negating his conjunction negates the law Your Honor, How exactly is that counselor, The *but* and its underlying foundation of shame states all that needs to be interpreted in the law and that specifically the agent enforcing or acting upon the law can with all due conscious amend to the law during enforcement or enactment, But the law can't so easily be interpreted counselor, Your honor we can presume that those who execute the law are at the tail end of legislative interpretation, And so, I object Your Honor, Overruled, And so the roads inspector was following rules he no longer saw fit for society, But I understand the law quite well, Your Honor I would like the record to show the roads inspector agrees.

The Studious Man looked up to meet the Chief Librarian's stiff, concerned face, some understanding and processing expression that attempted to repeat the details of the hearing the Studious Man just described but probably in her own words, I'm not certain it's in the English we need, English there is English everywhere ma'am, But it's not our English, But English is no longer a property any more than sky or water, But it must certainly be ruled and lorded by someone, English ma'am no longer belongs to people like you and me, That's an awful thing, It's the only thing, Is this the world we live in, It's certainly the one we die in.

The Chief Librarian nodded, And so what do you make, That I can file my clients' self-satisfying complaints so long as I consider attaching the right code, Surely the same as all suits in all jurisdictions, Most certainly the same as all suits in coded jurisdictions, But something must be different, I'm afraid it's all too much the same, Do you mean if it wouldn't have been this then it would have been that, As it pertains to the law ma'am it's always what it must be.

The Chief Librarian leaned back in her chair when she was suddenly interrupted by the Assistant Librarian who'd rushed up the steps breathless as if ghosts had suddenly consumed his face, Ms. Nikemi, Mr. Palomar, We have visitors, Do they need help, Not at present, Then is there a problem, It's that our guests are not here for the library per se, Then why are they staying, It seems something from the outside has seeped into the inside, But I've heard no warnings about a plague, It seems something altogether unnameable Ms. Nikemi, What exactly are they asking for Mr. Palomar, Nothing Ms. Nikemi, And what are they looking for, Nothing they've made clear, Then what are they waiting for, Perhaps someone or something to see or touch or speak with or feel, Where is this coming from, I'm not sure, Then why are you concerned, Precisely because I don't know.

The Chief Librarian leaned forward, I believe the line is coming from across the street Ms. Nikemi, Then it's a line, It's certainly a formation that elongates with age, And where is the tail end of the snake, At the stairwell now Ms. Nikemi, Goodness they're at the circulation desk, They're certainly past the information desk, From across the street then, Perhaps but I cannot confirm that at this time.

The Chief Librarian turned to the Studious Man across the table, What do you know, That my clients have found me, Then where will you go, To my clerks who are currently taking names, Do you have what you need, I certainly have more than I had, Then what is going to happen, What is going to happen is that I can no longer remain a stranger.

The Studious Man rose from the table, Where are you going, I must go, and as the Chief Librarian considered her options, reserving volumes, keeping something on hold or processing a library loan, the Studious Man, book in hand, removed his tie completely, unknotting and then rolling it up, and then he disappeared down the stairs with his collar up and hair on the back of his neck.

LOOP ELEVEN: THE DINER

From outside the diner, the storefront windows looked barred. The curtains, pulled tight and tied, spilled fluttering shadows onto the glass. Like all diners, the open seating welcomed walk-ins, but shadows against the back wall, revealing and concealing a far horizon, illustrated an in-between, phases of morning and night that never knew on which side of the coin to sit. Most infamous in all this was the front door. On it hung an open/closed sign so bleached by the sun, the one side seemed perpetually uncertain about whether to lock us in or keep us out and the other never knew when to face us.

On this night, the booths were sparsely filled. A handful lay asleep across cushioned seats as if tables were seasoned bungalows. Another handful sat hunched over sugar cubes, tea in hand and inhaling steam like history hung in the smell. Busboys dealing cards at the register played pepper packets as betting chips. The proprietor sat at his usual table with his usual newspapers and coffee, the cleared floors a testament to a time when the whole place wasn't simply another something in the City waiting to disappear.

A long time ago, the diner had been very busy. Shoes squeaked, spoons clanked cups from kitchen to front door, and the chairs had been so thoroughly pushed and pulled, they wobbled even when no one was in the room. The era had been marked by waiters serving coffees so alien, the Proprietor pasted pronunciation charts on menus just so people could order.

The City went mad for the taste, and probably because of the craze, confusion was the most popular item. Pronunciation was never easy, and too many of us resorted to hand gestures miming vowels and aping impatience for languages that weren't ours. Misunderstandings transformed lunchtime hours into aggravations. The Proprietor attempted to fix the headache with alternate pronunciation charts embedded in the actual tables, definition scales in tablets along the walls, and professional training for his servers, requiring certifications in translations across languages just to work the floor.

But because Furies always return in manic episodes across the Caucuses, the Proprietor's attempts to alleviate the situation only infuriated the most powerful people in town, the local Lions Club and City Council, their demands heavy and in unison clamoring that the Proprietor shouldn't have so swiftly abandoned local culture to satisfy some greed, And how dare he I say how dare he refuse outright those coffee beans produced in the backyards of our own backyards.

The Proprietor was sued to no end, according to commissioners, for neglecting his own. Despite indictments dismissed on insufficient grounds, the charges kept coming, and among the many hearings, one particularly horrible plaintiff blamed the Proprietor for being selfish with his sacrifices and with the common good, And though I love thinking upon the things our heroes do in war Your Honor I cannot abide by this man's blatant lack of respect for those men and women whose deaths have promised our goods a brighter future than the world over and I say Your Honor I say this man of a diner's perspective must have no respect Your Honor no respect for the good in every heart that dies bleeding in the soil for our freedoms to choose between that which is right and that which is right for us.

After months of staged protests, the Proprietor shut down under auspices of renovation. When he returned, the diner walls stood lighter where frames used to be and older, stiffer chairs had replaced the swivels. Enough haranguing in courts of public opinion and things disappear. The Proprietor wanted nothing of distant places anymore, nothing of distant tongues, despite the City's slow certain infusion of faces even the commissioners could no longer map onto a mirror.

On the night a man was found hanging by a noose from a plumbing pipe in a basement, the Proprietor passed time with neutral coffee. Having remade so much in the place, including renaming the booths' engravings from Peruvian Pearl to Swiss Sterling, it was difficult to tell what had originated where and which stories he'd suppressed in the name of objectivity. For more than a decade, the Proprietor ran a middle-of-the-road passage through time, careful to leave waters unstirred and emphatic about cutting historical narratives at their ankles before they revealed too much of the names that bore them and the influences that shaped them.

Even the newspapers he read, all twelve of them, had their titles ripped out. There was something about names he could no longer stand. He ordered his longest-serving waitress every day to tear from the top of every headline page the registered name of *Such-and-Such Chronicle* or *This-and-That Times*, Because I don't want to know where it comes from or what it's all for or how something becomes or who knows all about why the world is so disheveled. We always used to hear from him that news is just news, news here no different than news there, news everywhere nothing more than accounts of details people hear but never remember, mothers bearing children here much the same as mothers burying their children there.

That night, every time the Proprietor flipped a newspaper, he rattled the air. The time inside had passed timidly for so long that even the busboys dropping cards, however softly, and sliding packets into ante piles, however slowly, cut through breaths like a whip.

Leaning over the table, the Proprietor adjusted his spectacles. Despite the running fans above every third table, sweat collected thinly across his face. His glasses slipped regularly, and so he scratched his nose just as much and he pushed his glasses up the bridge of his nose even more.

At some point, a set of stragglers peered into the windows. They pulled at the handle but the door was locked. They tried getting someone's attention inside by waving and when that didn't work, they shook the door. When that didn't work, one of them pounded the storefront, pressing her face into the glass as if trying to walk through it. She pointed at her watch. She tapped its face. She screamed her time. And then she pointed inside the diner, as if she could meet the Proprietor's eyes with her own, warning him about leaving anyone, especially on that night, to fend alone in the heat.

The Proprietor glanced to his storefront but returned to his paper. He wiped his nose and adjusted his glasses and then shielded his eyes. His dog, tied to a table leg, wagged its tail, and one of the busboys set his hand down and turned around. The Proprietor avoided them. He coughed into his hand. He rattled the next newspaper.

A waitress came around to refill his cup. Anticipating annoyances he'd be unable to name, he preempted her, Don't tell me about what's happening there, I wasn't going to say a word boss, Just let them knock, I'll let them knock boss, There's a mess out there, Don't we all know it boss, And I'm not letting the shames of out there get anywhere inside here.

She settled his sugar cubes on the saucer, What have you heard boss, Naïve isn't a good color on anyone, Then what do you think about it boss, It's what they all get, Are you sure you know what you're talking about boss, How can you ask me such a thing, Because being an expert takes time boss, What happened is what everyone deserves, You mean we all deserve to see someone go boss, What I'm saying is it's what they get for feeling him go without feeling him at all.

She left napkins by his cup, But are we jumping to conclusions boss, I'm telling you I'm not afraid of these people, But it's not about being afraid boss, The door isn't opening for any of them, What I'm saying boss is that you're eventually going to have to forget things, I'll repeat it the door isn't opening, What I'm saying boss is you're eventually going to have to get over it.

The Proprietor composed himself, took a napkin, wiped his neck. Curly hair jutted from between buttons struggling to withhold his shirt, Did you see that they just went away, That's not what I'm saying boss, Everyone here crazes over unusual things and then forgets them the very next day, But that's not what I'm talking about boss, They worry about someone gone for a night and then forget he ever existed, You have to deal with it boss, They're not going to get me tonight, They're not coming after you boss, They're not coming in tonight, This isn't about you boss.

Another straggler stopped at the front door. He crouched to read the working hours sign. He then squinted to see through the glass. Inconsistencies begging for an explanation sometimes treat us all like thieves, and when the man's sneering inspection of the diner through the glass seemed to make him upset, he raised his chin, looked down on everyone, and dismissed them all with a backhand wave. He gleaned his reflection in the storefront before walking away, and even though the Proprietor had tried to shield his eyes, the stranger's face seemed etched in the glass.

Without notice, the Proprietor swung his stiff leg into the aisle and rattled the table, I'm going to pee. He grimaced, leaning forward, pressed into the cushioned seat just to get up with bearable pain. Only after he'd finally stood, reached for a newspaper and rolled it under his arm did one of his busboys and the Waitress rush to him, Why did it take you so long, Because you didn't prepare us boss, Would you have preferred I collapse, You didn't say you needed help boss, Do I always have to remind you, It would be helpful boss, Couldn't you just hear the table shaking, Hearing the tables shake is already too late boss.

The Busboy and Waitress helped the owner straddle his way to the bathroom. They loomed over him as he reached for the knob, You don't have to wipe my ass too, We'd like to see you inside boss, Well I'm already here aren't I, We've come this far so we're here the whole way boss, People don't need that they don't need the extra mile, It's only concern boss it's only decency, I don't like it and I don't need it, We're here boss we're already here.

Ten minutes later, when the Proprietor emerged from the bathroom, a commotion at the front door was rattling the rickety, old fans. The Waitress was explaining from inside the diner to a group of us outside the diner that the whole thing was closed, that the few people inside were uncurious friends of the owner, and that everyone would soon be leaving, that they'd all soon be gone, and that unfortunately there are always orders to be taken as well as those to be given and still others yet to be had, And I'm sorry but I can't help you now I'm really very sorry.

The Proprietor stood by his table for as long as he could stand the situation, and then he forewent appearances, limped to the door, nudged the Waitress aside, and pressed his palms to the glass, They can see right through me boss, They're coming for me, This isn't about you boss, Stay where you are. His palm turning white imposed a map, accounts of places where everyone is alone and where being alone is also a complicated tug of war between the things we need and the things people need of us even when they don't ask.

The stragglers stood on the opposite side of the door, chins back and waiting, moves and words past introductions. At some point, the shouting began, Let us in, You're staying there, There are no other places, There are many other places, Those places are closed, Because it's a right to be alone, This isn't about being alone, Solitude is an unmistakable human right.

The Proprietor's dog started circling his feet, What happened out there isn't coming in here, We don't bring it with us, This whole city takes everything to wild places, You don't have to be so unyielding, And you don't have to be so uninvited, Do you even know what's happened, I'm aware of the consequences, Then you must know it's only down the road, I'm aware enough that there's nothing in here, Then you have to know well enough this isn't something we can bear alone, This isn't a place for any of your stories, The story about what happened is only an idea, Then I don't want your ideas to shake this place up, But we just want a place where we don't have to talk, I've been through liars and jokers and tellers and seers, But we aren't those people, Everyone in this place is that kind of people.

Tired of arguing, one of the stragglers picked up a brick and turned to hurl it into the glass when someone reached for her arm. The Proprietor didn't step back. The Waitress had raised her hand to fight the broken glass, and when she opened her eyes again when nothing shattered, the Proprietor pressed the tip of his cane to the window, Get off my sidewalk, Why do you have to be such an infection, Because you're all a concert, Certainly there's shame but don't make us all the same, There's no one out there who really cares, Then you must be a living stain of yourself, At least I know what's mine, Shame as a useless pain is the only thing that's yours, Do you know what your fathers did to me, We don't carry their guilt in quite the same way, Learning it means it can teach you to mind your own selves, But that old way isn't the only way anymore, The alternative is to lose what's mine and share it with you, But that's not what we're trying to say, Because here you are ready to make everything yours, But that's not what this is about, I don't have to care about what happens to somebody else, We're not saying it's the absolute way, Then I can stay in here and mind my own things in the dark, But you have to come out to know what this is really about, I've been through what everything and more is all about, But you've only been minding your own and keeping things closed, And the process alone keeps me busy enough, But tomorrow is already dead if we're still only doing this alone, Then tomorrow begins with more of the same dead.

The Proprietor waved the stragglers away, shooed us to nowhere. At first only his dog listened, though it returned confused when no one paid it the mind it expected, precisely the glare or sympathy it always expected. The Proprietor stared at the stragglers until we slowly walked off, one at a time, some of us glancing back, some of us shaking our heads at him, the Proprietor, a sentinel whose glass always felt, to even the dog that followed him everywhere, like walls verging on storefront in shards.

LOOP TWELVE: THE NEWS DEPARTMENT

Complications are tepid. They can leave broken stories. We can discard or stitch them, but no matter what we choose, we have to keep at least something to grasp, like confession, like the spaces between the stories, real or white.

The journalist sat in his chair, leaning back. Outside the window, an oak tree towered still, its thinnest branches rustling, as if, like sleeping cats, the trunk sighed to prove the bark and burrowing roots were still alive. The night's cicada drone accompanied the leaves and so loudly that we couldn't discern it from the machinated hearts beating in the basement, the printers, the bundlers and stackers. Two floors beneath the Journalist's chair, the heart of the heart of the News buzzed, impressing headlines of City routines, murder and the police and the law and the horrors of reaction, a syncopation of circuits and gears marrying sixteenth-century revolutions with a digital circus.

The Journalist sat writing his news story. He meant something about this place, about the night, but flicking his pen, his thigh a drum, he'd written a lot or maybe not enough, always begging questions about where to start or stop and whose story to tell. Curt echoes jabbed the windowpane. Outside, a pigeon leapt off leaves. A squirrel scurried between branches.

The Journalist returned to his notes, his questions and the answers he overheard, strangers stammering about the night and assessments he didn't trust, Something like flurries, he told us, And I don't know what to make of all that damned white noise. He pushed one notebook aside in place of another, his desk covered in slips and receipts, post-its and index cards, envelopes and markers, spirals and binders, notebooks and notebooks, a stationary salad that threatened to shit information without the paper to wipe.

He'd encountered his problems, you see. He tapped away and then he tapped his pen against his lap, against his boots, against the dead radiator. He tapped. The editor had limited him to two hundred words, and because he hadn't paused to smoke or tend his desk, he'd already accrued a thousand. There was too much he didn't trust, and so the Journalist amended to the story until he cut it too short, and then he bled it dry because he wanted more, more of the street than he saw and more of himself to go around and more of us than we were willing to make sense of and enough of the man who'd been taken away, But I hadn't expected everyone, he told us, to be taken aback to the point of being gone. And so he typed to no end. It was all that was left.

He leaned back, shut his eyes, scratched his lips, cleared his throat. When he looked up, the ceiling was an eternal wandering, ventilation grates meeting long overhead lights meeting plywood tiles, a consortium of stories in mazes about where the News always went when it took so long to go anywhere.

It wasn't until nineteen eighty that the editorial floors were separated from the plumbing and ventilation ducts in the ceiling. Before then, flushed water and heat circulated above everyone openly, without barriers to separate a columnist with a bowler from a conduit with insulation. Accompanying busy typewriters and drafts and chatter were all manner of tubes releasing steam through pressure gauges and draining toilet water through switched valves and bulged currents through ground wire. All of it splashed across the editorial floors like cymbal crashes to punctuate a measure. Occasionally, drops of water sprayed onto front page proofs or a singed piece of rubber from an erupted wire would jam a keyboard. Other times, stop-jammed gas would spew unexpectedly from a pipe above someone's desk and frighten the writers writing, effects of which always found themselves in misspellings and syntactical mistakes in the following day's edition. Editors and illustrators and even the mail crew felt the heat, and the conditions were exemplified in one Sunday edition by a cartoonist who equated the functioning state of the News Department to working inside someone's body, beneath the left ventricle, atop the fifth rib, white cells launching raids all around you, lungs expanding and blowing papers away, one's working desk feeling the ripples of a pulse verging on a heart attack. *The anxiety,* read the caption, *is enough to end a cat's lives in one rude awakening.*

However, it was here the metaphor expanded into a controlled suffering, a contemplation that, in the words of one editorialist, *finally welded together the two irreplaceable wellsprings of our news: the worldly foundation of our stories and the inner workings of the process that disseminates them.* And so the headache effectuated by all that exposed piping eventually over the years eased into a steady jitter, the fascinating kind, the kind that keeps us breathing.

But by nineteen eighty, the publisher had had enough of sloppy upkeep and the summer cooling bill and the winter heating bill and the spelling mistakes. And so the ceiling was tiled. Frame by frame, square by square, the editorial floors gradually separated from pulsing arteries and veins, and as if on cue, everyone working on the summer day that the last tile was embedded stopped what they'd been doing just to watch. In the following day's edition, a cartoonist hung an illustrated newspaper copy from an illustrated noose, along with a caption that made no mistake about returning to work: *There will be no more mistakes.*

And with barriers in place between reports and the machinations that publicized them, we came to see that the News Department seemed more disconnected every day, filling pages with gaping holes where real stories used to be, and the Journalist's desk slowly lost whatever clear picture of the streets it used to have, a horrid reminder that we will always prefer the spirals of our own mess over the real stories of our neighbors.

Like all cases of neglect, some stories will get filed and others will never get finished, a disgrace of language that will always drive an editor mad and tyrannical and curt, as in *Cut the story down to where I need it to be cut down.*

The Journalist tapped his notebook, tired of trimming, tired of story, I guess everything is not always a story, he told us before he slipped past the police, Sometimes it's just news. He pressed his fist to his forehead. He closed his eyes.

The landline rang. The whole base jumped, threatening to shake the paper potpourri on his desk loose. Three rings later, the Journalist picked up, and his hello laid him bare, What was that, What was what, You breathed so hard like your soul escaped you, It was just a breath, You breathed so hard like you didn't know what else to do but to give your life to me, I was just working, Then are you finished, Not quite, And why not, Eyewitness accounts aren't so easy to pare, But you're paid to manage all that, And I'm still adding the fragments.

It was the Editor's turn at a frustrated sigh. There was a buzz and then a clank on her end, and then a hinge and a click, and then it was suddenly quieter, Why don't we just bury the story, We could still run it tomorrow, But the story happened tonight, And we could run it tonight as news, But I'm paying you to make a story, Are you really going to force it where you want it to fit, It's always like you to fight something it's your job to do.

The Journalist pulled the phone away when a piercing clack echoed at him from the Editor's end of the line, I'll be right up to help, I don't need to be edited, This isn't a choice, This isn't a story, We don't publish in parts.

Soon enough, the Editor slammed the stairwell door by the elevator. The Journalist leaned into his desk. Sneakers trampled the carpet. The cubicle wall shook. The Editor stopped beside him, hands pressed to her hips, Stop riding me with talk, You weren't at the place and you didn't see everyone there, We don't debate authenticity here, You have to have been there to be able to pull this together, A story doesn't need you for you to say something about it, But you have to hear the stories yourself, No because people don't want to read what you were there to hear, Then what's it all for, To let people read what they wished they'd been there to see.

She leaned into the screen, shielding her eyes as if the sun were beating them tame, Your listening is too keen for its own good, I've already cut it, This isn't a painting, Then what's it all for, To begin a story and then to cap it, But this is only a breath, Then make it feel like a story, Anything less and it's only the news, Then make it what I tell you to make it.

He held his tongue, I'm sure I've been trying, I'm sure you have, I can give you the details, Then give me the details, But then there's the picture, Just give me the words, It won't be enough, It's an obscenity to always have to understand you.

The Editor leaned back on the cubicle wall, Tell it to me, How much of it do you want, Start with what keeps you awake, I'm under a deadline, Well I'm not printing it tonight, Then why are we talking, Because histories start with encounters, But you're not printing it tonight, Tell me the things that you saw, That's just it I only saw what I saw, Then why isn't that enough, Because I'm struggling to make you to see that it's also about the things I neglected to see.

The Journalist crossed his arms, We have deadlines in the business, Yes I'm privy to them all, Then let's just stop here and I'll see you in the morning, But you wanted to know the things that I saw, I don't care to know the things that you saw, And so you've changed your mind already, Only one of us should lie sleepless tonight and it's not going to be me.

The Journalist dropped his elbows at the edge of his desk, Fine then, I'll be downstairs if you need me, Fine then, I'll call you if I need you, I understand, Drafts are a process, I understand that, So leave it where it is and I'll see you tomorrow. He nodded.

A summer breeze rattled the windowpane. The Journalist opened his notebook and then closed it again. Timelines stopped mattering, and his charts were sure to contribute to mills churning nobodies into stories that would never make it into the news.

The phone rang, Have you packed up to go, I'm getting there slowly, It's the nature of all stories to have working constraints, That isn't the issue here, And it's certainly the nature of all things to think you belong in there when it's not about you, But that's not what I was saying, Don't lie to yourself, I'm getting my things, These things aren't always about the stories we hear, I'm leaving now, You're eventually going to learn that these things are only about the words we can tell and nothing more.

The Journalist dangled the receiver. On her end of things, the Editor was interrupted after a hinge and a sudden swell of machine, and it was then the Journalist finally hung up the phone and reached over his desk to open the window.

LOOP THIRTEEN: THE POLICE DEPARTMENT

Police stations often find themselves entrenched in city blocks on streets with little if any walking traffic, where, as street lights approach the precinct steps, bulbs dim and cars slow as if an interrogatory lamp shone accusingly on the pavement, doubting not only a traveler's direction but also questioning whether her mapped path was the best way to get there. After all, there is certainly everything to hide when every step forward lies drowned by the moon.

The Police Department rests approximately one hundred feet from City Hall, where the trinity of flags, that is, the striped national cloth, the state's quadrangular polyester coat of arms, and the City's emblematic twinned goat-twine and rosebush emblem, hangs limp in the summer. The Police Department's rear steps release into an automotive alley byway, where on most mornings almost no sunlight trickles to the ground, the building's height nipping sun even in the afternoon. It's only evening when the sun casts orange purple onto curb and gutters, and before night drapes the buildings completely, sunset hues cover the windowpanes well past eight.

It was just after this that the Police Chief glanced out his window. Even though few if any municipal employees crossed the alley at night, he saw two of his employees meeting in the street, one with an envelope. The Police Chief stood and leaned into the pane. Whatever they did, they did like ghosts, and after the Police Chief stepped away from the window and sat back down, there was no way he could tell, no matter how far his glare inspected the street, where his ghosts would go and what his employees would do. By all accounts, he didn't care to know.

At his desk, he bit into his ham sandwich. He sipped his tea. He forked lettuce and then tomato but then bypassed the salad dressing. In fact, he didn't use it at all, and it was left as nothing but a wonderful, creamy ornament at the edge of his plate. He didn't dip anything, even though, as he did that evening, he always requested at least a quarter cup of dressing for its own sake, just to have, and the interrogation by the waiter, by the cashier taking his order, always culminated in the same confusion, But sir why do you order condiments in vain, Please garçon I enjoy it when people do as they're told, But sir you don't touch the dressing and we should use what we can for others, Please garçon waste is not waste if it provides the empowering knowledge that I have the power to waste as I please.

At his desk, the Police Chief brushed aside a court document and then opened a folder. He flipped through pictures inside that folder, and he stopped at the thirteenth picture, a photograph of a long signature with eccentric arches that underlined the middle initials and with wild curves that encircled the full name. The Police Chief was a known authority on loops, and files from cases involving bank fraud and questionable certificates and licensure misrepresentations were often left at his desk for his professional perspective or simply to outright discredit whosoever's signature, real or imagined, had found its way onto some official form.

The Police Chief was an expert at signatures. He could identify embellishments in a scripted *R* that suggested its signee's psychological state or hidden desires, and he knew how to classify various possible edges of an *O* by personality type, confidence level, and social status. He was particularly skillful at categorizing dots above the *i*, which either alluded to someone's wasteful spending or economic priorities, a person's brash ego or public humility. Generally speaking, the Police Chief's skills left its distinct impressions on others, most notably the county's official forensic document examiner who described the Police Chief's adept abilities in this way, The man's methods of classifications don't exactly follow standard field protocol or learned wisdom and I must say while still respecting the man's hard-earned reputation as an oracle guided by instinct that the man's purportedly expert opinions are nothing but big and often excessive words accessorizing unproven techniques that even if they do prove useful cannot be wholly reliable all the time. When asked for his perspective on the matter, the county probate judge put the

Police Chief's abilities this way. The man is a garnish upon the delicacy of this court an unnecessary taste that is also irremovable from the meals of justice.

At his desk, the Police Chief jotted down an observation in his notebook. He paused to take a big bite of salad, and as he chewed he noted that the curve width in the signature he was analyzing had *some kind of scope for sure.* He also added, in less delicate writing, that *the s downplays the effectiveness of the d which should be standing head and shoulders above the a but which doesn't because it gets pinned to the floor by the f.*

At his desk, the Police Chief's academy diploma hung on the side wall above his filing cabinets. Beside the diploma were a series of bowlers hanging on nails. Even though there hung six hats on each side of the frame, an additional one, a lonely bowler like an amended afterthought, hung on the far wall above the picture of a fisherman's rope loose on a pier. The fisherman's rope was being held by two hands whose arms, elbows, and shoulders seemed not to be a concern for the photographer's frame.

Shortly after nine o'clock, the Police Chief's phone blinked. He always left the phone on mute while he worked. In addition to the lack of volume, two sheets of paper covered the red blinking red light that blinked for ten minutes after the phone calls. In those ten minutes, the Police Chief sat assessing the state of the signature at hand, particularly a lower-case *e* so lavishly written it seemed to swallow the *l* and the void that followed.

At approximately nine fifteen, a detective knocked on the Police Chief's door. The Police Chief had left the door ajar. The door's openness, however, never truly spoke of openness in the traditional sense, because we all knew that, for the Police Chief, an open-door policy has never really meant what it does in common circles beyond law enforcement, as it would, say, for a principal's office or a priest's confessional or the editorial cutting floor. The Police Chief's open door simply meant that his ears could be open to passing sounds, available to the clamor of phones and desks outside his office but only as purveyor and voyeur. And so, if we ever wanted or needed his attentions, he required that we knock before entering his room. More specifically, he required specific patterns of knocks, a tapping Morse code, if you will, but with an ornateness in volume, rhythm, and exactness that bordered on excess, which he always described when we asked about its misconceptions in this way: the code of hard knocks is like a song that confirms one's attention to general detail and one's adeptness to understanding particular details.

The Detective knocked "Good evening, Chief," and the Police Chief responded with taps on his own desk "Good evening, there." The Detective knocked "I need to speak with you, Chief," and the Police Chief responded "I see and do you plan to take much of my time?" The Detective knocked "We have had an incident," and the Police Chief responded "You don't say." The Detective knocked "It is under our control, yes, but we might need counsel," and the Police Chief responded "Don't we all need counsel from time to time." The Detective knocked "But we could benefit from specific advice and a particular set of skills." The Police Chief responded "It is always polite to ingratiate before taking from someone their time and their energy." The Detective knocked "Thank you, chief," and the Police Chief responded "Will that be all, then?" The Detective knocked "May I come in, sir?" and the Police Chief knocked, "[heavy] Sigh."

From his desk, the Police Chief beckoned the Detective to enter his office. As he brushed his files aside, he caught the blinking phone light, and his double-take did not go unnoticed, The messages are mine Chief, I see, I called just a few times, And did you leave a message, Ergo the blinking light sir, I don't like people who play the smarts Detective, Indeed sir I don't enjoy such games myself, Then if you've come here this must be grave a situation, It's merely that we've spent longer on this particular street corner than we had initially believed necessary, Then you should shut things down immediately Detective as there are boundaries to our time in the same way there are limits to our patience, Yes sir of course it's just this particular set people have not yet been convinced to find their way home Chief, Then you should tell them Detective that the night is done and that there is no room outside to go to sleep, Of course sir and if it were only that easy Chief we would, Indeed things must be appearing difficult or nameless if you have made yourself into my office, Indeed they have Chief, Then I'm going to have to hear more from you Detective, I can share all that you need Chief, Then please Detective tell me all.

The Detective updated the Police Chief on the essentials of the situation, that is, the hour that each moment happened and the place where it took place and the stares that had been exchanged, searching, stubborn, and wild stares, and that continue to cover the street despite all reason having disappeared from the pavement and from the street corner's lights, From what you say Detective it's clear that hangings impressed a unique signature of consequence in this case, That's very insightful Chief what else do you know about hangings, Well Detective I have heard that they exacerbate death and fear and that sometimes our excuses for them are not enough, That's very interesting Chief because I didn't know that when people speak too much they are accounting for excuses to pardon their lack of memory and their lack of anticipation, However Detective a hanging that people talk about too much can unintentionally excuse everyone's silent hands in that hanging and which can sometimes only be resolved with another hanging, But that's awful Chief, Such is life Detective, Does the signature of a hanging suggest that anything about the stories people tell each other are the things they have always been afraid to tell each other, Sometimes Detective a happening has a funny way of churning grief into a narrative that can only make sense when there is more than one point to form a plot, How then are we supposed to tear the pages out Chief how then can we end this story, I believe you must consider Detective that only a permutation of what is already overwhelming these people can turn their voices into a rightful fear of death so that everyone can run back home where they always believe there is little to no death to be found.

The Police Chief leaned back in his chair, fingers to his chin. As the Detective watched him, he nodded an absent nod, perhaps to some unnameable agreement between them, or perhaps to sign off on something that had only begun taking shape in his mind, a certain suggestion or advice that hopes to contain stories by brutally ending them before anyone is ready, Have you tried Detective to let these people know that the night has only so many hours, We have not and I'm not so sure that these people know everything that there is to know about time, People have been known Detective to get tired of stories when they're reminded as we all must be from time to time that there is a place called the end and that they're better served being the protagonists of that end, Do you mean Chief that stories eventually find themselves at odds with the names that initiated them that is the names that no one talks about anymore, What I'm saying Detective is that authors are the product of this process and not the other way around, Does this mean Chief that you want us to assume another approach in dealing with these people, Have you tried telling them Detective that sometimes too many words only emphasize the differences and the distances between us, We have blared our sirens sir and our horns and we have tried with our sirens and our horns to make songs that should be known to these people, But people have been known Detective to resist words and meanings that they can't understand or that they don't like because there are words in them like *no* and *do not* and *exile* and *hero*, I understand that Chief but in the face of a signature event like this whose name has already been made a mess of what's left to us authorities other than to fill in the blanks with words that these people simply can't scramble correctly.

The Police Chief turned to his window. He licked his lips as if set to whistle a prophecy few people are ever privy to. He clasped his hands and then he pressed them to his mouth, Do we know who the man was Detective that was found hanging, We have made no official statement Chief at this time and his name seems to be many things at once, What do you mean Detective because as far as I'm aware we are all born with one name, Well Chief there is evidence on the streets that everyone knew him but that no one can remember his name, Who are these savage demonic people Detective, Well Chief there is evidence in the streets that no one dares to speak his name or to remember it, Then what are these people doing Detective if not consuming our breathable air with lies and with petty prayers for gods they probably can't even name, Well Chief there is evidence in the streets that both men and women and children and the saints among them believe in ghosts and are as afraid of their walls as they are of their floors, This sounds like a war narrative Detective, You say that often enough Chief that I am starting to doubt its veracity in all situations, I was a warrior once Detective so I know well enough about the ghosts and the walls and the floors we should all be afraid of, Then what do we do Chief with these people when all they want to do is to tell their stories with characters that don't have names, We do what I believe we always have to do now Detective when there is a signature without a name to call home, Which is why Chief I would like your earnest advice on this, Detective you must acknowledge the tragedy before us all and close the book once and for all, But how do we do that Chief, We move on Detective because that's all we can do, But the crowd Chief seems to want to breathe a eulogy every time they talk, I was a warrior once Detective I know well enough about the formalities and confessions of procession and penitence, Then you must know Chief that the only words we can use are words that people sometimes just can't read, People aren't always the smartest prunes Detective, I'm sorry Detective but I have not always understood your metaphors of food, What I'm saying Detective is that I was a warrior once and I know well enough how to sustain a narrative and how to end one.

The Police Chief leaned forward. Briefly distracted, he checked the pins on his breast pocket, all four of them, three squarely on the stitching and the fourth set to one side which the Police Chief removed to pin straight again, I'm tempted to believe Detective that the man who was hanged had been a callous man, Why do you think so Chief, Because Detective the fool has left us to pick up the pieces of a narrative he was too weak to bury himself, But there is evidence in the streets Chief that he was a warrior just like you, Not all warriors are the same Detective, How are you all different Chief, Firstly Detective some of us know how to handle the callouses we accrue on our hands, And secondly Chief, Secondly Detective some of us warriors are smart enough to make sense of stories that don't make any sense, I once believed Chief that all warriors belonged to one family if not always then at least once, You are wrong Detective because I am no friend of a warrior who can't get his story straight, Wow Chief I learn something new every day from you, The most important thing to learn Detective about warriors and people like me is that when it's my turn I'll know how to die with my secrets if I'm ever in a tomb without a name.

The Detective nodded, seemingly unsure, as if in those places where the damned don't cry, it was just fine to close the book on words we may not understand. The Police Chief pulled his phone to the center of his desk, Go on now Detective, To where sir, To the scene above all other scenes tonight, And do what sir, I will handle what needs to be handled you just be on site when it needs to be handled, Which will be what exactly sir, To console the fear that will inevitably arrive when these people don't know how to return quietly into the night.

The Detective hesitated in her seat. She watched the Police Chief's hand, Go now Detective, Yes sir, and then she left. When she was gone, the Police Chief dialed and let the call ring for a while, until his call was answered, though a reasonable person would have already hung up the phone because it had rung too much. When whoever it was picked up the other end of the call, the Police Chief initiated a conversation of pleasantries, a *Hello* here and a *Yes* there, followed by a second *Yes*, which was then followed by whispers between them, a careful exchange that incorporated a focused *Yes that* and then a specific instruction from the Police Chief *Yes I'll need your signature on this*. Immediately after his last words, the Police Chief hung up the phone and slid it across his desk, far away, to where it didn't crash onto the floor but hung enough over the edge to where it threatened to balance itself for eternity. For all we know, basic English in some people's hands becomes a decree in someone else's hands, a command that precipitates other commands and initiates an about-face of image and shape. That is, something that had once been one type of message before history began could be co-opted for a different kind of message, so that a story can be made to end, so that ghosts lose all discretion, so that a people know how to pick up their mess and their hearts out of fear they might lose both.

At his desk, the Police Chief watched his open office door, the ceiling fan tussling what remained of the hair behind his ears. The Detective had left the office door ajar, and it shook back and forth oh so slightly, almost imperceptibly but not such that the Police Chief could not notice. And even when it didn't move, even imperceptibly, he could imagine the miniscule breaths it did budge, the footsteps that shook the door and the telephone calls that nudged it this way and that, shifts of wind and hearsay that alter stories in grades so acute, no one could trace how a vast transformation of events that would threaten to turn the end into an utter disaster had actually begun.

After all, just because we can't see the steps that happen to make something happen doesn't mean they never happened. What it does sometimes mean, though, is that we can't really judge them. After all, we don't know what really happened. We can't really cry foul because then we would be calling the end a lie, and no end is ever a lie in the strictest sense, and we have to imagine the end in a general sense so that we can render a term of judgment. As such, we can imagine an approximation of those steps, a middle amended by degrees with appendices that slowly shut the door. After all, if we know the instructions, and we know they can't be rescinded, then we can trace our steps to the end. It's this imagination, this endless train of thought, that always leaves us amazed at the man, at his outcomes and at his stories and as witnesses to his outcomes and as bystanders to his stories, so much so that, because we are always in a place with no power, we can only critique the man where he stands, and we can only critique him in the kind of platitude that in the right hands can be its own flattery, *The man really enjoys a show*, we can watch ourselves say, *The man really knows how to put on a show*, we can listen to ourselves say.

Within the hour on Mystic and Pyre, someone no one saw made a show of himself, really only to himself, of climbing the fire escape and trudging to the roof of the apartment building, wearing a black leather coat despite the heat and heaving up all those more than a hundred yards of rope. By the time he got to the top, he felt the burn on his shoulder. He felt the burn on his hands. With his age, he felt the burn on his knees. At the top, there wasn't a cloud to impede the stars. The old man pulled out a revolver and set it down by the ledge. It shivered and almost fired when he let it go. When he pulled out his knife, he collected a few breaths. And then he set the knife by the fire escape ladder and proceeded into the instructions he'd been told would mark some kind of end.

His muscles strained and he scraped wrists when he unwound the rope and curled it in two and then wiped his brow. His face shone like a plum in the dark. He coiled and twisted and turned the rope, first one loop and then a second, and then a third loop, a fourth loop, a fifth loop, a sixth loop, a seventh loop, and an eighth loop so quickly that the twine fibers felt like they were crawling on his skin, and his neck shivered when a soft breeze brushed his hair. And then a ninth loop and a tenth loop, and he did these so tirelessly that it indeed felt like more bugs had crept onto his nape. And then an eleventh loop, and then the twelfth loop, and then he could barely collect himself because his arms wanted to hang limp for a moment, but he didn't allow it, how could he, there was an end and he had to get there. And finally the thirteenth loop, the last one, which could barely manage to curl and slide through, which even he knew was only a decorative loop which made its coiling and insertion that much heavier, weighed down as he must have been by the meaning embedded in things that were never intended to be necessary or even useful. And then before he tossed the whole construction over the ledge, he curled his fingers around the rope like they belonged there, unlike the people on the street who didn't belong there, the Police Chief quite clear about that, They don't belong there and they never will, all those people on the road with all their doors open and their voices colliding into each other without intention or definition or any hope that they could make a name for themselves.

The old man tossed the noose off the roof and he held tight to his end as the rope stretched as far as it could, and the force of it all made him slide to the ledge just to keep from letting go. The noose slapped the building's front doors. It slapped somebody's open window. It slapped the brick wall as it settled where it would finally hang so everyone could see it and scream that silent loud threat that did not go unnoticed. First one person pointed and then the next noticed until finally what had shown itself had been shown whole and people started mumbling and then muttering and then shrieking and then stammering, the *Oh my god* and the *Good lord* and the *Is there nothing sacred anymore* hollered everywhere as everyone began to scramble out of the way, into each other's way, into cars and doors, into the unthinkable, into news that buildings crumble and windows shatter when people aren't allowed to see their own ends, forever entombing even the unspoken words that only wanted to clear the smoke for the sake of peace, for a sense of an air of peace.

The old man struggled to tie his end of the rope to an exhaust pipe on the roof. It took almost more energy than he had left but he did, he did it, and he reholstered his pistol and reached for his knife and he limped to the corner of the roof where he sat against the ledge and waited for the sounds to die. But they didn't. They only turned into more intentional shouts and calls for meaning, calls for quiet, calls for an account of everyone's names to make sure he or she was who was there and who they said they were. But at least the street cleared, and after it did, an engine roared and a truck turned the corner. It rolled its way slowly down street, its wide-load siren beeping. Its tires were something of a blue heartbeat for the summer wind. Its brakes steamed. One of its doors slammed. Somebody barked a couple of orders. Somebody else started a mechanism that started other mechanisms so that the power company cable truck, which had arrived much earlier but which had never made it to where it needed to be, had finally managed to start its work to bridge service wires to bushings to breakers to upraised transformers to turn the lights back on.

JUAN CARLOS REYES's stories, poems and essays have appeared in *Ascentos Review, KGB Lit,* and *Hawai'i Review,* among others. He is a 2018 Jack Straw Writers Fellow and is currently an Assistant Professor of creative writing at Seattle University. He is also the chief editor at *Big Fiction* magazine. He is the recipient of the Artist Trust 2018 LaSalle Storyteller Award in Fiction.

Hinton

Current Hinton publications

Still True: The Evolution of an Unexpected Journalist
by Reagan E. J. Jackson

———————————————

Future Hinton publications

The Sylvan Hotel: a Seattle Story
by Frannie James (2025)

A String of Apologies: essays
by Danielle Marie Holland (2025)

———————————————

Hinton is

Marcus Harrison Green, Publisher

Marcus@hintonpublishing.com

Maggie Block, Deputy Publisher

Maggie@hintonpublishing.com